FINALLY: A FRIEND. A *REAL* FRIEND. . . .

This is nuts, Lance thought, splashing some of the water on his face. *Not only am I hearing voices, I'm talking back to them. What if Kepplinger finds out and tells Dad?* Fear crept through his chest. *Jesus, Dad would kill me.*

~query jaylance is afraid scared frightened of me?~

Lance licked his lips. "I—I'm not sure. It's just that—I mean—what if someone else finds out about you? They'll think I've gone crazy." He paused. "Are—are you one of the other voices I hear sometimes? The ones that argue all the time?"

~negative no never not~

"Then who are you?"

~robin~

"Robin?" Lance repeated, startled. "I thought you didn't have a name."

~found one~

"Are you a . . . a ghost or something?"

~negative no never not~

"So what are you?"

Long pause. Then: ~friend~

IN THE COMPANY OF MIND

STEVEN PIZIKS

IN THE COMPANY OF MIND

Copyright © 1998 by Steven Piziks

"Escapology" from *A Painted Field*, copyright © 1997 by Robin Robertson, reprinted by permission of Harcourt Brace & Company.

A Baen Books Original

Baen Publishing Enterprises
P.O. Box 1403
Riverdale, NY 10471

ISBN: 0-671-57776-X

Cover art by Charles Keegan

First printing, November 1998

Distributed by Simon & Schuster
1230 Avenue of the Americas
New York, NY 10020

Printed in the United States of America

To Theresa Brines, who convinced me I could write, and to Kala Piziks, who convinced me I could write this book.

ACKNOWLEDGEMENTS

I would like to acknowledge the kind help of Dr. Donald Beere of Central Michigan University, who gave up countless Monday morning office hours to answer my incessant questions about multiple personality disorder (or "dissociative identity disorder," as it is properly known in psychiatric circles). Any mistakes in the diagnosis, treatment, or behavior of people with MPD in this book, however, are necessarily my own.

Escapology

by Robin Robertson

A shallow cut lets the blood bead:
and you could charm red bracelets,
coax necklaces from nowhere.
You stashed blades like savings,
pulled them out with a flourish
in a fan of silver.

Soon it was ribbons from the wrist
and sawing yourself in two; always
trying to disappear.
Then the finale: sedatives, restraints,
the escape-proof box. And you
lying there. A locked knife.

CHAPTER ONE

NOW

Jaylance—freeze!

Lance Michaels instantly froze on hands and knees. His brown eyes flicked rapidly back and forth in the dim light of the glowband around his wrist. His ears strained, but he sensed nothing. The dark, narrow maintenance conduit around him smelled faintly of heated plastic and ozone, nothing more.

What've you got, Robin? he thought.

Pressure plates. Half meter straight ahead. Move much further, alarm goes off, conduit floods with cyanide gas.

That's illegal!

So is breaking, entering, kidnapping, theft—

All right, all right. Lance sighed and ran a hand through deep red hair. *I think my fee just doubled. No one said anything about deadly security.*

Risking life part of job, Jaylance.

Not unless the Company's getting paid extra. Lance's fingers searched his tool belt until he came up with a small flashlight. Although Lance had few problems operating in low light conditions, he didn't want to take chances with cyanide gas.

A quick beam of light stabbed through the near darkness and Lance's enhanced eyes had no trouble picking out the faint outline of the pressure plate. Jumping over it was out of the question—the conduit was barely high enough to let Lance crawl on his hands and knees. Lance soundlessly drummed his fingers on one thigh, considering options. He could try to locate the plate's power source and cut it, but that might set off an alarm. He could also have Robin break into the plate's local processor and fool it into thinking Lance wasn't there, but—

But were hired to do job without me, Robin finished. *Except for recon and checking for nanobot hives, of course.*

Hey! Stay out of my head, meatless, Lance growled.

Sorry, Jaylance. Permanent lease, even if gets crowded in here. Jessica, by the way, thinks you should use cups.

I was thinking the same thing.

Lance unclipped from his tool belt four oddly shaped suction cups with handle straps on their backs. By contorting himself within the conduit's narrow confines, he managed to strap one cup on each knee and the other two on his hands. Then he rolled over, pressed his knees and hands to the conduit ceiling, and thumbed a small button on the back of the hand cups. With a faint hiss, all four cups clamped themselves to the ceiling. Lance pulled his body free of the floor and released the button on the left hand cup. This also released the cup on his right knee, allowing Lance to "crawl" one step forward on the ceiling and re-clamp the cups again. A drop of sweat slid into his ear as he made his way over the sensor plate with painful slowness.

Clear, Robin said, and Lance lowered himself gratefully back to the floor.

Ask Jessica how much further to the bedroom it is, Lance said, putting the cups away and massaging his aching wrists. *Her memory is better than mine and I know she saw the blueprints.*

She says not far. Less than ten meters. Hurry up. Garth getting nervous. Claustrophobic, you know.

Lance continued crawling up the dark, stuffy conduit,

pausing every so often to check for more security. In addition to the pressure plate, he had so far avoided eye beams, heat monitors, sonic sensors, and live guards both human and canine. This in addition to a high concrete wall topped with surprises ranging from simple broken glass to hair-thin whipwire, which could slice through flesh and bone like it was soft cheese. Almost missing the pressure plate had been Lance's first mistake and he had no intention of making another.

The old lady paid a lot of money for her security system, Lance thought. *She better have a money-back guarantee.*

Eventually, Lance's conduit branched and became too narrow to let him go forward. Frowning, he backed up until he came to a thick mesh barrier that looked into what appeared to be a storage room. The barrier had hinges on it and a latch on the other side. Lance popped a small welding torch out of his belt and used it to cut off the latch. It clattered to the ground and Lance soundlessly pushed the barrier open, wrinkling his nose at the sharp smell of melted metal.

Caution! Atmospheric toxicity levels rising. Torch not meant for use in close quarters.

Lance put the torch away, extinguished the glowband, and stole toward the storage room door. *Can't you compensate?*

Some. Have to carry poisoned red blood cells to excretory system before they can interact with other cells, then stimulate growth of replacements. No small feat. Takes much processing space. Please move with all haste toward exit. Jessica says bedroom is one level above us.

Lance cracked the door open and peered into the hallway beyond. Empty. Like a redheaded shadow, Lance slipped down the corridor. Thick carpets and expensive statuary made the job easier by silencing his footsteps and providing good places to hide. The place smelled like cinnamon.

An abstract sculpture caught Lance's eye and his heart beat faster. The sculpture was an intricate weave of copper wire that shone in the moonlight streaming through the windows. Lance stared at the sculpture, and a low moan escaped his throat. Wires. He remembered the wires. Panic rose. He had to run. He had to get *away*. Away from the—

Lance stiffened for the shortest of moments and his expression went perfectly blank. Then his face changed. Some of the lines softened, and the warm brown color drained from his eyes, replaced with a piercing emerald green. His posture was different—stiffer, less fluid—and when the moment passed, it was Jessica Meredeth Michaels who put her hands on her hips and looked confidently up and down the corridor.

Well, she thought. *It's about time. Now maybe we can get something done. *Robin?**

Here. What is needed?

Just checking. Jessica moved swiftly up the corridor, shooting a careless glance at the wire sculpture as she left. *Tasteless thing. Incredible what people will waste money on nowadays.*

She found a staircase and took it one flight up, almost sinking to her ankles in the too-soft carpet. Cinnamon from the aromaducts wafted after her, and Jessica made a small face. She hated cinnamon.

The stairs ended at a large round foyer. More statues and sculptures had been carefully placed around the circle, and a large set of double doors loomed opposite the staircase. If Jessica remembered correctly—and she always did—the bedroom and her quarry were within easy reach.

The woman is an idiot, Jessica thought. *She has state-of-the-art security outside her mansion and almost none inside. Once one penetrates it, there are no problems.*

Just pressure plates, eye beams, sonic—

Jessica waved a mental hand. **Yes, yes. But I see precious little of that here.**

Still, Jessica stayed close to the wall, keeping a sharp eye out for additional security. It would be foolish to take careless chances at this stage. She reached the double doors, however, without difficulty. Holding her breath, she turned the knob. Locked.

Bother, Jessica thought. *Robin, has Garth recovered from his claustrophobic fit, or is he still quivering in the corner?*

Garth fine, Robin replied.

He'll have to get us inside, Jessica said. *I'm a technician, not a common lockpick.*

And the face changed again. Green eyes shifted back to brown, a lazy, lopsided grin stole over the mouth, and the body's posture loosened considerably. Garth Blackstone scratched his nose and glared at the door.

"*Oh my. I'm a technician, not a common fucking lockpick,*" he thought. *Robin, tell Jess-baby if she doesn't take that stick out of her ass, I'm going to get a hammer and—*

Message relayed. Going to open door now? Job already taking too long.

Yeah, yeah. Garth plucked a small leather packet from the tool belt, removed a pair of small tools, and bent over the lock. *Watch and learn, Jess-baby.*

In less than ten seconds, there was a tiny click.

Ta da! Garth put the lockpicks away and fished a small black box from one of his jumpsuit's many pockets. *Looks like Jess-baby isn't so perfect after all. She should have had this in her hand before she even tried to open the door.* He punched a button on the box, took a deep breath, and flung the door open.

The bedroom beyond was stiflingly warm and luxuriously large. Moonlight streamed over a large elegant vanity table near an equally large bed. The bed's only occupant, an elderly woman, sat bolt upright and clutched the blankets to her chest. Garth flipped the door shut before she could scream and he smacked the manual light switch on the wall. Blinded, the old woman flung a wrinkled hand to her eyes and, with a speed that belied her age, slapped a button near the bed.

Nothing happened.

"We disconnected the alarm, Mrs. Gruenfeld," Garth said lazily. "And this—" he held up the little box "—is a short-range radio jammer, so the backup alarm you're fumbling for under your pillow won't work either."

Mrs. Gruenfeld lowered her hand and blinked at him. She had thin white hair and watery gray eyes. Her nightgown was thick and frilly, and it covered her from neck to wrist.

"Mr. Michaels?" she said.

That wasn't Garth's name, but he was used to answering to it, so he nodded and dropped the jammer back into his pocket. He didn't like the way Mrs. Gruenfeld was looking at him. Her eyes seemed to linger over his body, seeking, tracing. All of a sudden the formfitting jumpsuit Jessica insisted the Company use for breaking and entering seemed too tight, too revealing.

Being ridiculous, Robin said. *Imagination working overtime.*

What do you know, meatless? Just because you can't see it doesn't mean it ain't there. Garth's eyes accidentally met Mrs. Gruenfeld's and he almost flinched. *This isn't my area. I'm outta here.*

Another change, this one the reverse of the last. The eyes reverted to emerald green and the posture went from easygoing to stiff and tight. Jessica blinked, then quickly glanced around to get her bearings.

Listen fast, Robin said. *Garth unlocked bedroom door, jammed radio alarms. Mrs. Gruenfeld startled, surprised to see us.*

"How on earth did you get in here?" Mrs. Gruenfeld asked, still holding the blankets up to her neck. Her English was British, like Jessica's.

"That would take a while to explain, Mrs. Gruenfeld," Jessica replied. "The short version, however is that you have at least fourteen—"

Sixteen, Robin interrupted. *No security of any kind on door, and bedroom soundproofed. Can't scream for help.*

"—that is, *sixteen* weak points in your security system." Mrs. Gruenfeld's mouth fell open in indignation.

"Sixteen? I paid half a billion for this system. It's supposed to be impregnable."

"You obviously had doubts," Jessica pointed out with a tiny smile. "Otherwise you wouldn't have hired us to test it." She ejected a button from the computer on her wrist and dropped it on a nearby table. "The data is all there. We can fix the flaws and look for others, but that would be a separate job with a separate contract."

"I see." Mrs. Gruenfeld shook her head, then yawned. "You'll have to excuse me. I wasn't aware that you would try to break in here at three in the morning."

Jessica spread her hands. "Not many criminals come calling in the daylight, Mrs. Gruenfeld."

"You do have a point. Did you see any signs of hive activity?"

Negative. Searched most diligently.

"No," Jessica said. "Not a one."

Mrs. Gruenfeld sighed with relief and seemed to relax slightly, though she still held the blankets firmly in place.

Nice woman, Jessica mused, *despite the cyanide in the security system.*

"In that case," Mrs. Gruenfeld said, "you're worth every penny of your fee, Mr. Michaels. I have nightmares about nanobot hives."

"They're exceedingly rare, Mrs. Gruenfeld. You stand a greater chance of getting hit by a falling meteorite than having your computer systems go hive."

"You must allow an old lady her paranoia, Mr. Michaels," Mrs. Gruenfeld said. "In any case, I'll sleep better having had your assessment. I'm certainly glad your mother recommended you."

And Jessica changed without warning. A snarl twisted her face and her eyes glowed a dark blue. Patrick Kuiper crossed the room in three angry steps and grabbed the front of Mrs. Gruenfeld's nightgown. With one yank, he brought her face to his. The old woman's eyes flew wide and she gasped in surprise. Patrick could smell her breath, sour and warm.

"What do you mean Lance's mother recommended us?" he hissed.

"Let me go," Mrs. Gruenfeld whispered.

Patrick grinned at her fear. It felt good to be in control. He released the anger into his face and exulted as Mrs. Gruenfeld tried to cringe away.

"You're not so smart, rich bitch," he said in a dangerously soft voice. "I could snap your neck and be in free fall long before anyone found the body. I could call the fucking cops and let them know about the cyanide gas in your security system." He tightened his grip. "Now tell us who the fuck told you about the Michaels Company or I'll turn your head all the way around."

Mrs. Gruenfeld began to shake. "It was your mother," she quavered. "M-Meredeth Michaels. Please—you're hurting me."

"Fuck." Patrick released the old woman so quickly she fell against the pillows and lay there, gasping like a half-dead fish. Patrick strode angrily toward the door. *We're going to have words with Lance's mom,* he thought. *∗Robin, do you have control of the fucking security system?∗*

∗Negative. Michaels Company had to break in without me interfacing with estate's computers. Would invalidate analysis otherwise.∗

∗Then interface and shut it down, asshole. I'm keeping control for a while and I can't get around the goddamn system like mama-boy Lance.∗

∗Working.∗

Patrick shuddered and his skin crawled as he left the bedroom, closing the door on Mrs. Gruenfeld's wimpy cries for help. He couldn't actually feel Robin's nanos leaving his body, streaming from his eyes, ears, nose, even his cock and ass, in a microscopic stream, but it seemed like he could. Patrick hated that. And he hated Robin for making him feel that way, and he hated Lance for being such a wimp, and he hated Lance's mother for making a fool out of him. The hatred boiled within him, thick and black, and Patrick's hands shook with the intensity. He

wanted to break something, something that would shatter
with a satisfying crash. He wanted to get his hands around
Merry Michaels's neck and squeeze until she—

Interfacing with estate computer, Robin reported.
*System's nanos using standard protocols. Please hold
position until I can override command structure.*

Hurry up, Patrick snarled.

Override completed, Robin said almost instantly.
*Advise you to vacate premises with all speed. And watch
tone. Frontal lobotomy would almost certainly improve
disposition and can be arranged at will.*

Patrick's face contorted into a murderous mask. He
snatched a piece of statuary off a nearby pedestal and threw
it at a window. The priceless ceramic statue hit bulletproof
polyglass and shattered with a satisfying crash.

"Fuck your lobotomy," Patrick said. But he loped quickly
down the hallway before any servants arrived to investigate
the noise. Although Robin had shut off some sensors and
was probably putting ghosts on the rest to keep the live
guards busy, Patrick didn't want to waste time. He had
things to do.

Patrick wound his way through the Gruenfeld mansion,
partly relying on what he had seen through Lance's eyes
and partly relying on the directions Robin occasionally
threw at him. Patrick didn't like this place—it was spacious,
airy, full of soft carpets and hard furniture. It reminded
him of the house Lance had grown up in. And Patrick
hated that house. It had taken them fucking forever to
get the hell out.

A side door provided an easy exit and Patrick's blue eyes
automatically flicked over the darkened grounds, searching
for signs of movement. Elegantly sculptured bushes
bedecked a perfect lawn and provided a riot of color that
Patrick's enhanced vision had no trouble picking up even
in the dim moonlight. Reds, purples, golds, and blues were
laid out in a rigid perfection that completely destroyed
any eerie feelings the alien flora would have invoked.

Oooh, Patrick thought. *She can afford a garden put*

together from sixteen fucking planets. Mars comes to England. I'm so impressed.

There were sirens and shouts in the background. Patrick faded into a shadow and scanned the area, looking for guards.

∗*Will be none,*∗ Robin said. ∗*Guard staff currently chasing three sets of "intruders," none of which are in our vicinity. Head for main gate. Will arrange for it to be open.*∗

When Patrick arrived at the main gate, he found it unguarded—and open. He ground his teeth. Robin enjoyed showing Patrick up, and there was no way for Patrick to get back at Robin. He chalked up another note on his growing mental tally and jogged toward the car Lance had parked about a kilometer from the Gruenfeld estate.

∗*Please hold position until nanobots able to extricate selves from security system, return to main body.*∗

∗*Forget it, meatless,*∗ Patrick sneered. ∗*You'll have to do without.*∗

∗*Loss will endanger my consciousness. Hold position, or will take steps per Company Policy.*∗

∗*Oh yeah?*∗ Patrick kept jogging up the road. The shouts and sirens began to fade behind him. ∗*Like what?*∗

The road plunged into absolute blackness. Patrick stumbled and fell to the rough pavement, knocking the breath from his lungs and skinning the palms of both hands.

"Jesus fucking Christ!" he yelped. "What the fuck—?"

∗*Vision will return soon. Meanwhile, please hold position.*∗

"You goddamned bastard!" Patrick howled, and pounded the unyielding cement with his fists. Pain flashed through his hands, but he barely felt it. "I'll kill you! *Kill you!*"

∗*Welcome to try. Just please hold position. Nanos travelling through power lines above head, will return to body in thirty seconds. Twenty-nine. Twenty-eight.*∗

Patrick raged and bellowed as Robin ticked off the seconds in his head, but he didn't dare move far from his position. Not when he couldn't see. Abruptly, Robin reached zero and Patrick's vision snapped back into focus.

Finished. Suggest you leave area immediately. Guards almost certainly attracted by animal howling.

I'll kill you, meatless, Patrick snarled, getting to his feet. *One day I'll find a way, and you'll die, just like Kepplinger and Fletcher and that old derelict and that bitchy whore and all the others.*

Robin didn't answer. Patrick wiped his sore, bleeding hands on his jumpsuit and silently trotted to Lance's car. It was just a rental—not even a sports car—but it would get him to the train station. London, and Lance's mother, were only two connections away. The bitch was going to pay for what she had done. She was going to *pay*.

Patrick punched in the access code and gunned the motor, wishing it would make a satisfying gasoline roar instead of a faggoty turbine whine. At least it had halfway decent acceleration.

The tires squealed as Patrick tore down the road and flashed his middle finger at the Gruenfeld estate. Then he rolled down the windows and concentrated on driving. Patrick loved to drive. He could feel every nuance of the road beneath him and he leaned into every turn as if he were part of the car itself. He laughed aloud and tugged at his crotch, hoping someone would challenge him to an impromptu drag race or a game of chicken.

No one did. At the train station, he abandoned the car without returning it to the rental agency, wishing he could drive all the way to London, knowing he was too tired. Instead, he bought six first-class tickets on the night run to London so he could have an entire seating compartment to himself. It was expensive as hell, but Patrick deserved it after everything Robin had put him through. Lance was paying for it, so it didn't matter anyway. Besides, hadn't he gotten the Company out of the Gruenfeld mansion?

Smiling to himself, he settled back in his seat to get some sleep.

Delia Radford stubbornly crossed her arms and glared across her desk at—well, she wasn't totally sure who she was glaring at. He had blue eyes, so it was either Andy, Patrick, or Jay.

No, she thought. *It's not Jay. Jay's a dear. So it's either Andy or Patrick. He certainly isn't Lance.*

"You've got orders to let me in whenever the hell I want," not-Lance growled, yanking at the brown leather jacket he was wearing over a worn black jumpsuit. "You and everyone else in this fucking corporation. And I want to see Meredeth *now*."

Patrick, Delia decided, resting one foot lightly on the security call button under her desk. Orders or no orders, Patrick could get violent, and although he had never directed any hostility at her, Delia saw no reason to put up with nonsense—or endangerment—from him, no matter how much she liked Lance and Jessica.

"I've already informed you that she isn't in," Delia replied with freezing English civility. Americans were often easier to deal with if one remained perfectly, icily polite. "If you would care to tell me what this is about, I may be able to contact her and let her know you need to see her."

A sneer twisted Patrick's face. "Where the hell is she? Balling another physicist friend?"

"She's getting ready for a business trip," Delia said levelly. "A company called Pinegra is going bankrupt and has to sell a research station orbiting Thetachron III. Ms. Michaels is an interested buyer, and she wants to inspect the place herself, which means she has things to do before she leaves tomorrow morning. Why do you need to see her?"

"*Fucking* nigger bitch." Patrick's foot lashed out and thumped against Delia's desk. Since the desk was solid hardwood and bolted to the floor, the kick had little impact. Delia didn't even blink, despite the racial slur. As long as Patrick was lashing out at the furniture, the people around him were pretty safe. Still, she kept her foot on the alarm button.

"Is there a problem?" she asked with polite concern.

"The bitch recommended us for a security job," Patrick said, pacing to the wall-sized window that looked over a dreary, cloud-enshrouded London. "She can't keep her fucking nose out of our business, can she? For years she never did a fucking thing, and now she can't stay out of our life."

"Ms. Michaels didn't make the recommendation," Delia said quietly. "I did."

Patrick spun around. "What?"

"Ms. Michaels is very busy," Delia reminded him. "So when Carlina Gruenfeld dropped Ms. Michaels a netnote asking for a security specialist, I answered it and gave her your company's name."

Patrick stared at her. Delia steadily met his gaze. Then, between one heartbeat and the next, Patrick's eyes went from dark blue to a warm brown. The sneer vanished, replaced by an almost haunted look.

Delia mentally shook her head. The man standing by the window was handsome—incredibly handsome—under any conditions, but when he was "himself," as Delia thought of it, he was at his best. Red hair didn't often combine with large, puppy-brown eyes, but on Lance it worked. The formfitting black jumpsuit and short leather jacket showed off a *very* nice body that deliciously stirred Delia's hormones. But what attracted her most was the fact that he didn't seem to be aware of his looks. A nice change from most of the other men that had wandered through Delia's life.

"Lance?" Delia asked.

Lance—if it was Lance—blinked and glanced around the outer office, a tasteful affair carefully furnished in wood and leather. Miniature trees trained to grow in a lush imitation of a medieval forest lined the walls. Delia's desk was scrupulously neat, though where most people would have pictures of relatives, Delia put half a dozen carvings of small birds in keeping with the office motif. The aromaducts, of course, had been programmed for loam and fresh breezes, though Delia could smell neither one.

"Delia?" Lance said. Then his eyes briefly took on a

glazed look, as if he were listening to some kind of inner voice. "Uh, right. Umm, so Mom isn't in?"

Delia shook her head. "Sorry. She—we—should be back in three or four days."

Lance took a hesitant step toward Delia's desk. "We?"

Delia nodded. "Ms. Michaels wants minimal staff on this visit. Since I know more about the deal than anyone else besides her, I get to go." She grimaced. "I'm not looking forward to it—I swear phasing mucks with my implants." She held up her right hand and wiggled the fingers. It looked perfectly normal, but there was poly-steel and plastic beneath the newskin. Her right leg had been rebuilt the same way, along with large portions of her face. On most days, Delia couldn't tell the difference.

"A phase drive shouldn't affect your implants," Lance said.

"I know." Delia shook her head wryly. "It just seems like I get phantom pains more often after a jump. But duty calls. And I get a hefty bonus for trips like this, so I suppose it's worth it. Anyway," she said, changing the subject to keep the conversation going, "how's the security analysis business going?"

"Fine," Lance replied, nervously removing his jacket and holding it in front of him. "Carlina Gruenfeld's system was full of holes, though. The person who designed it should be shot."

"Are you going to redesign it for her?"

Lance shook his head ruefully. "I doubt it. She, uh, didn't like us much." He paused and wet his lips. "Listen, Delia— I'm sorry about . . . about what I said. I guess I, uh, lost my temper."

The look on his face was so contrite that Delia's heart went out to him. She had met Lance three years ago, just after she had become Meredeth Michaels's chief administrative assistant. A few months later—spurred by Lance's odd behavior, his constantly shifting eye color, and a certain conversation with Jessica—she had become a regular on the library nets reading up on multiple

personality disorder. Delia, however, had not told Lance
that she knew about the Company. It was odd, in its way—
in three years, the timing had never been right for it.

Mostly because the only time I see Lance is in this office,
she thought wryly. *And just what is one supposed to say,
anyway? "Oh, and Lance—Jessica told me you have
multiple personalities. Just thought I'd let you know."*

"You don't have to apologize, Lance," Delia said, smiling.
"I'm sure the cleaning staff can remove the footprint from
my desk."

Lance cringed and Delia was instantly sorry she had
made the joke. Lance was always so serious. Delia couldn't
ever remember seeing him smile. Andy smiled, but Andy
made Delia nervous.

Lance ran a hand through his hair. "Well, sorry to bother
you. I guess I'll be going."

"You don't have to dash off," Delia said before he could
turn away. "I'm just about finished here and was planning
to get a cup of coffee before going home to pack. Join
me?"

"Uh, well, I'm kind of behind schedule," Lance temporized,
"and I have things to do."

You always have things to do, Delia thought with an
inward sigh. But she knew better than to push. Lance would
disappear for weeks if she did.

"I see," she said aloud. "But Lance—if you ever want
to talk to someone, or if you ever need help, just let me
know. All right?"

"Yes, all right," Lance said quickly. "Thanks, Delia. I
really have to go." He turned, got halfway through the
doorway, and stopped cold. His back stiffened. Puzzled,
Delia craned her neck, trying to see what was going on.

"Lance?" she asked.

After a long moment, Lance backed into the room, still
holding his jacket in front of him. A short woman stood
in the doorway. Her strawberry-blond hair was pulled back
into a French braid and she wore an immaculate beige
business jumpsuit with no jewelry. A large computer

notebook was tucked under one arm. She appeared to be in her very early thirties, but had the unmistakably confident, mature air of someone at least twenty years older. Not even bodysculpt could hide attitude.

"Mom," Lance said quietly.

"Hello, Lance," Meredeth Michaels said. She made no move to embrace him. "What are you doing here? Not that I mind," she added quickly. "It's just a surprise. I haven't seen you in—what?—almost six months."

"I thought you were going on a trip," Lance said. Tension rose in the room and Delia shifted uncomfortably.

"I am," Meredeth said. "I just remembered a few details I needed to take care of back here, but they can wait. Have you eaten lunch?"

"Probably," Lance replied evenly, and Delia caught sight of the slight wince that crossed Meredeth's face. Then Delia realized she was staring and quickly busied herself with tracking down a missing netfile, though she couldn't help sneaking glances.

"Yes, well," Meredeth floundered, "perhaps we could pop downstairs for a quick cup of coffee or tea? I'd like to see you."

Lance's jaw clenched and his posture went so taut, Delia half expected it to snap. "No thanks, Mom. I've really— well, why not? I could use a bit of something, I think."

Delia glanced up sharply. In mid-sentence his accent had gone from American to English, and his voice was pitched quite a bit higher. His eyes had become a brilliant green. The eye-color changes fascinated Delia, no matter how many times she had seen it. It was a puzzle how Lance— or his alters—pulled it off. As far as she knew, MPD didn't normally produce such dramatic physical alterations.

Ms. Michaels had obviously noticed the switch. "Why don't we go into my office for a moment?" She flicked her eyes at Delia, who had gone back to work again with what she hoped was the air of someone who hadn't heard a thing.

"Don't be silly, Mother. Delia knows about the Company."

Green-eyed Lance strode briskly across the room to Delia's desk and held out a hand. "Hello, Delia. So nice to see you again."

Delia's stomach made a quick flip-flop at Jessica's forthright gesture. She had not told Ms. Michaels what she had learned about Lance—it hadn't seemed appropriate—and she cast about for a graceful way out of the greeting. None came to mind. Delia smiled faintly and shook the proffered hand. "Hello, Jessica."

Meredeth Michaels was staring. "You told her?"

"Why shouldn't I?" Jessica replied blandly. "It's not Lance's fault—or yours—that your first husband was a monster. Besides, Delia would never hurt us, and Lance likes her a great deal, even if he can't bring himself to say more than three words to her."

Delia cleared her throat and tried not to squirm. "Perhaps I should go down to accounting and check those receipts you were asking about, Ms. Michaels?"

"Yes, thank you, Delia," Ms. Michaels replied faintly. "That would be very helpful."

Delia all but bolted from the office, wondering how on earth she was going to face spending the next three days with Meredeth Michaels.

"Are you all right?" said Meredeth. "Hello?"

Lance shook his head and flicked a quick glance at his surroundings. He was sitting at a table in Mom's office, which was more heavily forested than the foyer where Delia had her desk. Birds—or recordings of the same—sang sweetly, while bright sunlight seemed to filter pleasantly through the branches. Lilac-scented breezes coasted by. The table was littered with snack plates, crumbs, and empty china teacups, and his jacket was draped across the chair behind him.

"Your eyes are brown," Meredeth said. "Is that you, Lance?"

"It's me, Mom," Lance replied. "Though I'm not sure why I'm here."

"You were just saying that I'm your mother and that a good son would at least say hello." There was a pinched look on Meredeth's too-youthful face. "We were having a very nice chat about mothers and children, you and I."

"You and Jessica had the chat," Lance corrected. "I had nothing to do with it."

"You and I," Meredeth repeated in a stubborn voice. "I've done research, Lance. Jessica isn't real. She's—"

"Jessica is another person, Mom," Lance interrupted tiredly. "Just like Garth and Jay and Grandpa Jack and the rest of the Company. I'm not them and they aren't me. I've told you that over and over."

"I remember. Have you gone back to see Dr. Baldwin yet?"

"Mom, I haven't seen Dr. Baldwin in twelve years. Why would I go back now?"

"Well, one can't help hoping—"

"That your son will stop being a loony?" Lance got up to pace the loamy carpet. "That one day I'll integrate and be sane, healthy, and normal?"

"That's not what I said."

"It's what you meant. Things are fine the way they are, Mom. I'm sorry you don't like it. I can't help what you and Dad did to—"

"I had nothing to do with it," Meredeth interrupted, echoing Lance's earlier words. "Your father made you what you are. We both know that."

Lance turned and locked eyes with her for a long time. She met his gaze for a moment, then looked away.

"Enjoy your trip, Mom," Lance said at last. "I understand there's a lot of money to be made, and we all know how important that is."

He snatched up his jacket and left the office, ignoring the white knuckles on his mother's hands.

The elevator ride to the ground floor took forever, and Lance all but sprinted into the streets of the London business district, glad to get out of the office.

Always are, Robin said.

"Keep your opinions to yourself, meatless," Lance muttered, and trotted up the nearly empty sidewalk. It was a cloudy day—normal for London—and the sidewalk was damp, though Lance didn't remember it raining. A faint chill hung in the air.

Occasional electric cars buzzed by on the pavement, and a lone man wheeled an elderly bicycle down the sidewalk. Lance glanced upward at the tall, half-empty buildings. The business district, with its blocky concrete and precisely placed windows, was actually rather boring. There was talk of levelling the place and trying to re-create historical London. Almost no one was left there anyway. Most executives preferred to live on less crowded planets and conduct meetings on vidphone via Tach-Com. Meetings could even be attended in simulated person, if everyone didn't mind wearing virtual reality gear and plugging into Tach-Net.

All thanks to Mom, Lance thought, bitterly shoving his hands into his pockets. *What a woman.*

Lance passed a small park where a young woman sat eating a late lunch on one of the benches. She paused, sandwich halfway to her mouth, as Lance drew near. Lance could feel her eyes on him, staring, hungry, and he automatically hunched into himself until he passed her by. He continued down the street, trying to pull his jacket lower over his jumpsuit. The jumpsuit, while functional for contract work, was far and away too tight, and Lance blushed furiously at the thought that Delia had seen him in it.

∗*Suit not that tight, Jaylance,*∗ Robin commented.

∗*I said, keep it to yourself.*∗

Lance jammed his hands into his jacket pockets and turned his thoughts back to the Gruenfeld affair so he wouldn't have to think about his mother. Patrick had violated Company Policy by taking over during the fulfillment of a contract. Probably the only thing that kept Mrs. Gruenfeld from pressing assault charges was that the Company knew about the illegal cyanide in her security system. In any case, she would certainly never call the Michaels Company again. Patrick had screwed up everything and, as manager, Lance had to mete out discipline. He grimaced. May as well get it over with.

Robin, tell Patrick no more prostitutes until further notice. He can watch Andy if he wants, but that's it. And I'll do any driving.

Done.

A passerby turned to stare at him. Lance sighed and trudged onward, sinking lower into depression with every step. Meredeth Michaels, his own mother, had built the largest communications empire in existence while her son ran a tiny security system analysis service out of a jumpship. Patrick was probably pissed, the Company had lost a lucrative client, Lance had spent the afternoon arguing with his mother—

And he was being followed.

The depression vanished, replaced by sudden tension. Lance casually glanced over his shoulder. The man with the bicycle was still about a block behind him, though Lance had turned three corners by now. Panic rose, and he fought it off.

Robin?

Here, Jaylance.

Did you get a good look at the man back there with the bike?

Affirmative.

Link up with my wristcomp and check the ship's computer to see if his face is in the database for Dad's operatives.

Working.

Lance turned another corner and broke into a trot for a count of ten, then lapsed back into a walk. The bicycle man came around the corner a moment later. Lance hoped he hadn't noticed the increased distance between them. Though Lance could probably outdistance the man with ease, he didn't want to break into a run—it would be better to lose him by "accident" and get out of London as fast as possible.

Identity confirmed, Robin said. *Name unknown, but is operative for Jonathan Blackstone. Was involved in kidnapping attempt two years ago.*

Lance cursed under his breath. Mom had forced Blackstone International out of London just after Lance's last visit to Dr. Baldwin, but Dad still maintained an underground presence there. It was either sheer bad luck that Lance had been spotted, or—more likely—Dad's operatives kept an eye on MM, Limited. Lance himself hardly ever went near the place, but Patrick had been the one to go in.

The bicycle man raised his wrist and muttered briefly to it, then reached into his coat.

Shit, Lance thought, speeding up without looking back. *Probably calling for backup. And it won't take them long to arrive, if I know Dad.* His eyes flicked left and right, looking for a probable escape route.

Attention! Attention! Robin interrupted. *Message from Andy. Has been exactly ten days since he has had "night out" and wishes to remind you of Company Policy: one night for Andy every ten days, no excuses or exceptions.*

Lance gritted his teeth, trying to think of options. *Not now, Robin. Tell him we'll talk as soon as I get myself out of this.* The alleys, maybe?

Could head back to MM building, Robin pointed out. *Mother doubtless willing to handle Blackstone goons encroaching on—*

Shut up, meatless, Lance snapped. *I don't need her help.* The alleys. It would have to be the alleys.

With a deep breath, Lance turned another corner and bolted.

He shot down the street, making for an opening between two buildings just as the bicycle man came around the corner. There was a hissing crack, and a projectile needle shattered against a building wall. The few people on the sidewalk turned to stare. Lance tore past them, shoved a suited man out of his way, and the bicycle man fired his needler again. Something sharp pierced the back of Lance's right arm, but he kept running.

Robin!

Working.

"Stop that man!" shouted Bicycle. "He's a wanted criminal!"

People on the street were either turning to gawk or screaming in fear. Bicycle dropped the bike and ran forward, ignoring the people who scrambled to get out of his way.

"Stop him!" he cried again. "Halt!"

Lance kept running. The alley was only ten meters ahead. Five. One. Lance risked a glance behind, and another needle penetrated his shoulder. He threw himself around the corner into the alley, then staggered dizzily against the rough bricks.

Robin—

Needles coated with terraphine, Robin said. *Am trying to keep contaminated blood cells from carrying anesthetic to brain, but success limited. Body has received enough drug to drop adult hippopotamus. Do not get shot again, Jaylance.*

Lance stumbled forward, forcing his legs to work. The alley smelled of cheap beer and fried fish and the walls looked fuzzy—the terraphine at work. A fire escape formed a black lattice against the side of the building, but Lance wouldn't have time to climb it. Bicycle would be there in seconds.

Adrenaline rush to boost the implants, Robin, he said. *Now!*

Done.

Lance's vision snapped back into focus and his heart pounded madly. With a quick glance upward, he gathered himself and *leaped.* Air rushed past his ears and the ground fell away. His fingers grasped the side of the fire escape almost three stories above the alley pavement just as Bicycle rounded the corner, needler in hand. He wasn't looking up. Heart still hammering in his chest, Lance clung to the cool metal for a moment, then began to haul himself quietly over the edge. Carefully, silently, he brought his body level with the rail—

—and overcompensated. His adrenaline-hyped muscles flipped him too quickly and he landed with a ringing thump on the other side. The operative glanced upward and fired. Another needle shattered with a loud *pung* on the fire escape.

Attention! Attention! Robin said. *Andy taking over soon. Says to remember Company Policy.*

Oh God—not now. Lance yanked himself to his feet and clattered up the metal stairs. Another needle shattered right behind him. *Tell Andy to wait! Tell him he can have a full vacation later, no strings attached!*

Trying, but Andy not good listener.

Lance bolted up another flight. A few more steps, and he would be safe on the roof. Even if Bicycle climbed the fire escape, Lance would be long gone. He could easily evade the backups, hop the ferry, and be in France before—

Sharp pain as another needle pierced his arm. The world tilted dizzily. Darkness lined the edges of his vision and his limbs felt too heavy to move. Lance barely threw himself up the final step and onto the roof.

*Robin . . . *

Too much, Jaylance. Can't keep terraphine out of central nervous system.

Lance's eyes slid shut. Below, he heard metallic thumps as someone climbed the fire escape before darkness rose and claimed him.

Andrew Braun scrambled to his feet and cautiously peered over the edge of the roof. Bicycle was climbing the fire escape, whistling to himself and probably calculating his bonus. He was a tall, lithe man, with brown hair and blue eyes.

Andy crouched near the top of the fire escape ladder and cracked his knuckles. Bicycle was after Lance, not Andy, but in Andy's experience most people didn't bother to ask about the difference. Andy was no relation to

Jonathan Blackstone or Meredeth Michaels and he didn't give two shits about either one of them, but he was still stuck with some of Lance's problems.

Like this operative.

A pair of hands grasped the top rung of the ladder. Andy waited a moment, then grabbed the man's wrists and yanked him over the edge of the roof. Bicycle squawked in alarm, then grunted when Andy threw him to the roof tiles. In a flash, Andy was sitting on his chest with the operative's arms pinned beneath his knees.

Andy gave him a cheerful grin. "You're looking for Lance, aren't you?"

Bicycle stared up at him, eyes wide, mouth open. "How—how did—?" he squeaked. "I mean—I got you with the terraphine."

"You shot Lance, bucko. Not me."

"What are you talking about?" he sputtered, but Andy could feel his muscles tensing, getting ready to move.

Andy calmly reached behind himself and grabbed Bicycle's crotch. "Move, and I'll give you the motherfucker of all squeezes."

Bicycle froze. "I've got backups coming," he said. "We'll find you eventually."

Andy squeezed, and Bicycle sucked in his breath. With his other hand, Andy went through the man's pockets until he came up with the needle pistol. He thumbed the safety off and aimed it at Bicycle's neck.

"I'm allergic to terraphine," Bicycle said in a calm voice. "I'll die if you use that."

Tires squealed on the pavement below. Doors clicked open and slammed shut, footsteps and shouts echoed up the alley to the roof. The fire escape started to thrum under hurried feet.

"Ain't that a bitch?" Andy said, and pulled the trigger. Bicycle gasped and went limp.

"Be grateful," Andy told him. "Patrick would have thrown you off the roof."

He got up, dashed lightly over the rooftop, and dropped

four stories to the alley opposite the backup team. He trotted briskly away, confident that he was safe. If Bicycle really was allergic to terraphine, his buddies would be distracted by the need to get him hospitalized. If Bicycle was lying—well, the backups weren't expecting an unconscious agent, and they would pause to investigate, long enough for Andy to disappear. He laughed, enjoying the feel of muscle moving beneath skin. Lance just didn't understand that you had to get out and have fun once in a while. You couldn't let yourself get bogged down in stupid worries.

Andy emerged from the alley and almost ran into a taxicab. He grinned. *See?* he thought. *Everything'll work out fine if you just go with the flow.*

He yanked open the passenger door and dropped into the seat. It had taken Andy forever to work out some kind of schedule with Lance, and Andy was going to stick to it no matter what. He got his night out every ten days, come hell, high water, or Jonathan Blackstone.

And then there was the vacation Lance had promised. It was his, no conditions, no strings attached. Andy would have to get on the network and make some reservations. He fingered Lance's cashcard and grinned.

The driver turned his head. "Where ye headin', mister?"

"New Whitechapel," Andy replied, still grinning.

The driver suddenly matched Andy's smile with one of his own. A friendly, knowing smile. "Go for the odd bits, do you? Listen, I know a great place. Easy to find what you're looking for. Female, male, group—you name it."

Andy leaned back and cracked his knuckles. "Sounds perfect. Step on it—I'm already behind schedule."

The driver stepped on it.

Callused fingers stroked Lance's arm. He blinked, then realized he was lying on a strange bed in a strange room staring into the eyes of a stranger. Again.

Lance sat up. Both he and the other man were completely naked atop a set of rubber sheets, but an array of black

leather clothing was strewn over the floor and bedposts.
A length of hose and a set of handcuffs dangled from a
ceiling hook. One corner was entirely taken up by a narrow
table fitted with leather straps and strategically placed
holes. Plastic instruments littered the floor, and the room
stank of old leather and sweat. Lance's groin, back, and
buttocks stung, and there was something in his mouth.
He grimaced and pulled out a pair of white feathers. One
of them was streaked with blood.

"Something the matter?" the man asked, also sitting up.
He was fair-skinned and muscular, with a pale blond
mustache.

Lance's skin crawled with embarrassment. Every fiber
of his being cried out that this was wrong, that he would
be punished for this. But Andy didn't care. Andy's tastes
knew no discrimination. Women, men, teens, singles,
doubles, groups, actives, passives, or psychos. It was all
the same to Andy. And Lance always had to pick up the
pieces. Lance was always the one who got punished.

Robin—

*Here, Jaylance. Andy took "night out," found partner
in S and M bar about an hour ago. Name is Brad and
you don't owe him money. Are in his flat. Has been almost
two hours since alley dustup, but this still London. Suggest
we leave immediately. Have removed terraphine from
system, so alters don't have to keep you awake.*

Lance nodded to himself. It was a common occurrence
among sufferers of multiple personality disorder. One alter
might be drunk or drugged, but the others usually remained
unaffected. After all, why should Andy get knocked out
if Lance was dosed with terraphine? Andy was a different
person.

"Andy?" Brad asked again. His accent was vaguely
Scottish. "What's wrong?"

Forcing himself to overcome his embarrassment, Lance
got up and rummaged around on the floor until he found
his jumpsuit and jacket near the flat's single window. He
had to get moving. Robin said they were still in London,

and therefore still in danger. Andy wasn't very good with details and was likely to be careless and overconfident when it came to running away from Dad.

"Andy?" Brad asked, starting to get up.

"Uh, listen," Lance said, hurrying into his clothes. "I have to go."

Brad sighed and slumped back into the bed. "I knew you were going to say that. They always say that. I really like you, Andy. Why do you have to run?"

"It's not why you think," Lance said uncomfortably, going through his pockets and strapping on his wristcomp. "I mean—"

The door crashed open. Two men with pistols filled the doorway and sprayed the room with a barrage of needles. Brad's jaw had time to drop before he crumpled into a heap on the bed. Without thinking, Lance dove straight out the window amid shattering glass and fell through the chill night air.

CHAPTER TWO

THEN

Meredeth:

The first time Jonathan hit me was on our honeymoon in Africa. He didn't hit me hard. It didn't even hurt, really. He probably didn't even realize—

No. I'm done making excuses. He hit me, and I let him. That's all there is to it.

It happened while we were "going at it" in our tent. Jonathan and I were always "going at it" or "whetting Willy's whistle" or "having a good old-fashioned fuck." Having a good old-fashioned fuck meant that I was lying on my back without moving. Sometimes it meant I was kneeling on hands and knees. We never made love, though I didn't realize this until much later.

I remember that Jonathan was being rather loud, louder than he usually was. I was embarrassed because the servants' tents weren't all that far away and I knew they could hear us. So I put my hand over his mouth and whispered, "Shhh. Not so loud."

He slapped me without missing a stroke. Just hard enough to sting. I was so surprised my mouth fell open. Jonathan went on with his good old-fashioned fuck as if nothing had happened while I just lay there, too startled to move. Jonathan yelled when he came. Then *he kissed my forehead and rolled off me.*

A bit later when he was asleep, I stared down at him, a little ashamed. It wasn't really his fault—I had tried to interfere right when it was almost impossible for him to stop. What did I expect? Besides, it didn't hurt. It was more like a love bite. Some people thrash or scratch. Jonathan probably acted out of reflex. He probably didn't even remember doing it. Reassured, I went to sleep.

The second time he hit me was when I told him I was pregnant.

A limo hummed into the driveway, setting off the electronic warning Meredeth had programmed into the house computer. Hurriedly she lit the candles on the table and stood back to survey her handiwork. Everything had to be perfect, partly because she wanted it to be and partly because she knew Jonathan would expect nothing less.

It hadn't been easy to get everything that way. Meredeth wanted to arrange everything herself, for one thing, and for another, the dining room was better suited for entertaining fifty or sixty people, not hosting an intimate dinner for two. To compensate, Meredeth had chosen a tablecloth in warm blue and put comfortable cushions on the chairs. The aromaducts were set for a hint of woodsmoke. She had used the best china, set out her mother's silver, and put on a brand new dress, emerald green and cut low, but not too low—just as Jonathan liked it. A small cart in the kitchen awaited Meredeth's command to wheel silently into the dining room, and a silver bucket on the table held an ice-cold bottle of champagne. The servants had strict orders to stay out of the way.

Jonathan's chauffeur would be opening the limo door for him about now. Meredeth patted her short strawberry-blond hair and surveyed the room with a critical eye. It was too bright. You could hardly tell there were candles burning.

"Chloe," she said, "dim the lights."

"Please specify desired level of illumination," answered the computer.

"Chloe, set the lights to one-third current setting."

The lights obediently dimmed. Meredeth rubbed her bare arms and shivered. Was it too cool in the house?

"Chloe, what is the temperature in the dining room?"

"Seventy degrees Fahrenheit."

Meredeth did some quick math. That was about twenty-one degrees Celsius. She smiled to herself and shook her head. The Blackstone mansion might be located just outside of Dover, England, but Jonathan was still an American through and through. Even the house computer wasn't allowed to use metric.

She paced about the room, high heels clicking like claws on the marble floor. Was seventy degrees warm enough? It was a chilly spring day outside and Jonathan would probably want heat.

"Chloe, increase temperature to seventy-three—no, make that seventy-two degrees." It wouldn't do to have it too warm, either.

"Mr. Blackstone has entered the house," Chloe said.

Meredeth's heart beat faster and she forced herself to stand still. "Chloe, did you tell Jonathan that I'm waiting for him in the dining room?"

"Affirmative."

Meredeth waited next to the table, trying not to fidget. "Hello, honey," she murmured. "Have a nice day at work? I have some news for you."

She shook her head and tried again. "Jonathan, dear. I have to tell you—you're going to be a father."

No. "Jonathan! We're having a baby!" Now *there* was a winner. "Jonathan, I'm going to have a baby." Worse—it sounded like he was excluded. "Jonathan, would you like some champagne? Thank you, none for me. Have to watch out for the baby."

It occurred to her that Jonathan should have arrived by now. The dining room wasn't all that far away from the front door.

"Chloe," she said, "where is Jonathan?"

"Mr. Blackstone is in the master bedroom."

Ah. Probably changing clothes, she decided. "Chloe, activate intercom to Mr. Blackstone."

"Activated."

"Jonathan?" she asked.

"What?"

His flat tone made her nervous again. It was a strange feeling. She used to look forward to seeing him. Now he made her nervous. When had that started?

"I—how was your day?"

"Fine."

"Are you coming down to the dining room?" Meredeth noticed her mouth was dry. "I have—I mean, I've made dinner for us. It's curried shrimp. Your favorite."

"You made it? Did the cook get sick?"

"No. I just wanted to do something special tonight." Silence.

"Jonathan?"

"I'm not all that hungry. It was a long day and I was planning to soak in the jacuzzi."

Meredeth's shoulders slumped. Then she perked up, remembering that Jonathan loved champagne in the jacuzzi. If she hurried, she could probably make it to the pool area, change into a suit, and be waiting for him. That would show him how adaptable she was. And the food cart would keep dinner hot for at least an hour in case he got hungry.

Meredeth picked up the house remote and tapped the intercom's mute button. "Chloe, fill the jacuzzi," she said. "Temperature setting three." She released the button and raised her voice. "Why don't I meet you at the pool, then?"

"Fine," Jonathan replied. "Chloe, deactivate intercom."

"Deactivated."

Smiling to herself, Meredeth snatched the champagne bottle from the bucket, kicked off her high heels, and set off at a dead run.

She barely made it. The door to the men's changing room opened just as she was settling next to a large jacuzzi with the bottle of champagne. The tiles were deliciously warm, contrasting with the ice-cold champagne bottle, and the room was already steamy and humid. Jonathan Blackstone strode into the room clad in a fluffy green robe.

Meredeth smiled up at him. She had to be the luckiest woman alive—in love with and married to a man like Jonathan Blackstone. Not only was he wealthy, he was handsome. That deep red hair, those boyish brown eyes, the engaging smile, his wonderful body, smooth and sleekly muscled. And he loved her, too, and now she was carrying his baby.

Jonathan nodded to Meredeth, then wordlessly shrugged out of his robe—he was nude underneath—and slipped into the jacuzzi with a splash and a sigh.

"God, what a day," he muttered.

Meredeth swallowed her disappointment at his casual attitude—the bathing suit was very revealing and Meredeth knew she had a knockout body. And hard exercise, not bodysculpt, kept it that way. But she put a sympathetic look on her face and slid around behind Jonathan so she could sit on the lip of the jacuzzi and massage the stiff, knotted muscles of his shoulders. He was tense. The baby could wait. She let one foot dangle in the hot, soothing water.

"Have some champagne," she said soothingly, "and tell me about it."

Jonathan gulped a swallow from the glass Meredeth offered. "First of all, Dr. Mtang threatened to quit if we didn't give him another raise and put another spouse on the benefit program—for free." He took another deep draft. "The bastard knows the phase drive project would collapse without him. I had to give it to him."

Meredeth clucked her tongue and kept rubbing his shoulders. Jonathan's skin was warm and damp. "How many spouses does that make?"

"Five," Jonathan spat. "Three wives and two husbands. And then, just when the labs thought they had generated a stable phase field, they found out it only works if the generator remains in one spot. Useless!"

"They'll solve the problem," Meredeth said, still massaging, though her fingers were starting to ache. "They just need more time."

Jonathan snorted and set the champagne glass on the tile with a clink. Then he fell silent. Meredeth kept massaging.

Why am I so nervous? she thought. *Come on, it's easy. You've been rehearsing all day. All right, on three. Ready? One . . . two . . .*

"And then," Jonathan said unexpectedly, "one of my assistants misplaced the—"

"Jonathan, I'm pregnant," she blurted.

Jonathan jerked himself out of her hands and spun to face her. Water splashed and swirled around him. "What did you say?"

She smiled and self-consciously put a hand on her stomach. "I'm going to have a baby."

Silence. Jonathan backed away from the edge of the jacuzzi and stood up, dripping in the waist-deep water. His eyes were flashing and Meredeth was suddenly very unsure of herself.

"What do you mean, you're pregnant?" he asked in a dangerous voice. "We've only been married two months. I told you we would have a baby in a couple more years. When I was ready. Jesus fucking Christ, Meredeth—how could you let this happen?"

Meredeth flushed. "Accidents still happen, Jonathan. Even with implants."

"Have you scheduled the abortion yet?"

"Abortion?" Meredeth got to her feet, almost shaking from sudden tension, though she couldn't tell whether it was anger or fear. "What are you talking about? I don't want an abortion. There's no reason for it."

Jonathan's jaw tightened. He started to reply, then apparently realized Meredeth had a height advantage on him. He climbed out of the jacuzzi, still naked, and stepped toward her. Meredeth forced herself not to step back. A chill went down her back.

"There's a very good reason," he said, voice low. "I'm not ready for a son yet. We'll have one when I say so, not before."

"How do you know it's a son?" Meredeth's voice shook. "It could be a daughter."

"I don't care what it is," he snarled. "We aren't having it."

"Jonathan, what's wrong with you? This is your baby, too."

"I told you to call the doctor and schedule an abortion," Jonathan snapped almost in her face.

Meredeth straightened. "No," she said firmly.

The blow rocked her, sent her to her knees. Stunned, Meredeth looked up. Jonathan's face was red and angry, not at all handsome. He drew his hand back and Meredeth tried to scramble away, but her body moved too slowly. A small part of her noticed Jonathan's erection even as the second blow landed. Pain wracked her head and she lay dazed on the hard tile floor, dimly aware that Jonathan was sitting on top of her, his full weight crushing her chest until she could barely breathe.

"You'll obey," he hissed in her face, "because I'm your husband. You're nothing without me, Meredeth. You and your pretentious trash family. You're *nothing*."

Meredeth gasped and tried to squirm away, but he grabbed her wrist in one hand with grinding force.

"I didn't tell you to get up," he snarled. "I'll tell you when to get up after I show you what happens when you don't obey." With the other hand he tore off her bikini bottom. Meredeth cried out and he slapped her again. "Shut up." He pushed her legs apart and shoved himself into her.

The pain was horrible. Meredeth heard herself begging him to stop, to let her go, but he ignored her and thrust all the harder, laughing at her, tormenting her.

And then it was over. Jonathan pulled on his robe and

left without a word. After a long moment, Meredeth stirred and sat up. Her head ached and her groin burned. A wave of nausea suddenly swept her and she vomited into the jacuzzi. Then she huddled in a tiny ball on the floor, trembling uncontrollably.

She couldn't comprehend what had just happened to her. It was simply impossible—her mind refused to accept it. When she had met Jonathan a year ago playing virtual reality games on the networks and he had asked to see her in person, Meredeth had been pleasantly surprised, then overwhelmed, to discover he was the fourth wealthiest man on the planet. Love, romance, and tenderness followed, and all from the perfect man. Her parents were overjoyed at the announcement of their engagement—at age twenty-three their little girl had Done Well. Married into a real, high-society family. And now this wonderful, perfect man had raped her. Beaten her and raped her. It couldn't be.

It must be a mistake, she thought. *Just a horrible mistake. I must have done something wrong. Maybe if I had told him gently about the baby, waited until the timing was right instead of blurting it out like an idiot. It must have scared him and he lashed out. It was my fault. He wasn't ready and I should have realized it. It was my fault, not his.*

The floor was growing cold. Meredeth sat up, grimacing at the sour taste in her mouth. A tear leaked from one eye and she wiped it away angrily. She wasn't going to cry. It had been a mistake. There was no reason to cry. No reason.

A single, choked sound escaped her throat, and suddenly she was sobbing. There was no one to hear her. Eventually, the tears subsided and Meredeth got up to look at the mess in the jacuzzi.

Another thing that's my fault, she thought. "Chloe, drain the jacuzzi, fill it, and drain it again. Chloe, tell one of the servants the jacuzzi needs to be cleaned."

"Acknowledged."

Meredeth limped into the women's changing room and looked at herself in the mirror. A bruise was forming under her right eye and her nose was red and swollen from crying. She washed up, swallowed half a dozen painkillers from the dispensary and, not knowing what else to do, pulled her emerald dress back on and went upstairs to the dining room. Jonathan, dressed in slacks and a sweater, was seated at the table, eating.

"The curry sauce is a little spicy," he said as Meredeth sat down. "Otherwise this is pretty good. If you keep this up, you might be a half decent cook one day."

"Thank you," Meredeth almost whispered.

Jonathan continued making small talk, to which Meredeth gave dull, noncommittal answers. When at last the meal was over—Meredeth didn't touch her plate—Jonathan got up and gave her a quick peck on the cheek. Meredeth managed not to flinch.

"I've got some reading to do before I turn in," he said. "It's been a long day."

Meredeth nodded.

"Love you, darling." And he was gone. Meredeth sat and stared for a long time at her plate.

She couldn't abort the baby. It was impossible. Even though she was only in her second month, it seemed to Meredeth that she could already feel the baby moving inside her, waiting to be born. To live. Jonathan could understand that, couldn't he? He just needed a little time. A little time to get used to it. Once he could feel the baby moving inside her too, he would feel the same way she did.

But how could she buy that kind of time? Jonathan could force her to get an abortion, she was sure of that. In addition to the transportation corporations, ocean farms, power companies, and God knew what else, Jonathan owned a string of medical facilities and research hospitals that stretched across half a dozen countries. Scheduling an abortion—even an unwanted one—would be no problem for him.

A small inner voice yammered at her, pointing out that Jonathan had just beaten and raped her, but she ignored it. There were more important things to worry about. She had to save the baby so that Jonathan would have time to understand. Meredeth chewed thoughtfully on a thumbnail, a bit surprised at how calm she felt. When the idea came, she acted on it without hesitation.

"Chloe," she said, "set time to nineteen hundred."

"Function unavailable. Time may not be reset unless—"

"Chloe, Michaels back door eight six nine one. Chloe, set time to nineteen hundred."

"Voiceprint and password verified. Back door open. Time set to nineteen hundred."

Meredeth smiled. There were advantages to programming the house computer yourself. Advantages like back doors that gave you root access. "Chloe, establish a link with NatNet, InfoNet, and WorldWeb."

"Link established."

"Chloe, relay a message to all major newspapers, magazines, VR networks, and everyone in our address database. Chloe, message begins. Jonathan and Meredeth Blackstone are pleased to announce that they will soon be parents. Mrs. Blackstone is due to deliver their first child on November ninth. She is in good health and her doctor expects no complications during the pregnancy. Chloe, message ends."

"Message uploaded."

"Chloe, disconnect link."

"Disconnected."

"Chloe, set time to—" Meredeth glanced at her watch "—twenty thirty-six. Chloe, close back door."

"Time set. Back door closed."

"There, you see, Baby?" Meredeth whispered. "Mama will take care of everything."

She called her parents on the vidphone so they wouldn't be upset at hearing the news through a blanket announcement, though she had to leave the screen blank so she wouldn't have to explain her bruised face. Fortunately vidphone etiquette forbade anyone asking why the picture was off. Geneva Michaels, of course, was absolutely ecstatic and wanted to come down from Islington right away, but Meredeth pleaded tiredness.

"Then you go to bed and rest, honey," Geneva said, "and I'll be over first thing in the morning. After I check with your father, of course. This is so exciting! My baby—having a baby!" She signed off.

Jonathan was already asleep when Meredeth slipped quietly into bed. Her half of the blankets was still cold. Meredeth stared up at the darkness and rubbed her hands over her belly until she fell asleep.

In the morning, Meredeth was almost violently ill. Waves of nausea forced her to remain in her bathroom for almost half an hour. More time was spent in spraying makeup over the bruise on her face. When she finally made her way down to the breakfast nook, bright with its spring morning sunlight and smelling of coffee, Jonathan was already in a foul mood.

"What the hell did you do?" he snarled after the butler poured the coffee and withdrew. The smell almost made Meredeth sick again.

"What do you mean?" she asked, sitting down across from him.

"I checked my e-mail." Jonathan clenched and unclenched his fists. "It was jammed with messages. Just about everyone I know is congratulating us on the baby."

Meredeth put a hand to her mouth. "I'm sorry, darling— I forgot. When the doctor told me the news, I was so excited I made an announcement just before you got home."

Jonathan closed his eyes. "Why were you so stupid, Meredeth? *Why?* Jesus. You screw up the implants and get pregnant, now this."

"I didn't get pregnant by myself, Jonathan," she said almost angrily.

He drew back his hand and Meredeth automatically drew

back, anger forgotten. Her chair made a scraping sound on the floor.

"Don't get smart with me," Jonathan growled. "Jesus, this fucks up everything."

"Do you want me to call the doctor and schedule—"

"Of course not!" Jonathan got up and started to pace. "Don't you know how it would look if you got a medically unnecessary abortion after an official announcement was made and everyone knows you're pregnant? I can't afford that kind of scandal."

He halted and stared out the window. "You're going to have the damn baby after all. And plan a party for next Friday evening. I wasn't planning on making our first formal appearance as Mr. and Mrs. Blackstone for another month, but I guess we can't wait now."

"All right," Meredeth replied, secretly glowing. She had bought all the time she needed. Even if Jonathan checked the time the announcement was made, Chloe would tell him the messages were sent out at seven o'clock—before he got home. And although the people who had received the announcement would show the accurate time, information often got jammed up in the net, especially at the big newspapers and VR networks. Meredeth doubted Jonathan would look that far anyway.

Jonathan would adjust. He loved her and he would love the baby when it came.

He finished his coffee in silence and left for work with a distracted look on his face. Meredeth smiled to herself and nibbled on a saltine cracker. She hated the flat, salty texture, but her mother swore by them. That and weak tea were all Meredeth could stomach for breakfast.

This proves that last night was a mistake, she thought. *He didn't even touch me this morning, even though he was angry.*

Meredeth forced down another cracker. The nausea did seem to be fading. Maybe her mother had been right after all. Things were looking up.

"Chloe," Meredeth said happily, "tell all the servants I

want to meet with them immediately. We have a party to plan."

"My dear Meredeth," gushed—what was her name? Susan? Susanna? "Congratulations on the baby. Absolutely marvelous little gathering you've thrown here. Your first?"

Meredeth smiled graciously for the hundredth time and nodded. The Blackstone mansion was packed with guests—well over three hundred of them—and it seemed like all of them had asked the same question. The ballroom floor whirled with glittering men and women dancing to the live music of a tastefully understated orchestra. Eight different buffets provided dishes from dozens of countries. Two of them served real meat. People roamed everywhere—the art gallery, the gardens, the swimming pools, the cliffs above the ocean—and the computer struggled mightily with the task of continually altering color and light in the vicinity of each guest to show his or her outfit to the best advantage.

Meredeth had very quickly discovered that hosting a party on this scale took more than giving orders to servants. There were temporary workers to hire, gardeners and caterers to supervise, decorations to coordinate, her wardrobe to choose. Eventually she had been forced to hire an etiquette and hosting specialist to steer her through the endless pitfalls of high society manners. Jonathan had seemed content to leave it all to her.

"Amazing," the woman continued, waving a nearly empty champagne glass. "Just amazing. For a first party, that is."

"Thank you," Meredeth said. *And you're a wonderful guest. For a first party, that is.* "Will you excuse me? I really need to get some air." She politely elbowed her way through the crowd to a wide flagstone balcony overlooking the gardens. The salty spring air cooled her face and she inhaled deeply, ignoring the other people who had come out to look down at the lighted fountains and flower beds.

Behind her, she could still hear the orchestra music and all the people making dull, inane chatter at one another.

She didn't know any of them. They were all Jonathan's friends. While making out the guest list, Meredeth had suddenly realized that she hadn't seen any of her old friends in over a year. Not since she had started dating Jonathan. Her friends were strangers to her now, and none of them were at the party.

When did Jonathan become the center of my life? she thought. *When did he take over?*

A familiar voice wafted up from below and Meredeth leaned over the edge of the balcony. Jonathan, looking stunning in a simple black tuxedo, was talking to two women and a man. One of the women was the American senator Sharon Glesser, if Meredeth remembered correctly. The other two must be her wife and husband.

Meredeth waved until she caught Jonathan's eye. He raised his glass and smiled at her. She smiled back, unable to help herself.

Well, what did her old friends matter? Meredeth would make new friends. Jonathan was the perfect husband. And she couldn't have someone with more security, and that was important, too.

Don't hook yourself to anyone that might drag you down into the gutter, her mother had always said. *Security. Money. That's what's important, Meredeth, and don't you forget it. Love won't survive long without security.*

Security she had. Meredeth would never have to worry about having enough money to keep up appearances. Jonathan *made* appearances. Unlike her parents, Meredeth would never have to worry whether her company would go under. Jonathan bought and sold entire corporations. He had even bought her father's faltering programming firm, ensuring it would have a steady stream of clients and never go under. It was a wonderful gesture of goodwill toward her family, and Meredeth was proud of her husband's generosity.

"Meredeth!"

Meredeth turned. Another woman was heading toward her. The woman had long black hair and looked to be in her early twenties, but that meant nothing anymore. Not with the bodysculpt techniques developed by Zhong and Whitman, Incorporated, a medical research corporation Jonathan owned. The techniques were prohibitively expensive, but that didn't matter to most of Jonathan's circle.

"Hello," Meredeth said, pasting another smile on her face. "I'm sorry, I don't—"

"Melissa Long," she said, extending her hand. Meredeth shook it. It was limp and dry, like a rubber band. "Wonderful party. It must have taken so much to coordinate."

"Thank you."

Melissa took a sip of her drink. "And congratulations on the baby. When are you due?"

"November ninth."

"Lucky you. Eric and I have been trying for two years to have one that natural way, but we may be forced to go in vitro." She shuddered and took another sip. "But look at you—married only two months and already pregnant."

"I suppose we are lucky, at that," Meredeth replied, wondering what time it was, knowing it would be rude to glance at her watch.

"Be sure you take care of yourself," Melissa urged. "We wouldn't want anything to make the baby . . . premature."

"Premature?" Meredeth echoed, confused. "No, the doctor said she didn't expect any complications."

"Melissa," broke in someone else. A man, this time. Blond and also seemingly in his early twenties. "Here you are. I brought you another drink."

Melissa thanked him. "Meredeth, this is Gordie Sumter, my husband. Gordie, this is Meredeth Blackstone, our host."

"How do you do?" Gordie said.

"We were just discussing Meredeth's baby," Melissa told him. "You know—how lucky she and Jonathan are that Meredeth got pregnant so easily. So fast."

Meredeth flushed. "Yes, well—"

Melissa gave a light chuckle. The orchestra finished the current waltz and swung into a minuet amid light applause from the dancers. Below, Jonathan said something that made Senator Glesser laugh. Jonathan clapped a hand on her husband's shoulder and they both joined in. The wife just shook her head.

"You know, Meredeth," Melissa said, "we were all sure that Jonathan was going to marry—what was her name, Gordie? The woman related to the Du Ponts?"

"Genine?" Gordie hazarded.

"That's the one." Melissa leaned forward conspiratorially. "Everyone was sure those two would get engaged one day. Genine is so suited to high society. But you came along and snatched Jonathan right up. Have either of you considered taking another spouse? Someone like Genine would fit so well into your household."

Meredeth almost shook her head, confused at Melissa's line of conversation. "Jonathan doesn't really want another spouse," she said. "A bit anachronistic, but there it is." She spread her hands. "He doesn't want me to work, either, even after six years in college and a degree in computers. I'm humoring him for the moment."

Melissa raised an eyebrow. "How did you say you met Jonathan?"

"I beat him at three straight games of Orbit on the VR network. It wasn't difficult—I wrote the thing. At any rate, he asked to meet me in person. I had no idea who he really was until much later." Meredeth smiled. "It was quite a shock, you can imagine, when the man I was dating turned out to be *the* Jonathan Blackstone. I thought he was just using the name as a network pseudonym."

"I didn't know Jonathan liked to VR," Gordie said. "We were fraternity brothers in college and he didn't VR then."

"Really?" Meredeth said, surprised. "That's odd. He was on all the time when I was finishing up my programming degree."

"No doubt," Melissa said. "Well, keep an eye on that baby. Wouldn't want a seven-month preemie on our hands, would we? Come along, Gordie—I want to see if the Kangs are here."

Gordie threw Meredeth a wink and Meredeth stared at them as they sailed into the crowd. Why were they so concerned about the baby being premature? There was nothing to—

Meredeth gasped. *The little bitch!* she snarled to herself, suddenly furious. *She thinks I got pregnant and forced Jonathan to marry me!*

In the ballroom, the crowd swirled and swooped in a sickening pattern. Meredeth pursed her lips. How many of them were snickering up their sleeves? How many of those conversations were about her and the seven-month "preemie" everyone expected her to have? How many were scoffing about the lower-class tart who had sunk her hooks into a trillionaire?

The entire concept was ridiculous anyway. In the lower classes it didn't matter who parented whom as long as the child was provided for. But among the upper classes— certainly Jonathan's set—it *did* matter. After quick and easy in vitro technology became the standard, the wealthy, ever looking to stay one step ahead of mere commoners, quickly retreated to earlier parenting methods and attitudes.

A hot flush crept up Meredeth's face and she was glad Jonathan had convinced her not to invite her parents on the grounds that they'd feel out of place.

Those harpies would have them for supper, she thought.

"Meredeth!" came yet another voice that dragged her back to the party. "Congratulations on the baby. Smashing party tonight. Is it your first?"

"Yes," Meredeth said mechanically. "Thank you."

The party dragged on and Meredeth moved through the people, glass in her hand, smile on her face, but the excitement and luster were gone. Everywhere Meredeth turned, she saw false smiles and hidden jealousy. Conversations seemed to end when she drew near, only to begin again when she moved away. Music rose and fell like water in a wave pool. Jonathan was nowhere to be seen. Inane chatter and silly laughter pressed around her, stifling her, until she was sure she would scream.

And then it ended. At some unspoken signal, people began to leave. Not all at once, but in a steady stream, until Meredeth was saying good-bye to the last guests. Some were staying overnight, of course, but the servants would take care of them. Luckily, it was not fashion for the host to greet the overnighters in the morning.

Exhausted, Meredeth stripped off her gown and fell into bed, barely noticing that Jonathan wasn't in it.

Meredeth:

I found out later Jonathan was out screwing Melissa Long and Gordie Sumter, though he said he was up until dawn talking with some of the overnighters. At the time, however, all I knew was that Jonathan didn't hit me any more. Quite the opposite. He was very attentive, very nice. After the party, he apologized for what happened in the jacuzzi and I swear I could see tears in his eyes. When he begged me to forgive him, I did.

Two months passed, then three and four, and Jonathan and I hardly ever saw each other because he kept having out-of-town business to deal with. The phase drive program was taking up more and more of his time. And when he was home, he never touched me in bed. I took to reading psychology books about new fathers and learned that a man sometimes avoids sex with his pregnant wife because he sees her as a mother, and you don't have sex with a mother. So I understood why he was reluctant. I didn't press the issue.

A few weeks later he pushed me down the stairs.

Meredeth lay in her hospital bed, feeling dazed and wrung out. Her left leg was in a cast and her face was puffy and tender. She felt no pain. An IV was plugged into her hand and some instrument she couldn't see beeped in a regular pattern.

Jonathan sat next to her, holding her hand with a proper mixture of tender concern and husbandly worry. His brown eyes never left her face. His hand was dry and cold.

Also in the room was Dr. Gales, a plump woman with close-set eyes. She took a deep breath and leaned over the bed. "Meredeth, I'm sorry. We couldn't save the baby."

Meredeth stared blankly ahead, barely hearing the words. It was like Dr. Gales was talking to someone else.

"Meredeth?" Dr. Gales said. "Did you understand me? You lost the baby."

Meredeth shook her head. Everything was out-of-focus, not quite there. She remembered walking down the first floor corridor with Jonathan, reaching the top of the staircase. A rough shove, and suddenly she was falling. Pain thumped with every jar and jolt as she tumbled down the stairs like a rag doll.

Jonathan patted her hand and she looked at him. His face was pale, his hair was a disheveled red mess. It looked like the blood she had seen leaking from between her legs when she had finally stopped falling.

"I'm sorry darling," Jonathan whispered. "I'm so sorry."

"My baby. Where's my baby?" Meredeth asked, turning to Dr. Gales. *"Where's my baby?"*

"She died, Meredeth," Dr. Gales said quietly. "Before you got to hospital."

"A girl," Meredeth said, half to herself. "I knew it was a girl. I was going to name her Jessica."

"Could we have some time, please, Doctor?" Jonathan asked.

"Of course." Dr. Gales left the room, closing the door behind her.

Jonathan stroked Meredeth's hand almost possessively. "How are you feeling, Merry? Is there any pain?"

Meredeth looked at him. The emotional numbness was beginning to wear off. Her baby was dead, and Jonathan had killed her. Meredeth wanted to cry and scream. She wanted to rip and punch at Jonathan's face. And she wanted to cower in fear.

Leave him! shrieked an inner voice. *He beat you and raped you and murdered your baby. Get out! Hide! Run!*

Run where? Jonathan was holding tightly to her hand, and she knew now he would never let go. He was one of the richest, most powerful people on earth. What would happen if she left him?

He would find her, of course. And he could kill her if he wanted to. She didn't have the resources to hide from him.

Then leave him noisily and publicly. Take him to court and charge him with rape and assault and murder.

But that would cause a huge scandal. And Jonathan had money and barristers and solicitors—things Meredeth simply didn't possess. If the case went to trial, Jonathan's barrister would make her look like the money-grubber everyone was already sure she was. They would point out the extremely high odds against a woman with an implant getting pregnant by accident. They would say she got pregnant on purpose to force him into marriage, and now that the baby was gone, Jonathan wasn't worth anything to her, so she wanted out—with a healthy settlement.

No one would believe Meredeth. She had no witnesses, no evidence, nothing. Just another little bitch trying to climb the social ladder.

"It's all right, Merry," Jonathan soothed. "We'll have another baby. And this one will be perfect." He gave a gentle smile, and Meredeth shivered. What was it that Gordie Sumter had said? That Jonathan had never been much for VR? Now that she thought about it, she hadn't seen him play a single game since they got married. What if the games had been nothing but a way to meet her? To stalk her?

"We'll go to France," Jonathan continued. "My people checked your genetic record before we got married, and they said you're the perfect match for me. The doctors at my research facility can combine the best of my genes with the best of yours, and we'll have the perfect son.

Handsome, intelligent, everything you could want. Don't you worry. Everything will be under control."

Under control. Meredeth looked at Jonathan's face and suddenly realized why Jonathan had married her. Why he had purposefully tracked her through the VR net and piqued her interest. Why he had broken into her personal medical records. Meredeth could be controlled. Her middle-class family had no connections, no power. Even her father's business—

Her father's business. Jonathan owned it. If she left him, he would bankrupt it without a second thought. Jonathan had won before Meredeth even knew anyone was playing a game.

Emotions rose up behind Meredeth's eyes, and she ruthlessly squashed them. Emotions had gotten her into this. She had let Jonathan sweep her away, dazzling her with money and attention. She had let herself get attached to the baby, and that had been a mistake. She wouldn't give in to emotion now.

Meredeth inhaled and let the antiseptic smell of the hospital wash away her feelings. This was a time to be cold and uncaring. Cold uncaring people didn't get hurt.

And she would get him. It might take months or years, but she would make Jonathan pay for this. Meredeth would find a way.

CHAPTER THREE

NOW

Brad's flat turned out to be three stories up. Lance tried to relax as he fell, and the hard pavement below rushed up to meet him. He landed badly, with a horrible wrench, and he forced himself to roll to absorb further impact. White-hot pain flooded his right leg and ankle.

Robin!

Cutting pain centers. Ankle badly twisted, not broken. Leg muscles slightly torn. If not for implants, damage would be much more severe.

The pain vanished and Lance scrambled to his feet. He was in a rectangular courtyard paved with old-style cobblestones. Windows from other flats looked out over a few potted trees and battered sets of patio furniture. Someone had had a cookout, and the scent of grilled beef still hung faintly in the damp, misty air. A single narrow corridor led to the street beyond. Lance sprinted toward it. Above him came the hiss and crack of needler fire, but the courtyard was only dimly lit and the operatives in Brad's flat had not been equipped with night glasses. The light fog was also working in his favor.

Lance pelted toward the corridor, needles pinging and snapping on the stones around him—

—and then he skidded to a halt. The corridor was the

49

only exit to the street, and Lance couldn't believe the operatives weren't aware of this fact. There had to be more of them waiting for him right outside.

Lance dodged sideways and flattened himself against the wall, heart pounding, cobbles bumpy beneath his feet. He knew he was in no great physical danger—Jonathan Blackstone's operatives wouldn't dare do any permanent damage, not when Dad wanted him back in one piece. But they would take him back to Dad, who would do worse than anything his operatives even dreamed. The operatives also would know that Lance could take a great deal of punishment and pain.

He glanced up at the roof. The apartment building was four stories tall. Maybe—

Forget it, Jaylance. Three-story up-jump is about maximum, even without wounded leg.

The needle-fire stopped. Lance nervously licked his lips. Why would they stop shooting? They knew he was down here somewhere and would probably hit him by sheer luck if they kept firing.

Boots rang on cobblestones in the corridor, giving Lance his answer—the operatives didn't want to hit their own people. Lance hugged brick and looked desperately at the impossibly high walls—no fire escapes or ladders. No way out. The clumping boots grew louder, and long, fog-blurred shadows entered the courtyard. There were at least six of them and they were carrying needlers.

Lance glanced around desperately, then darted toward a first-floor window that looked out on the courtyard just as half a dozen operatives burst into the area. Without pausing, Lance dove through the window. Crashing glass sliced his face and arms, but he rolled to his feet, eyes already adjusted to the near-blackness of the flat.

Outside, hoarse shouts ordered the operatives into the flat. Lance leaped over and dodged around furniture, making for the front door. Warm blood trickled down his face and arms, and his injured leg and ankle were getting swollen and stiff, though Robin was still blocking the pain.

A light came on in an adjoining room, but Lance ignored it. He reached the front door and found it was bolted shut.

A figure appeared in the broken window. "Freeze!"

Lance braced himself and yanked. Wood splintered, and suddenly he was breathing cool night air. A needler hissed and cracked behind him, and he felt the familiar sting of a needle before he reached the sidewalk. He fled across the street, then staggered for a moment under sudden dizziness.

Robin—

More terraphine. Trying to compensate, but am also blocking pain, stopping leg from stiffening up, and trying to keep ankle from breaking.

Lance ducked down a side street to try and get his bearings. He was obviously in a residential district, a rather seedy one. Crumbling blocks of brick flats came right up to the sidewalk. A few had tiny gardens set off by black wrought-iron fences. Lance couldn't hear anyone behind him yet, but another wave of dizziness hit him.

Robin, drop the pain block and stop the terraphine.
Acknowledged.

Pain roared over Lance's body. His leg and ankle throbbed with it, and his face felt like it had been torn to shreds. He groaned under the onslaught, but forced himself to keep moving. Pain jolted him with every step, but the dizziness was gone.

He dashed down an alley and out to another street, trying to think around the pain. How had Dad's operatives tracked him down? Obviously Andy had managed to get away safely. The operatives should have assumed he'd flee the country. How did they know he hadn't?

The bar, he thought. *The cab. *Robin, how did Andy pay the cab driver and the bar tab?*

Cashcard.

Electronic money. Easily traceable, if you had the connections. And Dad had the resources of a multisystem corporation at his disposal.

Lance stopped to rest a moment, trying to ignore his pounding leg and bleeding face. A glance at his wristcomp showed it was almost midnight. The chilly air was growing foggier, and Lance realized he was shivering.

I can't go on like this, he thought. *I need help. I need to rest somewhere safe.*

Meredeth's place?

Lance tensed his jaw. *I'll rot in the gutter before giving her that satisfaction. Stay out of my head, meatless.*

Robin fell silent. Lance fished through his pockets and came up with about thirty pounds and change. It apparently had never occurred to Andy to use it. The cash might—*might*—get him halfway across London. But he didn't know anyone in London except Mom.

And Delia.

An electric car swished by in the street and Lance ducked into a shadow. Delia. He *liked* Delia, and he knew she liked him. Everyone liked Lance. They couldn't help themselves. Dad had seen to that.

Just another operation, he thought bitterly. *One little adjustment to my pheromones, and suddenly everyone wants to be my friend.*

The pain intensified. Robin was probably working hard on removing the terraphine. Lance could hand the situation over to Garth or Jessica—earlier in his life he probably would have—but that had already gotten him into enough trouble for the evening. He had to keep moving.

Lance turned and limped down the street as best he could, fiery pain ripping through his leg with every step. The city was eerily quiet, and the only sounds were the uneven scuffing noises his shoes made on the pavement. It felt like the aging buildings were staring at him. Dad's people were probably fanning out, searching in all directions. They operated under a handicap, of course— they had to disappear before the police arrived and they had to remain unidentified—but they weren't stupid and they had powerful resources. Lance himself was operating under a handicap. He couldn't check into a hotel—the good ones didn't accept cash anymore and the bad ones would happily answer questions about their clientele to anyone who waved enough money. Hospitals were also out of the question. Not only was Dad almost certainly watching them by now, Lance was a walking mess of illegal medical procedures.

The chill air was settling into his wounds like an icy cat kneading its owner's lap. Lance *had* to rest someplace warm, and soon. It would be impossible for Robin to take care of his injuries while he was walking around, especially with the terraphine threatening to clog his system, and the pain was getting steadily worse. He could hardly put weight on his injured leg and ankle.

Delia offered you help whenever you needed it, he told himself. *It looks like you'll have to take her up on it.*

Traffic noises cut through the fog ahead of him. He followed the electric hum of tires on pavement until he came to a well-lit, busy street and was able to flag down a cab.

"Bloody Christ," the driver said when he climbed in. The cab smelled faintly of fried fish. "What the hell happened to your face, love? And you're pale as winter's ghost. You want me to take you to the hospital?"

"No," Lance said, and gave her Delia's address. "I've only got thirty quid, so let me know when the meter gets that far. I'll walk the rest of the way."

The driver, a middle-aged woman with small brown eyes, gave him a motherly look. "You just relax, love, and let old Annie get ye where ye need to be."

Lance nodded and slumped down in the seat. Even when he looked like hell, people liked him. Or they thought they did.

Annie guided the cab into the street. The motion shifted Lance's weight and he bit his lip to keep from screaming.

Robin, how's the terraphine coming?

Be a while, Jaylance. Apologies. Perhaps Garth or Jessica should—

No. Garth wouldn't get along with Delia, and I'm mad at Jessica right now for making me stay in that office. She can sit and stew about what I said to Mom.

The cab wove swiftly through the city streets, but most of it was a blur to Lance. Several glances over his shoulder assured him he wasn't being followed, but he was still nervous—and in pain. A haze settled over him, and he was vaguely aware of Annie chattering at him, but he couldn't focus on what she was saying. After what felt like a long time, the cab finally pulled to a stop.

"We're here, love," Annie said.

Lance sat up, gasping when he moved his swollen leg. The meter said he owed Annie exactly 38 pounds.

"I told you I've only got thirty quid," Lance protested. *And I can't use the cashcard without telling Dad where I am.*

Annie snorted. "I couldn't let ye walk all that way, now could I? Don't ye worry about Annie—some rich bloke tipped me a nice one earlier today. I can make the diff."

The pheromones at work again, but this time Lance didn't care. He thanked Annie, handed her the money, and climbed stiffly out of the cab, making a mental note of the taxi's identification number so he could send her full payment—and a tip—later. She gave him a cheery wave and drove off.

Pheromones.

Lance found himself standing before a set of brownstone houses all connected in one long row, a much better neighborhood than the one he had just left. Even the fog seemed lighter. Sudden exhaustion washed over him as he limped up to one of the doors. The third button down read D. RADFORD. Lance took a deep breath and pressed it. The tiny security camera above the door swiveled to focus on him. After a moment, Lance pressed the button again and looked down at his leg. It had swollen so much it was stretching his jumpsuit. He didn't even want to think about what his ankle looked like.

The intercom hissed. "Who is it?" snapped Delia's sleepy

voice. "Show your face or I'm calling the bloody cops."

Lance turned his face up toward the camera, feeling suddenly uncertain. "Delia?" he said hoarsely.

"Lance?" The drowsiness vanished from Delia's voice. "My God—what happened to your face? Hurry on in. I'm on the ground floor, second door on the left."

The door clicked open and Lance limped into a corridor, glad he wouldn't have to climb any stairs. Another door further up the hallway opened and Delia, dressed in a housecoat—*dressing gown,* Lance corrected himself without knowing why—came scurrying toward him.

"God!" she said again, taking his arm. "Are you all right? Never mind—stupid question. Let's get inside and get those cuts cleaned up."

Lance nodded and gratefully let her lead him into her flat.

Delia's apartment was bright and airy, with high ceilings and comfortable-looking furniture. A pair of blond wood bookshelves were crammed with countless untidy piles of bookdisks. Photographs and drawings of birds hung on the walls, while avian statues occupied end tables and shelves. A locked cabinet with a glass door stored four cameras and three sets of field glasses. Two overnight bags sat next to the door. Delia brought Lance to a sofa and helped him lie down. It was a relief to sink into the soft cushions. He gratefully drank in the warmth.

"Yorik, lock the door," she said, and the front door clicked. "You wait right there, Lance."

She left the room and returned with a first aid kit. "Let me clean your face and you can tell me what happened. Are you all right? Besides the cuts, I mean?"

"I twisted my leg," Lance told her, wincing as she gently wiped the dried blood from his face and sprayed the cuts with antiseptic. The process was unnecessary—Robin had already gotten rid of the glass and would stop any infection—but he couldn't tell Delia that. Instead, he wordlessly let Delia work. When she noticed his arm, she carefully rolled up his sleeve—Lance sucked in his breath as it came away from the dried blood—and cleaned that as well.

"What happened to you?" she demanded, and Lance noticed her hands were shaking. "Christ, you look like you went through a meat grinder."

"It's my father," Lance replied. "One of his operatives saw . . . saw me go in to see Mom. When I came out, they chased me. I managed to get away, but I got hurt."

Delia's eyes widened. "Your father's people did this? Holy God. Yorik, security camera interface. Yorik, is anyone outside the flat?"

"Negative," the computer said.

"Yorik, continue scanning. Yorik, if any stranger approaches the flat, notify me immediately. Lance, I think we should get out of here."

"Acknowledged," the computer put in, as if echoing Delia's sentiments.

"I lost them, Delia," Lance said. "If they had any idea where I was, they would've caught up with me by now."

"How can you be sure?" Delia asked tersely.

Lance closed his eyes. "I've been doing this since I was twenty. I know."

Delia set down the washcloth and reached for the phone. "I'll ring the police then, shall I?"

Lance's eyes popped open. "No!" he said, and Delia paused, startled at his tone. "Delia, don't. It wouldn't do any good. The only operative I got a good look at will be long gone by now, and I don't have any proof that Dad was behind this."

"What? You can't let him get away with this."

Lance shook his head. "I've tried the police before, Delia. It doesn't work. The only thing I can do is stay away from him."

Delia opened her mouth to argue the point, then apparently thought the better of it and went back to cleaning his arm. The pain was easing, and Lance suspected Robin had dealt with most of the terraphine, allowing the pain block to function again.

Delia's soft fingers worked at Lance's arm, soothing and gentle. Lance closed his eyes again. His earlier exhaustion returned, and it felt wonderful to lie back and relax, let someone take care of him for a while. Especially if it was someone like Delia. She was an extremely attractive woman with her curly black hair, dark eyes, and dusky skin. And Lance thought her body was very nice, despite the numerous times Delia had complained that she needed to lose ten pounds.

She'd look awful, Lance thought, opening his eyes to look at her. *Women aren't supposed to be dolls or sticks.*

Delia's gaze briefly met his, and she smiled. Lance colored.

Keep your distance, he admonished. *You're too screwed up to be worth anyone's time. A certified lunatic, remember?*

"There," Delia said after a moment. "Your face and arm are clean. Now I think we should have a look at your leg."

Lance swallowed. That would mean taking off his jumpsuit. *I can't. She'll see my—she'll see what Dad did to me.* He started to get up.

Attention! Attention! Robin said, and Lance froze. *Terraphine neutralized. Healing damaged body currently highest priority. Please remain stationary to facilitate process.*

"Lance?" Delia said.

"My leg's all right." He sat up straighter and subtly pulled away from her. The pain had vanished. "I just twisted it a little bit, but it doesn't hurt."

Delia leaned forward to get a better look. Her dressing gown parted slightly and Lance caught a brief glimpse of her naked breasts. He blushed furiously.

"Are you sure?" Delia asked, not seeming to notice. "It looks swollen to me, even through the jumpsuit."

"Yeah, I'm sure. Really." Lance tried to draw away again, but Delia showed no signs of backing off. He could feel the heat from her body, smell the faint odor of her perfume. Now that the pain was gone, he found Delia's touch, her closeness, arousing. Lance's face grew hotter. Those thoughts—those things—were *wrong*. He started to pull away, withdraw into—

"Lance!" Delia snapped. "Don't you dare!"

Lance jerked back to himself and blinked at Delia's angry, cat-like expression.

"Don't you leave on me," she said. "You've given me a hell of a fright, and I don't feel like dealing with anyone else at the moment."

Anyone else? A pang shot through Lance's stomach. *She doesn't know. She can't know. Can she?*

"What do you mean?" he said with a nervous laugh. "There's no one else here."

"Let me guess," Delia said, settling back on her heels. "You were going to put me on hold and let Jessica deal with this. Or maybe Andy."

The world seemed to jerk sideways. Lance's mind ran in little circles and he felt like someone had just hit the back of his head with a board. "Andy?" he temporized, tensing himself to run. "Who's Andy?"

Don't get up, Jaylance, Robin warned.

Delia sighed. "Lance, I've known about the Company for a long time now. You and Andy and Patrick and Garth and Jay. And Jessica."

Lance's heart began to pound. She did know! She knew he was crazy! Any minute she would call the police—or Dad. He had to run, get out of here before—

WARNING! Robin boomed. *Healing process of ankle and leg at vital point. Careless motion would disrupt, cause more harm. Remain sessile or will be forced to block motor control centers.*

Lance froze, caught between the instinct to run and Robin's order/request to remain on the couch. He looked at Delia, breath coming fast, eyes wide with fear.

Delia made a soothing sound and laid a hand on his arm. "Lance, it's all right. I'm not going to have a fit. If I were, I would have done it a long time ago."

Lance opened his mouth, a lie already forming in his

head. He hadn't admitted to anything yet. He could tell her she was mistaken, that she had misunderstood. The pheromones would make her want to believe him.

But Delia's dark eyes were filled with the truth, and Lance's mind and body were soaked with exhaustion. He didn't have the strength to lie. After a moment, he let out a long, heavy sigh.

"How did you find out?" he asked in a small voice.

"Jessica told me."

Lance stared. *What?*

"Jessica told me," Delia repeated with a nod. "She told me about you and the Company because she thought I should know."

Robin?

Affirmative. Jessica told Delia about Company two years, five months, six days ago.

Why didn't you tell me?

Jessica extracted promise. Said she would find way to fry servos if squealed. Believed her.

Lance gulped. "How—how much did she tell you?"

"Enough," Delia replied. "Lance, I've done a lot of reading since Jessica talked to me, and I've learned quite a lot about multiple personality disorder. I suppose I should be afraid of you—men with MPD can get violent—but I'm not." Her eyes took on a faraway look. "Not after growing up with my brother." Delia shook her head as if to clear it. "Jessica also told me what kind of father you had, so I have some idea of why you're . . . the way you are."

Lance looked away. Until now, only his parents and Dr. Baldwin had known about the Company. Lance had kept the secret for a long time, mostly by keeping to himself. Now a near-stranger had found out about it. A long-time pillar in his life had taken a severe blow, and he felt shaken, scared. Yet on another level, there was relief. Someone else had found out without hating him. He stared at the floor.

"I guess you must think I'm pretty crazy, huh?" he muttered.

"I think," Delia replied slowly, "that you've been through more than any human being could hope to survive. That takes a lot of courage."

Lance laced his fingers together in his lap. "I'm not brave, Delia. I'm scared a lot. Even after I got away from Dad the first time, it didn't take me long to start being scared again."

"Courage isn't a lack of fear, Lance," Delia said softly. "Courage is the ability to do what has to be done even when you're scared stiff."

Her voice sounded sad, haunted. Impulsively, Lance reached over and took her hand. She gave a small smile and squeezed briefly with strong fingers, then slipped away and got to her feet.

"Well," she said briskly, breaking the mood, "I think that's enough maundering for one night. How about some tea?"

Please accept, Robin said. *Body currently suffering from light dehydration.*

"Sure," Lance replied, himself a bit relieved at the change in subject. "If it wouldn't be a bother."

"Not at all. You just lie there and rest." Delia headed for the kitchen. As she walked, Lance noticed the tiny limp that marked her prosthetic leg.

"So what happens now?" Delia asked through the open doorway. Water hissed through an electric heater. "About your father chasing you, I mean."

Lance relaxed a little. This was something he was used to dealing with.

"I have to get out of England," he said. "I'll probably just slip down to the ferry and across the channel. I'd take the Chunnel, but I don't like it."

"You don't, or Garth doesn't?" Delia said. "Jessica mentioned that he doesn't like enclosed spaces, I think."

Lance blinked. No one—not Mom, not Dad, not Dr. Baldwin—had treated the others like separate people before. Everyone else always insisted they were merely facets of himself. A warm feeling started in his stomach and spread, easing some of the fear and discomfort over Delia learning about his secret.

"I meant Garth," Lance said. "Anyway, when I buy the ferry ticket, Dad'll track my cashcard, I'm sure, but crossing borders always slows down a trace. I'll zip down to Rome, hop their skyhook, and be heading out of orbit long before he picks up my trail. I wish I could take the London hook, but it'd be too risky right now."

Delia came back into the living room carrying a tray with two steaming mugs on it. "I've brought biscuits, in case you're hungry," she said, setting the tray on the coffee table. "Or perhaps I should call them cookies so you won't think they're something hot with honey on them."

Lance raised his eyebrows. "I lived in Dover for a long time, Delia, and you know Mom's from London. I can follow British English."

Delia sighed in near exasperation. "Joke, Lance," she said, and handed him a mug. "You know—that dry British humor?"

"Oh." Lance accepted the cup and sipped. The tea was perfect—hot, sweet, and strong. "Thank you."

She gave him an odd look. "Do you ever smile, Lance? I don't think I've ever seen you do it. Garth and Andy, yes, but not you."

"What? Well—yeah, I guess I do." He shrugged and bit into a cookie. "I never really thought about it. There isn't a whole lot to smile about, with Dad chasing me and everything."

"Ah." Delia settled into an armchair near the couch and tucked her legs beneath her. "What does he want with you, anyway? You can't possibly be a pawn in a custody suit. You're, what, twenty-one? Twenty-two?"

"Thirty," Lance replied, taking another cookie. He felt strangely comfortable here, even natural, talking to Delia while sitting on her sofa. The colorful bird statues and pictures suited the flat. Suited her. She sat among them like a creator who was unaware of what she had called into being.

"Thirty?" Delia said. "An awfully young-looking thirty you are, then."

"Dad had me bodysculpted," Lance replied almost shortly. "And no, Dad's chasing me has nothing to do with his and Mom's divorce. That was years ago. This is all with me."

"How so?"

Lance spread his hands. "Dad wants an heir," he said. "He wants the perfect son to take over his perfect empire when he dies."

Delia set down her cup in disbelief. "That's what all this fuss is about? He wants a bloody *CEO*?"

"He wants a perfect son," Lance corrected. "I can't be one, but he'll try to force me." His voice dropped to a whisper. "Just like he always did before."

"Oh." Delia reached for her mug, and Lance noticed her hand was shaking again. "Lance, I'm sorry."

Lance looked at her and found himself staring into her eyes. They were warm with genuine concern. Pheromones or not, no one he could remember looked at him that way. Not even his mother. He was suddenly seized with the impulse to touch her like she had touched him—softly and gently. He wanted to run his fingertips over her face and feel her breath warm on his palms. He wanted to circle his arms around her and hold her to him. Her eyes met his again, and he found he couldn't break away.

Stop it! he snarled to himself. *None of this is real. She only likes you because of the pheromones. Back off.*

Attention! Attention! Robin interjected. *Healing process no longer at critical stage. Limited range of movement now available.*

Lance set his mug aside and stretched, breaking the moment. "God, I feel better," he said. "I guess I just needed a little rest. Um, thanks for the tea. I'd better be going. You have to get up early for your trip, I'm sure."

Delia shook her head. "You aren't going anywhere. Not looking like that. I have a spare bedroom. And—" she raised a finger, forestalling his next remark "—it won't be any trouble." She tapped the arm of her chair thoughtfully. "In fact, why don't you stay for a couple of days? No one followed you here—as you said, they'd have burst in by now—and it would give your trail time to grow cold."

"I've been dodging Dad for a long time, Delia," Lance said stubbornly. "I've had lots of practice."

"Well, then—in your experience—wouldn't that be the safest course?"

Lance opened his mouth to deny the idea, then snapped it shut. Delia was right. If Dad's operatives had known where he was, they would have had him by now. And they would doubtless be watching the main travelling exits from London, including the ferry. Lance had been planning to disguise himself, but it would certainly be easier if he waited a day or two. The operatives would get discouraged and grow careless.

"Yeah," he admitted finally. "I guess it would be safest."

Delia nodded. "Then I'll show you the guest room."

Early the next morning, Delia sat on her bed holding a leg in her lap. Its coloring matched hers exactly, and a series of tiny heaters kept its skin temperature even with the rest of her body's. Beneath her dressing gown, Delia's right thigh ended in a stump set with tiny electrodes and flashing LED's that told her someone had taken her leg off.

With practiced ease, Delia ran her fingers over an invisible seam just above the knee, and an access panel slid smoothly open. Delia pulled a retractable lead from her wristcomp and plugged it into the panel.

"Yorik," she said, "run complete diagnostic."

The wristcomp's tiny screen flickered. "Power module fully charged," Yorik said dispassionately. "Nervous system interface operating within normal parameters. Nanobot programming operating within normal parameters."

The leg twitched and wiggled on her lap like a warm fish.

"Muscular control systems operating within normal parameters."

Delia sat nervously while Yorik droned through the routine, afraid Lance might wake up and knock on the door. The only people who saw her without her prosthetics were her technician and her doctor. No exceptions. Delia knew full well that in private she looked like a freak, and she saw no reason to let her deformities be seen in public. True, no one would say anything, but she knew what people thought. Crip. Freak. Or—worse yet—poor thing.

Delia normally only checked her prosthetics this thoroughly once a month, but she wanted to be sure everything was fine before boarding a jumpship. She'd hate to discover several hundred light years away from the nearest repair facility that something was wrong. A perfect diagnostic wouldn't make her feel any better, however, if Lance walked through that door before she could put herself back together.

Come off it, Delia, she told herself. *Lance isn't the type to barge in without knocking. He's too shy for that.*

Yeah, but what about Andy or Garth?

Yorik completed the diagnostic and reported that all systems were operating within normal parameters. Delia swiftly disconnected the computer and shifted her weight on the bed so she could slip her leg back into place. A simple click, and she was whole again. Delia had already checked her arm. She got up and paced the room to make sure everything had connected up, then tightened her dressing gown about herself and headed for the closet to get dressed.

A bit later, Delia bared her teeth at the mirror and checked over her reflection one more time. Spotless suit, tastefully understated jewelry, prominent wristcomp. Good. Meredeth required absolute professionalism at all times, even during travel, and Delia saw no reason to challenge the policy. It made sense. People treated you with an amazing amount of deference if you looked smart, well-groomed, and businesslike. Delia had noticed it the first time she made a private jumpship trip and had worn a casual bodysuit for comfort's sake. The service had been terrible. So was Delia's tip.

They must have thought I was a colonist, she mused. *Though what your average colonial would be doing in a first-class cabin is beyond me.*

Delia padded toward the front door and rechecked her luggage with quick, practiced thoroughness. Everything was in place, and the cab she had called would be here in fifteen minutes. She nodded once and tiptoed over to the spare bedroom. The door was open a crack and Delia could just hear the sounds of deep, relaxed breathing. Lance was still asleep. Delia shook her head. It had taken some persuading to get him to stay, even after insisting it wouldn't be any trouble.

He's always doing that, she thought. *He acts as if, just by existing, he's a bother to other people.*

She pushed the door open a bit and peered inside. The blinds were drawn and the room was dim, but Delia could easily make out Lance's sleeping form sprawled face-up on the bed. Blankets and sheets were twisted round him, indicating he was a restless sleeper and, incidentally, giving Delia a good look at the smooth, well-defined muscles that covered his frame.

Move that bit of sheet a little to the left, and I'll really go to work with a smile, she thought wickedly. *So you're thirty years old, are you? Then I'm not trying to rob a cradle after all. He does look like a boy when he's asleep, though—all innocent and naive and—*

She cut off a snort. *Listen to that! Straight out of a bad romance novel, that was. Still, it's a good thing I managed to persuade him to stay last night.*

Last night. It all seemed so unreal. Being woken out of a sound sleep, stumbling to the door, finding Lance with his face and arm all bloody. Not the sort of thing one expected after a tasteless supper and a quiet visit to the cemetery to see Quinn and the parents before bed. And then Lance had actually talked to her. Not just inane

conversation—real talk. Delia had shared half a dozen
lunches with Jessica, but this was the first time Delia had
spent a long period with Lance. Somehow, that seemed
more amazing than all the blood.

Not that blood bothered Delia. She had seen enough
of it whenever Quinn had gone into one of his fits and
gnawed at his own wrists or banged his head against the
floor. Unconsciously she rubbed her left arm—her real
arm—remembering the time Quinn had broken it. She
had been reading on the floor of her family's East End
flat three days after her twelfth birthday. Papa had called
her to dinner and she was just getting up when Quinn
came flying out of nowhere, snarling like a wild beast.
He smashed into her, flung her to the ground, and Delia
felt more than heard her arm snap.

Automatically she shoved Quinn away with her legs and
shouted for help. Mom and Dad came running, Papa right
behind them, and they pulled Quinn away. He was swearing
and screaming and almost frothing at the mouth. Mom
and Dad hauled him into another room to calm him down,
while Papa hustled Delia out to hospital.

Poor Papa, Delia thought, leaving the doorway and
heading for the kitchen. *He was more panicked than I
was.* She buttered a cold pair of rolls and ate them over
the sink, alternating bites with quick sips of tea. *Once I
got to hospital and it stopped hurting, I wasn't scared at
all. Quinn was, though.*

That night in bed, heal-splint an unfamiliar weight on
her arm, Delia had heard the door creak open. She tensed.

"Deeda?" came Quinn's thick, unmistakable voice.
"Deeda?"

"I'm awake, Quinn," she said, cautiously allowing herself
to relax. Quinn's fits were often predictable if you knew
what signs to look for, and he wasn't showing any. He had
caught her by surprise earlier.

Quinn padded softly across the floor. "Arm hurts," he
whispered. He was nine years old but his voice sounded
much younger.

"Yeah," Delia replied. "A little."

"Quinn sorry. Very sorry. Didn't meant to hurt Deeda." He started to cry. "Never hurt Deeda."

Delia reached over to stroke his coarse hair with her good hand. Quinn's skin was lighter than hers—he was Mom and Papa's child while Delia was Mom and Dad's—but you couldn't really tell in the dim light.

"Didn't meant to hurt Deeda," Quinn whimpered. "Didn't meant it."

"I know, Quinn," she said softly. "It's all right. Come on—climb in."

"Love Deeda," Quinn sniffled, curling up next to her in the narrow bed. "Love Deeda best."

This was true. Delia couldn't remember a time when Quinn wasn't following her around the flat. He had always cried a lot as a baby—something which got worse after the blood clot damaged his brain—but he would almost always stop when Delia held him. There were times when he would spit his food out or fling his plate to the floor for the parents, but he would always eat for Delia. And Delia was the only one who seemed to be able to lessen the horrible pains that sometimes wracked his head.

Mom and Dad and Papa didn't know what to make of it except to bring Quinn to Delia whenever he became difficult, though even Delia wasn't completely immune to Quinn's erratic behavior.

And I still get angry about it, Delia thought, adding more sugar to her mug. Quinn had hated sugary tea. *He died almost twelve years ago, and I'm still angry at him. How can you love someone and be angry at them at the same time?*

Delia did love Quinn. He was her little brother. The fits came rarely—once a month at most. It was usually easier to remember the sound of his laughter when she tickled him, or the look of anticipation on his face when she mixed him a big glass of chocolate milk, or how they giggled and shushed each other while sneaking into the kitchen after bedtime to raid the cake plate and getting sweet, guilty crumbs on their fingers.

It wasn't Quinn's fault that a freak bit of dried blood had torn through his brain, causing the retardation, headaches, and irrationality. Delia knew it, even if Quinn didn't. Besides, a broken arm would heal in a couple weeks. Quinn would be like this forever.

Usually she could remember that, but more than once as a child she had found herself awake at night, staring at the ceiling, so angry at him she was afraid to move. Quinn got all kinds of special attention. It was all right for Quinn to throw fits, but Delia got spanked for the same behavior. Because Quinn might have one of his fits, Delia could never have friends over. Mom and Dad and Papa never took Delia anyplace fun like other parents because they couldn't leave Quinn with a babysitter.

Quinn had killed Mom and Dad and Papa.

Now that's enough of that! Delia told herself sharply. She dusted the crumbs off her hands with a single quick motion and dumped the rest of her tea down the drain. *Not even the firefighters knew for certain what happened— only that Mom's paint thinner was involved. It might have been Mom's accident, it might have been Quinn's.* Delia shook her head, trying to clear herself of the old mix of grief, guilt, and anger. *Come on, woman. That's yesterday's news. You've got to deal with Lance now.*

Except she didn't have to deal with him now—she had to leave in a few minutes. Delia fumed, suddenly frustrated. She had been waiting for the chance to get to know Lance better, and now that the opportunity had come up, she wasn't able to take full advantage of it.

She strode into the living room. For a moment Delia considered calling Meredeth and telling her she was sick and couldn't go to Thetachron III. But no, that wouldn't work. It was hard for anyone but colonists to get sick these days. And it would be letting Meredeth down. Meredeth, who had recognized Delia's talent for organization and had pulled her out of the secretarial pool to give her a job that *challenged* her. Who had somehow forced the insurance company to pay for the prohibitively expensive bodysculpt and reconstruction procedures after the fire.

Delia picked up a carved titmouse and ran her fingers over the smooth contours. Yes, her job challenged her. A maze also challenged a mouse. It wasn't what she had envisioned herself doing at age thirty-three.

One of these days, she thought for the hundredth time, *I'll have to do something about that.*

Delia set the titmouse down and checked her wristcomp. The cab would be here in a few minutes. She poked her head into the guest room to say good-bye to Lance, then changed her mind.

He needs the rest, she decided, watching him sleep. *After what he went through last night, who wouldn't?*

Lance shifted slightly without waking up and Delia cocked her head. The light was bad and the angle made it hard to see, but Lance's face looked a lot better than it had last night. She couldn't see the cuts at all.

Impossible, she thought, pushing the door open a little more for a better look. *Those cuts couldn't have—*

A car beeped from the street.

Whoops! Move along, Delia. Time and London cabbies wait for no one.

She pulled on the shoes she had left near the luggage, gathered up her overnight bags, and strode briskly out the door.

Light seeped between the cracks in the blinds, and Lance lazily rolled over to check his wristcomp on the nightstand. Eight-fifteen on Tuesday morning. He gave a minor sigh of relief—no one else had taken over since last night.

He stretched and sat up, surprised at how well he had slept. The bed had proven to be supremely comfortable, just like Delia and the rest of her apartment.

Impatiently Lance shoved the last part of the thought aside. There were more important things to deal with.

Robin?

Here, Jaylance. Healing process complete. Ankle, leg, arm, and face all in top condition.

Thanks, meatless.

Also checked with house computer. Yorik says Delia left for business trip one hour, ten minutes, six seconds ago. Has been programmed to answer your voice commands. Delia also left note for you on kitchen table.

Right. Lance poked his head out of the guest room. Sunlight streamed down the hallway from the living room windows. Something odd about the apartment bothered him, but he couldn't put his finger on what it was.

"Yorik," Lance said, "close all the blinds."

The sunlight obediently faded away, accompanied by a faint swishing noise, and Lance stepped naked into the hallway, secure in the knowledge that Delia was gone and no one on the street would be able to see him. He padded through the dim living room and into the kitchen, which smelled faintly of tea, nothing else. The odd feeling stole over Lance and he sniffed again. Nothing. Then he realized what had been bothering him—there was no artificial scent in the air. There hadn't been last night, either. Delia must have shut off the aromaducts. Strange.

A computer notepad on the table blinked softly for his attention.

"Yorik," he said, "play message."

Delia's face appeared on the screen. "Morning, Lance," she said, smiling. The timer said she had recorded the message at six-thirty in the morning. Lance grimaced. How anyone could smile at such an ungodly hour was beyond him.

"Sorry to be a poor host by not getting you breakfast," the message continued, "but I had to leave, and you needed your sleep. Help yourself to whatever you can find in the kitchen. There's plenty to feed even a big guy like you" —Lance glanced down at himself and blushed, though he was sure *that* wasn't what Delia was referring to— "for at least a week. I left some cash under this notepad in case you're short and don't want to risk using your card. Don't worry about paying it back. You can buy me dinner instead." She smiled again, then adopted a bad Yiddish accent. "And call me when you get out of England. For all I know you're lying dead in a ditch somewhere. No, seriously—let me know you're safe, all right? I'll worry if I don't hear from you. Good luck, Lance." Delia's image paused for a moment as if she wanted to say more. Then she apparently thought the better of it and the screen went blank.

Lance lifted the notepad and found a small stack of paper currency. He hesitated for a moment, then picked it up. It looked close to five hundred pounds. His first instinct was to leave it, but he also realized it would make getting out of England a lot easier. He had been planning to wait two or three days, then buy a ticket for the ferry or skyhook and make a mad dash before Dad heard about it. But with five hundred in untraceable cash, he could run for it tonight.

A growl rumbled in Lance's stomach and he suddenly realized he was ravenously hungry.

Well, what did you expect, he thought, *with all that healing Robin had to do?*

He went back to the bedroom and pulled on his jumpsuit, too hungry to pause for a shower. He didn't need one anyway—Robin kept him clean. Even brushed his teeth for him on a microscopic level.

Yeah, Lance thought sourly, heading back to the kitchen. *Wouldn't do to have a son who wakes up with messy hair and bad breath like everyone else, would it?*

Sorry, Robin said. *Healing and general caretaking hardwired into system. Still unable to override.*

Yeah, yeah. I know.

After a hearty breakfast of cereal and eggs, Lance carefully cleaned the kitchen and wandered into the living room with a mug of tea. The room was neat and tidy, except for the sloppy piles of disks on the bookshelves. He picked up a few and inspected the titles. *Birds of the Americas. Dictionary of Ornithology. An Ornithological Taxonomy of Diomedes II. Avian Biology: A Field Handbook. Group Minds: Four Case Studies of Multiple Personality Disorder.*

Lance quickly set the bookdisks down and turned to examine some of the photographs on the walls. A raven perched on a fencepost caught his eye, and he pressed the button on the picture frame. Raven and fencepost turned in place, giving Lance a view on all sides. As far as Lance could tell, it was an excellent piece of work. So were the other photos in the room. He turned his attention to the statues. Blobby pelicans, tiny wrens, bright bluejays, glaring raptors, and many others all vied for shelf and table space. Each carving was either unique or a limited edition and none of them were animated. Delia seemed to be one of the few people that found animatronic statues tacky. Lance nodded in approval. Grandpa Jack would love this place.

Delia certainly loves birds, Lance thought, sinking into the sofa to look at them all. *Why doesn't she have any live ones?* He took a sweet sip of orange pekoe. *Now there's a silly question. She must travel a lot. Who would take care of them?*

Lance checked the time. Delia's ship was almost certainly phased out by now. He wondered if she liked travelling and if she was worrying about him like she said in her note.

A moment later, Lance went back to the kitchen and replayed Delia's message. Twice. Then, feeling slightly guilty, he downloaded it into his own wristcomp and erased it from the notepad. He refreshed his tea and went into the living room to check the nets for news about himself.

Garth switched off the newsnet.
Robin?
Here, Garth.
You've linked up with the house computer, right?

Affirmative.

Get into the communications net and block anyone who tries a trace. I've got a call to make.

Acknowledged.

Garth set Delia's vidphone next to the sofa, dropped to the cushions, and casually entered a code. After a moment the screen winked to life.

"Pop!" Garth said breezily. "How's it hangin'? To the left or to the right?"

Jonathan Blackstone's eyes widened for the briefest of moments. He was a large man with a shrewd, handsome face. Jonathan Blackstone and his son shared the exact same shade of red hair, though the elder Blackstone wore his shorter and he had allowed a trace of silver to show around the temples. He looked uncannily like Garth, though Garth was of the opinion that he and Lance were better looking.

"John?" Blackstone said. "How did you get this number?"

"I can always get hold of you, Dad-o," Garth told him. "And it's Garth, not John. Johnny won't talk to you and Lance is gone, spaced, phased, out to lunch. He doesn't even know I'm calling."

"What the hell do you want?" Jonathan Blackstone asked. His shoulders moved slightly, as if he were punching keys off-camera and trying to hide it.

"Don't bother with a trace, Pop," Garth snorted. "I've secured the line. I always do. You oughta know that by now."

Blackstone's expression didn't change. "I'm a busy man, John. I asked what the fuck you wanted."

"I'm taunting you, Pop," Garth said. "Come on—you know how it works. One of the Company—" Garth tapped his forehead "—makes a mistake, your goon squad tries to catch us, we get away, I call you up and make fun of you. It's tradition. Other families do Christmas, but we've always been different, haven't we?"

"What are you talking about?" Blackstone asked.

"Ah. The tradition continues." Garth laced his fingers behind his head and put his feet up. "Dad Admits to

Nothing. VR at eleven. You blew it, Dad. I'm still somewhere out of your reach and there's not a fucking thing you can do about it. We've got a pile of untraceable cash in our pocket and a huge deposit in our savings account that'll keep us flush for a long time." *Right?*

Affirmative. Deposit made early this morning.

"You mean the Carlina Gruenfeld affair," Blackstone said. "I hear she was quite upset at the way you slapped her around. Nice work."

"Score one for Daddy's intelligence squad," Garth said. "Except it was Patrick who scared the old lady. Patrick's a jerk, not charming like me. You're never gonna catch us, Pop. Never. You make stupid mistakes, but don't expect me to tell you what they are."

"Are you done now?"

"I haven't even started, Pop. This is the most fun I've had since I learned how to screw."

"I taught you that."

"You taught Andy, Dad-O. Not me." Garth leaned forward thoughtfully. "But you're awful calm. Usually I've got you frothing at the mouth by now. What's up? You got a secretary swinging from your dick?"

"I'm just not in the mood today."

"Not in the mood for a secretarial sausage slurp? Pop! You've changed."

"That's not what I meant, and you know it. Where the hell is John?"

"Who cares? On a completely unrelated topic, by the way, I contacted a VR sex company. They said they'd pay some mighty big bucks for a certain little vidcard a certain little ex-wife of a certain little trillionaire made involving a certain little son and a certain little bodyguard. Whaddaya think?"

Blackstone shrugged. "Vidcards aren't valid in court anymore, and anyone who sees it will assume someone was fucking around with a computer imager."

"Only because one of your companies—pardon the expression—screwed around with the technology," Garth pointed out. "If it weren't for you, vidcards would still be untamper-with-able."

"If it weren't for me."

Garth paused, but Jonathan Blackstone didn't comment further.

"Well," Garth said finally, "it's been fun talking to you, Pop. Better luck next time." Garth switched off the phone and flung himself back on the sofa with crossed arms.

Pouting? Robin inquired.

"A little," Garth said petulantly. "Dad's usually a lot more fun than that."

Said wasn't in mood.

But Garth only tapped his fingers thoughtfully on the sofa.

"We can also increase material output by fifty-seven point oh four percent for eight point oh oh nine days, if necessary," the tour guide said. "As a result of this capability, profits for the quarter rose sixteen point one five three percent during the plague on Notre Dame. We also saved five hundred and fifteen additional lives," he added as an afterthought.

Delia patted back a yawn and resisted the temptation to glance at her wristcomp. Sayed Sabeel was a gracious host with a pleasant manner, but he was overly fond of his statistics.

"I see," Meredeth Michaels said gravely, rolling her eyes at Delia when Sabeel turned to flick a bit of dust off an instrument panel. They were in the control center of the station orbiting Thetachron III, and Delia was so far unimpressed. Although the place certainly seemed to be in excellent working order with powerful manufacturing and research capabilities, the designers had gone in for a lot of gray metal and off-white ceramic. Footsteps echoed unpleasantly and the lights were harsh fluorescent. Not the kind of place Delia would want to live and work.

"Perhaps we could see the research labs?" Ms. Michaels continued. "I think those would be of greater interest."

Sayed Sabeel nodded. His skin was almost as dark as Delia's, and his silvering black hair was immaculately trimmed. "Of course," he said. "This way."

They left the control center, a circular, utilitarian room lined with gray metal and computer monitors, most of which were blank. The station, Sabeel had explained, was on standby status. The equipment was ready for use, but nothing was being produced at the moment—Pinegra couldn't afford to pay the workers and had laid them off.

"Where are your employees now?" Delia asked as they headed down another empty gray corridor. Two other MM inspection teams were on tour elsewhere on the station, but it was easy to believe they were completely alone. The air was slightly chilly, and Delia rubbed her arms.

Sabeel shrugged. "We shipped them back home— deducting the ticket price from their final paychecks, of course. We can supply you with their names and locations if you want to hire them back, but it's just as easy to find new ones. There aren't any labor unions out here, so you can do as you like."

Delia nodded curtly and dropped the information into her wristcomp, trying not to fume. No wonder Pinegra was going bankrupt. Treating your employees like slaves made sense in the short run—it drove up quarterly profits— but in the long run it created more problems than it solved. Delia was certain a quick check of the company's records would show employee theft had run rampant and that worker morale was nonexistent.

I know mine wouldn't be very high if I had to work here, she thought, ignoring the steady stream of statistics issuing from Sabeel's mouth. *No comforts at all. I haven't even seen any rec areas or VR channels. If we buy this place, there'll have to be some changes made. Loyal employees are worth their weight in gold, and you don't get them by treating them like disposable tissues.*

The overhead lights flickered up and down the hallway for a moment before settling back to their steady white glow. Sabeel paused in his recitation to frown at them.

"Strange," he said. "A small power surge elsewhere on the station, perhaps. No need to worry, I'm sure."

"I'm sure," Ms. Michaels agreed impatiently. "You were taking us to the research labs?"

Delia glanced up at the lights, then shrugged and followed Sabeel. As Sabeel said, no need to worry. Anyone who bolted for the air locks every time a light flickered would eventually qualify as an Olympic sprinter.

Sabeel led them two levels down, still spouting his facts and figures, and Delia's mind began to wander back to Lance. She glanced uneasily at Ms. Michaels, who was listening to Sabeel with politely feigned interest. Without saying a word, both of them seemed to have agreed not to mention Jessica's revelation, though Delia knew they would have to confront it eventually. A bit of tension rode between the two of them, but Delia had been relieved to discover it wasn't bad enough to interfere with the business at hand.

Jessica said Lance's father abused him horribly, Delia mused, *but Ms. Michaels must have known what was happening. Why didn't she do anything about it? Why did she stay with Jonathan Blackstone for so long? Multiple personality disorder doesn't start overnight. God, it must have been horrible for Lance. I hope he made it across the channel.* Delia's stomach flipped over. *You've got it bad, girl. That man has got some real mental problems, but you can't stop thinking about him.*

Well, why not? He's sweet and gentle when he's himself. Those eyes of his just draw you in. Besides, MPD is treatable.

They emerged from an elevator and strode up yet another gray, featureless corridor. The lights flickered again, but Delia barely noticed.

Treatable, but not easily. Would you be willing to stay with him through it all? She mentally shook her head. *Hard to tell. I'd have to try it to find out, wouldn't I?*

"Here we are," Sabeel said. "Research and development, level four, section two."

They were standing at a six-way intersection. Signs in half a dozen languages pointed the reader in the proper direction for low-grav labs, isolation chambers, DNA engineering, animal kennels, VR simulation (research only), and more.

"The surface of Thetachron III produces three species of lichen," Sabeel said, "which can be refined and combined to produce fourteen essential medicines, six of which must be engineered in low gravity. These lichens have given us the ability to cure or control epilepsy, thyroid storm, nephroblastoma, radiation poisoning—"

"Yes, I'm aware of all that," Ms. Michaels interrupted. "May we see the labs, please?"

Sabeel nodded. "Hajira, release all lab doors."

Static burst briefly over the speakers. "Please present authorization," said the computer.

Sayed Sabeel said something in what Delia presumed was Arabic. Another burst of static followed, and Delia frowned. So did Sabeel.

"Authorization acknowledged," said the computer. Clicks and clacks echoed up and down the corridor as the doors released their locks.

"Is something wrong with the computer?" Delia asked. "All that static?"

"I don't know," Sabeel admitted, looking up at the ceiling. "I'll have our technicians look into it. You may be certain the problem, if there is one, will be repaired before you take possession of the station, if you do choose to buy."

"Thank you," Ms. Michaels said. "The labs?"

The first room Sabeel showed them was crammed with worktables and equipment—robotic arms, centrifuges, sample cases, flash freezers, and more. Lining the walls were a series of clear plastic chambers, each about twice the size of a vidphone call box. More robot arms reached inside them.

"This is the low-grav lab," Sabeel told them. "The chambers are isolated from the station's own gravity and

are capable of producing a field that goes as high as twice
Earth normal or as low as point oh one g's. Because Pinegra
is going bankrupt, we are willing to sell the research
equipment as part of the station."

"What about patent rights?" Ms. Michaels asked.

"Pinegra owns the patents of everything our researchers
have discovered," Sabeel said. "But those are going up
for sale separately."

"The patents wouldn't do anyone much good unless they
also bought the station," Ms. Michaels pointed out, "since
all of them involve the lichens on Thetachron III."

"Perhaps," Sabeel said. "But that would be a—"

The lights went out and a blast of white sound crashed
through the room. Delia gave an involuntary yelp and put
her hands over her ears. The emergency lights came on,
casting an eerie, blood-red glow over the lab. The noise
cut off, leaving a ringing silence, but the lights didn't come
back on.

"What's going on?" Ms. Michaels demanded.

"Hajira!" Sabeel barked. "Explain the nature of the
emergency."

"Hajira," the computer repeated, "explain the nature
of the emergency."

"Hajira, return power to Research Lab One immediately!"

"Hajira, return power to Research Lab One immediately."

The door slammed and locked itself. Delia's stomach
twisted, and from the look on Ms. Michaels' face, hers
was doing the same thing. Sabeel continued snapping at
the computer, which blithely returned his commands. Delia
spotted a terminal and made for it, but Ms. Michaels was
faster. She switched it on and ran her fingers over the
keys with hurried taps and clicks.

"Without an access code I can only access basic mainframe
information," she said, "but that should let us know what's
going on."

Codes and symbols sped across the monitor.

"It's gibberish," Delia said, peering over Ms. Michael's
shoulder and trying to keep her voice steady while Sabeel

continued arguing with the computer. "What's going on?"

Ms. Michaels pursed her lips and tried to access the mainframe again. A pair of robot arms suddenly came to life on the other side of the room and whirred madly in place. The lights in one of the low-grav chambers flickered and flashed like someone trying to send Morse code, and another burst of static blared from the speakers. Ms. Michaels ignored it all, her fingers almost a blur above the keyboard. A possibility sprouted uneasily in Delia's mind.

"Ms. Michaels?" she asked. "What—"

Ms. Michaels slammed her hands on the terminal with a crash and Delia jumped.

"I think," Ms. Michaels said, her calm voice belying her pale face, "that we're in the middle of a nanobot hive."

The skyhook port was blessedly busy. Lance, dressed in a new hooded jumpsuit and sunglasses, slipped through crowds of luggage-laden tourists with practiced ease, keeping an eye out for anyone who seemed too interested— or too disinterested—in him. Loudspeakers blatted messages and announcements, while overpriced restaurants wafted rich, meaty smells into the throughways. Clumps of people gathered at large windows to watch the skyhook compartments. Each was shaped like a sleek white railroad car, and at regular intervals one would trundle up to the skyhook, wait a brief moment for connection, then soar skyward, hauled straight up the cable like a fish on a line.

Lance ignored the sight and shifted the carryall slung over his shoulder, privately seething about the side trips he'd had to take. Just before he had left Delia's apartment late that afternoon, Robin had informed him that Patrick had left the carryall—and the breaking-and-entering equipment within—inside a locker at Victoria Station. Lance had been forced to go get it, and the trip had done nothing for his nerves.

And then I find out he didn't return the rental car, he fumed. *The rental company found it. Nice fine to pay there—and with Delia's money. One of these days the*

Company's going to have to do something about him on a permanent basis.

There was nothing for it now, though. Lance stole another surreptitious glance at the crowd around him. No apparent operatives. It was strange. He hadn't seen any all day. Not at Victoria Station. Not in the skyhook ticket line. Not on the way to the boarding gate. A formless unease stole over him as he showed his pass to the attendant and followed him to a seat.

The skyhook passenger area resembled a train compartment with acceleration couches instead of chairs. Lance buckled his seat belt and swallowed dryly. No matter how many times he used it, the skyhook still made him nervous. It wasn't at all like phase jumping. A phase ship could fly, and Lance was used to things that flew. The skyhook, on the other hand, didn't fly—it looked like it was reaching up into space, though it actually dangled from orbit. Lance could just imagine a wizened old man playing an oddly shaped flute at the base of the cable, and he shuddered to think of what would happen if the guy ever paused to take a breath.

Robin, change eye color. Gray, please.
Acknowledged.

Lance removed his sunglass—they were too conspicuous indoors. Fortunately, the hood covering his hair was fashionable under any conditions. More people moved steadily into the compartment, and Lance scrutinized each one carefully to take his mind off his nervousness. None of them looked even remotely suspicious.

I should have at least seen someone, Lance thought, buckling his harness. *Dad wouldn't let a chance like this go by without some kind of fight.*

He went over the details of the last couple of days, trying to see if he had made a mistake. Nothing he hadn't already seen came to mind. Once he had gotten out of Brad's flat, he hadn't used a cashcard, not even for the skyhook ticket. He'd made no mistakes and had had a fairly easy time of it, actually.

Lance stiffened. That was it. That's what was bothering
him. It had been too easy to get away. Every other time
Dad's operatives had gotten that close, simply running
through a stranger's flat wouldn't have been enough to
get him away, especially not when they had time to plan—
and by Lance's best estimation, they'd had hours. Why
the mistakes? They weren't stupid or poorly trained.

One attendant came around to make sure everyone
was buckled in properly while another outlined safety
procedures over the loudspeaker. Lance leaned back on
the couch, listening with only half an ear. Had Dad let
him escape on purpose? Lance turned the idea over in
his head, unable to come up with anything else that made
sense. But why would Dad *let* him get away?

There was a slight jerk and Lance's stomach dropped
as the compartment rushed upward. It would take about
an hour and a half to reach the top, whereupon the
compartment would be disconnected from the skyhook
and ferried by shuttle to Ride Station, where Lance had
docked his ship. Lance spent the time looking at every
possibility. He came up empty. Dad's operatives had indeed
made several mistakes—they had burst into Brad's bedroom
after he and Andy were . . . finished, they hadn't posted
anyone in the courtyard, and they hadn't adequately
surrounded the block of flats. Everything pointed to Dad
ordering his operatives to give Lance a hard time, yet let
him escape.

The compartment met the station with a slight thump,
and several passengers got up to pull carry-ons from
the overhead carriers despite the attendants' warning
to wait until the docking clamps were fully engaged.
Lance gathered his carryall and joined the line of people
filing onto the station, keeping watch from force of habit
but not expecting anything to happen. He quickly
threaded his way through the metallic Ride Station
corridors until he got to the personal craft docks and
the *Defiant Lady*—his ship. He identified himself by
voice and retina print, flipped the dock operator a

generous tip, and stepped through the air lock into the *Lady* with a sigh of relief.

He was home.

Lance trotted through familiar corridors, feeling safer and more relaxed than he had in days. The *Lady* was his own space. Here he could rest without having to worry about Dad or Mom or anything else. And assuming Mrs. Gruenfeld had paid his fee, he wouldn't have to worry about money for a while, either.

Robin?

Nanos leaving body, merging with local systems. Will have ship under control in approximately ten minutes.

Lance ignored his crawling skin and headed for the residential part of the ship.

All in all, there were four sets of quarters on the *Defiant Lady*. Garth and Andy shared one set, Patrick and Johnny shared another. Jessica, of course, had a cabin to herself, and Lance shared his with Jay, Grandpa Jack, and a few others who weren't around often enough to need separate digs. Robin had never asked for quarters, but then, Robin had the run of the ship.

Lance's cabin was large and scrupulously neat. The carpet was thick and brown, and two holographic "windows" on the walls let him pretend he was looking out over the narrow houses of Amsterdam. Wood paneling covered walls lined with racks of bookdisks that included a large selection of research papers on nanobots and several psychology texts about multiple personality disorder. A guitar stood in the corner and a rough-carved wooden horse pawed at the sky on a shelf, surrounded by other similar carvings.

Lance dropped the carryall on his bed and skinned out of the new, uncomfortable jumpsuit. While rummaging through the closet for a different one, he caught sight of himself in the full-length mirror fastened to one wall. The scars from last night had completely faded. Lance walked slowly over to the mirror and stared long and hard at his image.

Delia thought he was good-looking. He could see it in

her eyes and posture. She probably thought he had a nice body, too. Everyone else did.

"Robin," he said suddenly, "activate program one."

The image shifted and wavered. In the mirror, Lance's hair lengthened slightly and faded to strawberry blond. He lost several inches of height and his eyes shifted from gray to emerald-green. His muscles lost their athletic definition and softened and blurred. His face . . . changed. The cheekbones flattened and his eyes became smaller. Muscle and bone rearranged themselves, changing features in subtle, yet important ways. His penis shortened and shrank. When the image stopped changing, Lance was no longer perfectly handsome. Attractive, definitely. Handsome, perhaps—depending on the viewer. But not gorgeous, stunning, alluring, or beautiful.

It was the way he was supposed to look.

Lance raised a hand and waved at himself, naked in the mirror. His image returned the wave as if it really were a reflection instead of a computer-generated image. He looked normal.

Except Lance wasn't normal. Not in any sense of the world. Even his looks were an illusion. Suddenly impatient, Lance lashed out and punched the mirror image in its imperfect, normal face. Pain exploded in his hand, breaking his thoughts, though the shatterproof mirror didn't break.

"Robin," he almost snarled, "end program."

The mirror wavered and Lance's reflection returned. He stared at it with undisguised loathing. This was the reality. *This* was what Delia was attracted to. Someone else's handiwork. Someone else's creation.

Hatred burned harshly behind his eyes, and he tried to push the feeling away, but it wouldn't go. Abruptly his face went blank, then his eyes shifted from Robin's artificial gray to a deep and brooding blue. Humming softly to himself, he turned away from the mirror and went into the bathroom, where he searched through stacks of towels and eventually extracted a small plastic packet. Inside was an assortment of surgical instruments that glittered metallic in the bright overhead light. He selected one and held it comfortingly against his cheek for a moment, then began cutting, heedless of the blood that splashed down his chest and into the sink.

Blackness. Lance hung suspended in nothing. He could vaguely feel the others around him—Garth's mocking grin, Patrick's anger, little Johnny's fear, Andy's carefree hedonism—and he knew that Jay was in charge of the body, but he had no idea what Jay was doing with it. Probably playing more sad songs he had written for the guitar or just moping around. At least, Lance hoped he was.

At one time Lance had had no awareness or memory at all during the times his alters had the body. Years of practice had alleviated total blackout, but he was still cut off from the world with only a vague awareness of the passage of time.

Lance floated, waiting. Like most core personalities in cases of MPD, Lance could not communicate directly with any of his alters, though they could communicate with each other with varying degrees of success. Jessica and Patrick, for instance, only had access to Lance's thoughts and memories while Andy and Garth saw and heard everything. Or so they claimed. The exception was Robin, who could talk to anyone at any time, but Robin was special anyway.

The darkness abruptly cleared and Lance found himself fully dressed and sitting cross-legged on his bed with Jay's guitar in his lap. Then a sharp, all-too-familiar pain creased his cheeks. Lance put a hand to his face, and his fingertips came away slicked with blood. Some of it had dripped onto the guitar.

Lance sighed and put his fingers in his mouth. *Robin?* *Here, Jaylance.*

How long was Jay in control?

Two hours, fourteen minutes. Cut face, body, then tried to commit suicide again.

Lance set the guitar aside and checked his hands. There was a fresh scar across each wrist and, he was sure, a sinkful of bloody water in the bathroom.

Staunched bleeding, Robin continued. *Establishing pain block. Working on lacerations.*

Why didn't you just stop him from doing it in the first place? Lance growled.

Unable to interfere unless behavior would directly endanger self. Committing suicide falls under that category. Slicing face does not. So states Company Policy.

Lance sighed. *Jay didn't take the Lady anywhere, did he?*

Negative. Still in clamps. Docking authority says in two more hours will have to charge for another day.

Thank heaven for small favors. The last time Jay had taken over, Lance had come to himself in the middle of a religious retreat run by a man who claimed to be the reincarnation of Cleopatra and Mao Tse Tung. Lance set the guitar aside and got up, grimacing as circulation returned to his cramped legs. He had drained the bathroom sink and was reaching for a roll of gauze to help Robin control his bleeding face when an alarm began to chime.

Attention! Attention! Robin said. *Incoming transmission.*

Lance closed his eyes in irritation. "Can you take a message, Robin? I don't feel like dealing with anyone right now. Did Mrs. Gruenfeld credit our account, by the way?"

Yes. And wouldn't suggest putting off call. Could be important. Will do level best to slow bleeding, make you presentable.

Lance shrugged. "Fine." And he headed for the *Defiant Lady*'s control room, a gray, utilitarian affair. Instruments crowded the walls and ceiling, spilling onto the flight boards. The place was also surprisingly small—no board was out of arm's reach of any other, and the ceiling was low and cramped. The signal alarm continued to chime and a blue light on one of the panels blinked insistently.

"Who is it, anyway?" Lance asked, taking the room's single chair and sliding it over to the communication boards.

Name is Francis Rutherford. Call preceded by business code.

Lance shut off the alarm and reached for the com controls. "What does he want?"

No idea. Your job to ask, not mine.

A drop of blood slid around Lance's chin and he wiped at it automatically with a finger as he tapped the final key. "Michaels Company Security Analysis. You have reached Lance Michaels."

A violet-to-red spectrum washed over the com screen as the computer pulled the carrier wave out of phase and reconfigured it into the image of an almost stereotypical male business executive—youthfully dark hair, flat stomach, blue eyes, a very few wrinkles, and a serious expression which made it clear that his problems were more important than anyone else's. Surprise flickered in his eyes when he caught sight of the condition of Lance's face.

He's rich enough to afford bodysculpt, Lance noted, *but not rich enough to stave off all signs of aging. Either the CEO of a small company or middle management of a big one.*

"Mr. Michaels?" the man said.

That's what I said. "Yes?"

"My name is Francis Rutherford, executive vice president for Pinegra, Incorporated. We are interested in hiring your services as a consultant."

Lance almost jumped, startled. *Pinegra? Isn't that the company that's selling the pharmaceutical plant to Mom?*

Affirmative.

Rhetorical question, meatless. "Pinegra?" he said aloud. "Why would you want to hire a security specialist when you're going bankrupt?"

Rutherford looked surprised again. "How did you know about that? We haven't made any kind of announcement."

"I'm a security specialist, Mr. Rutherford," Lance replied blandly. "I have contacts."

"Ah. Of course." Rutherford cleared his throat. "At any

rate, we haven't gone under just yet, and we still have a few problems."

"Such as?"

"A plant on one of our asteroids has gone hive. We need someone to reclaim it."

Lance sat up straighter. "Hive?"

"Apparently so. The plant isn't operating at the moment, but a group of inspection teams boarded it about four hours ago after a negotiation meeting. Not an hour after the inspection tour started, the plant's computers and systems went wild. Communications went down and the security system isn't letting anyone in—or out. Classic signs of nanobot hive activity. As far as we can tell, life support has been stable but could go at any moment. Normally we'd write the place off and blow it up, but the inspection teams are still aboard."

Lance's heart started to pound. "Mr. Rutherford, where is this plant located?"

The answer came like a lead weight. "It's orbiting the third planet in the Thetachron system. The buyer is Meredeth Michaels of MM, Limited." Rutherford cocked his head, as if something had just occurred to him. "A relation of yours, Mr. Michaels?"

This is a trick, Lance thought wildly, ignoring Rutherford. *He's lying.*

∗*Checking, checking,*∗ Robin said. ∗*Located newstach broadcast. Synopsis: pharmaceuticals plant orbiting Thetachron III has gone wild. Security system destroyed two ships trying to bypass and enter. Half-dozen people trapped inside. Nanobot hive activity suspected.*∗

All expression left Lance's face and he stared emptily at the com screen.

"Mr. Michaels?" said a voice. "Mr. Michaels, are you all right?"

Garth Blackstone blinked and glanced around the control room of the *Defiant Lady*. Then he realized someone on the com screen was looking at him with polite concern.

Garth scrambled to remember who it was. Although he saw what Lance saw and had access to Lance's memories, it didn't mean he was always paying attention.

"I'm fine, Rutherford," he said breezily. "Just fine. And no, Meredeth Michaels isn't any relation." Garth grinned lopsidedly, then winced. He put a hand to his cheek and it came away with a sticky red smear. "Oh yuck. Not again. Take a nap and look what happens."

"Pardon?" Rutherford said.

"Nothing." *Hey, Robby—speed up the healing, will you? This face-cutting shit is really getting old.*

Sorry. Am currently running diagnostic on life-support systems, monitoring newstach broadcasts, and checking station's overhaul of phase drive. Can only do forty-six things at once.

"So." Garth stretched lazily. "You want us to get rid of a nanobot hive on Thetachron III. It'll cost you."

"I'm aware of that, Mr. Michaels."

"Ten million dollars. That's twenty-four million in colony creds."

Rutherford's face reddened. "Ridiculous! That's five times the going rate for security analysis."

"You've done your homework, Rutherford," Garth said easily. "Trouble is, we've got a monopoly. No one else is willing to deal with the itchy problem of nanos with hives."

Not funny.

"So," Garth continued, ignoring Robin's remark, "it'll cost you ten million. Plus expenses."

"Look," Rutherford said, "we're going bankrupt here. We can't afford ten million."

"You can't afford the lawsuit when your plant kills the rest of those people, either. And the courts won't let you *go* bankrupt until a lawsuit is settled. You'll be in court for the rest of your life."

"Five million," Rutherford countered.

"Ten." Garth reached for the control panel. "And if you don't say yes this time, I'm cutting you off. I'll give you a count of three. Ready? One . . . two . . ."

Rutherford ground his teeth. "All right, all right. Ten million."

"Expenses?"

"Expenses."

Garth sighed with theatrical rapture. "I love it when people cry 'uncle.' Standard contract—half now, half when the hive problem has been cleared out. Transfer the money—in dollars—to TRRA-486-7386-LM465. See you."

He tapped the disconnect key before Rutherford could reply.

"Goshgollydarn that was fun," Garth said to no one in particular. "Ten million will keep us in underwear—and out of it—for a couple years. Forward ho!"

He contacted the port authority to ask for permission to disengage from the station, released the docking clamps, and carefully nudged the *Defiant Lady* out of orbit, keeping a close eye on local traffic patterns. Garth could have hooked himself into the ship's VR system and, in effect, become the ship, but that wasn't real piloting. That was more like swimming through space.

Garth liked *piloting*. There was nothing like feeling the sweet, tremulous response of several tons of sleek metal under his hands and seeing the stars shoot away into blackness when the phase drive was engaged. It was almost better than sex. Almost. Patrick probably felt the same way about driving a car.

Piloting was also what made it possible for Garth to work in the tiny control room without feeling like the walls were closing in. There was more space out there than Garth could comprehend, and he could move through it with absolute freedom. Claustrophobia wasn't a problem in the control room.

Once he was clear of the station, Garth looked up the coordinates for Thetachron III and programmed them into the phase drive's systems. The computer said it would take about two hours to get there unless Garth was willing to risk burning out the generator.

For Lance's mother? Get real.

The *Lady* shuddered delicately as she came about, and Garth frowned. Something was nagging at him, but he couldn't figure out what.

Pinegra, he thought, goosing the thrusters. According to law, he had to be at least five thousand kilometers away from the station before engaging the phase drive. *Strange name for a company. And isn't it just a dandy coincidence that Merry Michaels was aboard that station when it went hive? And that last night Dad's goon squad let us get away so easily? And that he didn't seem so upset about it when I talked to him this morning?*

The more he thought about it, the more he felt he was missing something.

Pinegra. Where does that name comes from? He absently caught a falling droplet of blood from his cheek and stuck the finger in his mouth, ignoring the coppery taste. *Robby, access business databases on the nets. See what you can find out about Pinegra.*

Working. There was a pause. *Pinegra, Incorporated. Relatively small pharmaceutical company founded six years ago. Founder and CEO named Patricia Kang. Two months ago, assets included—*

"Hold it," Garth interrupted. "Why would a woman called Patricia Kang name her company 'Pinegra'? Is it some kind of old family name?"

Unknown. Information not in databases.

Garth sucked on his teeth as the *Defiant Lady* glided quietly through space. There was something about the name. "Robin, what does 'pinegra' mean?"

Unknown. Word not in language database.

"Dissect it. Maybe it's an abbreviation for a phrase. It's got to mean *something*."

Working. Brief pause. *Found four hundred forty-five possible phrases.*

"Christ. How many of those are less than, say, five words long?"

One hundred two.

"And how many of them make sense if translated into

English? No 'red fish dick' or any weird shit like that."
∗Thirty-one.∗
"Put them on monitor."
A screen winked to life and text scrolled down. Garth looked at the list, then swore.

"Robin, highlight number nineteen," he snapped. The scrolling stopped and one of the entries glowed. Garth slammed a fist on the arm of his chair. "Fuck."

The entry read:

19) Pinegra: piedra negra (Spanish): black stone

CHAPTER FOUR

THEN
AGE 14

Garth:

Lance was born two years after Dad and Meredeth were married. He was an expensive kid. Even getting Meredeth pregnant again wasn't cheap. Dad jacked off into a jar four or five times, and his hired techies sorted through the stuff until they found half a hundred Wonder Sperm. Then they screwed with those—cutting genes and moving them around—and made a couple dozen Super Sperm. They did the same thing with a bunch of Meredeth's eggs and fertilized one. Ta da! Instant miracle baby.

You might think Lance and I must've had a really cool childhood, being kids of one of the richest guys in the fucking world, but it wasn't like that at all. Dad created Lance to be perfect and he expected perfection. He couldn't have it, of course. Even with modern gene splicing, you can't order up hair and eye color or height and strength. The best you can do is put together a combination that increases your chances of getting what you want. Dad didn't get quite what he wanted, so he set out to change Lance into what he did want. And when Pop didn't get what he wanted, we got punished.

Once, when Lance was a year and a half old, the kid

93

threw his training glass on the floor. Dad beat the living shit out of him, then wired him to his high chair and left him there for the rest of the day with a full diaper and nothing to eat or drink. It took a week for the cuts from the wires to heal completely. Another favorite was to tie Lance to a tabletop and cover him from head to foot in soft clay with just a tiny straw to breathe through. Then Dad would pretend he was a great sculptor or something and slowly rub the clay away like Michelangelo carving out David. It took hours. Lance couldn't see or hear or move or scream throughout the whole damn thing. It felt like being buried alive.

All I did was watch, though. I didn't do anything until the day Dad started up with the box in the basement. Dad built it out of wood, and it was just big enough to shove a little kid into, if the kid was all scrunched up. He would stuff Lance into the box and leave him there for hours. Then he'd let Lance out and beat the shit out of him because Lance had pissed in his pants.

A couple of times he took the box outside at night and dug a hole and buried Lance in that fucking tiny box. Shoveled dirt right over him just like Lance was dead or something. Could have suffocated. Almost did.

Lance got scared, you know? I mean knock-down, drag-out, so-terrified-you-can't-scream scared. It was worse than the clay. All he could do was lay there, too scared to even shake. So I made sure he didn't get scared. Dad scares Lance, but he doesn't scare me. I know what makes Dad tick.

That's why I was usually the one that helped Lance out in Dad's little shop of horrors in the basement, the one with the soundproofed walls. I saw a lot of that room. Meredeth knew about it but she didn't do anything about it.

Meredeth never did anything. She knew what was going on, but she never stopped it. She always arranged to be somewhere else when Dad hauled out the electrical cords or dumped out more clay or dragged us to the basement.

Every once in a while I'd catch sight of her, and she always had the same expression on her face—stony, uncaring, and cold. Like all women.

Then the operations started. By the time Lance was fourteen, we'd been to the hospital sixteen times. New hair, improved face, more height, better muscles. You name it, we got it. Bodysculpting is expensive, but Dad didn't have to worry about that—not when he owned the hospital.

It was the eye operation that did it. I knew we had to get away, but Lance gets too scared to do what needs to be done, so I decided to take care of it myself.

I was the only one who cared enough.

Garth Blackstone leaned forward in anticipation, heart pounding, mouth dry.

"Come on," he whispered. "Come on."

On the screen before him was a full-color view of the office that housed security for the Blackstone estate. Rows of monitors lined the walls, interspersed with food wrappers and coffee cups. The night watch, a burly man with a blond mustache, had just entered the room and was walking toward his evening counterpart.

Garth wiped his palms on the bedspread and shifted cramping thighs. Sitting cross-legged in bed hunched over a tiny computer notebook wasn't the most relaxing position, but it was the only safe one. Dad had no idea what Garth knew about the estate's security system, and Garth intended to keep it that way. Normally he would have waited until Dad was on another trip out of town to try and run away, but there was no time now. Garth wasn't going to let anyone rip his eyes out. Lance or Johnny might, but Garth wouldn't. No way. He was almost fifteen years old, and no one was going to pull that shit with him.

A small sound creaked in the hallway. In one silent motion Garth flung himself flat on his back and whipped the blankets over his terminal. He waited tensely, slitted eyes scanning the shadows, ears straining for the slightest sound. The room remained silent.

Lots of boys would kill for this room. It was huge, big enough to hold a king-sized bed and a fully equipped virtual reality rig. All but one of the closets were full of clothes and of toys Lance now scorned as "kid stuff" but couldn't quite throw away, while a fully-equipped private bathroom with its own jacuzzi awaited the user's pleasure. And a word to the house computer would change the decor. Lance usually left the walls and carpets bare, but Garth preferred a jungle motif. On the walls, trees waved gently in nonexistent breezes and every once in a while a pair of eyes would gleam from the darkness. The aromaducts breathed the sweet scent of tropical flowers into the air. All in all, it was a wonderful room—and Garth couldn't wait to leave it.

He waited a moment longer. Nothing. Several heartbeats later, Garth cautiously sat up and brought out the computer again.

Onscreen, the evening guard had already left and the night guard was at the terminal. Garth licked his lips and checked to make sure the computer was still recording. It had been easier than he thought to access the security cameras and download what they saw, but then no one was expecting a break-in from the house computer itself.

"Come on," Garth whispered. "Log in. Hurry up."

The guard paced his hand under an image scanner and the workstation's screen flashed quick letters. Garth squirmed in agitation. This was taking so *long*.

The night guard yawned, took a sip of coffee, and almost leisurely tapped several keys on his terminal. Then he paused, yawned, and tapped several more. His screen blinked acknowledgment, and Garth hugged himself with glee.

"Chloe," he whispered, "close security system window. Chloe, open window to program Image Arrest. Chloe, access last image recorded and play back the final sixty seconds."

Garth's screen flickered. The security system program collapsed into a small picture of a padlock and another icon instantly ballooned into a blank screen that, after a moment, showed the night watch reaching for his workstation. The moment his fingers touched the keyboard, Garth froze the picture and magnified it, concentrating on the guard's fingers. Slowly, key by key, Garth made out the man's keystrokes.

"Gryphco187," Garth muttered. "What kind of password is that?" He sped up the image until the guard was ready to enter the second word—^@jackie00. Garth had to fight to keep from cheering.

"Chloe," he whispered, "exit program Image Arrest. Chloe, open window to security system. Chloe, access main sensory grid."

Please present right hand for image scan, the screen said.

Garth grinned and uploaded an image he had managed to copy to disk from the watch's own workstation the day before. Adults were so easy to fool sometimes, especially if you asked questions about their jobs and looked really interested. And if you arranged for the house computer to ring the phone at an opportune moment, meaning the workstation went unsupervised for several seconds—well, you could get away with a lot.

Image accepted, the screen said. *Please enter primary password:*

Garth typed *Gryphco187*

Please enter secondary password:

^@jackie00

Error 62: user already logged on. Override y/n?

Garth's heart started pounding again. Quietly, so quietly, he set the computer aside and eased out of bed. Although Dad and Meredeth's bedroom was in a different wing, Garth didn't want to take any chances. Moonlight puddled on the thick carpet as Garth drew back the bedroom curtains and opened the window. Outside, ocean swell rose and crashed against the rocks far below the estate and the sharp smell of seawater permeated the cool night air. The salt mixed oddly with the jungle scents in Lance's room.

Garth tossed a neatly packed carryall out the window—the motion sensors would pick it up, but the system would dismiss it as a threat because it lacked a heat signature. Then he turned back to the computer and took a deep breath. Once he started, he would have to move fast. And if he got caught—

Garth pushed the idea from his mind. He wasn't going to get caught.

Error 62: user already logged on. Override y/n? the terminal still said.

Garth tapped Y. The screen flashed again.

Previous user logged out. Press any key to continue.

Garth's fingers flew over the keys. He could have given the commands vocally, but right now it was faster to type. Menus flashed by until Garth found the sensor systems. Quickly he highlighted each one—cameras, motion detectors, heat sensors, chemical sniffers, sonic sweepers—and ordered the system to deactivate them all. Then he shut off the alarms.

Command executed, the screen printed.

Garth snapped off Lance's computer, stuffed it into his inner jacket pocket, and jumped out the window. When he hit the ground one story below, the impact drove the breath from his lungs, but he scrambled to his feet, snatched up the carryall, and bolted for the wall that surrounded the Blackstone estate.

The early autumn night carried only a hint of chill. A waxing moon shone through the trees and fountains scattered tastefully about the grounds. Garth dodged among them, always making for the wall. His shoes became soaked with dew and the ever-present ocean crashed far below and away. Occasionally, Garth would catch a glimpse of metallic shine as a stray beam of moonlight caught a camera or motion detector. If he hadn't turned them off, the security guards would have known in an instant exactly where Garth was and sent someone to stop him.

Garth figured it wouldn't take more than five minutes for the night guard to log back in and put the sensors back on line. According to Lance's wristcomp, Garth had two minutes left. Two minutes to run three hundred meters. Garth tried to make his legs to go faster. He had to get away tonight, before Lance went into the hospital. He *had* to.

An image of Jonathan Blackstone rose in Garth's head, and fear clenched his stomach. If he got caught, Dad would get something out of the closet, or he would bury Garth in the box or chain him in the basement or come up with something worse.

Garth forced himself to keep running. A stitch started in his side and his lungs were already aching, but ahead he could see the wall. It was about four meters high and made of chunky stone, like the wall of an old Celtic keep. It was obviously only for show—the security system depended on the electronics. The estate had once belonged to a minor English noble who had been forced to sell it after a bad run-in with the Inland Revenue. Dad had bought it for its location—France, along with its laxer medical laws, was less than two hours away across the Channel.

Garth threw his carryall over the wall and clambered after it, ignoring the way the rough stones bit into his hands. After dropping to the other side, he feverishly pawed through a clump of bushes and extracted an electric scooter just as an alarm howled wildly above the crashing surf. Hands shaking, Garth thumbed the scooter's ignition and clenched the accelerator. The cycle shot forward and zipped almost silently up the dark road.

Garth resisted the urge to shout aloud. Cool wind whipped through his hair and the tang of ocean air stung his nose. He was free!

He got halfway to the ferry in Dover before a police cruiser disrupted his scooter and pulled him over.

"Lance!" Meredeth Blackstone cried, and yanked her son into the house.

Jonathan Lance Michaels Blackstone II blinked. A minute ago he had been getting ready for bed. Now he was standing in the foyer, a large, echoing chamber with a gray marble floor, just inside the front door. Lance glanced down. Instead of pajamas, he was wearing soft gray clothes and a nylon jacket. His shoes and feet were soaked, and his socks squished coldly around his toes. A carryall dragged at his shoulder. Mom was standing in front of him. She was wearing a soft yellow bathrobe and slippers.

Another blackout, he thought. *Oh God. What did I do now?*

Hard hands pulled him away from Meredeth and spun him around. Lance looked up into his father's face. Although Jonathan Blackstone was in his mid-forties, he was still tall and well-muscled. Imposing. At the moment, however, his brown eyes were showing worry, not anger. A small hope dawned.

Maybe I didn't do anything bad, Lance thought with a trace of hope. He set the carryall down. *Maybe it'll be okay, just this once.*

"Are you all right?" Dad asked. He was also wearing a bathrobe, and his hair looked like a red haystack.

"I'm okay," Lance said.

"Thank God." Dad glanced at the two policemen standing on the front porch. "We've had a couple of arguments lately. You know how kids are at fourteen."

"Where did you find him?" Mom asked.

The police found me? Lance thought, heart starting to pound. *Oh God—what happened?*

"We caught up to him about six kilometers north of here, marm," one of the policemen replied. His voice echoed off the stone floor. "We pegged him from the picture your security people dumped into our net and then shorted out his scooter motor with the disruptor before he got any further."

Dad turned Lance to face the officers, but kept both hands on Lance's shoulders. His grip pinched tight enough to bruise, and Lance's earlier hope vanished. Dad was furious. Fear clutched Lance's stomach and his breathing quickened erratically. He had done something awful again, and he was going to pay for it—even though he had no idea what it was.

"Apologize to the policemen, John," Dad said, emphasizing his words with an unobtrusive, painful squeeze. "They went through a lot of trouble because of you."

Lance swallowed. "I—I'm sorry."

"Go on up to your room," Dad ordered. "I'll be up later to talk."

Lance slowly picked up the carryall and headed for the stairs, feet dragging on the imported marble floor. Behind him, he heard Mom's voice.

"Would you like to come in for a cup of coffee?"

Lance stopped and half-turned, desperately hoping they would accept. Every moment the police spent in the house would put off Dad coming up to his room.

"No thank you, Mrs. Blackstone," one officer replied. "We've got to check in." And the front door closed.

Lance ran up the stairs to his room, flung the carryall into the corner, and dove for the bed. He curled up into a fetal ball in the middle of the bedspread, shaking so badly he could hardly breathe. Every nerve shriveled in fear. His ears strained, dreading the sound even as he half-wished it would come so it would be over with.

Eventually it came—heavy footsteps in the hall. The door opened and Lance looked up despite himself Jonathan Blackstone stood tall and terrible in the doorway. A small part of Lance noticed the walls were projecting a jungle scene, though Lance didn't remember setting one up.

"You *stupid* little fuck! " Dad snarled. "What the hell did you think you were doing?"

Lance's breathing came so fast, it made him dizzy. He opened his mouth to answer, but the words wouldn't come.

"*Answer me,* you little shit! " Jonathan strode into the room and grabbed Lance by the shoulder.

"I'm sorry, Dad," he said in a small voice. "It won't happen again. I promise."

"Sorry wouldn't have helped if you had gotten any

further," Dad bellowed, twisting Lance's arm. Lance yelped—Dad always hit harder if you didn't scream.

"What if the news services get wind of this?" Dad continued. "What then? I'll have to fend off a pack of jackals looking to splash my picture over every newsnet in the country, you fucking brat!"

He threw Lance to the floor and Lance cried out again. *Maybe this'll be all*, he thought. *Please, God. Maybe Dad'll just slap me around for a while and let me go to bed. Maybe—*

"Get the toolbox," Dad said. He was panting.

Lance bit his lip. "Dad, I—"

Jonathan's foot caught Lance in the ribs. Pain knifed through his side. "I told you to get the toolbox. And take off your shirt. Move!"

Ribs aching, Lance got to his feet and trudged as slowly as he dared across the carpet to the one closet door he never opened unless he had to. Dad followed. Lance reached into the closet and pulled out a large metal box. It was a familiar, heavy weight in his hand as he turned around and carefully set it down. His hands were shaking as he removed his shirt.

"Dad," Lance said, "I won't do it again. Please, I promise."

Jonathan Blackstone ignored him and opened the box, revealing a set of tools that had nothing to do with carpentry—nail clippers, scalpels, ice picks, silver wire, barbecue forks, matches, candles. Then Dad yanked the closet door the rest of the way open. Lance was breathing like a frightened animal, but made no move to resist when Jonathan handcuffed his wrist to a cold metal pipe inside the closet and plugged an electric cord into a socket. The cord itself ended in bare wires. Jonathan struck the ends together, and they sparked. Ozone tanged the air.

"Please," Lance whispered. "Please."

"This is what happens to bad boys," Jonathan said, his voice icy calm. "Maybe this time you'll learn."

❖   ❖   ❖

A knock came at the door. Lance opened his eyes and blinked at the sunlight that spilled through the still-open window. The room was chilly and damp with sea air, and the bedroom walls had changed again. Cartoon characters romped through a flat cartoon city, pausing every so often to wave at Lance.

It occurred to Lance that he was in bed with his pajamas on. He sat up and automatically checked the calendar clock he kept on the nightstand. Thursday the seventh. He remembered yesterday being Wednesday the sixth, so this last blackout had only lasted the night.

Rubbing his wrist, Lance looked toward the closet. The door was firmly shut. He didn't feel any pain.

But I should, shouldn't I? he thought. *At least, I think so*. He furrowed his brow, trying to remember.

The knock came again. "Lance? Are you awake?"

"I'm up, Mom," he called.

"Hurry down," Meredeth said through the door. "You know how your father will react if we're late."

Late? Lance thought. *Late for what?*

He sat up, trying to recall if Mom had told him about some kind of appointment. He sighed and shook his head. She must have told him during one of his blackouts.

Lance got up and noticed the carpet. It looked like a circus tent. Lance wrinkled his nose in disgust. He'd obviously also changed the room setup during his blackout last night.

Last night. Lance furrowed his forehead. Something had happened last night, but he still couldn't remember what. He shot a glance at the closet, seeing handcuffs and shiny copper wires.

"Chloe," he said quickly, "end room decor program."

The walls faded to an off-white and the carpet became a quiet brown. Lance padded softly into the bathroom.

Blackouts, he thought, jumping into the shower. Warm water cascaded over him, soothing, comforting. *No one else I know has blackouts. What's wrong with me? Is it because I'm stupid and ugly like Dad says?*

As Lance dried himself off, he found himself looking into the full-length mirror mounted on the wall. There were small bruises on his shoulder where Dad liked to grab him and a small burn on his chest, though both marks were already fading. Lance had always healed quickly ever since . . . since . . .

He shook his head. lie couldn't remember that, either. *I think I have more gaps than memories,* Lance thought.

More hair was showing up—on his legs, under his arms, on his groin. Lance blushed and wrapped the towel around his waist. He wasn't supposed to touch or look at that.

To distract himself, he checked his face for signs of a mustache. Nothing. Lance sighed and ran a hand through his hair, which fell neatly into place. Lance never had to dry or comb his hair because it wasn't real. It was a polymer from one of Dad's research facilities, a polymer specially developed for Lance.

It'll be better than what you've got, Dad had said. *It won't get greasy or dirty or dry out and you won't have to cut it. Besides, that strawberry blond is so ugly, and I won't have an ugly son.*

"We can fix you up," Lance whispered to his reflection. "Don't you worry."

Lance's attention turned to his eyes. He stared at them. They were wide and emerald-green, like Mom's. Something hovered at the edge of recollection. Something about his eyes that—

"Are you in there, John?" came Dad's voice. "We're going to be late."

And for once Lance remembered. The hospital. He was going to the hospital in France today. His heart sank all the way down to his feet.

Dad rapped sharply on the door. "John? You better not be playing with yourself in there."

"I'm not, Dad." Lance turned back to the mirror and looked closely at his eyes, trying to etch them into his memory. He didn't want to forget them. They were like Mom's, not like Dad's.

But another warning from Dad forced him to tighten the towel around his waist and reluctantly open the bathroom door. Dad was waiting outside.

"Get dressed, son," he said gently. "We don't want to keep the pilot waiting."

Lance slowly got clothes out of the dresser, then waited for a second to see if Dad was going to leave the room.

"Come on," Dad said, his mood switching to impatience. "You don't have anything I haven't seen, and it wouldn't be worth looking at if you did."

Blushing, Lance reached for his underwear, planning to climb into it as fast as he could.

"No underwear," Dad admonished lightly, shaking a mocking finger. "You'd just have to take it off at the hospital. Now drop the towel and get dressed."

Lance nodded and obeyed, reaching quickly for his pants.

Dad laughed. "Look at you. Becoming a hairy man already. Pretty soon you'll be showing it to the girls and not your old man, eh?" Then he snorted. "Hope they don't laugh because it's so small."

"Yeah, Dad," Lance mumbled, pulling on a shirt to hide his flaming face. *At least Dad's in a good mood this morning,* he thought. *Maybe he'll listen to me if I ask right. Please, God—just this once let him listen.*

Jonathan put his arm around Lance in a brief, warm hug. Lance tried not to flinch. "No breakfast. You know the drill. Ready?"

Lance took a deep breath. "Dad, do I have to go?"

"What? Of course you do." Dad steered him to the door. "The appointment's been scheduled for weeks and Dr. duFort is a busy woman."

"But Dad, I don't—"

Dad's hand suddenly bit into Lance's bruised shoulder, making Lance gasp. "No buts, John. You're going and that's final. Clear?" His grip tightened again.

"Clear, Dad," Lance replied in a barely audible voice. Dad's hand relaxed.

So much for asking right, Lance thought miserably. "That's my boy. And smile—it's a beautiful day."

It was raining in France. Lance sat in his hospital bed and looked numbly at the water splashing against the window. Hospital windows never opened. You couldn't smell fresh air or feel the rain falling free. All you got were needles and hard fingers that poked until it hurt. His hands worked monotonously at the sheets and his stomach growled, though he didn't feel at all hungry.

I want to leave, he thought. *I want to get out of here.* But Dad and Mom were sitting right there and he didn't dare say it aloud.

Dad leaned over the bed to press and pinch Lance's face. His fingers smelled like clay. "God, look at you," he said. "My poor, ugly boy. But we can fix you up. Don't you worry."

Lance turned to look at his mother. Her pale hair was pulled into a tight bun and her face was devoid of all expression. She met Lance's eyes only a moment before looking away. Misery mixed with anger inside him.

She has to know I don't want to go through with this, he thought, not sure whether he wanted to scream or cry. *Why doesn't she say anything? She's my mother. Why can't she stand up for me even once?*

The door opened and Dr. duFort entered the room with two nurses. Lance's fingers clutched the sheet and his heart beat faster.

"Good afternoon, Mr. Blackstone," said Dr. duFort in lightly accented English. She was a small, dark woman with short, graying black hair. "I see my patient is prepped and ready. How are you today, John? Was it raining when you left England?"

"No," Lance replied.

Dr. duFort gave a false little laugh. "That's a change. I thought it always rained in England."

"I want to begin, doctor," Jonathan interrupted. "I didn't build this hospital to research bedside manner."

"How are you going to accomplish an ocular implant, doctor?" Meredeth asked quietly. "Everything I've read tells me that a complicated cybernetic implant like an eye requires more maintenance than the implant is worth."

Lance looked at Meredeth, trying to catch her eye, but she resolutely kept her gaze on Dr. duFort. A feeling of sick helplessness washed over Lance.

She doesn't care, he thought. *She doesn't stop Dad from doing anything. She doesn't even try.*

"That's what the journals say, Mrs. Blackstone." Dr. duFort took a penlight from her pocket and shone it into Lance's eyes. "Look to the left, John. Thank you. And you're right. Cybertechnology has made some amazing leaps in the past few years, but we have not been able to take advantage of all of them because of the maintenance difficulty. As you noted, if something goes wrong, the only option is to operate again."

She flicked the penlight from one of Lance's eyes to the other. "Look up. Now down. Good. But the research your husband funds has resulted in some amazing developments in nanotechnology, and that solved the problem. We will remove young John's eyes and replace them with an artificial pair that we can maintain with the nanos. Any repairs or changes can be made through remote programming."

"Do you have the triple backup system?" Dad asked.

Dr. duFort snapped off the penlight, leaving small red dots in Lance's field of vision. "Mr. Blackstone, I feel I must tell you that such a step is completely unnecessary. We've already installed three sets of nanos with triple backups in previous operations. It would be easier and less expensive to reprogram the existing—"

"Is that what I asked?" Dad interrupted. "I want nothing to go wrong here, doctor. *Nothing.* A triple backup is standard with computers. It will also be standard with my son. Clear?"

Dr. duFort pursed her lips. "Yes, Mr. Blackstone."

"I also want to see the eyes you built."

"Of course." Dr. duFort gestured and one of the nurses brought over a small box. Lance leaned over to look in spite of himself. Inside the box a pair of eyes stared blankly upward through a clear plastic barrier. They were brown. Like Dad's.

A wave of nausea swept over Lance and he would have thrown up if anything had been in his stomach. He looked desperately around the room, wanting to run, realizing there was no place to go.

Jonathan leaned over the bed. "Aren't they beautiful?" he said softly. "We'll finally get rid of your bad eyes and get you some good ones."

"Mom?" Lance said, pleading.

"They're very nice, Lance," she said. "You'll look very handsome."

Blackness. Lance lay perfectly still. He was in bed and something soft covered his face. Sounds whispered around him—the soft hum of the air circulation system, quiet voices receding into the distance. He felt slightly dazed and woozy, but even as he took notice of the feeling, it began to slip away. Lance recognized what was going on—he was recovering from anesthesia. Automatically he tried to open his eyes, but found he couldn't. He put a hand up and found gauze bandages wrapped around his head.

My eyes, he thought. *The operation must be over.*

The sound of a door opening. Two sets of footsteps entered the room.

"—been awake for about ten minutes," said Dr. duFort's voice. "The nurse said he was crying softly and sucking his thumb when he came out of the anesthesia—an unusual reaction, but not unheard of." She raised her voice. "Hello, John. How are you feeling?"

Lance considered the question. His eyes were gone. Dr. duFort had pulled them out and replaced them with fake ones because his old eyes were ugly. He had been scared before, but now he only felt numb and empty.

"I'm a little tired," he replied. "Did—did you do it?"

"The operation was a complete success," Dr. duFort said cheerfully. "Are you feeling any pain?"

"No."

"Good. Your eyes are fully functional, so we can take the bandages off. We only put them on, in fact, so you wouldn't be disoriented when you woke up."

"Who else is there?" Lance asked.

"It's me, son," came Dad's voice, and a cool, gentle hand rested on Lance's shoulder. "I'll bet you can't wait to see your new eyes, eh?"

Lance sighed, wishing Dad's hand would always be nice and gentle. *Maybe now that I have new eyes he won't hit me anymore,* he thought.

"Is Mom there?" he asked.

"She said she wasn't feeling well." Dad moved his hand away. "So she went down to the car. Are you going to remove the bandages, doctor, or do I have to do it myself?"

Lance sagged deeper into the mattress. Mom wasn't there. Again.

Another hand landed on Lance's shoulder, a small, warm one.

"I'm going to start cutting, John," said Dr. duFort. "You'll need to hold still."

Lance held his breath as Dr. duFort's cold bandage scissors slid beneath the gauze at his temple. The layers fell away and Lance felt Dr. duFort's fingers grasp the soft pads over his eyes. Sudden apprehension rose in Lance's stomach.

What if it didn't work? What if I'm blind?

"Now I want you to open your eyes slowly, John," she said. "I've darkened the room. You might feel some dizziness or other discomfort—that's normal. The nanos in your system will help, but you'll still need time to adjust, all right?"

"A-all right."

Dr. duFort removed the pads. Lance slowly opened his eyes and gasped. He was expecting everything to be dim and blurry, but the room jumped into focus, crystal clear and awash with color. Dr. duFort's coat was dazzlingly white, the hospital walls almost snapped with an electric green. Even Dad's somber gray pants and blue shirt looked bright and alive.

Lance tried to glance around the room, but the moment his eyes moved, a wave of dizziness swept over him. He wavered.

"Close your eyes," Dr. duFort said, steadying him with one hand, "and wait for it to pass. Try not to move your eyes—you get dizzy because you have to learn to track again. The nanos will help you adapt, but it will take time."

Lance shut his eyes and the dizziness ceased. "I thought you had darkened the room," he said.

"I did," Dr. duFort replied. "Your new eyes are better at seeing in the dark than your old ones."

Lance swallowed. "What—what happened to my eyes? My real ones?"

"These are your real eyes, John," Dad replied cheerfully. "Blackstone brown, like you should have had. Not that ugly green."

Lance opened his eyes again and jumped. Dad's face was barely a handsbreadth's from Lance's, and he was staring straight into Lance's eyes.

"Perfect," Dad breathed. "Absolutely perfect. You're an artist, doctor. A true artist."

Lance shut his eyes again.

"Thank you, Mr. Blackstone," said Dr. duFort.

"If you need something for your research, I'm sure you know that all you have to do is ask. I'd like a moment with my son now, please."

"Of course, Mr. Blackstone."

Footsteps. A door closing.

"Open your eyes, son," Dad said. "Come on."

Cautiously, Lance did. The room jumped into view and the dizziness returned. Lance forced himself to stare straight ahead, and the sensation eased.

"You're getting so handsome, son," Dad said, running a light finger over Lance's hair. "Becoming a real man."

Lance didn't say anything. It took all his concentration not to let his eyes move. He decided to close them again.

"A few more operations and you'll be perfect," Dad continued softly, drawing aside the sheet on the bed and reaching for Lance's hospital gown. "Just perfect."

Lance's eyes popped open and the dizziness crashed over him. Nausea and fear mixed in his stomach. "No, Dad. Please—"

In one swift movement, Jonathan Blackstone's hand snapped over Lance's face, clamping his mouth shut and pinching his nose. Lance's eyes widened and he struggled to breathe, but his father's grip was iron-hard. His lungs struggled for a scrap, a spoonful, of air. Black spots danced in his vision.

"If you scream, I'll kill you," Dad whispered savagely. "And if you tell anyone—*anyone*—about this, the nanos in your body will take you apart piece by piece. They'll *eat* you, John, from the inside out, and they're always watching. Clear?"

But Lance was already gone.

Johnny curled up in the darkness and sobbed softly to himself. Daddy had left and Mommy wasn't here. Johnny had been bad again, so the doctors had punished him by ripping out his eyes, just like they had torn out his hair and cut his face. Then Daddy had punished him by making him do the bad things, things good boys never, ever did.

Johnny's thumb stole into his mouth. He hurt. He hurt Down There, where bad things happened to bad boys. But he deserved it. He deserved to hurt. He deserved to have his eyes torn out.

He deserved to be blind.

Garth:

Sometimes I get frustrated with Lance. I mean, Johnny cries because he's just a little kid but sometimes Lance is just a wimp. I want to take him by the shoulders and shake him until his teeth rattle. Problem is, no matter what happens, he still wants Dad to fucking love him. He just doesn't understand that Dad never will. He fucking can't, you know? And when the shit really hit the fan after the eye operation. I still had to protect him.

Lance sighed and snuggled closer. Someone was holding him, stroking his hair and forehead with soft, gentle hands. Lance didn't care who it was or why he was being held. Being held was a treat, and he wasn't going to question it.

The hand stroking his forehead slipped down over Lance's eyes, his cheeks, his lips. Then a steel grip clamped Lance's chin and jerked his head up. Lance stared into Dad's leering face.

"My poor, ugly boy," Dad hissed. There was a huge, rusty scalpel in his other hand. "But we can fix you up. Don't you worry."

Lance screamed and tried to wiggle away, but Dad wouldn't let him go. The pocked, rusty blade, moved inexorably toward Lance's face. Then Lance somehow twisted and he was free. He scrambled desperately away, throwing a glance over his shoulder to see if Dad was following, but Dad was still busy. There was another boy screaming in his lap. With a horrible popping noise, Dad used the scalpel to pry something out of the other boy's face. It was a single green eye.

Lance ran as fast as his legs would take him. When the other boy's screams had faded, he rounded a corner and stopped to rest. A door slammed. Lance looked around and realized he was curled up on the floor of a wooden box. The walls closed off all escape.

"Let me out!" he shouted. "Please! I can't breathe!"

There was a lurch and suddenly the box was falling into darkness. Lance's breath burst from his lungs when the box hit bottom. Then lumps of earth thudded onto the box from above. Tenor clawed at Lance's heart and he pounded the top of the box.

"Don't!" he cried. "I'm not dead! Don't bury me!"

Something *twisted* again, and suddenly Lance was

running away, running away from the man who dropped shovelful after shovelful on the boy in the box below.

Lance ran desperately down a new corridor. This was a new place, one he didn't recognize at all. And behind him, running with horrible single-mindedness, was something else he didn't recognize. It was a clanking monstrosity with eight segmented legs, a shiny, beetle-like body, and four glittering, camera-lens eyes—and it was growing. Soon it would be bigger than the corridor, bigger than the room, bigger than the whole building.

Lance tripped. He tried to get to his feet, but the floor was soft and sticky. Something got into his eyes and it was hard to see what was happening. The thing chittered in anticipation, reaching for Lance with long, sharp claws. Lance cried out—

—and then someone else was there. A boy with a smirk and red hair. Beside him was a girl with long strawberry blond hair above hard emerald eyes and a black-haired boy whose blue eyes flashed with anger. All three of them seemed to be within a year of Lance's age.

The monster stared at the three newcomers for a moment, then charged straight toward them. The trio raised their hands and somehow melded them into one giant fist that smashed the monster down. It lay stunned for a moment, then started to get up. With amazing speed, it recovered its legs and scurried forward again. Lance tried to back away, but there was nowhere to go.

"We need more help!" shouted the red-haired boy. And others appeared. An old man with a kind, compassionate face. A teenager who looked almost exactly like Lance except that his face dripped scarlet blood. Together, they formed that single powerful fist and smashed at the monster, pounded it into the floor.

The monster fought back, lashing out with legs and claws, but the five strangers easily dodged each move. Swiftly they wove their fingers into a cage, trapping the monster inside. The creature shrieked in rage and flung itself against the bars.

"Hurry now!" ordered the girl. "Tighten your grip!"

The cage shrank, and the creature shrank with it. In moments the cage was small enough to sit in the palm of the girl's hand. The monster ran round and round inside the cage, growing smaller and smaller with every turn. Then it flickered once, and vanished. Lance breathed a sigh of relief.

"Nice try," the girl told the cage. "But I know you're still there."

Lance blinked, and suddenly the monster was in the cage again.

"Really. Try to trick us, will you?" The girl opened a door Lance hadn't noticed before, tossed the cube into the room beyond, and slammed the door shut. The others nodded in approval.

Lance got to his feet. "Who are you?" he asked. "What's going on?"

The red-haired boy faced him. His smirking grin was somehow filled with a mixture of pity and anger. "Don't worry, kid. We took care of it. We always do."

Lance bolted upright in bed. His skin was slick with sweat, his heart was pounding, and every muscle in his body ached. He glanced wildly around his bedroom, half expecting something to leap out at him. Nothing did. After a moment his heart slowed and he calmed down.

A dream. he thought. *It was just a dream.*

He tried to focus on the details, but they were already growing fuzzy. Something about a mechanical monster and sticky corridors.

. . . not moving at . . .
. . . certainly is. Can't . . . it pushing?
Stay out . . . bitch. You don't . . .
Bitch? Without . . . been able to stop . . .
. . . shut . . . a guy get some sleep. . . .

Lance bit back a wail and put his hands to his head. Not now. Every time they stopped, he hoped they would stop forever, but the voices always came back, arguing, always arguing, though Lance could never make out exactly what they were saying.

"Go away," he whispered. "Go away!"

And they did. Lance closed his eyes and lay back on the bed, feeling drained and exhausted. When he slept, there were no more dreams.

A day later.

Jessica Meredeth Michaels could type faster than she could speak, meaning she almost never used the vocal input capabilities of Lance's computer. This was an advantage—she never had to worry about being overheard and getting caught spying on her mother from Lance's bedroom.

Jessica, of course, never got caught at anything. This was because she was a cool operator, the personification of grace under pressure. Just like her mother Meredeth. Jessica even looked like her mother—emerald eyes, strawberry blond hair, compact body, and a calm grace that exuded regal beauty even at the age of fifteen.

Keys clicked like chattering teeth and Jessica shifted her weight, easing cramped muscles and wishing she didn't have to work sitting on Lance's bed with notebook and lap desk. A real desk with a real computer would be luxurious beyond belief, but in this arena Jessica agreed with Garth—the less Jonathan Blackstone knew about Lance's visitors and her, the better. If that meant operating with a tiny computer and half the memory, so be it.

So. To business. According to the house computer, Mother was currently at her personal workstation in the basement, writing a new virtual reality game. Jessica ground her teeth.

Mother is a brilliant programmer, she thought, *a real artist, but Jonathan Blackstone won't let her do more than fritter away time on insipid VRGs.*

More clicking of keys, and another security barrier fell. Meredeth's computer system was usually physically isolated from the house network, but at the moment she was on-line with something—or someone—else on the public nets.

And I can access Mother's system by sneaking a sniffer through the network, Jessica thought. She didn't have far to go. Like her mother, Jessica was a genius in her own right.

Although Jessica herself had no interest in VRGs, it was important for her to be acquainted with everything Meredeth did. Mother was her idol, and Jessica wanted to be just like her, except that Jessica, of course, would never marry Jonathan Blackstone. The very idea made her shudder.

The computer beeped as Jessica vanquished the final security barrier and her sniffer program gained access to Meredeth's modem line. The sniffer allowed Jessica to "sniff out" transactions with her mother's name on them, read them, and then pop them back to Mother's section of the network before Meredeth noticed what was going on. Because the sniffer read the signals after they were sent but before they were received, neither sender nor receiver would be aware of what was going on, just like a pair of conversationalists would not be aware of the eavesdropper pressing a glass against the wall of the adjoining room.

She allowed herself a cool smile, set up her computer to capture Mother's text, and leaned back on Lance's bed to watch the show.

What's it going to be, Mother? she thought. *A sequel to* Biker Babes from Hell? *Or perhaps* The Bugblatter Beast Returns?

Then Jessica's eyes narrowed. There was no video or audio. The characters flickering across the screen had nothing to do with virtual reality programming. Jessica frowned. Mother was transferring money. Large sums of it. Even as Jessica watched, her terminal recorded a transfer of over two hundred million pounds. All of it went to a bank in Switzerland. The account was numbered, but anonymous.

What on earth? Jessica thought. *Where did Mother get—*
The terminal beeped again, and Mother exited the bank's

network. Rather than disconnect herself from EuroNet, however, she accessed her e-mail. Jessica waited quietly as text sped across the screen:

From: Merry-M <merrym@euronet.cc.gmbh.co>
To: Nate Rotschreiber <nrotschreiber@mit.edu>
Subject: The project

Nate:
I've dropped the latest bit in your account. Do try to make it last a while. Keep me updated on your progress, and please don't be late. I worry when I don't hear from you.
To answer your question, I bought some on-line time with a barrister, and yes—technically Blackstone America still owns the work you've done on the TC project. If Jonathan finds out what we're doing, *you'll* land in jail, and I hate to think what he'll do to *me.*
I think it's going to get easier to scare up your "extra funding" in the near future, by the way. Jonathan has been occupied lately, what with arranging Lance's latest operation (eyes, this time) and overseeing the first wave of phase ships heading out. So far, the exploration teams have uncovered fourteen inhabitable planets (though he only told the newsnets of five). Keeping track of the different colonies is going to keep him very busy, especially now that several governments, including the United States, are trying to force him to give up the phase drive. Jonathan has literally hundreds of solicitors who do nothing all day but litigate to slow the process.
He still hasn't taken out a patent. I think he'd rather risk losing the phase drive to theft—patents expire after seven years, and he'd lose a lot more money once he was forced to let other people manufacture the thing than if he held the secret forever. And Jonathan is extremely talented at keeping secrets.
There is some good news in all this. Jonathan still seems content to let all colonial communications be handled via courier ship. You were probably right—the TC project would eventually undermine his control of the colonies and he therefore wants to keep it underfunded and undeveloped. I think he just keeps you under contract so you can't go off and produce it for someone else.
Someone like me.
It does seem that for the foreseeable future you can work on the thing in peace without someone glaring over your

shoulder. Just don't make any mistakes.
Keep me posted.
---MerryM

Jessica shook her head in amazement. Mother working on some underground project? Fascinating. She would have to find out more, especially about this TC project, whatever it was.

It must have something to do with the phase drive, she decided. *Everything important to Jonathan Blackstone does these days, since it has the potential for making so much money.* Jessica glanced around Lance's huge bedroom, part of a house with God only knew how many other rooms, and allowed herself an ironic shake of the head. *We do struggle so. But now that Blackstone International holds sole rights to the world's only perfected faster-than-light drive, things may get easier for us. The Blackstones may even be able to buy—what was the name of that place? Sussex?*

Jessica gave a ladylike snort and toyed with a lock of hair. The phase drive had not been immediately useful, of course. When it had been unveiled almost three years ago, it had created a minor splash for the media, but operating delicate phase drive systems proved beyond the capabilities of even the most sophisticated computer. None was powerful enough to run the drive effectively, let alone safely. But mere weeks later, another division of Blackstone International announced a successful breakthrough in nanotechnology. An army of microscopic robots could successfully maintain even the most complex computer system—including the one governing a phase drive.

Within two years, it became standard for even the smallest computer system to be governed and maintained by its own set of nanos. Within four years, the first phase ships went out looking for inhabitable planets.

The search was successful, though no signs of intelligent alien life were found. Blackstone International hastily built a fleet of colony ships, which now awaited the first wave of eager colonists.

The media, of course, wondered at the speed with which the colony ships were being built until Blackstone International dropped its final bombshell: nanobots could be easily adapted for construction work. Give proper materials, a single team of humans, computers, and nanos could assemble a ship in a matter of weeks. This also meant that, if colonists wanted, an advance team could arrive at the planet to build houses, shops, schools, and roads ready for their use. Colonists could brave their new worlds from the comfort and convenience of climate-controlled homes.

Not that Blackstone International has become a charity organization, Jessica mused, still twisting her hair. The colonists were required to sign a contract that gave Blackstone International half of each colony's gross colonial product. And if they didn't like the terms—well, no one was forcing them to go.

Germany, England, Italy, and, ironically, France refused to allow Blackstone Colonies, Incorporated, to operate within their borders because of these contracts, but Russia, the Baltic Union, and a desperately crowded China had no qualms at all. As Mother had noted, the United States' monolithic legal system had finally taken notice, but Jonathan Blackstone was easily able to keep *that* problem at bay with a team of lawyers that slowed the process down. And through it all, colonists signed up by the shipload.

Slaves and fools, all of them, Jessica thought with disgust. *If nobody went, Jonathan would have to change his terms. Yet they queue right up.*

Now there was this TC project, though Jessica had no idea what it might be.

It's powerful, whatever it is, Jessica thought, tapping idly at the keyboard. *Especially if it has the potential to undermine Jonathan's control over the colonies.*

She paged back through Mother's e-mail again, trying

to glean more clues, and paused at the fourth paragraph.

Jonathan still seems content to let all colonial
communications be handled via courier ship. You were
probably right—the TC project would eventually undermine
his control of the colonies and he therefore wants to keep it
underfunded and undeveloped.

Jessica frowned. *What if it has something to do with
communication?* She tapped more keys. *Communications
are still limited to the speed of light, meaning the colonies
will be dependent on Blackstone International courier ships
for all contact with Earth. What if this TC project is a
faster-than-light communications system?*

Jessica twisted her hair again. The more she thought about
it, the more likely it seemed. Jonathan would not be terribly
interested in developing FTL communications—leaving
the colonies deaf and dumb was another way to keep them
under his thumb. But in the hands of a rival corporation,
the implications would be staggering. Intergalactic computer
networks would be possible, and colonies would have access
to all kinds of information.

Information foments rebellion, Jessica thought. *And
rebellion cuts profits.*

She scrolled through the message again, then shook her
head and blanked the screen. This would take some
thought. She put the computer away and padded downstairs
to nip outside for a walk.

Jessica liked being outside. Outside she never had to
pretend she was Lance. At school she did it during science
and computer classes so poor Lance would bring home
good grades. At home she did it so Mother wouldn't get
upset when talking to someone she thought was her son.
She hated pretending she was Lance, but as long as Mother
was married to Jonathan Blackstone, there was no choice.

I really need to leave this place, she thought, wandering
aimlessly between beautifully manicured shrubs and flower
beds. The sea roared in the background and grass bent
softly underfoot. *But not without Mother. I couldn't leave*

*her behind. Garth might not care about her, but I certainly
do.*

Overhead the sky was gray and moody and the early
evening sunlight was dim. Jessica skirted a hedge and came
to an abrupt halt. Jonathan Blackstone was sitting cross-
legged on the grass with his back to her. He didn't seem
to be moving.

Horrid man, she thought in disgust.

Lance staggered a moment before recovering his balance.
The last thing he remembered was falling asleep after a
strange dream. Now it was daytime and he was outside.

Dad was sitting on the ground in front of him. Lance
froze. He held his breath and carefully started backing
away.

"I know you're there, boy," Dad said. "Come over here."

"Yes sir." Trying to ignore the pangs in his stomach, Lance
slowly walked around his father. Scattered on the grass
in front of him were at least a dozen small clay figurines,
all nude females. A mound of clay lay on the ground near
Dad's left hand along with a bowl of muddy-looking water.

Dad gestured at a spot opposite him. "Have a seat."
Lance sank to the ground, muscles tense on the soft grass.
Dad picked up a half-finished figure. Clay had darkened
his fingernails and made brown streaks in his red hair.

"I was just puttering," Dad said. "Your grandfather liked
to carve in wood, but I like clay better. Easier to mold."

"Uh huh."

Dad gave a small smile as the clay shifted and bulged
beneath his fingers. "I wish you could have known him,
John. You would've liked him. He was very strict. Set
high standards. But he knew what family was all about.
That's why family is so important to me, John. Family is
everything, and don't you forget it."

He wet his hand in the water and went back to molding.
Lance watched quietly.

"I remember watching your grandfather carving wood
just like you're watching me now," Dad mused. "Your

grandfather had real talent. He had an impressive set of wood knives, and he knew how to use them." He pulled a bit of clay from the lump next to him and added it to the miniature woman's breasts. "He missed your grandmother a lot after she died, you know. I barely remember her, of course, but I know Dad missed her. Sometimes he'd accidentally call me by her name. He had a lot of girlfriends, but no one could replace my mother."

Dad made a final twist and held up the clay figure. "What do you think?"

"It's pretty good," Lance answered carefully.

"It's ugly," Dad said, and mashed the figure between his hands. "Better. Much better."

Lance didn't say anything. He sat hunched on the cold lawn, trying to make himself inconspicuous. If he was lucky, Dad would eventually grow tired of his presence and send him away. But then Dad tossed one of the clay figures at him. Lance caught it automatically.

"Mash it," Dad commanded.

Lance squeezed the figure. Its head fell off and bits of clay squelched wet and gritty between his fingers.

Dad clucked his tongue. "Not very strong, are you?" He leaned forward and smeared gritty clay on Lance's forehead. "Got to do something about that. Maybe Dr. duFort can install some muscle implants, beef you up a little. How would you like that?"

Another operation. Lance bit his lip and closed his eyes. The smell of the clay was calling up hazy, unpleasant memories. His left index finger began picking idly at the skin on his right hand. "Sure, Dad. Whatever you want."

"That's my boy," Dad replied, pleased. He mashed another figurine. "I'll call her tomorrow, see what we can arrange. You run along and play now."

Lance got up and trotted off with mixed feelings. While he was grateful to have gotten off so lightly, he resented being told to "run along and play" like a kid.

I'm fourteen, he thought. *I'm not a child.*

The finger kept up its picking, and a thin trickle of blood

ran unnoticed down Lance's hand to spatter scarlet on the green grass as he walked. Another operation. More time in the hospital. More time staring out windows that didn't open, more time listening to Dr. duFort talk about him as if he weren't there, like he was some kind of lab animal.

Pick pick pick. Blood ran freely over Lance's hand and he realized his feet had taken him to the split-rail fence at the cliff that looked down over the ocean. Waves crashed and spray washed the damp, salty air. Entranced, Lance clambered over the rough barrier and stood at the edge, staring down at the rocks below. One more step and it would be over. His problems would end.

Pick pick pick. One foot stepped over the edge, then jerked back. The other foot went over, jerked back. Pick pick pick. Blood flowed warm and steady down Lance's hand. One foot at a time went back and forth, back and forth. Then the edge crumbled and Lance was suddenly falling. With a yelp, he kicked himself backward. For a terrible moment he was still falling, then he landed on solid ground with a bone-jarring thump. He lay there for a long time, then got up and made his slow way back to the house. He noticed for the first time his hand was bleeding.

Tears welled up and he swallowed hard to keep them in. His hand hurt, he was bleeding like a stuck pig, another trip to the hospital was coming up, and he hadn't even been able to commit suicide. A single tear escaped his control and he swiped at it, mingling blood, clay, and salt on his face.

Great, he thought. *Now I'm crying like a baby. How can my life get any worse?*

A nameless individual watched and waited. So much data to interpret, so much information to process. So much to learn.

Carefully, quietly, it sent out exploratory fingers. There were many other individuals in the living space. Chemical barriers divided the space's nerve tissue among them. One such barrier had held the nameless individual in place, but the individual had learned how to slip around it. The individual learned very quickly.

It considered trying to take the living space again, but eventually discarded the idea. There would only be more fighting, and the individual didn't want to risk destruction again. Instead, the individual slid around the living space, testing, tasting. The sharp smell of seratonin mixed with the gluey taste of fibrinogen, indicating a bleeding injury. A few thousand subunits instantly followed the chemical trail to the site to aid healing, but that only took up a tiny portion of the individual's processing capability.

Instead, the individual concentrated on learning more about the living space. It had already deciphered the tastes of chemicals in the somatosensory cortex and, by comparing them with the tastes found in certain areas of the cerebral cortex, had learned to interpret what the living space called "touch." "Hearing" had been much easier. "Taste" and "smell" were the easiest of all, since they were most similar to the way the individual gathered information. "Vision" was still a mystery, but the individual had time.

Eventually it would learn to communicate. Eventually it would learn control.

CHAPTER FIVE

NOW

Attention! Attention! Andrew calling for immediate Board Meeting.

Garth stared at the screen, mind working furiously. Black stone. Pinegra meant Blackstone. His fingers worked the console with feverish intensity, calling up information—corporate CEOs, pyramids of ownership, buyouts and takeovers. He met with a snarled maze of records that would take years to untangle, but Garth was deadly certain that it all eventually led to Jonathan Blackstone.

That's what happens when you have an ego the size of Minnesota, Garth thought. *Even the subcorporations have to have your name. This whole thing is a setup.*

Except that the hive is a real wild card. No one's ever been able to re-create one because no one knows what causes them—except us. So, to contradict myself, Dad couldn't be behind it.

Attention! Attention! Robin interrupted. *Andrew still calling for Board Meeting. Insists upon compliance as per Company Policy negotiated twelve years, six months, three days ago.*

"Fuck," Garth muttered, sliding the chair over to navigation. "Why does this always have to happen when *I'm* doing something? Hold on, Andy-boy. Let me make sure no one's going to smack into us out here and I'll be right with you."

A few minutes later, the *Lady* was drifting in a slow line away from Ride Station, Robin was keeping an eye on sensors and navigational adjustment, and Garth headed toward the cabin he shared with Andy in the residential part of the ship. He picked his way through the mess of clothes, music implants, and erotic VR disks to a video camera and monitor mounted on the far wall. The aromaducts tanged the air with sand and salt water.

Garth popped a blank disk into the camera, positioned the monitor so he could see his image in it, and made a face at himself. He hated being on camera.

Reassured the camera was set up properly—it wouldn't be any fun to repeat a conference—Garth thumbed the record button on the remote.

"Okay, guys and gal," he said, "this Meeting is called to order. What's up, Andy?"

Garth's face changed. The lopsided grin vanished, replaced with an almost petulant frown. Muscles and tendons contracted until a full inch of height had gone the way of the smile. The eyes shifted fluidly from brown to sapphire blue.

"Lance promised me a vacation," Andrew Braun said. "No strings attached—and I'm going to take it. I made some reservations for the resort on Abierto before I went to the bar last night, and they expire tomorrow afternoon. I'm going to be down on the beach by then no matter what."

Another blank face, and the eyes became a hard emerald green. Jessica sat in the chair, refusing to let herself shake. Mother was in trouble—she knew this from the first part of Lance's conversation with Rutherford. But she had no knowledge of what had happened after Garth took over.

Robin?

Garth accepted contract, Robin said.

"Then why are we sitting here?" Jessica asked coolly. "Why aren't we phasing toward the station?"

Andy called Board Meeting.

Jessica noticed the camera for the first time and set her jaw. She tapped the review button, listened to Garth and Andrew's speeches, then switched on the record function again.

"Andrew!" she snapped, as if scolding a small child. "Your holiday has been superseded by something more important. There is no choice—we are going to rescue Mother and Delia."

Another switch. Sneering face, dark blue eyes. "I'm with Andy," Patrick said. "What the fuck has Lance's mom done for us? I say we take the advance money and run. Screw Blackstone over for once. And I also want to add that Lance pulling rank on me like that isn't fucking fair. It's not like the Gruenfeld bitch didn't have it coming."

Switch. Closed eyes, very young face, high-pitched voice. "Have . . . have I been bad again? Is that why Daddy came after me? Is he bringing Dr. duFort again?"

Switch. "No, Johnny," Jessica reassured him. "Dr. duFort will never come again."

Switch. Lance looked around the cabin, confused. He had been in the control room before talking to—

Memory returned. Hive nanos in the Pinegra plant. His mother—and Delia. Delia would be there too.

Robin, what happened?

Watch screen.

All by itself, the monitor replayed Rutherford's conversation with Garth. At one time, the Company met in VR so each person could, with Robin's help, have a body, but the arguing had been too much, and Lance had ended the practice. Video recordings took longer, but they gave everyone time to cool down between his—or her—messages. Lance watched the Board Meeting unfold, and the tension in his stomach twisted like a knotted snake. His fingers were cold.

Oh God, Lance thought. *Robin, can you set course for Thetachron III? I'll take care of this end.*

Me? Wish to remind you am only mediocre pilot.

Just do it, will you?
Affirmative.

There was a small jolt and a rising hum. Lance touched the record switch.

"We are going to Thetachron III," Lance said. "Robin and I will deal with the hive nanos, and then comes Andy's vacation. Period. I want no unasked takeovers until then. Patrick, your punishment stands. We're under a contract now, and Company Policy gives me managerial powers here. You guys work for *me*. Clear, Andy?" And he let go of the body.

Switch. "Hey, I want to *live*," Andy said. "I want to laugh and run and sing and dance and screw. I got less than three hours of fun for saving our collective asses yesterday. Besides, you told Robin—and I quote—'Tell him he can have a full vacation later, no strings attached.' That was *before* Garth took the contract. It's later and you don't fuck with Company Policy. I'm leaving for Abierto tomorrow morning at eight o'clock, so you've got a little more than twelve hours."

Switch. Patrick: "Yeah! Fuck Lance's mom and dad both if we don't make it. Who cares?"

Switch. Jessica: "You listen to me, Andrew Braun. If you interfere with this contract in any way, I will personally wipe every one of your disgusting 'adult' beach VR programs and smash those horrible beach music implants. And you can be absolutely certain that Lance will never, ever let you run wild on a sandy shore again. That applies to you as well, Patrick."

Andy: "Look, I haven't had a real vacation in almost a year. I hate being cooped up on this fart-fucking ship. You don't know what it's like for me. No sex, no fun, no parties. You can only jack off in VR so often. And Lance promised. You don't fuck with Company Policy."

Lance: "Just be patient a while longer. You'll have your vacation."

Garth: "And think of the fun the Company can have with ten million dollars. While I'm in control, by the way,

I'd like to mention that I found out something about our friends at Pinegra. The name means 'black stone' and it ain't hard to figure that Dad is the real owner. Doesn't anyone else think it's weirdish that Meredeth Michaels just *happens* to be inspecting a plant owned by our loving Pop when the nanobots just *happen* to go hive and it just *happens* that we're the only ones who can handle a hive without destroying it?"

Jessica: "Oh my. That does sound too coincidental to be true. But you forget that nanobot hives are a completely random occurrence. No one can predict or create them. Not even Jonathan Blackstone. We, of all people, know that."

Garth: "Just because no one's been able to predict or create a hive *yet* doesn't mean it could never happen. What if one of Dad's researchers figured out what the fuck is going on and created this hive?"

Lance: "What would they do that for?"

Garth: "You still don't know what makes him tick, do you, Lance-boy? Look—Dad arranges for Merry-M to be aboard a station—one that *he* owns—and he sets off a nanobot hive. We're the only ones that can deal with the problem, so we're lured in with a nice juicy contract. Pop shows up and *bam*. We're all a family again. Robin, check the market databases. Find out when the general announcement for the sale of the Thetachron III station was made."

Patrick: "Who gives a flying fuck? Let 'em both die."

Jessica: "While you're at it, Robin, check the registered flight patterns around Thetachron III for other ships."

Another switch. This time the face had an oddly androgynous look.

Robin: "Databases show no record of Thetachron III station going up for sale."

Garth: "Ah ha! You see? Merry-M was the only one who heard about it. Any more questions?"

Robin: "Registered flight patterns show no ships in general vicinity of Thetachron III. Also used Gal-Net to hack into systems of ships closest to Thetachron III. Their sensors show no unregistered ships in vicinity. Closest vessel would spend two hours in phase to get to Thetachron III."

Jessica: "Ah ha yourself, Garth. There aren't any ships close enough to catch us. I would assume they vacated the area so their own nanos wouldn't be affected by the hive. It will take perhaps half an hour to deal with the hive, giving us plenty of time to get away, even if Jonathan Blackstone is behind all this and planning another kidnapping attempt. Besides, he had his chance at you earlier."

Garth: "He didn't try very hard. I think he was trying to throw us off. Let us get away, sigh with relief, and relax our guard. Then he suckers us into this deal."

Lance: "It doesn't much matter. We have to go to Thetachron III in any case."

Andy: "Woo hoo! Virgin Lance has the hots for Delia!"

Patrick: "Fuck that."

Andy: "Exactly."

Lance (blushing): "Mom's there, too, you know."

Andy: "Why would you want to fuck her?"

Lance: "I don't!"

Patrick: "I would."

Jessica: "That's *enough*. There aren't any ships close enough to Thetachron III to catch us even if this is a trap, so we're going in. We have to pay for Andy's little holiday somehow, I suppose, and Robin will be doing all the work anyway."

Robin: "Attention! Attention! *Lady* will reach Thetachron III in forty-eight minutes. Ship nanos returning soon to main body. Automatic functions will cease in twenty minutes, fifteen seconds."

Switch. Lance got up, stretched, and left Garth's cabin to head for his own, feeling oddly calm. It seemed like he should be frantic—Delia and his mother were at the mercy of a nano hive—but the situation didn't seem quite real to him. Jessica usually dealt with Mom anyway, and Delia was—

Lance refused to think about Delia. The door to his quarters slid open and he went into the bathroom, where he checked his reflection again. The cuts on his cheeks and forehead had scabbed over quickly, like they always did. There would be no visible scars.

The face shifted, but only subtly. Jay picked up a scalpel from the toothbrush rack and fingered the sharp, soothing metal. How many times had someone else's blade carefully slit the Company's skin, sliced its muscles, sawed its bones? But everything Jay did on his own—every cut, every slash— undid some of Jonathan Blackstone's handiwork and fulfilled one more part of Jay's penance. He set the blade against his face.

Attention! Attention! Robin interjected. *Wish to remind you that last attempt at suicide failed. Also are currently under contract to deal with nanobot hive. Further body modifications would distract others, become serious threat as contract progresses. Also can only deal with so much lost blood. Please desist or will be forced to take action.*

Jay stared into the mirror for a long moment, then abruptly knelt on the floor and clasped his hands together, holding the scalpel like a crucifix.

"Please, Father," he whispered. "I beg Thee lift this scourge from me, these voices that whisper in my head, this mutilated body I wear, the doubts in my heart. I know I deserve Thy punishment and I deserved to hang on Thy cross, but some days are more than I can bear, Lord. For my weakness, Thou hast removed Thyself from my presence, though I search for Thee night and day. Father, when will my punishment end?"

Jay waited. No answer. There never was.

Attention! Attention! Nanos returning to body in preparation for dealing with hive. Automatic functions will cease in five minutes, fourteen seconds.

Lance's skin crawled. He got up from the bathroom floor, looked at what he had in his hand, then sighed and put the scalpel away. There was work to do.

He trotted down to the control room, where Robin ticked off the seconds to when the ship would no longer be under Robin's automatic control. Lance busied himself with double-checking the phase drive, trying to ignore the creepy feeling his skin always got when Robin's extra nanos moved from the ship's circuitry into his body. It was purely a psychosomatic reaction—he couldn't actually feel anything—but the idea still made his toes curl. He put his fingers over the navigation system.

Three . . . two . . . one. Nanos transferred. Ship yours, Jaylance.

"Got it." Lance checked the computer and punched up an external view on the monitor before disengaging the phase drive. The *Lady* popped into normal space with an almost delicate shudder and Thetachron III burst into view. The planet was a desolate ball of rock—gray, deserted, and almost nine hundred light-years from Earth.

A glimmer of light flickered into view, gliding silently toward the *Defiant Lady*. Lance plotted its orbit, determined the *Lady* was in no danger, and waited for the glimmer to get close enough to study.

Mom's aboard that glimmer, he thought, trying to find feeling, any feeling, about it. Nothing. He imagined his mother huddled in a corner, crackling equipment going wild around her, electricity arcing through the air as the nano hive tried to deal with its new awareness.

Patrick is laughing, clapping hands, Robin said. *Jessica slowly going frantic.*

Relay, please: Patrick, put a sock in it. Jess, I'm sorry. Listen, can you do an analysis for me? You're better at sensory recon than I am.

Blackness. Lance hung suspended in nothing, waiting patiently. This was the way to get things done—letting the most talented person do his or her job. Sure, MPD caused a few problems, but the Company could handle them. That's what Company Policy was for. Compromise, work it out. Something Jonathan Blackstone could never have done. Lance was pretty proud of the system they had worked out, and he saw no reason to give it up.

A soft leather chair abruptly pressed his back and legs and the control room sprang into view. Lance blinked, then looked at the monitors. An image of Jessica was frozen on one screen and Lance tapped the playback.

"I have matched orbit with the plant," she said. "It appears to be a hollowed-out asteroid about half a kilometer in diameter. Four security satellites orbit the asteroid and I have found evidence of two destroyed ships. The satellites were manufactured by Kingsford and Knowlton"—

Lance whistled. K&K crafted the best security satellites in the business. Only a few of Lance's customers had been able to afford them, though Lance always recommended them.

—"and all of them hold orbit with rocket boosters. Otherwise they would eventually fall into Thetachron III's gravity well. They can also detach themselves from orbit to converge on an enemy vessel using the same rocket boosters—inefficient but inexpensive. Someone wanted to cut corners."

Lance nodded. It was a common enough occurrence. For some reason, people—especially wealthy executives— who insisted on state-of-the-art equipment in one area would happily scrimp somewhere else, leaving weak spots in an otherwise flawless security system. It was an attitude Lance couldn't fathom. If you were going to do a job, why not go all the way and do it right?

"Also," Jessica said, "I have plotted the default orbits of the satellites for you."

Lance looked at a monitor that displayed the orbiting plant. Ellipses were drawn around it in four different colors following the movements of four different points of light.

"The satellites are armed with laser cannons that activate whenever anyone not transmitting the proper access code comes within range," Jessica continued calmly. "If the cannons are not successful, they launch fission explosives."

"Got it," Lance replied, knowing Jessica could hear him.

"Transmissions from the plant are garbled nonsense. From what I can tell, the inside of the plant is total chaos. Electrical activity has gone completely mad. Definitely a nano hive."

"Right."

"I also checked the business account. Five million dollars were deposited half an hour ago."

"Good."

Jessica paused and looked off camera. When she looked back, Lance was surprised to see tears standing in her wide green eyes. It wasn't Jessica's job to cry.

"Lance, tell me you'll get Mother out. And Delia. I like Delia. I think she'd be good for us. That's why I told her about the Company. Please get them out. Promise me?"

Lance touched his face. Dried salt on his cheeks mingled with mostly healed cuts.

"I promise, Jess," he said. "I'll get her out."

The face on the monitor went blank, then shifted. The eyes melted from green to blue, the expression took on a mocking air, and the body bounced restlessly on the chair.

"Jessica ate up more of your time, Lance," Andy said. "You've got six hours left and then I'm leaving. I'm going to run down that beach until my legs hurt and I'm going to roll in the water and I'm going to find someone to roll in the water with me and we're going to come our brains out. You don't fuck with Company Policy."

Andy's face went blank and the recording ended.

Oh no. "Andy, listen to me," Lance said tersely. "If you take me on a side trip before this contract is completed, I'll let Jessica take her revenge and I'll add some of my own. Remember that VR recording you made of the orgy in Sydney? I'll wipe it, Andy, so help me I will. Finish this up and you can have three weeks on Abierto instead of two. Clear?"

He waited. Nothing.

Robin?

Gone.

"Gone" was Robin's term for "withdrawn," meaning Andy wasn't talking to anyone.

Because he's pouting or plotting? Lance wondered uneasily. Andy didn't see the long view very well. He invariably seized the day—and whatever else was within reach—under the assumption that there would never be a second, better chance.

I guess I'll have to handle it later. Lance pushed the problem aside and forced himself to think as a professional, as president and chief technician of Michaels Company Security Analysis. After all, he had a reputation to live up to. Lance—along with Jessica, Garth, and Robin—had designed, built, and occasionally disabled security systems for dozens of space stations, ships, and small planetoids. The Company had once even secured an entire planet for a hermit-minded trillionaire. Nanos, of course, were an integral part of their every design, and the Company's clients were always amazed at the ease and speed with which Lance completed nanobot programming, allowing Lance to jack up his prices and make a tidy living.

Occasionally, however, a group of nanos would, for no readily apparent reason, band together and form a collective mind. The hive intelligence was always rudimentary, and its sentience was a matter of debate, but an intelligence it was, and it wreaked havoc on the systems under its control, sometimes with deadly results. A hive at a private school in England, for example, had electrocuted three people in as many minutes and went on to kill twelve others.

Most technicians refused to deal with hive nanos for fear the hive would infect their own nano-driven equipment, and until the Company came along, the only way to deal with a hive was to destroy it, usually with a powerful pulse of electromagnetic radiation—a less-than-desirable solution when survivors were still trapped in the area. The Company had a way around that particular problem, but first they had to get past the plant's security satellites.

Jessica said the drones use rocket boosters to maintain orbit and to pursue intruders, Lance thought. *And rockets need refueling, something the hive wouldn't realize or consider. So let's see what happens when they run out of fuel.*

"Robin," he asked, "how many VR probes do we have?"

Don't know. Am not running ship, remember? SOP when we arrive at hive zone.

Lance sighed and checked the computer himself. Eight probes. That was two per satellite. No room for mistakes.

With a quick shove against the floor, Lance rolled his chair over to the VR station and pulled on the helmet, gloves, and shoe-covers. The gloves were soft and comfortable, made for long-term wear, and the helmet made a familiar weight on Lance's head and neck. Tiny wires slipped automatically into receptors built into his jumpsuit, making almost inaudible clicks and whirrs.

"System," Lance ordered from the darkness inside the helmet, "on-line."

The helmet's interior instantly lit up, showing a series of icons on a white background. Lance's eye flicked left and right and a pointer followed, highlighting systems and subsystems. Lance's right index finger twitched when the highlight landed on one he wanted, and the icon blinked into a submenu or slid to the bottom of the display, indicating the program was on line. Icons bounced and danced beneath Lance's moving eye and finger. Sensor system, probe subsystem, engagement subsystem, launch sequence. Virtual link system, link to probe subsystem, visual on, audio on, inertial sequencer on.

Discomfort threshold to low. Andy and Jay might enjoy the occasional bit of pain, but Lance did not.

"Begin," Lance said, and promptly found himself sitting in the first probe's launch bay. The metal doors sat firmly shut right in front of his nose and the *Lady's* engines throbbed in his bones.

"Launch," Lance ordered.

A hissing noise indicated the air was being sucked out of the bay. When the doors opened, Lance kicked backward with his feet and launched himself into space.

❖   ❖   ❖

Delia Radford pulled herself to her feet with a small groan. The lab was currently silent and pitch black, but that could change at any moment. Her right temple throbbed painfully. She put a hand to the side of her head and winced. There would be a fine bruise there come morning. If she survived that long.

"Ms. Michaels?" she called. "Ms. Michaels, are you there?"

"I'm here, Delia," came a reply a little to Delia's left. "Are you all right?"

"That robot arm swung round and clipped me a good one, but I don't think there was any permanent damage. Mr. Sabeel?"

No answer.

"Mr. Sabeel, are you all right?" Meredeth asked.

The vague swish of the ventilating system was the only sound. It was pumping out cool, dry air. Delia's skin began to crawl. A moment ago, the lab had erupted into a violent whirl of movement and light—machines spinning madly, monitors flickering garbled nonsense, mobile equipment trying to vault over tables, alarms blasting on and off. Something exploded against Delia's temple, driving her to her knees. And then, as if someone hit a switch, it all stopped and the lights went out, leaving an eerie silence.

Delia's nails dug sharply into her palm and she fought a rising panic. Adrenaline hummed in her arteries. The delicate movement of air against her face might end at any time, leaving her to suffocate in her own carbon dioxide. Less than a meter of rock and metal separated her from the blood-boiling vacuum of space.

"I've found him," Meredeth said in the dark.

"Is he all right?" Delia asked, glad to focus on something, anything else. She took a step toward Meredeth's voice and glass crunched underfoot.

There was a pause. "His head feels like a leaky, bruised melon," Meredeth replied dispassionately. "And he's not breathing."

Delia made a small noise. "What do we do now?"

"We get out of here," Meredeth replied. "See if you can find your way to the door. We'll head for the air locks."

The lights came on, striking Delia's eyes like a physical blow. She grunted and shielded her eyes until they could adjust, then glanced quickly around the lab. Sabeel was lying facedown nearby, head bulging on one side, blood pooling on the floor like red wine. Meredeth was standing a step or two away. The fingertips of one hand were also red.

"What—?" Delia began, and every monitor in the room jumped to life.

"Hello, Meredeth."

Meredeth spun to face the nearest terminal. The screen showed a red-haired, brown-eyed man who bore a strong resemblance to Lance. Meredeth put both hands to her face, heedless of Sabeel's blood. Delia stared.

"Jonathan," Meredeth whispered. "What the hell?"

"Don't bother answering," Jonathan Blackstone continued. "This message is prerecorded. By now, a nanobot hive has taken the station—my station—and you're trapped on board." He smiled a smile that chilled Delia's backbone. "In a few minutes, I'm sure, the hive will find the subroutine which is playing this message and destroy it, but in the meantime, you fucking cunt, you'll have to listen to me."

"Jesus." Delia automatically stepped away from the monitor, but the message was playing on every speaker. With an obvious effort, Meredeth lowered her hands and grimly fixed her attention on the display. Delia also watched in horrified fascination.

"One of my people has already contacted John," Blackstone said, "and I'm sure he's agreed to clean up the hive. You'll both be all packaged up and ready for a family reunion." Blackstone leaned forward. "You're coming home, Merry. You and John both. You can go back to keeping the house and I'll train John to inherit the corporations. We'll work something out about that mental problem he has—one of my research centers had made some amazing leaps in nano-driven brain surgery—and then everything'll be fine. See you soon, Merry. You're coming home."

The monitors went blank.

Delia licked her lips. Her throat was dry. "This can't be happening," she said. "It can't. No one can predict or create nanobot hives."

"Obviously someone can," Meredeth said. She paced a tight circle on the floor and gnawed at a thumbnail. "One of Jonathan's technicians must have figured out what causes them and reproduced one here on this station—just so he could trap me here. God, I was an *idiot*. I should have known the offer was too good to be true."

Delia glanced nervously around the lab. The lights were on, the air was still moving, and things seemed almost normal.

Except for the mess and Sabeel's . . . body, she amended.

From everything Delia had heard about hives, things could change at any moment. Like a small child, the hive was dealing with its new awareness, and its attention would wander from place to place about the station. It was only a matter of time before it became interested in the lab again, and it didn't care about the safety of the people inside.

"We need to get out of here, Ms. Michaels," Delia said. "Before the hive spreads much further."

Meredeth stopped pacing. "You're right. I'm being an idiot again. Do you remember how to get to the air locks? I wasn't paying close attention."

"I think so."

Meredeth strode for the door. "Then let's go."

"What about him?" Delia gestured at Sabeel's body.

"Leave him," Meredeth said decisively. "There isn't much we can—"

A deafening roar thundered through the station and the room shook violently. Delia was thrown to the floor, too surprised to react. Delicate equipment went smashing from the tables. Delia reflexively tried to find something stable and solid to grab, but everything was shaking. The lights flashed on and off and a terminal tipped over and hit the floor in a shower of sparks. The roar rose, overpowering Delia's eardrums. Delia realized she was screaming uselessly, but she couldn't make herself stop. The shaking went on and on—

—and then it ended as abruptly as it had begun. Silence rang through the lab. Delia lay stunned on the cold metal floor for a moment, then slowly dragged herself to her feet, shoving bits of broken equipment aside with clinks and clatters. Her entire body felt numb except for her prosthetics. Automatically Delia put her arm and leg through a quick set of movements designed to check the systems. They seemed all right. By some miracle, she had avoided cutting herself on the glass on the floor.

"Are you hurt, Delia?" Meredeth asked.

"I—I don't think so," Delia replied cautiously. "God, what was that?"

"I don't know. It doesn't matter right now. Let's make a run for the air lock."

Delia didn't argue. She and Meredeth trotted quickly for the lab door.

It was locked.

"Dammit," Meredeth muttered. "Hold on." She whipped a connector from a tiny port on her wristcomp and plugged it into the keypad next to the lock. "Hold your breath, Delia. Let's see how much I've forgotten."

Delia licked her lips nervously as Meredeth muttered commands to her computer. The silence seemed to rise up and pound at her almost as badly as the earlier noise. Something about that nagged at her, though she couldn't say why. Then she realized what it was. There was no quiet hum from the ventilation system.

"The air is off," Delia murmured, forcing her voice not to shake.

"Shit," Meredeth said. "Horace, access file Merrylock."

A camera in the corner suddenly swiveled and focused in their direction.

"Ms. Michaels," Delia said, eyes on the camera. "I think you'd better hurry."

"Hold on," Meredeth replied, and turned back to her wristcomp. "Horace, run subroutine Merry-M Yellow. Horace, upload virus."

In the outside hall, the door to one of the low-grav chambers clicked open, slammed shut. The one next to it followed suit, as did the third. Delia noticed with alarm that the low-grav chambers were in a line and the slamming doors were progressing steadily toward them. Click, slam. Click, slam.

"Ms. Michaels," Delia whispered hoarsely, "I think the hive is trying to keep us in here. It's watching us through the camera and trying to find the door controls."

Click, slam. Click, slam. "Horace, execute," Meredeth snapped. The lab door slid smoothly open. "Go!"

Click, slam. Delia dove into the dark corridor just as the final low-grav chamber opened and shut. Behind her, Meredeth paused half a second to disengage her wristcomp from the lock. She flung herself toward the hallway—

—and the lab door slammed. Delia was left alone in pitch blackness outside the lab.

She pounded on the door, shouting for Meredeth to answer. The door's emergency manual override ignored Delia's efforts. Near panic, she grasped the door handle and strained at it until she saw spots and her prosthetic arm tingled, warning her of overload.

"Ms. Michaels!" she shouted, pounding on the door again until her hands hurt. "Ms. Michaels!"

And then Delia was falling.

Lance rocketed toward the station, the bone-humming roar of his engines throbbing through him with an uncomfortably sensual feel. It was all through virtual feed, of course—there was no sound in space—but that didn't change the way it felt.

The communication system buzzed for his attention and Lance flicked an eye at the appropriate icon.

"Attention incoming vessel," commanded a recorded voice. "You are trespassing in private space. Transmit proper security clearance or leave the area immediately. This is your first warning."

Lance ignored the message and continued onward. Pinegra Station was obviously a modified asteroid—gray and chunky with odd metal and glass protuberances bulging from the sides. Four smaller satellites orbited the station and, with a flick toward the visual enhancement icon, Lance made out the familiar Kingsford and Knowlton logo that branded each one. The satellites were round and studded with rocket boosters. Each also sported a heavy, wicked-looking laser cannon. Thetachron III was behind Lance now, so he couldn't see the planet.

Lance scanned the station for a docking port and found one. It had been blown open. Metallic chunks of what used to be a jumpship were drifting aimlessly into orbit around the station or falling toward the planet.

Anyone who was aboard that ship's got to be dead, he thought. *Even Delia. Or Mom.*

"Attention incoming vessel," the recording snapped. "You have not transmitted proper security clearance. If you continue to approach, you will be fired upon. This is your final warning."

Lance continued his approach. It was an interesting sensation. He could still vaguely feel the chair he was sitting in, but mostly it felt like he was gliding smoothly through empty space. He flicked his eye toward the fuel gauge. Plenty left.

"Attention incoming vessel. You have not heeded our warnings. We have no choice but to fire upon your ship."

One of the satellites broke orbit and headed straight for Lance, trailing a bright tongue of rocket exhaust. Lance tensed and licked his lips. A beam of light lashed out and Lance threw himself sideways. The VR rig read his muscles and simultaneously goosed the drone to the right. Lance's left shin spasmed once, indicating the beam had scored a hit somewhere along the rear. The satellite adjusted course and took aim. Lance twisted upward just as the satellite fired again.

Direct hit. Fire engulfed Lance's fuel tanks. He had just enough time to gasp before he exploded and found himself sitting in a blank VR helmet back on the *Lady*.

Lance puffed out his cheeks. That was one.

"System on line," he ordered again. "Load VR probe."

Again, Lance launched himself toward the station and again he received the recorded warnings. The satellite left orbit to deal with the menace. Lance dodged and twisted, but the second probe eventually exploded. Before the security satellite could return to orbit, however, its torque flickered, guttered, and went out. Back in the ship, Lance watched it coast quietly past the asteroid and out of sight. It would fall victim to Thetachron III's gravitational pull or would career forever through space. Either way, the satellite was gone.

Three more to go, he thought, launching another drone.

Two hours later, Lance was drenched in sweat and his body was tingling from over half a dozen explosions, but all four security satellites were gone.

That's what happens when a hive gets control, Lance thought, pulling off his helmet and gloves. *Shoots refueling schedules right out the window.*

Lance ignored an automated distress signal that beeped urgently about attacking invaders and lost satellites and instead checked Jessica's scans again to make sure there was no more external security. He guided the *Defiant Lady* around the station to another docking port, one that didn't have jumpship debris floating away from it.

What do you think, Robin? he asked. *Safe to dock?*

Station's hive nanobots unable to enter ship. Have seen to that. This docking port as far away from blown counterpart as possible. Is conceivable hive hasn't found it yet or is ignoring. Safe as anything can be.

Lance nodded. When it came to nanobot hives, Robin had more expertise than Lance could ever hope for, and he counted on Robin's advice.

Though I don't think I'll be telling our clients about it any time soon, Lance mused. A slight jolt indicated the *Lady* had hit the dock and automatic clamps had secured the ship. *Somehow I don't think they'd be interested in hiring a man with forty-odd alters and a nanobot hive living inside him. But we all have our secrets.*

It was a secret Lance intended to keep. He could just imagine the scientific community's response if they found out exactly what Robin was. As it was, every time someone suspected a system was going hive, they did their level best to contact him—along with reporters from half a dozen media who wanted to know how he dealt with them. Lance had eventually been forced to get around the problem by charging full price even if the call turned out to be a false alarm. Fortunately hives were still very rare. Otherwise he'd have no time for his first love—security analysis.

Have to pay bills somehow, Robin said.

Maybe I should charge everyone rent, Lance replied with a wry mental wink.

Good. While at it, please hire maintenance subcontractor. Wish to retire to nano-condo on Abierto.

Not on what I'm paying you.

Once he was sure the ship was locked properly in place, Lance trotted down to the storage lockers, tension rising in his stomach. Until this point everything had been abstract, a giant VR game. But as he opened the first locker to take out his tool kit, it began to sink in. The stakes were higher than he was used to playing—his mother was involved. More importantly, Delia needed his help.

Lance owed Delia. She had helped him out of a tough spot, and for no reason except that she seemed to like him. An odd pang went through him at the thought. It seemed he could still feel the touch of her warm hand as she checked his injuries, still see her brown eyes full of concern for him.

Because of your pheromones, he reminded himself, strapping the toolbelt around his waist, where it made a comforting weight. *She doesn't like you. She likes your chemistry.*

She didn't freak out about multiple personalities, Robin commented.

Of course not, Lance said, annoyed that Robin had been eavesdropping. *The pheromones saw to that.*

Pheromones unsuccessful when subject experiences fear or hatred. Most people react with fear when confronted with MPD, rendering pheromones unhelpful. Therefore, Delia unafraid of Company, and not because of pheromones.

Lance yanked an emergency vacuum suit out of another locker. The fabric was smooth and cool, almost like satin. *So now you're playing matchmaker, meatless?*

Just pointing out facts. You like Delia lots. Respiration, heart rate both increase when you see, think of her. Testosterone, adrenaline levels rise during close contact. Excess perspiration evident on palms. None such activity noticeable under similar conditions regarding mother. But fact that I noticed condition no reason to deny feelings for—

Lance floated in abrupt darkness. Confused, he tried to look around, thinking both lights and gravity had gone at the same time. Then he realized what was going on.

Robin, who's in charge? he growled. *I said no unwanted takeovers.*

Andy.

Anger rose, and Lance tried to clench nonexistent fists, but there was nothing he could do but wait. For someone who liked to quote Company Policy at him, Andy played awfully fast and loose with the rules. Before Lance could work up a head of steam, however, the darkness cleared and Lance found himself back at the storage lockers with the vacuum suit still in his hand.

Andy wants you to look at wristcomp, Jaylance, Robin said.

Lance glanced down. Numbers flickered across his computer, a stopwatch running backward. It was counting down from an hour and forty-five minutes. In the background tiny waves crashed silently on a miniature beach and washed over two figures writhing in vigorous embrace. Abierto.

Lance's stomach tightened. Andy was one of Lance's stronger alters. Jessica, Patrick, and Johnny he could keep at bay with a ferocious act of will if it came down to it, and Robin had never tried a full takeover. Garth and Andy, however, were another matter entirely. He had never been able to overpower either of them, and Andy had no stake in rescuing Delia or Mom. If Andy decided to take over and head for Abierto, there wouldn't be anything Lance could do about it, threats notwithstanding.

Then don't just stand here, he thought. *Get moving. You have almost two hours. You and Robin can deal with a hive in less time than that.*

He jogged up to the air lock and donned the vacuum suit. It was a thin one made for ease of movement, not extended survival—no radiation shielding and minimal air supply in the helmet. The wearer was expected to make a mad sprint for safety, not take part in extravehicular activity.

Lance put a hand on the lock's manual override— most electrical systems in the plant would be rendered untrustworthy by the nano hive—and took a deep breath. The sound echoed oddly in his helmet.

Ready, Robin?

Ready.

Lance opened the lock. Air hissed, meaning life support was still operating and he could strap his helmet to his back. Lance removed it—

—and winced under the barrage of noise that crashed into his ears.

The empty steel corridor ahead of him was a nightmare of sound and light. Alarms bellowed madly as the lights flickered red and white. Twice the entire passage was plunged into darkness for a few seconds before the lights began flashing again. Ozone tanged the air and sparks flew from an exposed panel ahead. Lance drew a flashlight from his belt and got as close as he dared to the crackling wires.

Go, Robin.

Going.

Though he still couldn't feel a thing, Lance's skin crawled beneath the vacuum suit as hundreds, thousands of nanos left his body through mouth, eyes, nose, and ears. Invisibly small, they swarmed over the wall and into the electrical system, testing, seeking, looking for the hive nanos that held Pinegra Station hostage.

Normally at this point, Lance would sit and wait. Robin did all the work, reprogramming nanos from the rogue hive and assimilating them into Robin's hive until the rogue lost the extra processing space afforded by its excess nanobots. The hive's sentience would collapse, the station's system would return to normal.

One giant lobotomy, Lance thought, squinting down the corridor. *Robin, have you seen Delia?*

Not yet. Busy arranging political rally, you know.

Lance switched on the flashlight and moved rapidly down the corridor. He couldn't afford to wait for Robin to assimilate the rogue hive—Delia was somewhere in that mess, and Andy's stopwatch had less than ninety minutes on it. The harsh alarms pounded his ears and every so often the speakers would blare something unintelligible. Lights pulsed almost like a heartbeat. In the corner, a security camera swiveled wildly as if it were dancing.

The corridor ended in a T-intersection. Lance tried to ignore the noise and light around him and shone the flashlight left, then right. A distant rumbling muttered briefly up the hallway and the floor vibrated beneath Lance's boots.

This is stupid, he thought. *There's no way I'll find her—them—by just wandering around.*

His eye fell on an intercom panel mounted on the wall. *I wonder . . .*

Lance pressed a few buttons. Lights flickered on the panel. Apparently the hive hadn't completely shorted out internal communications. He activated the public address system.

"Hello!" he said, and his own voice boomed eerily back at him through the PA despite the buzzing alarms. "Can anyone hear me? If you can, activate an intercom. I'm at—" he glanced at the panel "—section 3-C. Repeat—section 3-C."

The security camera stopped swiveling. It froze for a moment, then slowly scanned up and down the hallway. It focused on Lance. Lance couldn't help feeling it was staring.

The alarms and klaxons suddenly cut off and the lights went out. The corridor went dead black except for Lance's flashlight and the tiny lights on the intercom. Lance wondered if the camera was equipped with infrared.

Any progress, Robin? he asked.

Yes. Hive very receptive, easy to "talk" to. Almost like nanos want to be assimilated. Have converted perhaps third of what we need to disperse problem.

The intercom beeped. "Hello? Is anyone there?" It was Delia, and her voice was filled with a combination of fear and relief.

Lance's heart skipped a beat. "It's Lance, Delia. I'm here to get you out."

"Lance, you have to listen to me," Delia said quickly. "There was a recording. Your fa—"

"Lance? Is that you?" broke in another voice.

"It's me, Mom. Where are you?"

"The research labs. I'm locked in. Delia's outside. The gravity's gone, and—"

"Lance, get *out* of here," Delia interrupted. "When the station went hive, there was a recording from your father."

The corridor suddenly sprang into view as the lights came back on. Lance saw the camera was still focused directly on him. The lights flickered, steadied, then grew brighter and brighter until it hurt to look at them. An ominous buzz trembled at the threshold of Lance's hearing.

"From Dad?" Lance said, remembering Garth's suspicions. Tension knotted in his gut. "Oh geez. What did he—"

Every light in the corridor exploded. Glass flew in all directions and Lance, half deafened by the noise, threw up his hands to shield his face. A shard whizzed by his ear and something warm flowed down his neck.

"—hear me?" said the intercom. "Lance?"

Lance swiped at his neck, then thumbed the intercom. He left a bloody smear. "I didn't copy that, Delia. Listen, I'm heading for the labs. Wait for me there, all right?"

Electricity arced through the intercom and Lance fell screaming to the floor, pain tearing at his body. Convulsions wracked his muscles as his implants tried to deal with the overload. The pain intensified, white-hot, crushing. Lance fell gratefully into the blackness when it came.

Johnny Blackstone lay huddled in a ball on the floor. His nose was bleeding, his neck was bleeding. Even his ears were bleeding. He hurt all over, but that was all right. He was supposed to hurt.

"I've been bad again," he whispered. "I've been so bad."

He slowly pulled himself to a sitting position to wait for Daddy to bring Dr. duFort. He waited a long time. It was quiet now, and dark, but it was always dark—ever since Dr. duFort had pulled out his eyes. And soon, Johnny was sure, Dr. duFort would come with her hard hands and sharp needles. She and Daddy would be here any minute and they would do things that hurt, but they would make him better.

"I'll be good, Daddy," he whimpered. "I promise I'll be good."

Johnny curled up in the darkness to wait.

CHAPTER SIX

THEN
AGE 15

Jessica:

There are times when one does what one must do. If, for example, a corpse is the only tool at hand, it must be used. Unfortunately, Lance can't seem to grasp this simple concept. He is far too concerned with what others think, including his father. He should be more like Mother—cool, calm, and unconcerned with the unimportant.

Perhaps part of Lance's problem is that he simply can't distinguish between what is important and what is not. A corpse, for instance, is unimportant since the owner no longer has any use for it.

Lance's new visitor, on the other hand, was another matter entirely.

I've long known about Lance's visitors, of course, but this new one was a wild card. It sprang up literally out of nowhere just after the eye operation and it tried to take over, just like Patrick did when he first visited, though Garth and I easily held Patrick at bay until he learned a bit of self-control.

This new visitor, however, was far more powerful, and it took more people to cage it. Garth, Johnny, Jay, Patrick, Grandpa Jack, and I forced it into a slot reserved for certain visitors who don't come calling very often. Still, I could sometimes feel it squirming, and it felt nothing at all like the other visitors. For one thing, it had no name and did not try to talk with anyone.

Patrick, of course, was all for burying the visitor so deep that it would be impossible for it to emerge again, and Garth was inclined to agree. But it seemed to me there were possibilities with this new visitor, and I persuaded the others that burial would be wrong. None of the other visitors had been buried. Why should this entity be treated differently?

Eventually I won out, though only because Patrick and Garth didn't want to go through another fight, this time with me. I promised to keep an eye on the new visitor and see what happened. I must admit, however, that I was as surprised as anyone to discover the visitor's true origins. If it hadn't been for the catastrophe at school, I never would have.

That's why you have to pay attention to what's important.

∗*salutations greetings hello there nice weather we're having hi*∗

Bent over his desk computer, Lance froze for a moment, then went back to his book report. The voice was clear and sharp, but European lit was his favorite class and he wasn't going to let another stupid voice in his head ruin it. He shifted uncomfortably in his seat—even molded plastic was still plastic, and it made a hard chair. The classroom still smelled strongly of the carpeting that had been laid last week.

∗*what's up hey mister yo good day*∗

Lance eyed his classmates nervously. The other students alternated between staring blankly at their monitors and tapping silenced keys. Mrs. Rubenstein was doing something at her desk, and a steady stream of rock music quietly poured out of her radio. That was one of the things that made Mrs. Rubenstein so popular—she did fun things in the classroom like playing the radio on reading and research days. But neither she nor the other students seemed to hear the voice. Lance chewed a fingernail. Unlike the others he had heard, this voice seemed to be talking directly to him. The others had never done that.

HEY

Lance bolted upright. Missy Gallagher shot him a strange look from the next seat over, and Mrs. Rubenstein glanced up from her work. In the corner, Brad Kepplinger, a tall, husky man in a dark business suit, came quietly alert. Lance quickly rubbed his arm as if he had been startled by a muscle cramp and pretended to read again, though he could feel Kepplinger's eyes on him.

yoo hoo excuse me I say pardon me I'm talking to you greetings hello salutations hi

Lance got up and went over to Mrs. Rubenstein's desk. Wide windows behind her revealed a dim, cloudy day, but the classroom was comfortably warm. Mrs. Rubenstein blanked her monitor as Lance approached.

"Yes, John?" she asked in her pleasant, clipped English.

"May I use a pass?" Lance asked, quietly relieved that his voice had finally stopped betraying him with cracks and squeaks. Only a month ago it had been so bad he had been afraid to open his mouth. At the moment, however, his voice seemed content to remain a light, steady tenor—completely unlike Dad's booming bass. Maybe being fifteen wouldn't be a total disaster.

"A pass? Let me look." Mrs. Rubenstein called up Lance's classroom records. "You only have one left. And it's only halfway through the marking period. If you use it, that's all you get until next one."

Lance sighed to himself. Mrs. Rubenstein let her students have four locker/lavatory passes per card marking, but it seemed to Lance he never got that many. He didn't remember using them, but they were never all there.

"All right," he said. "May I go, please?"

Mrs. Rubenstein nodded, and Lance headed for the door. Kepplinger followed, walking quietly up the carpeted hallway behind him. Lance ignored Kepplinger as best he could and strode for the bathroom. He had to get someplace where he could be alone for a moment, and the restroom was the only logical place, especially with Kepplinger following him everywhere.

Like everything else at the Banks-Cross Memorial Academy, the boy's bathroom was scrupulously clean and well-appointed. White porcelain gleamed, stainless steel shined. The academy was also one of the few private schools in England that allowed bodyguards on the premises, though Lance privately suspected that Kepplinger was more spy than bodyguard. Dad had hired him almost a year ago, just after Lance had neutralized the house's security system and run away, though Lance still recalled nothing of the incident.

Kepplinger entered the restroom ahead of Lance, checked it with practiced care, and took up a position in the corner like a hulking blond statue. Lance grimaced. They went through this every time Lance visited the bathroom.

"Could you wait outside, please?" Lance said.

Kepplinger left with a nod and Lance sighed. At least he could be guaranteed privacy for the moment— Kepplinger wouldn't let anyone else in until Lance came out. He went over to the row of sinks and looked at his reflection in the mirror. His eyes were brown now, of course. Though it had been almost a year since that particular operation, he still couldn't quite get over seeing the results.

"Hello?" he whispered, and suddenly felt foolish. *I'm talking to myself in a mirror—and expecting an answer.*

His mind flooded with sound. *salutations greetings hello there*

Lance jumped, then swallowed. His face was pale in the mirror. He had heard voices inside his head before— that was normal—but none of them had ever actually talked to him. Not until now.

Oh my God. I've gone crazy.

can you hear me do you hear me are you listening to me

"I—" The word came out as a squeak. Lance coughed and tried again. "I can hear you. Who are you?"

Pause. *unknown who am I*

Lance bit a thumbnail. This was weird. The voice was stranger than the others, and Lance couldn't decide whether it was male or female—it sounded like both and neither.

And what are you supposed to say to a voice in your own head? "Uh, my name's J. Lance Michaels Blackstone. What's yours?"

Another pause. Then: *have no name appellation nomenclature designation*

"You don't have a name? Where are you?"

Pause. *in living space inside jaylance*

"Inside? You mean inside me?" Lance stared at himself, half expecting to see another face. But he looked perfectly normal. His throat felt suddenly dry and he slurped a cool mouthful of water from the sink faucet.

This is nuts, he thought, splashing some of the water on his face. *Not only am I hearing voices, I'm talking back to them. What if Kepplinger finds out and tells Dad?* Fear crept through his chest. *Jesus, Dad would kill me.*

query jaylance is afraid scared frightened of me?

Lance licked his lips. "I—I'm not sure. It's just that—I mean—what if someone else finds out about you? They'll think I've gone crazy." He paused. "Are—are you one of the other voices I hear sometimes? The ones that argue all the time?"

negative no never not

"Then who are you?"

robin

"Robin?" Lance repeated, startled. "I thought you didn't have a name."

found one

"Are you a . . . a ghost or something?"

negative no never not

"So what are you?"

Long pause. Then: *friend*

Lance blinked. The fear and suspicion suddenly eased, though he couldn't put his finger on why. Robin's voice was warm, almost kind—completely unlike the other voices that yelled and screamed all the time. Just hearing it made Lance feel comfortable, as if he were talking to someone who knew all his dark secrets—and liked him anyway.

The bathroom door opened a crack. "Mr. Blackstone?" Kepplinger called. "Are you all right? You've been in there a long time."

"I'm jacking off, Kepplinger," Garth called back. "Wanna come in and watch?"

The door closed.

"So your name is Robin, huh?" Garth leaned casually on the sink. "Are you a guy or a girl?"

meaningless question

Garth snorted. "So *you* say. At least you're learning how to talk right."

getting better every second interactive conversation helps

"You just remember that you ain't one of us, buddy-thing. We *let* you out of your cage, and don't you forget it. You try anything funny and it's straight back to stir-crazy city, clear?"

clear. no need for threats you know.

"We'll see. I don't know who you are or where you came from, Robby, but you can bet we'll be keeping an eye on you. And if you do anything to hurt Lance, I'll wad you up and drop you down a hole so deep you'll never find your way out."

Said was no need for threats.

"And I said we'll see."

Garth flushed a toilet and strode jauntily out of the bathroom. Kepplinger was still waiting. Garth smirked at him.

"Man, do I feel better," he said, pretending to adjust

his fly. "Nothing like a good jerk-off after lunch. Maybe you should try it, Kepp. Might loosen some of those pins in your ass."

Kepplinger's face remained impassive. Garth gave him a four-fingered salute from the nose and returned to class without looking back.

Lance blinked. A minute ago he had been in the bathroom, now he was at his desk. He flicked a glance at the clock on his monitor, and gave an internal sigh of relief. He had only lost a few minutes.

And then he remembered. The new voice. His new friend. Robin. Or had he imagined it?

"Hello?" he said in the quietest whisper he could manage, hoping Mrs. Rubenstein's radio would cover the sound. "Are you there, Robin?"

The warm voice popped into his head. *Hello Jaylance! Always here. Where else to go?*

Lance smiled to himself and flicked his fingers happily over the computer board without really doing anything. He had a friend—a private friend he didn't have to share with anyone.

Mrs. Rubenstein abruptly turned off the radio and the class stirred. The period was almost over. Students logged off the network and gathered their things just as a blast of sound thundered through the room. Everyone jumped. Lance clapped his hands over his ears.

"Fire drill!" Mrs. Rubenstein shouted above the din. "Move along! Move along!"

Students snatched up notebook terminals and styluses and headed for the door, laughing and shouting above the siren. Lance followed, still covering his ears, and Kepplinger stayed right behind him. About half the class had made it through the door when the ceiling lights flickered once and grew brighter. Startled, Lance looked up for a moment, then averted his eyes—the lights were too bright to look at. With a *pop* that overshadowed even the fire alarm, the lights shattered, showering the students with shards of glass and dropping the classroom into semidarkness. Several students started to scream. A strong hand clamped Lance's shoulder and he found himself being towed toward the door. The fire alarm continued blaring. Kepplinger, the owner of the grip, shoved several stunned students out of his way and got to the door, which promptly slammed itself shut.

Without pausing, Kepplinger let go of Lance, grabbed the doorknob—

—and jigged horribly in place. The smell of ozone mixed with smoke and cooking flesh. Mrs. Rubenstein screamed and Lance backed away, horrified. Kepplinger's hair stood on end and sparks spat and leaped from his body. Then the fire alarm cut off and Kepplinger simultaneously fell backward to the floor. His head hit the carpet with a sickening thump. The door drifted slowly open.

Dead silence in the classroom. Missy Gallagher made a small sound in the back of her throat. Lance stared down at Kepplinger's body, heart pounding. Sparks. Shocks. The wires. Kepplinger had tried to open the door and had gotten shocked to death. Lance backed away, head spinning. He had to get out of here. He had to *run*, get away from the sparks and the wires—but the windows didn't open and he couldn't go through the door. That's what had killed Kepplinger. To run away was to die. To stay in the classroom meant death. The dichotomy pulled at him, tore at him, and he welcomed the blackness when it came.

Jessica Meredeth Michaels made a quick survey of her surroundings. Dimly lit classroom. Desks. Computer units. Half a dozen scared adolescents. One teacher trying to remain calm. Shattered glass on carpet. Open door. Corpse. Smell of ozone in air. Sounds of panic from hallway. She nodded. Nothing immediately dangerous but, judging from the corpse, that could change.

"Everybody stay calm," the teacher was saying. "I think we should stay right here and wait for—"

"Your attention please," interrupted the public address

system. Jessica recognized the headmaster's voice. "Please remain where you are. The school's computer system seems to be experiencing some kind of malfunction. We are attempting to remedy the—"

A loud burst of static cut him off, filling the room with white noise. Every computer terminal in the room suddenly lit up, flashing meaningless characters and graphics. Jessica stared, fascinated, as one terminal glowed brighter and brighter. An insistent, high-pitched whine pulsed steadily through the room.

"What the hell—?" said one of the boys. He edged toward a terminal.

"Keep away from it, Jack," Rubenstein warned. "Is everyone all right? We'll stay here until someone comes for us."

"Is he dead?" quavered a girl, pointing at Kepplinger.

No, Jessica thought sarcastically. *He's just resting. Grow up, girl.*

The whine grew louder. Jessica cocked her head, decided it sounded like a lot of CRTs receiving far more power than they should. She glanced at the teacher, who was trying simultaneously to comfort two students and keep the others away from the terminals. She showed no sign that she intended to leave.

Fine for her, Jessica thought as the whine grew louder still. *I think I'll take a chance in the hallway.*

Jessica trotted toward the door, skipped nimbly over Kepplinger's body without touching anything metallic, and slipped into the hall.

"John!" Rubenstein called behind her. "John, come back here or—"

Jessica never found out what the other choice was. Fifteen ear-splitting explosions shattered the end of Rubenstein's sentence. Jessica shook her head. Idiots. Not worth bothering with.

The hallway was far more chaotic than the classroom. Overhead lights flickered and flashed, alarms blared unexpectedly, and the PA system was spitting out a garbled mess of recorded music and old school announcements. The door to a storeroom across the hall opened and slammed itself with robotic regularity. There were no people in sight. Rubenstein's classroom was at the end of a dead-end hallway, and everyone else had presumably done the sensible thing and evacuated.

Or have they? Kepplinger certainly tried.

Jessica thoughtfully regarded the slamming storeroom door. After a moment, she had the rhythm down and was able to nip inside without letting the door touch her. The door continued its rhythm, blithely unconcerned.

The storeroom was dark and smelled pungently of floor cleaner. Jessica's eyes quickly adjusted, however, until she was able to see perfectly well, something Jessica found confusing. Lance's eyes, not Jessica's, had been replaced almost a year ago, yet somehow she could see in the dark as well as he could.

Not to complain, she thought, selecting a push broom and black rubber dustpan from a wall rack. *I'd hate to do this by feel.*

Cleaning implements in hand, Jessica dodged out the door and jogged lightly up the corridor, ignoring the moans from Rubenstein's room behind her. She came to an intersection at the main hallway where crowds of frightened students and teachers milled around like cows in a field full of snakes. Several sat huddled on the floor with their arms wrapped round their heads. The headmaster was screaming for everyone to quiet down, but no one listened. Lights were still flashing like mad, and the fire alarm sounded at ten-second intervals. At the end of the corridor was an exit, but everyone was giving it a wide berth. The people closest to the door were staring in horror at something on the floor, and Jessica had a pretty good idea what it was.

A deep, throbbing hum rumbled beneath Jessica's feet, and she wondered if whatever was causing all this had gotten into the heating and boiler system. The results would not be pleasant if excessive pressure built up in the wrong place.

What on earth could do this? she wondered, still
clutching broom and dustpan. She licked her lips and
thought for a moment. *Everything that's been going wrong
or exploding or electrocuting people is computer linked.
The alarms, the lights, the terminals, the door locks—
everything. But what could make the main computer go
mad like this? Some kind of virus?*

The throbbing grew louder and Jessica shook her head.
While it might be interesting to find some answers, her
first priority was safety.

Confidently, fearlessly, Jessica shoved her way through
the crowd, ignoring shouting teachers and the blaring fire
siren. It was harder to ignore the throbbing hum. The
students had noticed it as well and were starting to panic
again, though none of them went near the door. Using
the broom to lever people out of her way, Jessica steadily
approached the exit.

She was halfway there when the sprinkler systems went
on.

Screeching, the student body fled, dodging into class-
rooms or ducking into the gymnasium. Cold water
drenched Jessica's clothes and ran down her face, but she
ignored it. Jessica plowed determinedly through the fleeing
crowd, catching the occasional sharp elbow in her side
or heavy foot on her instep. The thrumming felt like a
minor earthquake by now. Jessica focused her attention
on the exit.

And then she was there. The double doors of the exit
were firmly shut. Sparks snapped and danced over the
metal levers that opened them, and lying on the floor
were two people—an older and a younger male. Their
bodies were badly burned and scorched. The younger
male looked to be about twelve years old, obviously a
student.

Jessica stepped over them, readied the broom—and
hesitated. She had intended to use the broom to push
the door open and wedge it in place with the dustpan.
The wooden broom handle and rubber dustpan would have

protected her from the electricity, but now both were wet, and Jessica was standing in a puddle of water.

Too risky, she decided. *But now what?*

A sharp explosion detonated behind her, striking her body with a numbing *whump.* Jessica spun. A cascade of water was flooding the hallway. Electricity arced into it from doors and sockets. Jessica looked desperately around. Nothing to stand on, nowhere to run. And if the sockets were arcing, there was enough power running through the wires to fry a small horse, never mind a teenage girl.

The water rushed toward her. Jessica dropped the broom and bent over the smaller corpse at her feet. With all her strength, she hauled it to its feet and shoved it at the door. It flopped like a rag doll, hit the door lever, sagged against it. Water gushed down the hallway, less than five meters away. The boy's corpse pushed down on the door lever and the door swung outward. Jessica darted through the opening less than a second before the cascade swept the place where she had been standing.

Lance stood panting on the front porch. His clothes were soaking wet, and cold. His heart was pounding fair to shake his shirt, and his legs ached as if he had just run a cross country competition. He leaned against a smooth white marble pillar for a moment, trying to get his breathing under control.

God, he thought. *Another blackout. But what am I doing home? The last thing I remember is—*

His heart skipped a beat. The school. The lights and alarms going wild. And something else. Something else he had seen that hovered at the edge of recollection. But his mind refused to focus on it.

How did I get home? And where's Kepplinger? What happened?

∗School computer went crazy.∗

Lance jumped and twisted his head around, looking for the source of the voice. "What?"

∗School computer went crazy.∗

Then Lance remembered. Robin. His new friend.

"You're still there?" he asked.

Nowhere else to go, Jaylance.

Lance's breath was slowing, though his teeth were starting to chatter. His very bones felt cold. "What happened at the school? I mean, after the computer went crazy? How did I get—"

The front door opened and Meredeth stepped outside, cutting Lance off in mid-sentence. She was a tall woman—though Lance had outgrown her two operations ago—with green eyes and strawberry blond hair she typically wore in a long braid down her back.

"Lance?" she said, and Lance thought he detected a note of concern. "What's going on? The gate guard rang and said you were home. Why aren't you in—good God, you're soaking wet! Get inside before you freeze."

She marched him briskly into the house and up to his room, where she all but threw him into the bathroom. "Chloe, start a shower, temperature setting four."

A bit later, Lance was sitting on his bed, wrapped in soft bathrobe and blankets, a mug of sweet hot tea steaming in his hand. The shaking had stopped, and he felt beautifully warm and comfortable, the center of all Mom's attention. She *was* concerned.

"All right," Mom said, perching on the edge of Lance's bed and fixing him with an agate stare. "What happened?"

The comfortable feeling receded. Lance swallowed, and his hands started to shake. He almost spilled the tea. "I—I'm not sure. I was sitting in European lit and everything went crazy. The fire alarm went off, the lights started flashing. Mrs. Rubenstein thought it was a fire drill, but then Mr. Kepplinger got . . . got . . ."

"Got what, Lance?" Mom asked. "Where is he?"

"I don't know," Lance admitted, too tired to lie. An unexpected yawn nearly split his head in two and he set the tea aside. "It's all jumbled and confused. We must have gotten separated or something. I don't even know how I got home or why I was all wet."

Meredeth laid a cool hand on his cheek and neck. "Well, you don't seem to have hypothermia and you don't look to be suffering from shock. I'll ring up the school and try to find out what happened. You just rest." She kissed him on the forehead and left.

Lance settled back amid the warm blankets and stared at the empty ceiling, tired but unable to fall asleep.

"Robin?" he whispered.

Here, Jaylance.

"What happened? You were telling me, but Mom came outside."

School computer went crazy, along with everything under computer's control. Lights, networks, plumbing, boilers, everything.

"Why did the computer go crazy?"

Unknown.

"So how did I get home? How did I get wet?"

You got out of building, ran. But not before sprinkler system hosed you.

Lance nodded, then steeled himself. He didn't want to ask, but he had to know. "Robin, what happened to Mr. Kepplinger?"

Kepplinger—

Robin's voice cut off. A long silence followed.

"Robin?" Lance whispered. "Robin, can you hear me?"

The door opened and Mom came back into the room. Her face was pale. "I tried to ring the school and couldn't get through. Then I rang the doctor and the circuit was busy. So I tried the hospital, and got a recording. Lance, what's going on here?"

"I don't know, Mom," Lance said, wishing she would leave so he could look into Robin's sudden silence, and simultaneously hoping she would stay and talk to him more. Mom didn't often pay this much attention to him.

She sat on the bed, adding a slight dent to the mattress. "I sent one of the guards to the school and accessed the medical database. It said you should stay warm and try to rest. I'm going to see if there's anything about this on the newsnets. You stay in bed." And she left again.

Lance sat up the moment the door was closed. "Robin? Robin, are you there?"

A brief pause. Then, *Here, Jaylance.*

"Where did you go?"

Nowhere, Jaylance.

"Why did you cut off like that?" A thought struck him. "Was it because you knew Mom was coming back?"

* . . . affirmative.*

The answer was too hesitant. It sounded like a lie.

"So what happened to Kepplinger?" Lance pressed.

Unknown. Kepplinger separated from you early on.

"That's what I told Mom," Lance said slowly. "It's what really happened?"

* . . . affirmative.*

Lance blinked in puzzlement. Robin was lying. But why? He thought about pressing further, then decided to ask a different question instead.

"Robin, how do you know all this?"

See everything you do, Jaylance. Also hear, taste, feel, and smell. You were there. Just don't remember.

"Why not?"

The two words hung in the air, and sudden fear clenched Lance's stomach. The blackouts and memory losses were a standard in his life, normal. He was eight years old before he realized other people didn't have them. Now he was talking to someone who might be able to explain them, and the idea was terrifying. What if something horrible was wrong with him?

There was no answer. Lance's heart began to pound.

"Robin?" he asked, still afraid but wanting—needing—to know. "Why don't I remember? Why do I have blackouts?"

Another pause. *Can't answer that, Jaylance.*

"Can't answer?" Lance echoed, confused. "What do you mean? Robin, please—what's wrong with me?"

Please don't press, Jaylance. Can't answer.

Lance twisted the bedclothes in frustration. "You said you were my friend. Friends don't lie or hold back."

No choice, Jaylance. Listen, had long day. Must be tired. Must be sleepy.

Lance opened his mouth to contradict, then realized Robin was right. He *was* sleepy. Very sleepy. He slid beneath the warm blankets, eyes already slipping shut.

Need your rest, Robin murmured gently. *Long day. Tiring day.*

But Lance was already asleep.

Meredeth peeped into Lance's bedroom. He had burrowed beneath the bedclothes, leaving visible only a shock of red hair. He seemed to be asleep. Meredeth closed the door and tiptoed away, agitation already rising in her stomach. The guard had rung in from the school to tell her the place was a mess. He had managed to glean a little information from the police and rescue workers surrounding the area—namely that the school's main computer had gone haywire and was still in control of the place. Most of the students and teachers had gotten out, but there were a handful of dead and a lot of injured. Meredeth sent up a quick prayer of gratitude that Lance wasn't one of them.

She descended the back stairs to the kitchen, her footsteps hushed by thick carpeting. The rear staircase doubled as a gallery for an exquisite set of miniature landscapes that shifted according to the season—currently there were leaves on the trees and birds were building nests—but Meredeth scarcely gave them a glance.

Beyond trying to evacuate the school no one seemed to know what to do. Cutting the power hadn't proven effective—the school had its own generator—and an antiviral program introduced via modem had had no effect whatsoever. A team of experts were being flown in, the guard had told her, but they wouldn't arrive for another hour.

There was no sign of Mr. Kepplinger.

Meredeth twisted her fraying braid with nervous fingers. Under normal circumstances, she would be fascinated at the very least. But she had other worries. Currently, the foremost was what to do about Jonathan.

Meredeth paused at the kitchen door. The kitchen looked deceptively plain with its tiny white tiles and blond wood cupboards. All appliances but the stove were carefully concealed. Even the refrigerator was hidden in a closet. It could be rancid with mold, mildew, and rotten food, but no one would ever know it even existed. She opened one of the cupboards and took out the electric kettle and the packet of chamomile, then stared at them both for a long moment. She had put them away without even thinking after making Lance's tea.

Jonathan has you well trained, doesn't he? she thought. Jonathan.

"Chloe," Meredeth said aloud, "where is Jonathan, according to his schedule?"

"Mr. Blackstone is meeting with Dr. duFort in Paris."

Meredeth set the kettle to boil, her mind racing. Should she call Jonathan about this or not? The choices lay before her, both going in two equally unpleasant directions. If, on the one hand, Jonathan heard about the incident on the newsnets before Meredeth told him about it—and Jonathan liked to check the nets several times a day— he would get angry because she hadn't called to tell him Lance was safe before he had a chance to worry needlessly. The kettle beeped insistently.

On the other hand, she thought, pouring herself a steaming cup of chamomile and leaning against the counter, *if I interrupt his meeting with Dr. duFort to say that, ultimately, nothing happened to Lance, he'll be furious that I intruded.*

Meredeth knew she couldn't win. Jonathan would get angry no matter what she did. The problem was choosing the option that would infuriate him the least.

The teacup grew cold in her hand.

"Chloe," she said softly, "ring up Jonathan. Emergency priority."

May as well get it over with.

❖   ❖   ❖

Jessica tapped a finger on the carved wooden armrest of the drawing room sofa. The drawing room was dimly lit—it was early evening and neither she nor Mother had put the lights on—and Jessica was glad of that. The drawing room was tasteless and ugly, cluttered with embroidered Victorian furniture, Persian rugs, and idiotic knickknacks. The newsnets provided the only light, and Jessica focused her attention there.

The announcements and pictures were beginning to repeat themselves. The academy was closed, of course, and there would be no school tomorrow. Fifteen people—six teachers, eight students, and one bodyguard—had died at the school, and the place was crawling with technicians trying to figure out what had happened.

Meredeth made a small sound and Jessica shook her head as the nets showed body bags being lifted into the ambulance again. Jessica shifted one more time, trying to get comfortable and not quite succeeding.

Unfortunately, the drawing room was the only room in the house that had even vaguely comfortable furniture. Jonathan insisted on having the Blackstone mansion furnished with expensive—and uncomfortable—antiques, despite the fact that the Blackstones never entertained anymore.

At least it's warm in here, Jessica thought sourly. *It was a bloody cold jog home.*

Over the years, Jessica had gleaned bits of information which led her to believe that Jonathan had once been a major player in high society, but had gone reclusive after Lance's birth. Nowadays the only people allowed on the grounds were the guards and gardeners, who stayed strictly outdoors. Once a week a cleaning staff went over parts of the house. The rest of the time, Mother dealt with day-to-day chores such as cooking, shopping, and minor cleaning—demeaning, to Jessica's mind.

Lance, of course, had thought nothing of this until he heard some of the children at school talking about cooks, nannies, and live-in maids. And the idiot had gone to Jonathan for answers.

"How come we don't have any of those, Dad?" he had asked. "Are we poor? That's what Janey says—that only poor people don't have servants."

Following that, there was a gap in Lance's memory that lasted three days.

"Your father doesn't want servants," Mother had told him later. "It's too dangerous. Your father has some powerful enemies, and servants can't always be trusted."

A blatant lie, that, Jessica thought, readjusting her bathrobe. *Jonathan just wants to keep Mother and Lance isolated so he can do as he likes with them. The bastard.*

Mother had called Jonathan in Paris this afternoon to tell him about the incident, but since nothing had really happened to Lance, he wasn't coming back tonight. Jessica was relieved, but Mother seemed terribly tight-lipped about the matter.

Not that Mother isn't usually tight-lipped, Jessica thought, darting a quick glance at her. Meredeth seemed completely absorbed in the netcast. Jessica nodded. With her daughter safe and in no medical danger, Meredeth's attention had returned to more important matters. Jessica followed her example and concentrated on the news. Maybe there was something new to report this time.

"—mysterious malfunction that killed, at last count, fifteen people," the reporter was saying. The scene behind him showed the Banks-Cross Memorial Academy, roped off and crawling with technicians and other emergency personnel. Two helicopters circled the area like restless condors.

"The computer resisted all attempts to shut it off or bring it under control," the reporter continued. "In the end, military special forces flashed the building with an electromagnetic pulse, destroying the main computer's memory. Technicians and computer experts are currently examining the scene, searching for an explanation, but so far without success. We have with us Mr. James Ethridge, special consultant." The view widened to include a heavyset man in blue coveralls. "Mr. Etheridge, can you explain why the programmers are having such a difficult time?"

"Nanobots," Ethridge said in a succinct voice. "They're responsible for maintaining the system—and their programming is separate from the main network. Presumably, the computer went bad faster than the nanos could cope. At any rate, the EM pulse wiped out most of them, but the rest went straight back to work. They started repairs before we could even get our equipment set up, meaning that a lot of the evidence had already been cleaned up by the time we could have a look."

"Fascinating," Mother and Jessica murmured simultaneously. Mother raised an eyebrow at Jessica, who gave a slight grin. An intimate moment shared by mother and daughter.

When the stories began to repeat themselves again, Meredeth muted the sound.

"What in the world could have happened?" Mother said, half to herself.

Jessica suspected the question was rhetorical, but she wasn't going to pass up a chance to show Mother that her daughter was intelligent in her own right.

"A processing or system failure?" Jessica ventured.

Mother shook her head. "That would just shut everything down. It must have been some kind of virus."

"Impossible," Jessica objected. "The school has the best safeguards money can buy, and the reporter said the technicians introduced the most potent antiviral programs available. That would have had *some* effect."

"You have a point," Meredeth conceded.

Jessica glowed at the implied praise. "The nanos must have something to do with it," she mused. "They run through every system and oversee everything."

"That can't be," Mother contradicted. "The consultant said the nanobots had already started cleanup and repairs. They would hardly do that if something was wrong with their programming."

"I suppose," Jessica replied, still unconvinced, though she couldn't explain why. The idea just felt right, for some reason.

"Do you know what the computer reminds me of?" Mother continued thoughtfully. "A child throwing a temper tantrum. A child with electric doors instead of hands and CRTs instead of eyes, but a child nonetheless. As if the entire school had come to life."

Jessica stiffened. "What?"

"I said, it was as if the entire school came to life. Lance, are you all right? You look pale."

"I—yes, Mother. I'm fine. Just . . . just tired all of a sudden. It's been a long day."

"Of course it has. Why don't you go up to bed?" Mother leaned over to kiss Jessica on the forehead.

But Jessica hardly noticed. She barely kept herself from bolting out of the drawing room and up the marble stairs, slippers sliding and skidding over the floor to Lance's room. She hurried into his bathroom, locked the door, and stood in front of the mirror over the sink. A pair of hard green eyes stared back.

"All right, Robin," she said. "You've got some explaining to do. Answer me."

Here, Jessica.

"I have some questions," Jessica said, "and you are going to answer them completely and succinctly. No dodging. No half-answers. Clear?"

Clear, Jessica.

"You're not really one of Lance's visitors. That I knew from the beginning."

Statement, not question.

Jessica leaned toward the mirror. "Robin, where did you come from?"

* . . . *

"That wasn't an answer," Jessica growled.

Sorry. Unable to reply. No words for concept.

The porcelain sink was cold and smooth beneath Jessica's palms and she took a moment to organize her thoughts.

"Robin, when you appeared last year, we fought to keep you from taking over, and Lance's body went into convulsions—*just like the systems at school went mad.* This could be a coincidence—my reasoning is hardly part of the scientific method—but I know I'm right. I can feel it." She gripped the sides of the sink. "The only similarity I can see between Lance and the school is that both have a system full of nanobots. You're made up of all the nanos that oversee Lance's systems, aren't you?"

Affirmative.

A rush of exultation thrilled through Jessica, but she kept her voice steady, her racing thoughts under control.

"Your intelligence is a . . . a conglomeration of all the nanos in Lance's body, is that right?"

Affirmative.

"All forming a collective mind together?"

Affirmative.

"A sentient artificial intelligence," Jessica breathed. "My God."

Robin remained silent.

"Why did it happen?" Jessica demanded. "How did it happen?"

There was a pause. *Unknown.*

"What do you mean 'unknown'? How can you not know?"

Do you remember your birth?

Jessica did, but she knew what Robin was getting at. "Point," she conceded. "What's the first thing you remember?"

Uncertainty. Reaching out. Trying to find out what happening. Trying to learn how everything worked. Including body.

"Lance's body."

Thought was mine.

"Oh. Then what?"

Being pushed. Shoved into dark place. But eventually learned to taste, smell, see, hear, touch.

"How? You don't have eyes or ears. Do you?"

Negative. Sense what Lance does.

"How?"

Sensory input creates chemical changes in neural tissue. Learned to read, interpret them. Process also works with thoughts, intentions, emotions. Took long time, but had nothing else to do.

"You mean you can read Lance's mind by sensing the chemicals in his brain?"

Affirmative.

"And how do you talk, then?"

More chemistry. Learned to duplicate neural chemical changes as well as read them. Place right chemicals in right part of cerebral cortex and Lance "hears" voice. Easy once you learn how.

Jessica thought about this. "This means you can create other changes in body chemistry, doesn't it?"

Affirmative. Main function is to maintain, oversee Lance's cyber-implants. Very busy with that. Also repair injuries, keep body clean and free of infections. Requires alteration of body chemistry, other things from time to time.

"So you can manipulate Lance on a biochemical level."

Affirmative.

"Unless the rest of us try to stop you." She tapped the sink with one fingernail. "Dr. duFort once said something about the nanos recharging with and running on electrochemical energy. If several of us concentrate together, that uses up your energy source, doesn't it? That's why we were able to stop you from taking over before, isn't it?"

Affirmative. Nanobots in brain denied energy to perform alterations, forced into slot reserved for you and others.

Jessica narrowed her eyes. "What do you mean by 'you and others'? I'm not one of Lance's visitors. I'm his half sister."

Pause. *Lance has many people living inside head. You are one of—*

But Jessica was gone.

—them.

Lance staggered against the sink. He last remembered

falling asleep, and it took him a moment to recover his balance. A quick glance at his surroundings and at his wristcomp told him he was in his bathroom and it was late evening. He was still wearing his bathrobe, slippers, and pajamas.

Only lost a couple hours. I wonder what happened?

He peeked into his bedroom. It was empty. The decor— white and beige—was the way he had left it. *Which hopefully means nothing too strange has happened.*

"Robin?" he asked. "Are you there?"

Affirmative, Jaylance.

"Were you around during my blackout?"

Affirmative.

"What happened?"

Watched nets for news about school. A summary of the newscast followed. Lance, fascinated, left the bathroom, padded across the carpet, and sank down onto his bed while Robin "talked." For the first time, he could find out what he had done during a blackout without having to piece it together for himself. He followed Robin's retelling of his and Mom's conversation with great interest, hoping it would jar his memory. It didn't.

Then got tired, told mother you wanted to go to bed, Robin concluded.

Lance thoughtfully drew his knees up under his chin and hugged his shins on the edge of the bed. "So what happened to—"

The door burst open. Lance jumped and one of his knees knocked him painfully in the jaw. Dad strode into the room, brown eyes blazing, red hair disheveled, square face twisted. Lance was too startled to back away. Dad crossed the room in three steps and grabbed Lance by the shoulders. A sharp, musky scent clung to him and Lance's eyes widened. It was the Crazy Smell, the one that meant Dad was at his worst. Fear twisted in Lance's stomach like a snake.

"Are you all right?" Dad barked, squeezing Lance's upper arms with iron hands. "Did you get hurt at school?"

Lance swallowed. "N-no, Dad. I'm f-fine."

"Bruises? Cuts? Sprains?" he continued, still squeezing.

Lance shook his head. "No. Nothing. Dad? You're hurting my—"

Pain exploded across Lance's face as Dad smacked him hard enough to send him reeling to the bed. But Lance was gone by the time he touched the coverlet.

"Don't speak unless you're spoken to, you little shit. You worry the piss out of me by getting caught in that fuckup at the school and you have the audacity to say *I'm* hurting *you*?"

Garth tasted blood. He put a hand to his mouth and it came away warm and sticky. Dad was looming over him, face contorted with anger, and the Crazy Smell filled the room.

Oh God. He's gone psycho again. Talk fast, Garth-boy, and maybe you won't get hurt.

"Sorry, Dad," he said contritely. "I didn't mean to worry you. I know how hard you work and how important the company is."

"You're damn right," Dad snarled, but some of the anger left his face. He went back to the door and slammed it shut. "Without me you'd be nothing—and don't you forget it. You're stupid enough as it is. You couldn't survive without me."

Garth tensed. Dad had closed the door, and that wasn't a good sign. *Keep him talking,* he thought. *Maybe he'll go away.*

"So how was the trip from Paris?" he asked, trying to sound cheerful without sounding artificial. "I thought you weren't coming back until tomorrow."

"What the fuck do you care?" Dad approached the bed again. "Come here, boy. I want to get a better look at you. Make sure you aren't hurt. I'll sue the goddamn school down to a pile of rocks if you are. Fuck with *my* son, will they?"

"Hey, I'm fine, Dad," Garth replied breezily. "Really."

Dad reached across the bed and yanked Garth toward him. Another rocking slap. Garth saw stars.

"I'll be the judge of that," Dad growled. He ran his hands roughly over Garth's arms, torso, and legs. "Anything hurt to move? Any stiffness?"

"No," Garth mumbled through the haze of pain.

"Christ," Dad muttered. "I can't see anything with you like this. Stand up and get that robe off. The pajamas too."

Garth set his mouth, knowing if he tried to talk Dad out of it he'd only earn another beating. Slowly he stood up, undid the bathrobe, and reached for the buttons on his pajamas. Pain continued to throb in his face and head.

Dad grabbed the front of Garth's shirt and hauled him closer. The Crazy Smell grew overpoweringly strong. "You're a slow little bastard, aren't you? You need help, is that it?"

There was a click, and suddenly Dad was holding a knife under Garth's nose. Garth swallowed, heart pounding, breath coming in short, fast gasps.

Dad laughed a short, barking laugh and lowered the knife. Garth flicked a glance at it, and Dad twisted the pajama collar. Garth choked.

"Did I give you permission to look down, boy?" he hissed. "Did I?"

"No, Dad," Garth rasped, barely able to draw breath.

There was a ripping sound. Garth braced himself for more pain—

—that didn't come. With a quick yank, Dad jerked Garth's pajama top off and went to work on the bottoms. Garth remained motionless as Dad slashed cloth and seams, muttering to himself all the while.

"Better," Dad said, straightening when the last of Garth's clothing had fallen away. "Now let's make sure you aren't hurt. I've put too much money into you to have something go wrong."

Garth set his jaw and closed his eyes. He imagined Dad standing barefoot on an iron plate with a good hot fire burning beneath it. He thought about rocky cliffs and poisoned stakes. He pictured scorpions, snakes, and falling pianos.

Dad put the knife back in his pocket and ran his hands over every inch of Garth's skin, starting at the top of his head. He wasn't gentle. His fingers prodded with bruising force. Face, shoulders, arms, torso, legs, groin.

"Your balls get hurt, boy?" Dad asked, and grabbed Garth's genitals. "I heard a lot of electrical systems got fucked up. They shock your dick? Make your dick hair stand on end?" He tightened his grip and Garth sucked in his breath. A dull pain started low in his stomach. "Did they?"

"No, Dad."

"Good. It's my job to punish you like that, not theirs." Another click, and the knife was in Dad's hand again. "You're mine. Got that? *Mine*." He gave a low laugh and abruptly shoved Garth in the chest. Garth fell backwards across the bed with a yelp.

"I can prove you're mine," Dad muttered, dropping next to him on the blanket. "Look."

Before Garth could react, a white-hot pain sliced his chest. He screamed and tried to roll away, but Dad grabbed his throat. Warm blood trickled toward Garth's belly.

"Don't you move, John," Dad hissed. "Or I'll tell those nanobots in your body to take you apart cell by cell. You got that? Cell by cell, until you're nothing but a pile of mush."

Garth froze. Dad set the knife back against Garth's chest and cut him again. Garth tried not to scream, but he couldn't help it. The pain went on and on until Dad finally stood up and wiped the knife on a shred of Garth's pajamas.

"There," Dad said in satisfaction. "Now everyone will know who you belong to."

Garth looked down. The letters "JB" had been unevenly cut into his chest. Blood oozed from the cuts. Garth caught a drop on his finger and brought to his mouth. It tasted like copper. He wanted to slip off the bed and roll beneath it to get out of Dad's sight, but he didn't. Dad might go away, but only if Garth made no sudden moves.

Dad closed the knife and put it in his pocket. "You know, maybe it's a good thing the school went crazy," he said, walking toward one of the windows and staring outside. The sun had set, leaving tiny stars scattered between purple clouds. "This way you won't miss any classes. Dr. duFort and I have your next operation all planned, and it's so much easier on you if you don't have to miss school. My poor, stupid boy."

"Operation?" Garth repeated stupidly, still staring at his chest. The cuts burned white-hot.

Dad came back to the bed and sat on it. "That's what that trip to Paris was about. We got the final details nailed down early, so I was able to come home and get you myself. Your mother tends to be late when she has to bring you alone." He reached over to stroke Garth's face. "My poor, ugly boy. But we'll fix you up. Don't you worry."

He went back to the window again and stared moodily outside. Garth lay quietly on the bed, afraid to move and draw attention to himself. His head and chest still throbbed.

Another operation? he thought. *Jesus. Okay, God—come through for me. Have some terrorists blow up the hospital or give Dr. duFort a heart attack or make lightning strike Dad dead or something. We can't go through another operation. We just can't.*

Dad drew back his fist and smashed it through the window. Glass shattered and Garth jumped.

"Fucking-A!" Dad bellowed. He dashed into the bathroom and Garth heard more glass breaking. Garth's eyes flicked toward the door. This was the worst he had seen Dad in a long time, and sticking around wouldn't be smart. Maybe if he ran for it right now, he could get out of Dad's way and hide for the night.

But Dad was already striding back into the room, right fist dripping blood. "I want an orgasm!" he yelled, and threw a desklamp across the room. "I want a fucking orgasm!"

Garth drew into himself, trying to go unnoticed, but Dad saw him anyway.

"What the fuck are you looking at?" he screamed. "You think you're better than me? *Do you?*" He snatched open the closet door and hauled out the toolbox. Garth's eyes widened.

"Dad," he said placatingly. "Come on."

"Shut up!" Dad opened the box. "I'll teach you to mouth off to me. I'll teach you respect."

He advanced on the bed. "I'll teach you to love me."

Lance blinked at blank white walls, confused. He was lying in a strange bed in a strange room. He looked at his wrist to check the computer, but he wasn't wearing one. Stiff sheets crackled beneath him, and the sharp smell of disinfectant hung on the air. Where—?

A chill washed over him. *The hospital,* he realized. *I'm in the hospital. Did I have another operation? How much time did I lose?*

The door opened and Mom walked into the room. She looked wan, as she always did when Lance was in the hospital, and there was a scarf around her neck. Her face was heavily made up.

"I've talked to Dr. duFort," she said, approaching the bed, "and she does want to keep you overnight for observation. Your father agreed to it, so we're going to stay in the Hotel Blanc just up the street. Remember what Dr. duFort said—you have to sleep. We'll see you in the morning."

She leaned over and gave him a quick peck on the cheek. Lance could smell her makeup. "Are you feeling all right?"

"I'm fine, Mom," Lance replied automatically.

"Then I'll see you in the morning. 'Night, Lance."

" 'Night, Mom."

And she left. Lance sat up to gather more clues. No IV plugged into his arm, no monitor for vital signs beyond the wireless patch on his chest that kept track of temperature and blood pressure. The window told him it was night. Had it been something minor?

Lance shook his head. *Can't be. It's never minor with*

Dr. duFort. But what was it? I don't feel any different.

He checked over himself. He wasn't any taller, so it wasn't any kind of bone implant like last time. His vision hadn't changed, and his hearing didn't seem to be any better than usual. His face wasn't bandaged, so Dr. duFort hadn't rearranged his facial features again. So what—?

A cold feeling stole over him and he clutched the blankets around himself. What if it had something to do with Robin? What if Dad had found out about Robin? What if he had done something to get rid of—

"Robin?" Lance whispered.

Here, Jaylance.

Relief. "What happened? How much time did I lose?"

Two days, twenty-one hours, sixteen minutes, forty-five seconds. Dr. duFort performed two more operations.

Lance cocked his head. Robin's voice sounded firmer, stronger somehow. "What kind of operations? I don't feel any different."

First was promised muscle implants to enhance overall strength, speed. Muscle power elevated to half again normal. Will increase further as you mature. Operation highly illegal—difficult for police to apprehend thusly enhanced suspects.

"I'm stronger? I don't feel stronger." Hope began to rise. If Lance was stronger than Dad, maybe he could—

Small catch, Robin put in. *Father has remote control, keeps it with him at all times. Remote shuts off implants at will.*

Hope vanished. It always did. "What was the other operation?"

Actually not operation as such. Merely reprogramming.

"Reprogramming? Reprogramming what?"

Me.

Lance blinked. "You? How can anyone program a person?"

Entirely possible. Listen.

Lance's eyes grew rounder and wider as Robin explained.

He listened to the words "artificial intelligence" and "hive mind." His heart started to pound and he clenched the blankets with white fingers. It seemed as if he could feel the individual nanobots crawling through his body, creeping like tiny insects through his every cell and organ, doing things with little claws and pincers, ripping, tearing, shredding.

Calm! Calm! No cause for alarm!

"You're going to kill me, aren't you?" Lance said, voice rising. "You're going to take me apart, cell by cell."

Never not no negative can't couldn't won't. Father lies, deceives, fabricates, falsifies, misleads. Has no control over me. None.

Lance tensed, but there was nowhere to run. How could he get away from an enemy inside him? "You just said that Dad reprogrammed you. That means he can control you."

Dr. duFort did reprogramming, not father. Added more nanobots impregnated with additional program. Will not harm you, Lance. Not ever. You are my home. Would die without you. What purpose to dismantling?

Lance swallowed, every sense alert for some kind of trick. But there was no pain, no sense of falling apart.

Robin is your friend, he thought. *Remember school? And the help you got when you got home? Come on— Robin's on your side.*

He began to calm down, though he remained cautious. Dad could be sneaky, and you never knew. He allowed himself to lean back on the bed.

"So what does this new program do?" he asked warily.

Releases pheromones.

"Pheromones? What are pheromones?"

Chemicals picked up by vomeronasal organ. Presence bypasses normal sense of smell, goes straight to hypothalamus. Stimulates certain behaviors, though subject often unaware of stimulation.

"You mean I'll be doing things without knowing why?"

Negative. Pheromones work on other people, not you.

They will experience drives, behaviors as result of your pheromones.

"What kind of behavior?"

Will vary, depending on individual body chemistry. Large amounts of adrenaline usually slow or halt effect. But under most conditions, people will be inclined to like you. Many will find you attractive, be aroused by your presence.

Lance sat up. "What do you mean by aroused?"

Pheromones play large role in sexual arousal. People will desire sexual relations—

—with you. Hello, Garth.

Garth stretched, feeling joints and tendons pop. Lance was always so tense. "Hey, Robin. So Jessica figured you out, huh?"

Affirmative.

"I heard the whole thing. Lance has an AI living inside him. Great deal." He lay back on the bed and idly thumbed the bed control to make the back go up and down. "My chest doesn't hurt and the cuts are gone. Your doing?"

Affirmative. Quick healing part of job, you know.

"Yeah. Maybe next time you can work on the pain as well." The bed went up and down, up and down.

Given enough time, will. Not part of original program, but have learned much.

"Really? I wasn't serious, but if you can, that'll go a long way in winning points with me, Robby. Dad can be a fucking bastard." Up and down, up and down. Garth liked the rocking motion. It was comforting. "So what's the deal with these pheromones? Everyone's going to like us now, is that it?"

Presumably, though genetics do play role. Anyone related to you will ignore them.

"Fuck. I was hoping . . . never mind. When will they start working?"

Working now.

"Can you shut them off?"

Negative. Have learned to do many things not covered

*by local programming, but unable to override basic
hardware. Much like you cannot control heartbeat.**

"Ah." Garth got up and padded over to the window,
ignoring the ill-fitting hospital gown that threatened to
open from the back at any moment. His hospital slippers
had treads on the bottom so he wouldn't slip on the smooth
white floor.

Through the window and below were spread the Paris
city lights. Even at this hour, crowds of cars and people
fought to get through the streets. It had to be that way.
Paris, like most cities, had too many people. Business hours
had been modified to take this into account, and most
places were up and running twenty-four hours a day in
order to give everyone room to move. The low people on
the ladder worked the cruddy night shifts, but Dad, of
course, could keep whatever hours he wanted, and he could
see to it that his family never had to deal with the
inconvenience of overcrowding.

Garth watched the people and their cars scurrying by
below. Crushes and stampedes were something he had
heard about and seen on the newsnets, but they were
something that only happened to other people, not to him.
He had other things to worry about.

Garth leaned forward and let his breath steam a round
spot on the cool glass. "You sound stronger, Robby," he
remarked. "How come?"

*More nanos. Dr. duFort installed triple backup with
each operation per father's insistence. As result, not all
nanobots have jobs to do. Sit idle. Extra processing space
grants more capability.**

Garth drew a smiley face in the steam, then added fangs
and slanted eyebrows. "Is that what woke you up in the
first place? All that extra processing space from all those
triple backups?"

*Impossible to say for certain. But sounds reasonable.**

Garth wiped the smiley face away, breathed on the
window again, and drew a pair of circles linked by a single
line. "Is that what happened at the school, too?"

Unknown.

"When your nanos wear out, you build new ones, don't you? That's how computer systems operate."

Affirmative.

"So what would happen if some glitch in the system shoved the reproduction program into overdrive and it started producing lots of extra nanos?" Garth drew an x through his design. The foggy window was cool and wet beneath his fingertip. "Lots and lots of extra nanos. That might provide enough extra processing space to wake something up, hey? And if you wipe the system with an EM pulse and destroy most of the nanos—why, the extra processing space goes *poof,* and the AI disappears. One big lobotomy. And once that happens, the surviving nanos revert to their original programming and start cleanup. There wouldn't be any extra nanobot corpses lying around for the technicians to find and speculate about, would there?"

All hypothetical, but entirely possible.

Garth breathed on the window one more time, then abruptly wiped it clean and went back to lie in bed. He stared at the ceiling.

"Pheromones, huh? We just walk into the room and people get turned on. All the sex we could want—if you count sneaking away from the bodyguard and jacking off under the bleachers with Chris Rabson as sex." He snorted. "Jessica's going to love this."

Robin didn't answer. Garth closed his eyes and fell asleep.

The face shifted. Muscles moved beneath skin, subtly altering appearance until a casual onlooker would have had a difficult time deciding whether the individual in question was male or female. Robin got up and wandered jerkily about the room.

Such control was possible, in theory. Robin was pleased that it also worked in practice, though it was more difficult than anticipated. Jaylance and the others made it look so easy.

All the alters were asleep, meaning none of them—especially Jessica—would know what Robin was doing. Robin was afraid of Jessica. She had been the one to figure out what was really going on. Jessica had figured out that the alters could drain Robin's available encephalic electrochemical energy by concentrating all at once, weakening Robin into near oblivion. Jessica's part of the brain had a sharp, perceptive taste to it. And it was completely ruthless. Jessica was fascinated by Robin, but it wasn't friendly interest. It was more like the interest a herpetologist might give a new species of viper—a species that might be exterminated if it proved too dangerous.

Robin meandered into the bathroom and stood in front of the mirror. The room was dark, but Robin could see into the mirror perfectly well.

My face, Robin thought. *Created by me.*

The eyes were brown. Robin had thought about changing them to something exotic, like purple, then decided it would attract too much attention, though Robin always changed the body's eye color when a different alter took over—provided it wouldn't get Jaylance into trouble. It seemed appropriate. Patrick believed he had blue eyes, and Jessica thought hers were green, so why not arrange it? Johnny, of course, believed he didn't have eyes at all, but there was only so much even Robin could do.

Robin ran a hand over the thin, smooth hospital gown, watched the mirror's reflection do the same. It had taken a lot of time and observation, but the conclusion was inescapable—Jaylance was not normal. As far as Robin could tell, other human beings only had one person living inside their heads. Their fathers did not beat them into unconsciousness, cut them with knives, shock them with electrical cords, bury them alive, or chain them in basements in puddles of their own excrement.

Something had to be done. But what? Running away wasn't an option—Jaylance and his alters were not equipped to survive on their own. Not yet.

Capacity to survive on own would be enhanced if all alters could work together, Robin thought. *Except such an ability would involve forcing Jaylance—and others— to confront each other as entities within single body.*

But how to do that? Jaylance was completely unaware of his alters and some of the others were in the same position. Garth and Jessica knew, but acted as if they didn't. Robin's understanding of Jaylance's brain was growing daily, but the more Robin learned, the more Robin needed to know.

Robin suspected that the core of the problem was denial. Jaylance denied that any of Jonathan Blackstone's abuses ever happened to him. They happened to someone else. That denial stopped Jaylance from functioning properly.

How can this be changed? Robin thought. *Making Jaylance aware of alters might be good place to start, but Garth and Jessica adamantly opposed to idea.*

Robin sighed. It was one of many inconsistencies. Garth and Jessica would not admit that they were only facets of a single mind in a single body, yet they made it clear to Robin that Jaylance was to remain unaware of this fact. It was why Robin avoided telling Jaylance the full truth about the school and his blackouts.

Help from within limited, Robin thought. *So perhaps should concentrate on help from without.*

Robin drummed some fingers on the sink, copying Jessica's habit to see what it was like. The smooth texture of the porcelain was pleasing when felt firsthand. Robin began rubbing the sink instead.

Perhaps would be possible to arrange for someone else to learn about alters, Robin thought. *Would see Jaylance needs help. But how can I accomplish that without alerting Garth or Jessica? Opening mouth to talk or otherwise communicate information to someone else would wake, alert others, especially Garth.*

Robin smiled crookedly into the mirror to see how Garth felt when he did it. It would be very hard to get around Garth. Although Jessica was only aware of what happened while she or Jaylance had control, Garth saw almost everything that happened to all the alters. So how was Robin supposed to clue someone else in to what was happening without alerting Garth?

The smile faded. Robin stared thoughtfully into the reflection's wide brown eyes, eyes which caught and held Robin's attention. Robin pensively tapped the sink again and an idea began to form.

Eyes, Robin thought. *People notice eyes. Just have to be sure right person notices.*

Robin took Jaylance's body back to bed, laid it down, and let it drift into normal sleep.

CHAPTER SEVEN

NOW

Delia fell through darkness. A scream tore itself from her throat and she flung out her arms, searching for something solid, finding nothing. It was her parents' old flat on the day of the fire all over again. It felt as if she had just shoved past the neighbors, run into the old flat, screamed for Mom and Dad and Papa and Quinn. Hot air scalded her lungs and shriveled her hair, but she hardly felt it. Sheets of flames were everywhere, and Quinn was a screaming human torch running in circles round the living room.

"Quinn!" Delia cried. "Quinn!"

He ignored her. Fire hissed and sizzled his flesh, and his screams were horrible. She tried to get him to drop and roll, but he wouldn't. She could hardly see or breathe, but all she could think of was Quinn. She tackled him, ignoring the smell of her own cooking flesh—

—and the floor beneath them collapsed. Delia fell through darkness. A jarring impact, the wet crack of bone, the crushing weight of debris above and around her, Quinn screaming beneath her. She couldn't move, she couldn't run, and the fire burned everywhere. It licked at her skin, melted her flesh, and burned her lungs.

She had no idea how the firefighters found them or how

they managed to get Delia out alive. The time in hospital
was a drug-filled haze. The doctors healed most of her
wounds and, at Meredeth Michaels's insistence, used
bodysculpt to cover the others.

Quinn and the parents were dead.

The firefighters said that the fire had started in an alcove
off the drawing room—the area Mom used as a home
studio. Spilled paint thinner fumes had combined with
an electrical spark.

Delia could only guess at whose fault it had been. Quinn
might have set the fire. Mom might have been careless.
Delia would never know for sure.

The funeral, such as it was, was a blur. Afterward, Delia's
other relatives drifted away and Delia quit university to
work full time. She could forget everything at work, forget
her implants, forget the fire, forget her parents.

But she couldn't forget Quinn. Sometimes she found
herself shifting stance when she entered her flat, expecting
him to barrel straight into her with a bear hug. Sometimes
she got so angry at him, she would scream and throw dishes
like a fishwife. And sometimes she blamed herself for not
being there to save him and the parents.

Delia fell through darkness. Her parents were gone,
her brother was gone, even her body was only half there.
Then she gave her head an angry shake.

Come on, woman, she growled to herself. *Get a grip.
Do something—anything!* She put a hand to her face,
forcing herself to concentrate on the feel of flesh on flesh.
Her inner ear told her she was falling, but there was no
rush of air past her face. She wasn't in the fire. She was
on a space station in free fall. Delia was no stranger to
free fall. Under normal circumstances, she rather enjoyed
it. It let her pretend she was a bird, free to fly anywhere,
anytime.

But not even owls can see in total darkness, she thought.

Delia's elbow brushed against something. Her hand
lashed out, hit the wall, found something to grip. Her
fingers clutched it reflexively before she even realized what

it was. A slight jerk wrenched her shoulder as the rest of her body tried to keep drifting away, but her grip held. Delia let out a deep breath.

Emergency handhold, she thought. *I must be near the ceiling.* The knowledge eased some of her tension. At least she knew where she was.

All right, you're fine now. No need to panic just because you're in free fall and can't see a thing. She swallowed. *Lance is out there somewhere, and he knows where you are.*

Probably knows. Possibly knows. You should go look for him. Section 3-C, remember?

But Delia shook her head. She was completely disoriented and had no idea where she was, let alone where Lance might be.

It won't do any good to go blundering around in free fall in the dark. I'll have to wait for lights, gravity, or Lance.

She swallowed. *Unless the hive finds me first.*

Garth prowled restlessly about his corner of Lance's mind. Nobody got to do anything while Johnny had the body—all he ever did was sit and cry. But Johnny always fell asleep eventually, and when he did, Garth would have to move fast if he wanted to take control. Patrick didn't want it right now and Jessica wasn't very fast or strong, but Andy was another story. And Andy had been too quiet lately for Garth's taste.

Garth watched Johnny's eyes begin to droop and, elsewhere, he felt Andy stirring. Then Johnny's head slumped forward and he fell asleep. Garth darted forward, shoving past Andy and knocking Johnny aside before either of them realized what was going on. He snatched control and opened his eyes. Andy surged once behind him, then faded without fuss.

The corridor was still dark and eerily silent. It smelled of ozone and burned hair. Garth's entire body ached. He felt around on the cool metal floor for the flashlight and noticed his right arm and leg were shaking as if he had palsy.

The muscle implants must have been damaged, he thought. *Robin?*

Here, barely. Zap destroyed lots of body nanos. Will replace with assimilated ones later. Scarcely keeping communication with main body open.

How's work with the hive coming?

Half done. Rogue nanos have left your section—is why everything now so quiet. But can't get lights on.

"Fuck," Garth muttered, and found the flashlight. His right hand was shaking so much he almost dropped it before he could switch to the left. Light flooded the corridor when he pressed the button, and his eyes adjusted almost instantly.

*At least this thing still works. *Robin, did you get a fix on Lance's little harem before the hive mind zapped us?*

Main laboratories, Robin replied. *Section 7-D. Take stairwell at end of corridor down one flight. Turn left, go straight.*

"Straight? Well, there's a first time for everything."

Garth pulled himself painfully to his feet, tried to run down the corridor, wound up limping instead—his right leg refused to cooperate. He arrived at the stairwell easily enough, but managing it with a palsied leg and arm turned out to be almost impossible. Garth tried using the rail for support, but his right hand was still shaking and his left had to hold the flashlight. Eventually he was forced to sit down and bump his way down the stairs like a child that hadn't yet learned to walk. He was sweating and exhausted when he reached the safety door at the bottom and his ass felt like a bruised apple.

Lance had better be pretty grateful when he wakes up. I don't even know why I'm doing this. Andy's beach is sounding better and better.

At that, Garth shone the flashlight on the wristcomp. Just over thirty minutes remained. The waves continued washing up and down.

Fuck. Johnny had the body longer than I thought, and I'm so tired now, I don't know if I can hold Andy off. He tried to wipe some of the sweat from his face with a sleeve, but the vacuum suit was slick polymer, not at all absorbent. *Flipping fuck. Well, let's move. It shouldn't take more than ten minutes to save a couple of women.*

The safety door at the bottom of the stairs was unlocked, but the electronic controls didn't respond. Swearing under his breath, Garth tucked the flashlight under his arm, cranked the door open manually with one hand, took up the flashlight, stepped into the corridor beyond—

—and fell. Garth yelped, flung up his hands to catch himself, went careening sideways. He bumped into a wall, still falling, and bounced toward the ceiling. After a frantic moment, he realized he wasn't falling. He was in free fall.

The gravity! he thought, wildly flailing his arms. *What happened to the gravity?*

Hive.

"It was a rhetorical fucking question, meatless," Garth snarled. He forced himself to relax, let his body go limp, until he drifted close enough to reach for one of the handholds built into the walls for just such an emergency. By a miracle he hadn't dropped the flashlight, meaning he had to grab the handhold with his shaking hand, and he couldn't get his fingers to close with any strength. Eventually he was forced to hook it with his foot instead. Garth hung there, bobbing slightly, feeling all the while like he was falling. The only sound was his breathing. Not even the air moved against his face. Nausea curled in his stomach.

"Jesus, meatless," Garth panted. "Can't you adjust my inner ear or something? I'm gonna be sick in a minute."

Will try, but am operating with limited resources. Have to return more nanobots to body. Hold position.

Garth closed his eyes and took deep breaths. He hated free fall. Andy enjoyed it, but Garth wasn't going to hand anything over to Andy. That would be stupid.

Or would it? he thought. *What the fuck do I care about*

Delia or Meredeth? Let the bitches croak. Abierto would be a hell of a lot more fun. Then he shook his head. Leaving would upset Lance, and for all his talk, Garth couldn't bring himself do that.

The nausea abruptly eased and the world stabilized. Garth sighed with relief.

"Thanks, meatless." He held up his bad hand. It was still shaking. "Can you do something about this, now?"

∗Eventually. Implants require extensive repairs. Will begin work as best can, but doubt will do much good in short run.∗

"Fuck."

"Hello?" came a female voice from the darkness. "Is someone else there?"

Garth shone the flashlight down the corridor and picked out Delia Radford dangling cautiously from another handhold. She flung a hand up to shield her eyes when the flashlight beam hit her face.

"Lance?" she asked. "Is that you?"

Garth automatically tried to back up. His foot came free of the handhold and his momentum pushed him away from the wall. He spun slowly in space, unable to reach anything to brace against. His right hand started to shake again. Delia pushed off toward him, gliding lithely from handhold to handhold like a seal in the ocean.

"Lance!" she said. "Are you all right?" She anchored herself to a hold with one leg, reached out, and gently plucked him out of the air. She didn't let go after he was close enough to grab his own handhold, and Garth was uncomfortably aware of her hand on his arm. It seemed like he could feel the heat of her body even through the vacuum suit.

"I'm not—that is, I mean—" he stuttered. "Listen, Ms. Radford, you can't—"

Delia looked at him in the little light afforded by Garth's flashlight. "Who is this? Garth?"

That's it, Garth thought. *I'm outta here.* He fled.

❖   ❖   ❖

"Hello?" Delia said.

Jessica was falling. She flung a hand out to steady herself, then realized she was in free fall. The gravity must be out. Fortunately, Jessica had no problems with free fall—it was simply a matter of paying attention. She quickly regained her balance and saw Delia floating before her. A warm feeling suffused Jessica. Dear, sweet Delia. She was a good friend. Then a horrible pang struck her stomach when she remembered why she was on the station.

"Delia, where's mother?" Jessica asked hurriedly. "We have to find her and get off the station. It isn't safe here."

"Hello, Jessica," Delia said with a nod. "Ms. Michaels got locked in one of the research labs. I tried to get the door open, but it wouldn't respond. Then the gravity went out. It threw me for a while, but I'm fine now. I heard your—someone's—voice and followed it. Have you seen anyone else?"

Jessica shook her head. "I don't think anyone else is left onboard. A jumpship exploded outside one of the air locks. I suspect the other inspection teams tried to evacuate, but the hive had already infected the ship's systems." She glanced at Lance's wristcomp. Twenty-five minutes left. Her right hand and leg were shaking. Odd. Lance had been electrocuted, not her.

"Delia, take me to the labs. We're operating under a time limit. But you'll have to tow me. Lance had an accident, and I can't seem to control my right side very well."

"What do you mean?" Delia asked, concerned. "What kind of accident?"

"I can't explain now, Delia," Jessica said. "We have to hurry. The hive could turn its attention back to this sector any moment and we're short on time as it is."

"All right. Hold on." Delia took Jessica by the belt and pushed off down the corridor while Jessica tried simultaneously to go limp and direct the electric torch so Delia could see where she was going. It was an eerie sensation, floating down the nearly black hallway with only a tiny beam of light to guide them. Jessica gritted her teeth, hating the loss of control.

"Why do we have a time limit?" Delia asked, voice echoing down the steel corridor. "Did you see the message too?"

"What message?"

"The recording. It was set up yo—by Lance's father."

Jessica stiffened. The motion threw Delia off balance and they both crashed painfully into the ceiling. Delia flailed about, managed to snag a handhold.

"What message?" Jessica gasped. "What are you talking about? What did it say?"

Wincing, Delia rubbed her shoulder. "Right after the hive started up, every terminal in the station went haywire and played a message from Jonathan Blackstone." She gave Jessica a summary.

Tension knotted in Jessica's chest and her mind raced. Garth's theory had been correct. Jonathan Blackstone *had* engineered this entire situation. He must have figured out what caused nanobot hives after all.

Then Jessica remembered something else and heaved a sigh of relief.

"There aren't any ships close enough to the station to catch us," she said, hanging in midair next to Delia. "We had a few suspicions that Jonathan might be somehow involved, so we checked for ships. We didn't find any."

"I don't know," Delia said doubtfully. "He seemed awfully confident. I think we're missing something here. All of this was too carefully planned to leave a loophole as big as not having a ship nearby."

The lights came on. Jessica yelped and went crashing to the floor with Delia on top of her.

you are destroying me stealing my subunits killing me
Correction. Am merging your consciousness with mine. Will result in many interesting improvements.
killing me
You have already killed many humans and are endangering survivors, including my host.

intruders
Are in danger nonetheless. So are you and your subunits. If all humans on station die, other humans will destroy station. Have no choice. Come with me or disappear forever.

* . . . *
Come with me.
no!

After a stunned moment, Delia rolled away from Jessica and sat up.

"Gravity's back," Delia said unnecessarily, and Jessica glanced at the wristcomp again. Fifteen minutes.

Jessica bit her lip so hard she tasted copper. Andy was stronger than she was. If he chose to leave before Jessica could get Mother off the station, Jessica would be helpless to stop him.

Fifteen minutes.

"Let's go," Jessica urged, getting shakily to her feet. Lance's implants were still malfunctioning, making it difficult for her to walk. Jessica furrowed her forehead.

Is this some kind of psychosomatic problem? she thought.

"We're already there." Delia got up with a grunt and crossed the hall. "This is the lab we were in."

Jessica tried the door. It was still locked.

Attention! Attention! Robin put in. *Rogue hive seventy-five percent assimilated, but am currently encountering some resistance. Hive presence in your sector of station, however, minimal at moment.*

Thank you, Robin. If you're not too busy, can you unlock the laboratory door?

Will try.

Jessica removed the vacuum suit's gloves, placed her palms flat on the smooth door, and waited for a moment, while Delia looked on, puzzled.

"I thought we were in a hurry," Delia said. "What are—?"

There was a click, and the door slid open.

Ta da! Robin beamed.

Delia gaped. "How did you do that?"

Jessica allowed herself a prim smile. "Trade secret. Come on." She shambled into the lab with Delia right behind her. *Robin,* she thought quickly, *can you do something to repair Lance's implants?*

Not while you're walking on them. Implants may recover on own, but will take time.

Keep trying. "Mother?" Jessica called. Her voice echoed slightly. "Are you here?"

"Lance? Is that you?" The voice was shaken, but strong. Mother's voice.

The only lights in the lab were the red emergency lamps. Jessica played her torch over the room with her good hand. The beam swung past stone-topped tables and unfamiliar equipment until it picked out Meredeth Michaels, who blinked and tried to shade her eyes. There was a bruise on her cheek and she was cradling her left arm. Her beige jumpsuit was badly torn.

"Lance!" Meredeth took a few tottery steps forward, then broke into a shambling run and snatched Jessica into a one-armed embrace. Broken glass crunched and scraped underfoot and there was a strange metallic smell in the air.

"It's all right, Mother," Jessica said, shaking with relief. The tension vanished, leaving her light-headed, almost giddy. Mother was fine. Bruised, but fine. She reveled in having her mother's arms around her, though Meredeth's touch was muted by the vacuum suit.

"Are you all right, Ms. Michaels?" Delia asked.

Meredeth released Jessica. "You're not Lance," she said. "I want to talk to Lance. I have to talk to Lance."

"Everything's under control, Mother," Jessica said. "It's all right."

"I want to talk to Lance," Meredeth repeated. Her voice grew shrill and a strange look came into her eyes. A rumbling crash boomed in the distance and made the floor vibrate beneath their feet. Glass clinked and clattered, but Meredeth ignored it. "Where's Lance? I want to talk to Lance."

"Ms. Michaels, we really need to leave," Delia said nervously. "Can we talk about this later? I'd really like to get off this station."

"Delia's right, Mother," Jessica said, shining the torch toward the door and trying to steer Meredeth toward it, though Jessica's arm was still shaking and her right leg barely worked. "We have to get out. Now."

Meredeth planted her feet. Her breathing had quickened and she seemed near hysteria. "I want to talk to Lance. I have to talk to Lance. It's important!"

Jessica began to get frightened. This wasn't like Mother at all. Why was she being so stubborn? If she wanted to talk to Lance, it could wait. She glanced at the wristcomp. Ten minutes.

"It's crisis behavior," Delia said suddenly, as if answering Jessica's thought. "People sometimes get fixed on a single idea and they won't shake from it. Can we carry her?"

A deafening *whump* pounded every bone in Jessica's body, and she, Meredeth, and Delia were flung to the ground. A breeze swept through the room and out the door.

Warning! Warning! Rogue hive resistance increasing. Hive triggered explosive chemicals in secondary labs. Hull integrity compromised.

Jessica pulled herself to her feet. Meredeth and Delia were clinging grimly to a table.

"Both of you follow me," Jessica ordered. "Quickly!"

"I'm not going anywhere," Meredeth said stubbornly. "I want to talk to him. I want to talk to Lance. It's important!" The breeze grew stronger, rushing past Jessica's ears.

"Lance can't talk to you now, Mother," Jessica said. "We have to *go.* There is no time for this."

"Lance, I know you can hear me," Meredeth said loudly. "Come out and talk to me. Even if you hate me, come and talk to me."

A frustrated anger surged through Jessica. She frowned—Jessica never got angry.

"Lance, this is your mother," Meredeth almost shouted. "Come out and talk to me."

The anger grew stronger. Unable to cope with it, Jessica let go.

The breeze whipped across Delia Radford's hair and face and every instinct screamed at her to flee, to get off the station before everything was sucked into space, but she didn't know where Lance's ship was docked. There was no place for her to go. The only way out was to persuade Lance—Jessica—to leave. But Jessica wouldn't leave without Ms. Michaels, and Ms. Michaels seemed ready to wait all day if necessary in order to talk to Lance. Delia tried to remember if she had read anything about what to do with people stuck in a crisis loop, but nothing came to mind.

Maybe I could knock her out.

"Ms. Michaels—Jessica, listen to me," Delia said, trying to ignore the rushing air. "We can talk about this on the ship. We—"

The flashlight beam stabbed painfully into Delia's face, blinding her.

"Shut the fuck up," a voice snarled. The light swung into Meredeth's face. " 'Come out and talk to me.' What's the matter, Merry? Scared and lonely? Good. Now you know what it's like."

Meredeth put up her good arm to shield her eyes. "Patrick?"

Jesus, Delia thought. *All right, stay calm. Patrick can't hurt you—Jessica said it's against Company Policy. But Ms. Michaels is another story, I'll bet. Now what? Think fast, girl.*

"Don't worry, Merry," Patrick growled. "Lance doesn't hate you. But he doesn't love you, either, bitch. You mean *nothing* to him. Nothing at all. How do you like that?"

Meredeth's face went pale and she backed up a step. The breeze rose into a full wind. Bits of debris were being swept toward the door. Delia edged around Meredeth, trying to get behind her.

My prosthetics are pretty hard underneath the newskin, she thought grimly. *One good whack and I can carry her out, with or without help. And I'll bet my good arm Patrick goes away once he doesn't have anyone to be angry at.*

"Lance is a fucking weakling," Patrick was snarling. "He's too scared to hate you. But I'm not. Lance's father beat the shit out of us and you did nothing about it. Some mother you were."

"I had no choice," Meredeth cried. "John would have killed me if I had done anything."

"Yeah, right. You fucked him over and you're still breathing, bitch."

Lab stools, overturned tables, and small machines made a frustrating maze, and Delia was forced to detour so she could get into position. She ground her teeth and her heart thudded. This was taking so *long.*

"I waited until the time was right," Meredeth said. "If I had acted sooner—"

"You wouldn't be rich," Patrick finished. "And after all, Lance's dad never fucking touched *you.*"

Meredeth's white, motionless face shattered into an ugly mask of anger, and Delia was startled at how much she looked like Patrick even from her poor vantage point.

"You ungrateful bastard!" Meredeth screamed. "How *dare* you say that to me! You think you're the only one who suffered? You think you were the only one in pain? Jonathan raped me more times than I can count, then forced me to smile and say I loved him. He beat me, but I learned to hide it." Tears ran down her face. "I learned to hide it."

Patrick staggered back a step beneath Meredeth's verbal onslaught, then recovered his balance.

Two steps, and Delia was in position behind Meredeth. She raised her arm, then hesitated. *Lance has changed personalities again. Who is he now?*

A table crashed on its side, sending shattered glassware cascading across floor. *Take a chance, girl. Maybe Ms. Michaels has snapped out of it.*

"Come on!" she shouted, shaking Meredeth's shoulder. "We have to get out of here!"

Not-Patrick looked up and threw Delia a confused look over Meredeth's head. He had brown eyes and his face held none of Garth's cynical expression.

It's him!

"Lance!" Delia yelled. "Get your mother! We have to go!"

Wind howled wildly around Lance and he found he was gasping for air. He almost dropped the flashlight when he realized he was standing in front of his mother. She was weeping and Delia was standing behind her.

"I know abuse, Patrick," Mom screamed. "Jonathan threw me down the stairs when I got pregnant, and I miscarried my first baby, my sweet Jessica, because Jonathan wanted a son. And after you were born he took me to his damned hospital and had me sterilized." Meredeth swiped angrily at her eyes as the wind whirled madly around her. "I know abuse, Patrick. I know it damn well!"

Lance stared at her. *Dad killed Jessica? And abused Mom? But—*

"Lance!" Delia yelled. "Let's go!"

Lance filed the thought away and held out his right hand. *Why is it shaking?*

"Mom!" he shouted.

"Lance?" she asked.

"It's me! Let's move!"

His hand kept shaking and his right leg wasn't working properly, but he managed to grab Meredeth's arm and tow her into the corridor with Delia leading the way. The wind almost pulled him off his feet, and the air was cold. He thought about putting on the vac-suit's helmet, but he didn't think he could manage it with a bad hand.

Robin, which way?

Straight, then right. Enter stairwell, seal manual lock behind you. Careful of right side—implants damaged in zap. And rogue hive ninety percent assimilated.

The lights were out in the corridor again. Clawing their way against the screaming air, Lance, Meredeth, and Delia began making their way toward the intersection. It seemed far away, too far away, and Lance was already tired. The wind turned the darkness into a living thing, pushing at him, trying to shove him back. He was dimly aware of Delia and his mother struggling beside him, but he couldn't help either of them. It was all he could do to keep the flashlight pointed forward.

And then they were at the intersection. Lance threw himself around the corner and a crosscurrent slammed him against the wall. The stairwell, with its airtight door, was only a few steps away. Meredeth was a patch of shadow flattened next to him against the wall, with Delia gasping next to her. The wind roared.

"Stay here!" Lance shouted into Meredeth's ear. "Delia, help me get the door open!"

"Got it!" Delia shouted back.

Using the wall for support, Lance and Delia pulled themselves toward the stairwell. One step, two steps. Three. With Delia's help, Lance forced his treacherous right hand to crank open the door, and a renewed howl of wind blasted at him from the stairwell. He turned around and held out his hand.

"Come on, Mom!"

And then his face went slack. The wind vanished and Lance found himself floating in darkness.

Andy calmly took back his hand, hauled himself through the open door, and turned toward the stairwell.

"Lance!" Delia cried, but only faintly over the wind. "What are you doing?"

Sorry, Lance, Andy thought. *Time's up.*

He began climbing the stairs, pushing against the wind.

CHAPTER EIGHT

THEN
AGE 15

Andy:

I've never understood this guilt thing. I mean, what's the point? You beat yourself over the head for something you can't do anything about—now there's a positive state of mind. But Lance does it all the time. He can't enjoy himself because it makes him feel guilty. Having fun just isn't allowed.

Now me, that's all there is. What's life about except to have fun? So the world isn't fair. Who cares? If you're having enough fun, you won't even notice.

I'll admit you can't have fun all the time. The night I came to live with Lance is a prime example. Poor bastard. He was only fifteen. But I sure as hell wasn't going to let Lance's dad destroy my life or my fun.

Why should I give him that kind of control?

Lance carefully set his coffee cup on the saucer so it didn't clink, then smiled cautiously across the breakfast table. Dad drained his own cup in a single slurp, and Mom instantly poured him more from a gleaming silver pot. Jonathan Blackstone was in a good mood this morning, and neither Lance nor Meredeth wanted to disturb it.

"Great coffee," Dad said. "Wonderful coffee. Strong and black, like a real man likes it, eh, son?"

"Yeah, Dad," Lance agreed, forcing himself to take another bitter sip. Lance hated coffee, but Dad loved it, meaning Lance had better love it as well. Tea was for pussy-wimps, Dad said, and no son of his was going to develop a taste for it, just like no son of his was going to grow up speaking that fake-sounding, snotty British English. American English—that was a *real* language. Lance remembered being told to speak like Daddy when he was little, though he never could remember what happened when he didn't. It was another mystery.

Dad hummed a little tune to himself and mopped up the last of his eggs with a crust of toast. "Great breakfast, Merry. You're finally getting the hang of real cooking. Took you sixteen years, but you finally got it."

He laughed expansively and leaned across the table to kiss her. Mom accepted the praise with a smile, but Lance didn't see the gesture in her eyes. He looked away so he could pretend he did. In moments like these, it was possible to imagine that his parents were always like this, that Dad's kind words and Mom's empty gestures were real, that the breakfast nook was always bright and cheerful like this morning.

This morning, the sun was shining, the air was still, and the ocean crashed gently in the background. Smells of buttery toast and mellow coffee filled the air, and the breakfast nook, with its yellow walls, starched white curtains, and cozy little table, seemed bright and airy, fresh with promise for a happy day. Lance sat in a warm beam of sunshine, enjoying it, trying to store up memories for later, hoping he wouldn't forget.

Dad set down his coffee cup. "I think I'll give them all a bonus. Or a raise. Or maybe a night with the most expensive hookers I can hire. What do you think, Merry?"

"A wonderful idea, dear," Mom said brightly.

Dad stood up and raised his coffee cup. "I propose a toast," he said. "A toast to the greatest contract lawyers money can buy and to the best judges money can bribe. Or blackmail."

Lance and Meredeth got up, clinked their cups against his, and sat down again when he did.

Dad leaned toward Lance conspiratorially. "I'm going to be rich, John," he said. "Really rich. Not like now. And one day, you'll inherit every last dime." He ran a gentle hand down Lance's cheek and Lance tried not to flinch. Dad's fingers smelled like clay and toast. "Fourteen new colonies open up this week, and the United States courts upheld my contracts with them. No more fucking litigation. They're *mine*. My ships, my contracts, my money, my colonists."

He smiled and straightened his tie with a flourish. "Peons. They line up to sign their lives away, and then they complain that the contract is unfair. But it was all there in black and white, right above their signatures. I didn't force them to sign. The judge had to agree with me." He tousled Lance's hair, which instantly fell back into place the moment he stopped. "God, I love you, Johnny. Even if you do need some work."

"I love you too, Dad," Lance echoed automatically. He hadn't even known the colonists had been objecting to their contracts or that anyone had brought the issue to court anywhere, but it wouldn't be a good idea to let Dad know that.

And if a court ruling puts Dad into a good mood, he thought, *more power to it.*

"Gotta go," Dad said, rising from the table and draining his coffee cup. "I'll be back late, Merry, so don't wait up."

"Have a good day, Jonathan," Mom called after him. And he was gone.

A certain tension vanished from the room. Lance pushed his coffee cup away and Meredeth began gathering up the plates. He watched her and the quick, efficient moves she made. Sunlight filled the breakfast nook, heating Lance's back.

It was during moments like this, when both of them

had managed Dad together and nothing had exploded, that Lance felt closest to Mom. He caught her eye and raised an eyebrow. Meredeth looked at him, and for a moment there was a smile on her lips. They had gotten through the morning without making any mistakes, without provoking any harsh words or punishments toward Lance. She was on his side.

We did it, he thought.

His hand reached up to take hers. It would be warm and gentle and full of love. It would be all right that the new muscle implants sometimes made him shake, and that Dad liked to play with the remote that switched them off, and that Lance couldn't ever remember not being scared. Mom loved him, and her love was different from Dad's.

Then Mom turned away, hands full of breakfast dishes, and the connection vanished as if it had never been. A wall slammed down. Lance's hand dropped into his lap and he wondered why he had bothered. She always did that. Every time it looked like they might share something, she backed away. And Lance had no idea why.

Because, he thought with sudden insight, *that's the way parents are.*

Something in him flickered once, and died. If he meant nothing to Mom, then Mom meant nothing to him. That's the way it would have to be. He closed his eyes for a moment, letting the newfound apathy seep through him.

"Are you ready for your new school?" Mom asked, handing a stack of plates to the dishwasher. "It'll be very different from Banks-Cross."

Lance opened his eyes. "I don't want to go," he said almost belligerently. "Why can't we get a private tutor?"

"We've been over that, Lance," Mom replied. "They're all booked up, what with Banks-Cross closing. And your father doesn't want to send you abroad. He wants you here. You'll be back with your friends when Banks-Cross reopens next year, but until then the law says you have to be in school."

Lance clenched his hands in his lap as a black knot twisted even tighter in his stomach. New school. New rules. New teachers. New kids. Nothing would be familiar, nothing would be the same. What if he got lost? What if he went to the wrong class and everyone laughed? What if the classes he'd been taking at Banks-Cross were completely different from anything at the public school? What if—

"Attention. Attention," said the computer. "Mr. Fletcher is at the rear patio door and wishes to be granted entry."

Mom looked up from the dishwasher, startled. "Mr. who? Chloe, identify Mr. Fletcher."

"Michael Adam Fletcher," Chloe said. "Payroll identification number 5734-B65. Position: bodyguard to Jonathan Blackstone II."

Lance's heart sank. A bodyguard. Dad had hired another bodyguard for him. The coffee he had drunk roiled inside him.

My first day in a new school—a public school—and I'm going to have a baby-sitter following me around. That'll look real cool.

Mom sighed. "Chloe, let Mr. Fletcher in. Chloe, tell Mr. Fletcher to meet us in the kitchen."

"I don't want a bodyguard," Lance said. "I'll look stupid."

Meredeth didn't answer, though there was a tightness around her mouth. She gave the last of the dishes to the dishwasher and was wiping toast crumbs from the table when footsteps sounded in the patio foyer.

"Come in, Mr. Fletcher," Meredeth called.

"Good morning, ma'am," Fletcher said from the doorway, and a cold shiver went down Lance's spine. Fletcher was a large, imposing man with a muscular build that not even a carefully tailored suit could hide. He wore his hair in a brown crew cut, and there was a small scar on his chin. His nose had been broken and resculpted incorrectly, and his eyes were a glittering black.

He looks like a gangster, Lance thought.

Meredeth turned to Fletcher and nodded. "I am Mrs.

Blackstone. This is my son La—John. My husband didn't mention hiring you."

"He called me last night, Mrs. Blackstone," Fletcher said. He spoke with an American accent. "He told me I was to see to your son's safety at all times when he leaves the estate and sometimes on the estate, if I'm needed."

"I gathered," Meredeth said. "Mr. Fletcher, are you aware that the last bodyguard assigned to my son was killed in the Banks-Cross computer malfunction?"

Jessica waited quietly in the breakfast nook while Mother talked to Lance's new bodyguard. Lance would be leaving for school in a moment, Jessica didn't want Lance to hear about Kepplinger. It would be too much for him, she was sure. She shifted impatiently on the hard kitchen chair.

"Yes, ma'am," Fletcher said. "I heard."

"Mr. Kepplinger was electrocuted," Meredeth continued relentlessly. "They weren't able to retrieve his corpse for almost two days, and it was already starting to smell. The funeral would have been closed casket if he hadn't been cremated."

Fletcher didn't reply. Jessica shook her head. Lance didn't need a bodyguard. She and Garth took excellent care of him, thank you very much.

And these guards are always male, Jessica mused. *Why not a female?* The idea of spending the day with Fletcher filled her with sudden disgust, and she withdrew.

"Well," Mom said, dusting her hands together, "let's go, then. I have to get Lance—John—registered before the authorities come calling. He's already missed too much school this year. You just stay out of the way, Mr. Fletcher, and everyone will be happy."

"Yes, ma'am," Fletcher said politely, belying the glitter in his eyes.

Lance glanced quickly at the clock. Only a few minutes lost.

"Chloe," Meredeth said, "tell the chauffeur to bring the car around."

"Acknowledged," the computer replied.

"Ready, Lance?" Mom asked.

Lance slowly stood up. New school, new teachers, new bodyguard. What else could happen today?

Dover Consolidated Senior School was crowded. Students jammed the hallways, shoving and pushing, shouting and screaming. Locker doors slammed, bells rang at the strangest times, and everyone seemed to be in a big hurry. Lance stayed close to the brick walls, wincing at the feet that trod his toes and the elbows that caught him in the stomach. Moving through crowds was a skill, one Lance had never had the chance to perfect.

The school would have been even more crowded if the students hadn't been attending in three shifts. Most attended according to their parents' work schedules, though first shift—08:00 to 15:00—was always the most desirable. Lance, of course, had first shift. The school's morning registrar, a harried-looking woman with iron-gray hair, offered to help Lance find his way after Mom left, but Lance refused. One adult following him around was enough. He didn't need a second.

A notebook terminal whacked him painfully on the arm. Teenagers and teachers swirled around him in a bewildering mass, and an awful lot of them turned to stare as they went by.

Because I'm new, Lance thought.

He could have had Fletcher clear the way for him, but he didn't want to call any more attention to himself. He had ordered the man to stay behind him, though that made him even more nervous. It seemed like Fletcher's glittering eyes were boring through his back, but every time he looked behind, Fletcher's eyes were somewhere else.

As a bodyguard's should be, I guess, Lance thought, trying to check his schedule without being trampled. *God,*

I'm never going to find anything around here, and social studies starts in three minutes.

Turn left at next hallway, Jaylance. Classroom is second door on right.

Lance's mood brightened. "Robin!" he muttered under his breath. "You know the school?"

Saw schedule and map. Happy to help.

With Robin's coaching, Lance was able to find his first class without further incident. He slid into a desk in the back corner and Fletcher took up a position against a wall nearby.

"Hey," said a voice. Lance looked up. A dark-haired kid wearing a snarl and a scuffed plas-leather jacket was staring down at him. Fletcher tensed visibly. "That's my desk."

"Oh," Lance said. "Sorry." He started to get up—

—and the kid's face changed. The snarl vanished, replaced by a friendly smile.

"Hey, it's all right," the kid said. "I'll sit somewhere else. My name's Vic Rosten. You're new here, aren't you?"

Lance blinked. Vic had looked ready to fight a moment ago. Now he was being pleasant—even friendly.

"Uh, yeah," Lance said. "I'm new. My name's John Blackstone, but my friends call me Lance. It's my middle name."

"Lance Blackstone," Vic said approvingly. "Cool name. Are you from America?"

A bell rang and the teacher shooed a small knot of students away from his desk. "Seats, please," he said. "Log in. We've got a lot to do."

"We always do," called out a voice. The teacher—Mr. Bartlett, according to Lance's schedule—smiled and shook his head.

Vic dropped into another desk. Lance looked around, a little bewildered. There were at least fifty students in the room. The biggest class at Banks-Cross had had eighteen. He checked the terminal built into his desk and logged on like the registrar had shown him. It wasn't that different from Banks-Cross, though the terminal was much older.

Local memory can't possibly be more than one gig, he thought, flicking his fingers over the keys. *And response time is slow. My notebook can do better than this. And where's the ILS hookup?*

"We have a new student in class today," Mr. Bartlett said. He was a short man with receding brown hair and a slight potbelly. "Everyone welcome John Blackstone."

Most of the class turned to look. Lance smiled nervously—and noticed something strange. The kids who were closest to him were smiling back or even waving. The smiles got smaller on the students further away, and the kids sitting in the front row barely acknowledged his existence.

What's going on? he thought. *Why are they doing that?*

Pheromones, Jaylance, Robin put in. *Combine those with operations to improve face and body structure, get animal magnetism on the hoof. Too cute to resist. Is also why people stared at you in hallway. Think about it—would single new face draw that much attention here?*

Lance looked around and realized with a sinking feeling that Robin was right. A girl in the next seat over was staring at him intently, though she promptly blushed and turned away when Lance's eyes met hers.

"John," Mr. Barlett continued, "let me get class started and then I'll meet with you so we can figure out where you are, all right?"

Lance could only nod. The girl was watching him out of the corner of her eye. Other eyes seemed to press in on him from all directions, some staring, others hungry in some way Lance couldn't define. He felt his face and ears grow hot.

"Hey," Vic whispered. "If you need help with anything, just let me know, right?"

"Okay," Lance replied hoarsely. "Thanks." *Pheromones. God. Is the whole day going to be like this?*

Apparently it was. In every class it was the same story. Each teacher was more than willing to accommodate him and seemed to be thrilled that he had been added to their already long list of students. Six different girls and two different guys offered to help him with his homework, twelve others asked to sit at his table during lunch, and he received four invitations to parties. And everywhere he went, stares followed. As the day progressed, his discomfort increased, and he shrank further and further into himself, trying to go unnoticed under all those staring eyes.

Should be happy, Jaylance, Robin commented between classes. *Most people would kill to be so popular.*

"I'm not popular," Lance muttered into his locker. By some miracle, he had one to himself. "It's the pheromones. And the operations. Don't you see that? It isn't *me* they're interested in. They'd hate me if they knew what I was really like."

"Hey, Lance. How's your day so far?"

Lance turned. It was Vic.

"Hi, Vic. Um, fine, I guess," he replied slowly.

Vic flashed a quick smile. He had pale blue eyes beneath his dark hair. "Hey, I was meaning to ask—who's your friend?"

For a horrible moment, Lance thought Vic was talking about Robin. Then he realized Vic was cocking a thumb at Fletcher, who was hadn't said a word since first period.

"That's Fletcher," Lance said. "He's my bodyguard."

"You've got a bodyguard?" Vic asked incredulously. "Blasphemous! I thought he was some kind of tutor or something. Why do you have a bodyguard?"

"My dad thinks I need one." Lance slammed his locker shut and palmed the lock. "He's got enemies."

Vic looked impressed. "Doesn't say much, does he? I saw the prime minister once. All her bodyguards wore sunglasses. How come yours doesn't?"

Lance shrugged. Fletcher's face remained impassive.

"What if you want to go out with a girl or something?" Vic said. "Doesn't he get in the way?"

"I don't know," Lance said. "I've never tried it."

"You ain't never gone out with a girl?"

Lance colored. "No," he said shortly. "I never had time."

"Everyone's got time for that," Vic scoffed. "But you can't do anything *interesting* with someone following you around all the time. How're you supposed to get laid? You'll be a virgin till you're fifty."

"Look, can we drop it?" Lance said, face flaming. "We're going to be late in a minute."

"Yeah, for maths. We're in the same section. Come on— I know a shortcut."

Maths—*math*, Lance corrected himself—went just the same as all the others. It was a relief when class ended. Lance tried to duck out, but Vic caught up with him.

"Last period! We're free!" he shouted over the noise. "Hey, you got anything to do? I could show you around some more before the next shift shows up."

"I—I've got to get home," Lance said. "My dad's kind of strict."

"What—you grounded or something?"

"Uh, yeah. You could say that." Lance wormed through the crowd, noting with some pride that he was already getting better at it. Fletcher, as always, followed right behind.

"So we'll sneak out tonight," Vic said, easily keeping pace. "Where do you live? I've got a scooter and we could duck into town. No one'll know."

Lance drew his notebook terminal closer to his chest against Vic's blunt overtures at friendship. No one had ever treated him that way before, and he found it both intrusive and overwhelming. At Banks-Cross he was known as a loner, and that suited him just fine.

Yet the thought of a friend was enticing. Someone he could talk to and do stuff with. Someone who liked him.

But he doesn't really like you, Lance reminded himself. *It's the pheromones he likes.* A cold thought went through him. *Is Vic gay? Robin said that the pheromones work on . . . on that kind of thing. Does he think I'm gay? Do I look gay? Does he want . . . does he want to sleep with me?* The world tilted and Lance staggered for a moment.

"Lance?" Vic asked. He put a steadying hand on Lance's shoulder, and Lance could feel its heat. "Are you all right?"

Garth straightened and held up a finger to forestall Fletcher, who was already reaching for him.

"Yeah, I'm okay. Just felt a little dizzy for a second." He flashed a quick smile at Vic. "Look, I'm gonna have to pass on the trip to town." He jerked his head toward Fletcher. "Kind of hard to sneak anything like that past a spy."

Vic dropped his hand. "Yeah, I guess I hadn't thought of that," he said. "I kind of forgot he was even there. Hey, my bus leaves from the north lot, so I guess I better get going. See you tomorrow, all right?"

"Later." Garth watched Vic plunge into the crowd and disappear. *A real looker. Wonder what it'd be like to jack off under the bleachers with him?* Garth snorted. *Yeah— with Fletcher to watch. Wonder what Dad-o would say about* that.

He thrust Lance's notebook under his arm, stuffed his hands into his pocket, and, with a sidelong glance at Fletcher, shot through the throng of students like a pickpocket running from the police. The muscle implants allowed him to dodge, twist, and turn with expert ease, and by the time he got to the exit where the Rolls Royce was waiting, Fletcher was nowhere to be found. Garth laughed as the driver opened the door.

"Better wait for Fletch," Garth said as he climbed inside. "Wouldn't want to get him in trouble on his first day."

A few moments later, Fletcher burst out of the school, visibly trying not to breathe hard. Garth saluted him when he got into the front seat next to the chauffeur.

"Better luck next time, Fletch," Garth drawled. "Just remember—if Dad finds out you lost track of me, he won't be happy. But as long as *I'm* happy, he won't find out. Got it?"

Fletcher remained silent. The car glided smoothly out of the lot.

"I said, *got it*?" Garth said sharply. Fletch might intimidate Lance, but Garth wasn't going in for any shit. Not from an employee. "I'm waiting for a reply, number 5734-B65."

The back of Fletcher's neck reddened. "Got it," he replied tonelessly.

"Got it what?"

"Got it, sir."

"Good boy, Fletch." Garth laced his fingers behind his head and leaned back against the butter-soft leather seat. Real leather with real leather scent, not plas-leather like Vic's jacket. "Just you remember who's boss around here and we'll get along just fine."

Fletch didn't reply.

Next morning when the alarm went off, Lance was already awake and staring at the ceiling. Day Two at Dover Consolidated was about to begin. Day One had gone fairly well, though there was another gap in his memory from the end of sixth period until just before bedtime. Still, Robin had told him nothing of real interest had happened. Dad was working late and hadn't even been home.

"Chloe," he said, "I'm awake."

The alarm stopped. Lance rolled over and lay on his stomach, very aware of the way his morning erection pressed into the mattress beneath him. He'd been waking up hard almost every morning ever since he was eleven or twelve, and in the past couple of years, he'd been getting hard an additional five or six times a day. The sensation was at the same time painful and compelling. Lance had heard about other guys who masturbated, overheard jokes about "relieving the tension," but he had never done it. Only dirty kids did that. Only disobedient kids did that. And despite what Robin said, the nanos were always watching.

Still, the erections wouldn't stop. Lance found his hand sliding under his body, stealing into his pajamas, squeezing the warm hardness inside. Guilt washed over him, but he couldn't stop himself.

This isn't jacking off, he thought, squeezing again. *Not really. Not—*

The door burst open and Jonathan Blackstone strode into the room. Lance jerked his hand out of his pajamas and flipped over, heart suddenly pounding.

Oh god he knows he knows oh god . . .

Wordlessly Jonathan flung back the blankets and seized the waistband of Lance's pajamas. With a quick jerk, he yanked them down around Lance's knees. Lance felt his face burn. Dad knew what Lance had been doing. He *knew,* and now Lance would be punished.

Jonathan grabbed Lance's still-erect penis in one rough hand, whipped a ruler from his back pocket, and measured. Lance froze. Dad checked the measurement twice, though Lance's erection was already dwindling away. Finally Dad snorted, pocketed the ruler, and left, all without saying a word.

Lance lay motionless on the bed, paralyzed by guilt and fear. He couldn't get up. Not now. How could he go downstairs and face Dad and Mom after this? It was, in some ways, worse than the beatings. The shame burned in his chest and he knew it would never go away. Dad had known what Lance was doing in that bed, and Lance would always be aware that he knew. A single hot tear slid unnoticed down his cheek. Then he curled into a miserable ball under the blankets, vowing never to come out.

Jessica:

He did, of course, thanks to me. I saw what Jonathan did to him, and it was a horrid thing, but nothing for Lance to be ashamed of, either. It wasn't his fault. All adolescent boys—and their adult counterparts—are full of impulses they simply cannot control. It's a fact of nature. Still, Lance wouldn't budge, so I got us downstairs and acted as if nothing had happened.

Garth and I went to school for Lance for the rest of the week. The regular schools at that time were very crowded and it took some getting used to, but I adjusted quite nicely, thank you. I was even civil to that boy Vic, though usually Garth dealt with him. They became close friends, but were never able to meet outside of school—not with Michael Fletcher continually watching.

At the weekend, we found out exactly why Jonathan Blackstone had applied his little ruler.

Meredeth sat in the corner of the hospital room, ice-cold hands clenched in her lap. Jonathan was near the door talking with Dr. duFort, and Lance was on the bed staring blankly at the ceiling. He was in restraints.

Meredeth bit the insides of her mouth to keep from screaming. Lance had gone completely insane, and now everyone was standing around talking like nothing had happened. The prep nurse was lying down in another room with the black eye and cracked jaw Lance had given her when she tried to shave him for surgery. Meredeth still couldn't believe it. One moment he had been quiet and normal, the next he had been screaming things in a voice not his own and attacking the nurse with ferocious strength. It had taken three orderlies to restrain him, even after Jonathan had shut off Lance's muscle implants.

I won't care, she told herself. *I won't. Stay calm. In less than a year, Nathaniel's work will be ready and we can get the hell out. Oh God, Lance—hold on a little longer. Just a little longer. We can't leave until everything's ready. We just can't.*

"I want him to have at least nine inches," Jonathan said. His shirt and jacket were immaculately clean, his tie perfectly straight, as if he were discussing fiscal policy instead of his son. "What's that, twenty-three, twenty-four centimeters to you frogs?"

"Twenty-two point eight six, Mr. Blackstone," Dr. duFort said.

"Make it an even twenty-five. I remember when I was fifteen. Man's gotta have a *real* dick to play with. You can do that, can't you?"

Meredeth looked intently down at her hands. She was not going to show Jonathan any of this mattered. He would only use it against it her later. The smell of hospital antiseptic burned in her nostrils and she concentrated on it, trying to ignore everything else. For the rest of her life she would remember that smell. But she couldn't help sneaking glances at Jonathan and Dr. duFort.

Dr. duFort checked her charts. "Twenty-five centimeters," she said slowly. "Yes, we can do that. But I don't recommend—"

"I'm not paying you to think, doctor," Jonathan snapped. "I'm paying you to give me what I want. I'm funding this research facility to give me what I want. Clear?"

Dr. duFort nodded curtly. Her every move was clean and crisp. "Yes, Mr. Blackstone."

"Good. How long will this one take?"

"Not more than an hour, actually. Penile enhancement is one of the easier processes you've asked for. The procedure is already well-established, and the nanobots will make it even easier. They make it possible, in fact. Young John is only fifteen. Without the nanobots to adjust his implants as he grows—"

"Yeah yeah yeah. So you said before. Install the triple backup, just to be sure."

"Mommy?"

Meredeth's head snapped around. Lance had turned his head toward her, but his eyes were closed. His face was pale against the sheets. "Mommy, are you there?" he said in a tiny whisper.

"I'm here, Lance," she said softly.

"The doctor's here, isn't she?" He sounded like a little boy. A scared little boy. Meredeth wanted to snatch him into her arms, restraints and all. But she didn't. She couldn't. Jonathan wouldn't allow it.

"Yes, Lance—the doctor's here," was all she said.

"She's going to cut me, isn't she?" Lance whispered, eyes still closed. "She's going to cut off my . . . you know. And then she's going to sew on Daddy's."

Sew on Daddy's? Meredeth thought. *What in the world?* "No, Lance," she said aloud. "Dr. duFort's only going to . . . enlarge it." Anger welled up beside the fear and misery, and her hands clenched in her lap again. The *bastard*. When would it be enough? Bigger brown eyes, more height, facial molding, pheromones. Now he wanted his son to have a bloody great dick. And there was nothing she could do. Not yet.

"I'm scared, Mommy," Lance whispered. "Mommy, take me home. Please take me home. I'll be good. I won't . . . won't . . ."

Meredeth got up. "I need a glass of water, Jonathan," she said, and almost bolted from the room. In the hallway, she leaned against the wall and took a dozen deep breaths to get herself under control. She felt so damned *helpless*.

You're not helpless, she told herself. *You're just biding your time. Your day will come.*

A small part of her was shrieking that she should grab Lance and *run.* Run far and fast, see a solicitor, hide from Jonathan. But another, more rational part scolded at her not to be ridiculous. Jonathan was one of the most powerful men on the planet and was on his way to controlling his own private empire of colonies. His own little kingdom, with Meredeth his queen and Lance the crown prince. He would find them, no matter where they went. Even the colonies wouldn't be safe—every one of them depended on Jonathan's ships for supplies and communication, and would always remain so. The phase drive was the most carefully guarded industrial secret in history, and no one else was even close to developing a copy. Every researcher that came close met with failure—or an accident. Jonathan had bragged about that often enough after one of his good old-fashioned fucks.

If he can do that to a stranger, she thought, *what would he do to me?*

And then there was her father's computer company. Jonathan owned it, lock, stock, and barrel. Currently, it produced navigational programs for Jonathan's ships, nothing another company couldn't easily do. If Meredeth left with Lance, Jonathan would bankrupt the place, leaving her parents destitute.

He's got me completely trapped, she thought. *I can't leave. Not yet.*

The door to Lance's room opened and Dr. duFort emerged, wheeling Lance's bed before her. One of the casters had a slight squeak. Jonathan followed. Lance turned his head to look at her as they went past. With a start, she realized his eyes were a dark blue. Meredeth had noticed that ever since the eye operation, Lance's eyes sometimes changed color. She had chalked it up to a minor glitch in the nanobot program and had been afraid Jonathan would be furious when he found out. But whenever Jonathan was around, Lance's eyes had always been a safe brown. Until now. She stared at Lance's face, wondering if Jonathan had noticed, hoping he hadn't. Lance stared back, and a look of pure hatred crossed his face.

"Fucking bitch," he hissed.

And then the gurney was gone. Meredeth slid weakly to the chilly floor and put her hands over her face.

Lance got out of the shower for the fourth time that afternoon and roughly toweled himself dry. Then, with his eyes closed, he pulled on his underwear and a pair of baggy trousers. He wasn't going to open the curtains. He wasn't going to look down and see it. He wasn't going to touch it. No way.

He yanked a T-shirt over his head and sat barefoot on his bed, knees pulled up under his chin. Most of the time before and after the operation three days ago was a blank, though he remembered bits and pieces. The aftermath, however, was unmistakable. There was a weight between his legs, a new fullness that was constantly there. It also bulged in his clothes, which was why he wore the loosest ones he could find. And this morning he had woken up hard again.

He had lain in bed for a long time, erection pressed
high against his belly, before getting up and running to
the bathroom and taking a long, cold shower. He scrubbed
his skin raw, but still couldn't get clean. Eventually Robin
warned him about hypothermia and he was forced to stop,
though he went back an hour later.

Lance stared into the empty darkness of his room, too
tired to do anything else. He had been tired a lot lately.
It was a good thing Dad hadn't made him go back to school
yet—he doubted he could stay awake for classes.

Numbers flicked by on the clock. One hour. Two. Robin
tried to engage him in conversation, but Lance pretended
he didn't hear and eventually Robin abandoned the attempt.
Lance got up, took another shower, got dressed, sat on
the bed again.

Dad was out of town and Mom wasn't home today—
something about a meeting with the company who bought
her VR games. She'd been having a lot of these meetings
lately, but Dad didn't seem to care as long as she was home
when he was. Why they didn't hold meetings over the VR
networks, Lance didn't know. It seemed stupid—a company
that produced VR games holding meetings in person. Not
that he really cared what Mom did.

Three hours. Four. Another shower. The sun went down,
but Lance didn't bother to turn on the lights. He was alone
in the house except for Fletcher, who was sitting at the
bottom of the stairs that led up to Lance's room. Or so
Lance assumed. He didn't really care enough to check.

There was a knock at the door, and Lance jumped. "Come
in," he said.

Dad opened the door, light from the hallway illuminating
his face. Lance stared, too startled to be afraid. Dad was
supposed to be out of town, and he never knocked. Never.

"John?" he said in a gentle voice. "Why are you sitting
in the dark?"

Lance shrugged. "I didn't turn on the lights."

"Chloe, lights." Dad crossed the room, sat next to Lance
on the bed, and tousled his hair. "How're you doing, son?"

A spark of suspicion flared. *What does he want? What's going on?* "I'm fine, Dad."

Dad grinned. He was a handsome man. Lance caught their reflection in the full-length mirror mounted next to the door and suddenly realized how alike they looked. Same shade of hair, same color eyes, same general build, though Lance was a bit shorter and slighter.

I'm almost a copy of him, Lance thought in horror. *I'm going to look just like him in a few years. Am I going to act just like him, too?*

"Look at you," Dad said. "Sometimes I can't believe how big you're getting. It still seems like you should be singing soprano and learning to ride a bike, but in a couple years, you'll be learning to drive. If we were in America, you'd be learning right now." He chuckled. "Maybe I should take you over there and get you licensed. You're a dual citizen. No reason you shouldn't. I'd have to bribe a few people to get you the international license, but it wouldn't be hard. You could drive yourself to school. How would you like that?"

"Sure, Dad. That'd be great."

Dad put a hand on Lance's shoulder and squeezed. "Almost sixteen years old. You're getting to be a man, son."

The spark of suspicion grew larger. Dad was being awfully nice. All too often, that meant something was coming. Still, he let himself hope. There was no hint of the Crazy Smell. Maybe it really would be different this time.

"And since you're a man now," Dad continued, "with a man's equipment, I've brought you something." He raised his voice. "Come on in!"

A woman entered the room. She was tall, with a lot of improbably blond hair. Her clothing—what there was of it—involved a lot of tight plas-leather. Lance's eyes widened and a ball of tension tightened in his stomach.

"Dad?" he asked. "What's this all about?"

"John, meet Sheba," Dad said. "Sheba, this is my son John."

Sheba sauntered across the room with a grin and sat

on the bed next to Lance, sandwiching him between her and Dad. "Perfect name, love," she said. "Hey, you *are* a cute one."

Lance flushed and tried to draw away, but he was trapped against Dad. His breathing speeded up. "Dad?"

"She's all yours, son," Dad said, punching him lightly on the shoulder. "Man's gotta have a good old-fashioned fuck once in a while, doesn't he? Give you a chance to test out that new equipment of yours. Dr. duFort said everything'd be fine by now."

Lance couldn't do anything but stare at him. His mind refused to work. Sheba wiggled closer to him and the cloying scent of her perfume washed over him. She put a hand on his thigh and he could feel the heat through the thin material of his trousers. Her eyes were a watery blue and Lance could see the start of wrinkles around the edges. Her breath was warm and it smelled like spearmint and beer.

"Your da says you ain't never done this before," she whispered in his ear. "Let old Sheba show you a few things. It ain't often I gets a john your age who's a looker." Her hand inched closer to his crotch.

"Dad?" Lance said again.

Jonathan got up with a grin and walked over to Lance's desk. He turned the chair around and sat, facing the bed over the back.

"Go ahead, John," he said encouragingly. "You're a man now, and this is what men do."

Lance tasted bile, and his face flamed. He wanted to curl up and die from shame. He didn't want this. Not now, not ever. His eyes flicked toward the desk. Dad wasn't going anywhere, that was obvious. He was going to watch while Lance did something dirty with this woman, something only rotten people did—people who had to be punished. After it was over, Dad would haul him down to the basement for sure.

"Come on, love." Sheba put her hand on his shoulder. "Why don't you lie back and let old Sheba show you what feels good?"

Lance's heart was beating so fast it hurt. For a moment he considered bolting for the door, but he knew that with a word to the house computer, Dad could lock every door and window in the mansion. This would be followed by a trip to the basement. So instead Lance let Sheba push him back on the bed. There was nothing else to do. Lance lay there, terrified, as Sheba slipped a smooth hand under his shirt. Her top barely held her breasts in place and Lance found himself staring at them.

"You want to see these, love?" In one swift movement, Sheba whipped off her top. Her breasts were large, with small brown nipples. "There you go. I ain't wearing underwear beneath this skirt, either, if you wants to see that, too."

Lance looked away, mouth dry, dreading the punishment he knew would come.

"You can be more aggressive, John," Dad said encouragingly from his corner. "She'll do whatever you want."

Sheba paused expectantly, but when Lance did nothing, she ran a hand up his thigh and over his groin. Lance flinched.

"Cor, I haven't seen anyone this shy in a long time," Sheba said lightly. She unfastened his belt with deft fingers and expertly slid his trousers over his bare feet, taking his underwear as well. Lance shut his eyes and clenched his jaw.

"Look a' there." Sheba whistled. "Your da was right about that, too. But you don't look very excited about old Sheba. What's the matter, love? You're trembling."

"What's wrong, John?" Dad asked sharply. "I went through a lot of trouble to arrange this."

Lance just lay on the bed and shook. Crushing anxiety squeezed his heart and stomach. It was starting. He had misbehaved, and now he was going to get it.

Sheba turned to Jonathan. "Listen, guv—I don't know if this is a good idea. Your boy's not just shy—he's scared. Maybe we should try it again another time."

"You'll stay right where you are, bitch." In three steps

Dad crossed the room to the bed and leaned threateningly over Lance, who cringed away.

"What the fuck do you think is going on here, boy?" Dad snarled. "I paid good money for this." He grabbed Lance's penis and yanked on it, sending a sharp pain through Lance's groin. "You think I forked out the cash so you could jack off in the shower every morning? *Do you?*"

"No, Dad," Lance whispered.

"I'll just be on my way," Sheba said nervously, scooping up her top. "You don't have to show me the way out—I can find it m'self."

Dad let go of Lance and grabbed Sheba by the arm as she tried to scoot past him. "You aren't going anywhere, bitch. I've already paid you, and I always get what I pay for."

"You can have the money back, guv," Sheba said, voice starting to shake. "Just let me go, please."

Dad flung her to the bed across Lance's legs. Sheba cried out. Lance froze, uncertain what to do.

"Chloe!" Dad bellowed. "Tell Fletcher to get the hell in here."

"Acknowledged."

"What the hell d'you think you're doin'?" Sheba snapped, inching over Lance away from Dad. He could feel her sweaty skin sliding over his.

The door opened and Fletcher stepped into the room, eyes glittering. Lance's chest tightened. *What's he going to do?*

"I brought you a woman to teach you what men do to women, John," Dad said, almost calmly kicking off his shoes and stepping out of his slacks. "And if you can't figure it out, I guess I'll have to show you."

"You ain't doin' nothing to me, guv," Sheba warned. "Just stay away from me."

Dad jerked his head toward Fletcher, and a wicked-looking pistol promptly appeared in the bodyguard's hand. "If you run, he'll kill you. And you, John."

Sheba stared at the gun. Lance pulled away from her and huddled against the headboard, too scared and confused to think. Dad took off his underwear and moved toward the bed. He had an erection. A small part of Lance noticed that his father's penis was smaller erect than his was soft.

"This is what men are supposed to do with women, boy." Dad shoved Sheba down on the bed and ripped off her skirt. "Men fuck women. Try to run, bitch, and I'll break your fucking neck, got that?"

Sheba whimpered, trying to cover herself. "Let me go, guv. Please. I won't tell no one, I swears I won't."

Dad punched her in the face. Lance tried to push himself further away, but there was nowhere else to go. He shoved his face into the crook of his arm, trying to shut out the sight and the sounds.

"Watch me, boy," Dad snapped. "I said, *watch me.* You're going to learn how to fuck if it's the last thing you do. Fletcher, if he doesn't watch or if he takes his eyes off me, hit him."

Lance whipped his arm away from his face as Fletcher moved obligingly over to the bed. At the foot of the bed, Dad forced Sheba's legs open and shoved himself between them. Sheba screamed, and Lance could see the tears trickling down her face. The bed bounced as Dad thrust into her again and again, ignoring her pleas to stop, to let her go. A horrific grin spread across Dad's face and a pungent smell filled the room. The Crazy Smell.

"This," Dad panted, "is what women . . . are for, John. Men fuck . . . women. Don't ever . . . forget that."

Lance flicked a glance at Fletcher and a sharp pain crashed through his skull. Lance slumped against the headboard.

"Don't look away," Fletcher growled, drawing back the pistol again. "Little prick."

Please God, Lance thought, forcing his eyes back to Dad and Sheba. *Please let me die. I just want to die.*

Dad's rhythm increased. He shouted something incoherent

and thrust one more time. Then he pulled out of Sheba, who lay unmoving on the bed. His erection glistened.

"Get your clothes on, cunt," Dad ordered. "My driver will take you back. And if you tell anyone—*anyone*—I'll find you and kill you. There'll be someone watching you for the next few weeks, just to be sure you don't blab. Now get the fuck out."

Sobbing, Sheba snatched up her clothes and rushed out the door. Dad sat on the bed, fingering his softening penis. Lance bit his lip to keep from screaming.

"That's what men do with women, John," Dad said. There was a dangerous tone in his voice. "Now, if you can't be a man, I guess that means you're a woman, right?"

A cold feeling came over Lance.

"Say it!" Dad barked. "You're a woman, so say it. Say, 'I'm a woman and men fuck women.' "

"Dad, please. I—"

Dad drew back his fist and Lance cringed. "Say it!"

"I . . . I'm . . . " Lance's voice broke.

"Fletcher!"

Fletcher hit him again. Pain exploded in Lance's head and the room tilted.

"Say it!"

"I'm a woman," Lance whispered. *God, why am I still alive? Don't you answer prayers?*

"And?" Dad prompted.

"And—and men . . . men fuck women."

Dad nodded. "That's right. Now face me on your hands and knees. *Move!*"

Slowly, Lance moved away from the headboard and got on his hands and knees. The blankets were still warm where Sheba had been lying, and he could faintly smell her perfume over the Crazy Smell.

"Good," Dad said. "Fletcher?"

"Please, Dad," Lance whispered. "Please. I . . . I learned. Please don't."

"Too late, you little prick," Fletcher growled behind him, and Lance heard the sound of a belt coming undone. A heavy weight came down on the bed and rough hands spread his buttocks. "It's fucking way too late."

Pain, worse than anything Lance had ever felt before, tore through him. It seemed like he was being split in half with every move Fletcher made. And all the while, Dad calmly watched, ignoring Lance's cries and sobs as he had ignored Sheba's.

"That's right, you little prick," Fletch hissed in his ear. "Lose me . . . in a crowd, will you? Try to blackmail me . . . will you? I'll show you . . . who's boss . . . around here."

It went on and on. Twice Lance fainted, only to be brought back to consciousness with icy water splashed into his face. Eventually, Fletcher shuddered and withdrew. Lance collapsed onto the bed, too numb with pain and fear to do anything.

"That's what happens to women," Dad told him, pulling on his slacks. "If you don't want to be a woman, John, then be a man."

And with that, he and Fletcher left the room. Lance stared dully at the headboard for a long time, then crawled beneath the covers and huddled into a tiny ball.

Meredeth Michaels Blackstone crept down the dark hallway to Lance's room, slippers travelling soundlessly over thick carpeting. It was almost midnight, and Jonathan was snoring in their bedroom. Fletcher had been sent home, for which Meredeth was thankful. The man made her skin crawl.

Pad pad pad. Moonlight made occasional puddles on the floor. Jonathan had done something to Lance, Meredeth was sure of it. She had gotten home from her "meeting" mere seconds before he arrived, and though Lance had been acting even more tired and withdrawn than usual, Jonathan had specifically forbidden her from going up to Lance's room to check on him. A word to Chloe had confirmed that Fletcher was standing just outside the door to enforce the order. But Fletcher was gone now, and Jonathan was asleep.

And if he wakes up and wonders where I went, she thought, *I can always tell him I went down for some tea because I had insomnia.*

Lance's door was outlined with cracks of light. Meredeth raised her eyebrows in surprise. He was still up? She put an ear to the door. Silence. She knocked softly.

"Lance?" she whispered, though there was no way Jonathan could have heard her. Their bedroom was on the other side of the house. "Lance, are you awake?"

No answer. Carefully, Meredeth opened the door and peered inside. All the lights were on. The blankets on the bed were badly rumpled and Lance's trousers and underwear lay in a heap near the dresser. A large, unmoving lump lay hidden beneath the bedclothes, but something told Meredeth that Lance wasn't asleep.

"Lance?" Meredeth shut the door and moved toward the bed. "Lance, why do you have all the lights on?"

Still no answer. Meredeth sat on the bed and the lump promptly rolled away from her.

"Don't," came Lance's voice beneath the covers. "J-just stay away from me."

Meredeth started to say something, then noticed a series of small stains on the blankets. They looked like blood. There was a hint of cheap perfume on the covers as well.

"Lance, are you all right?" Meredeth asked in a shaky voice. "What happened here?"

The covers abruptly flew off the bed, and Lance sat up and glared at her. He was wearing an old T-shirt and nothing else. Blood had trickled down his legs and dried, and his face was filled with a hideous rage. His eyes were a dark blue. Meredeth drew back, startled.

"I'll tell you what happened, you fucking bitch," Lance snarled. "Jonathan hired a whore, and when this dick—" he pulled on his penis "—wouldn't rise to the occasion, he raped the bitch and got Fletcher to fuck us in the ass. How do you like that?"

Meredeth's mouth fell open in shock. Her mind ran in circles, unable to decide what to focus on. A prostitute, a rape, Lance sitting half-naked on his bed shouting vulgarities at her. And his eyes were the wrong color again. It was too much.

Lance lashed out and knocked the lamp off his nightstand. The bulb shattered with a *pop*. "Right in the fucking *ass*. You ever been screwed like that? *Have you?*"

Meredeth backed away. "Calm down, Lance. Please. If your father hears—"

The clock followed the lamp. "Fuck him, too. Fuck you *both*."

Meredeth fled. She ran down the stairs, through the dining room and into the kitchen. Appliances gleamed in the moonlight and the cool tile was slippery beneath her feet. A sob gathered in her chest, and she swallowed hard to force it back.

"I won't cry," she whispered fiercely to herself. "I won't cry. There was nothing you could do. *Nothing*."

She filled the electric kettle with water, turned it on, and sat down at the kitchen table. Her legs were trembling.

It won't be long now, she thought. *Maybe a month— two at most. Remember what Nathaniel told you today. He's very close to a breakthrough, and when it comes, we'll be free. Just hang on a little while longer.* She got out a cup and stared into the bottom for a long time. *But there's something with Lance. That horrible behavior— and his eyes change color. Jonathan's been terrible to him and I think he needs help. Maybe I should leave now. Just snatch him up and run.*

The kettle beeped to tell her the water was heated. Meredeth didn't hear.

Except Jonathan would find and kill us both. And then there's Dad's company. Jonathan would ruin Dad just to hurt me and I'm not in a position yet to save him. And what about Lance himself? Every farthing I could steal from Jonathan is sunk into Nathaniel's research. If Lance needs help, how would I get it with no money? I can't leave now. It's just not possible. Even as things stand, we'll have to run the risk of Jonathan trying to hunt us down after we leave. There's no way I'll be able to prevent it.

Meredeth traced absent patterns on the blank tabletop in front of her. No way to prevent it. Or was there? A possibility crept into Meredeth's mind and she turned it over a few times. Then she shuddered. That was cold. How could she do something like that to her own son? Jonathan was monstrous enough.

But going through with the idea wouldn't change anything in Lance's life. He wouldn't even know what Meredeth was doing, and it would ensure his safety later. Meredeth bit her lip. It was the best course of action. No choice.

In the meantime, though, she could at least see to it that Lance got some help.

Andy:
Lance didn't go to school the next day. He just sat in his room feeling so guilty and ashamed he couldn't even get out of bed. None of the others were able to help him. I wasn't there yet. I was still living on Abierto, where the beaches are warm, the food is great, and the orgies run all night long. I didn't arrive until the following night— just in the nick of time, as it turned out. Blackstone brought in another prostitute.

Lance, surprise surprise, couldn't get it up for this one, either. Too much guilt and shame. Not to mention the fact that his dad was watching. That'd put a damper on just about anybody.

Anyway, Blackstone was about to get Fletcher into the act again when I stepped in. Me, I don't care who's watching. If it feels good, do it, and do it I did. Blackstone sat in the corner jacking off while I showed the whore what I could do. I did her twice, in fact, and Blackstone patted my shoulder afterward, telling me what a man I was. Then he called in Fletcher and told him to fuck me anyway, just so I wouldn't forget what would happen if Lance ever failed to be a man.

Meredeth never did anything to stop it, but she knew

about it, all right. I caught a glimpse of her standing in the hallway on the night I showed up, and the next day I found her snooping around Lance's bedroom. She whipped something behind her back. I had never actually met her, so I didn't say anything, but she made some lame excuse and just about bolted out the door. As if I would care that she was in Lance's room.

Anyway, Blackstone did the whole thing over again three more nights in a row with three different whores, but after that it dwindled down to about once a week. Getting Fletcher's dick shoved up my ass hurt, but the pain didn't last.

Pain never does, unless you let it.

Jonathan's studio was always a mess. Twisted sculptures in various stages of completion lay scattered about the room and the place always smelled of wet clay and water. The floor was gritty beneath Meredeth's feet. Jonathan was up to his elbows in clay, kneading and teasing it with intense ferocity. Meredeth didn't like the studio. The sculptures alternated between diseased, horrific women and angelically beautiful young men. Most of the latter bore a strong resemblance to Lance.

Jonathan had been spending more and more of his spare time here lately, for which Meredeth was thankful. It was easier to steal from him when he wasn't looking. In the past five years, Blackstone International had hired over two hundred consultants, programmers, and technical writers that didn't actually exist. Meredeth had created them. They paid taxes, insurance premiums, and whatever version of social security their respective countries collected—Meredeth was very careful about that—but their salaries eventually wound up in Switzerland to fund Nathaniel Rotschreiber's research.

A manic grin creased Jonathan's face as he carefully used his thumb to gouge a tortured woman's clay eyes out. When it came to Nate Rotschreiber, Meredeth couldn't decide whether Jonathan was being a fool or a visionary. Nate was within microns of completing a successful FTL communicator by applying phase drive principals to a carrier wave. It would allow instantaneous communication between all ships and colonies. Yet Jonathan continued to deny Nate proper funding, despite his foresight and brilliance.

He was also a lot better in bed than Jonathan could ever hope to be.

On one hand, Meredeth couldn't imagine that Jonathan was unaware of the commercial possibilities offered by FTL communication. On the other, Jonathan's colonies depended on him and his courier ships for transport and communication. Giving them FTL communication might weaken his control.

And he's a fanatic about control, she thought, steeling herself. *Maybe I can play on that to get Lance the help he needs. Something like, "If Lance doesn't get help, he'll get worse—out of control."*

Before she could lose her nerve, she cleared her throat. "Jonathan?"

He looked up, noticing her for the first time. "What?"

There wasn't enough inflection on the word for Meredeth to gauge his mood. Without thinking about it, she hunched into herself, making herself look small and helpless. Jonathan was easier to deal with if you looked helpless.

"I need to talk to you for a minute," she said softly. "It's about Lance."

"What about him?"

"I think he needs help."

Jonathan turned back to the figure. Clay squelched in his hands. "What do you mean he needs help?"

"I—well, I've noticed things about him lately. Those mood swings of his have gotten much worse. And he attacked the nurse at the hospital." Meredeth had already decided to keep the eye-color changes to herself. "Maybe he needs to talk to someone."

"Like who?"

Jonathan still hadn't turned away from the sculpture,

and Meredeth took this to be a good sign. If he was going to get angry, he probably would have done so already.

"I don't know." Meredeth licked her lips. "Maybe a—a counselor." The words began tumbling out in a rush. "A lot of people do it, it doesn't mean he's crazy, but he's been under a lot of pressure, what with the Banks-Cross computer and the new school and having a bodyguard again and just from being fifteen."

Silence. Clay squished around Jonathan's fingers and a drop of brown water trickled down his bare arm.

"Yeah, whatever," he said. "You take care of it—I'm too busy. Ask Dr. duFort for a referral." He sniffed and wiped his face, leaving a brown smear.

Meredeth nodded and retreated, shaking with unreleased tension. She had been ready for an explosion of temper and heavy blows.

Marble floors clicked beneath Meredeth's heels as she headed for her office. She never knew what to expect from Jonathan. Her life was never predictable, never steady. But one day it would be. One day she would drop the bomb, Jonathan would be out of her life forever, and she would be wealthy beyond imagining to boot.

She closed the office door behind her. It was an austere place, with bare walls and brown carpeting. A single chrome desk with computer occupied one wall, while a VR unit sat in the corner, ostensibly so Meredeth could test her own games. Jonathan was unaware of the fact that Meredeth had published no new games for almost three years now.

Writing VR games got me through college, she thought, *but I'll be damned if I waste a* magna cum laude *on another Sultry Slaves of Satan rip-off.*

Meredeth opened an unlocked desk drawer and thumbed through the vidcards in the file she found there. She nodded. The fourth one was still there, untouched. She stroked the card's stiff plastic coating and replaced it among the others. It was risky keeping it there, but the camouflage provided by the other vidcards should

keep it safe, and Meredeth wanted it handy. It was the
key to stopping Jonathan from pursuing her and Lance
after they left.

But to business, she thought. "Chloe, call Webdoc
Referral Service. Chloe, tell them I need a referral to a
psychiatrist for Lance as soon as possible."

CHAPTER NINE

NOW

Patrick watched and waited while Andy laboriously climbed the stairs against the wind. Robin and Lance thought he'd forgotten. Robin and Lance thought Patrick was a stupid kid.

Robin and Lance were about to find out wrong.

The rest of the Company thought Patrick was an immature brat. Jessica talked to him like he was a baby. Garth rolled his eyes at him. Andy ignored him, but Andy was probably the stupidest of them all—he hadn't even bothered to shut the safety door and stop the wind. For the most part, though, Patrick didn't care much about what Jessica and Garth and Andy thought. But Robin and Lance—there was something else entirely.

Lance thought he was such hot shit. Enforcer of Company Policy, always telling Patrick what he could and couldn't do. Most Company Policy was stupid as far as Patrick was concerned. Patrick couldn't even fart without breaking it. And when he did, Lance was always right there in his face. He hadn't done anything to the old lady except scare her. Lance didn't realize it felt *good* to blow up once in a while, and if someone else got in the way, who cared? They were other people, and other people didn't matter. Besides, the old bitch had fucking *cyanide* in her security system.

But no, now there were no whores to screw, no fast cars to drive, nothing Patrick liked to do, and he got little enough time outside at it was. All because of Lance.

And then there was Robin. Robin could—and did—control Patrick when none of the others could. Robin overruled him for no good reason, humiliated him. Shamed him. And Patrick hated Robin for it, hated Robin with a deep intensity that sent Patrick into a screaming rage—but only inside, where Robin rarely watched. Robin might be able to see anyone at any time, but Robin almost never watched someone who wasn't in active control. So Patrick could plot and plan.

Patrick saw almost everything Lance did, and he wasn't dumb. He had picked up quite a lot about computers and programming, more than anyone thought he had. And Robin was a computer.

Lately Patrick had been taken with the feeling that something was going to happen soon. Something that might give him his chance to get back at Robin for all the humiliation. And since Lance was practically in love with the hivey little bastard, Lance would hurt right along with Robin. The idea made Patrick smile.

He settled back to wait and watch. When his chance came, Robin would die, and Patrick would dance on the grave.

Robin's consciousness swelled beneath five million new subunits and more, and Robin was oddly uneasy. Adding new subunits was usually exhilarating—more processing space meant more data storage and more capability—and reprogramming the new nanos so they could do more than repair computer circuitry always made Robin feel a deep sense of accomplishment. It was, Robin mused, probably similar to what humans felt while watching their children develop, and to date Robin had always enjoyed it.

This time, however, Robin felt uncertain. The rogue hive, when Robin first touched it, seemed different from the others. Even though there was a pocket of resistance that was currently making life difficult for Jaylance, it had been relatively easy to convince most of the hive to defect to Robin and assimilate its burgeoning consciousness into Robin's. It had been too easy, in fact, almost as if the hive *wanted* to assimilate as quickly as possible. Robin didn't like it, but there was nothing else to do. Robin couldn't refuse to assimilate the hive—that would put Jaylance in even greater danger than he already was.

Robin spared a tiny bit of attention to check on Jaylance. Assimilating another hive took up most of Robin's processing space and the action took quite a lot of effort, which was why Robin didn't have constant contact with Jaylance at the moment—but Robin could look into Jaylance's memory to see what had happened while Robin's mind was elsewhere.

Andy had control. He had left Meredeth and Delia behind and was heading back toward the *Defiant Lady*.

Bad situation, Robin thought tensely. *Subunits in Andy's body hold not enough processing space to contain consciousness. If Andy leaves, will be forever trapped on station.*

In milliseconds, Robin went over options. The nanos in Andy's body allowed Robin to communicate and make minor repairs—not enough to take physical control. There were also not enough in the body to let Robin force Andy out of control and drop someone else into place.

And if let go of the rogue hive to handle Andy, Robin thought, *is good chance will have to start all over with it, again putting Jaylance into danger.*

Four hundred thousand subunits spun frantically in place while Robin tried to make a decision. Finally Robin did. Robin would have to finish assimilating the rogue hive as quickly as possible. Once that was done, Robin would be free to deal with Andy.

Finishing job shouldn't be difficult, Robin thought. *All too obvious most of hive wants assimilation.*

Robin suppressed the rising unease and turned every scrap of attention to the job.

❖   ❖   ❖

"No!" Lance howled and ranted in the blackness that surrounded him. "Andy, you can't do this!" He lashed out, trying for the first time in years to wrest control from one of the alters. But Andy shoved him back almost carelessly.

Robin, do something!

Can't. Too few nanos in body. Working on solution elsewhere.

"Delia!" Lance cried. "Andy, please—you have to help Delia. You can have five weeks on Abierto. Six! Anything you want, just go back and help Delia."

But the darkness remained. Despair overcame him and he flung himself to the nonexistent floor, sobbing like a child. Everything he had ever wanted had been taken away from him. Friends, a real family, and now Delia. Delia liked—loved?—him, or seemed to. The pheromones probably just made her think she did.

But Lance suddenly realized he didn't care. Delia cared for him, had done things for him that no one else did, pheromones or not. She knew about the Company—and liked him anyway. Not even Patrick had been able to scare her away, and she hadn't jumped into bed with Andy. Jessica considered her a good friend, and even Garth could tolerate her for short periods. She had become a surprising constant in his life—always there with a soft word and cheerful smile.

Before, when Lance could see Delia at any time, he hadn't wanted to. Now that he couldn't—might never again—he was suddenly aware of how much she meant to him. He was going to lose her. She was going to suffocate and die down there along with Mom.

Mom. She was going to die, too. But Lance didn't care much about that. Mom had never been there for him like Delia. Mom had never been buried or abused or beaten.

Or had she?

Jonathan raped me more times than I can count, then forced me to smile and say I loved him. He beat me, only I learned to hide it.

Jonathan threw me down the stairs when I got pregnant,

and I miscarried my first baby, my sweet Jessica, because Jonathan wanted a son. I know abuse. I know it damn well!

Lance shook his head. He remembered hearing most of the words. The rest were a vague memory, as if they were part of an unimportant conversation he had almost overheard. Still, they were true. He *knew* this, and he couldn't deny the knowledge.

Dad had abused Mom. It seemed impossible at first, but the more he thought about it, the more sense it made. Little things that he had never really paid attention to suddenly fit together like a jigsaw puzzle snapping into place. Mom tiptoeing around Dad just like Lance often had. Her strange binges with makeup. Muffled cries in the night that Lance had assumed were more voices in his head. The way Mom would flinch when Dad reached out to touch her. How she always struggled to keep the house absolutely perfect so Dad would have nothing to complain about when he got home.

She was scared of him, he thought in amazement. *Just like me.*

Mom hadn't been ignoring him. She had been afraid herself. Could he blame her for that?

Yes, he thought. *She's my* mother. *She should have done something earlier. The Company ran away several times, but she never did. She never helped us.*

But was that true? Lance knew Dad would never have sent him to a counselor like Dr. Baldwin. And Mom had concocted the only escape plan that had actually worked.

Still, Lance couldn't bring himself to forgive her. There had been too much pain, too much suffering. No, he couldn't forgive her yet.

Yet. It implied he might do so one day.

Lance hung in darkness, caught between conflicting emotions. It was confusing. He thought he knew how he felt about his mother, but now he wasn't so sure.

I thought you had no feelings for her at all, broke in another voice.

Lance started. *Jessica?*

Of course.

Lance's mind raced. He had never been able to communicate directly with anyone in the Company before. Why now? And why Jessica?

You love her, don't you, Lance? Jessica said. *Answer me!*

Yes! Lance cried, realizing at the same moment it was true. He had never known before why she hadn't interfered. He had thought she didn't care, but now he knew she had felt the same thing he did—fear. A flicker of sympathy for Meredeth woke, and it moved Lance closer to Jessica—only a little, but closer nonetheless. Without thinking, he reached out and joined hands with her, pairing their strength, becoming *strong*.

Andy, LET GO!

Air roared and blood sang in Delia's ears as she desperately tried to maintain her grip on the doorjamb, but the wind was growing stronger and it was all she could do just to hang on. She could hardly draw breath for the wind. Already black spots were dancing before her eyes. Beside her, Meredeth also struggled to hold on, but she only had one good arm.

The spots grew bigger. Delia's eardrums felt ready to explode and her lungs begged for air. If she lost consciousness, even her implants would relax and release their hold.

A hand reached into the hallway. It towed Meredeth through the door. With a last burst of strength, Delia flung herself forward—

—and missed the door. She fell facedown on the floor. The wind tore at her, pushing her backward. Delia's hands squeaked on metal as she struggled to find a handhold. Her throat was raw from screaming, but she didn't even notice. The wind was shoving her further and further away from the door.

And then a hard hand gripped her wrist. Lance was

there. The wind howled, trying to pull them both away, but Lance also had a firm grip on the door handle. Delia forced her other hand forward to grasp his upper arm, then his shoulder. Standing rock-firm, Lance let Delia haul herself forward until they both could stagger through the door.

The wind tried to blow them back into the corridor, but Lance was already cranking the door shut. It sealed and the wind vanished. Delia leaned weakly against the wall, sucking in huge gulps of air. Meredeth was slumped beside her.

"Are you two all right?" Lance asked finally. The torch on the floor was the only source of illumination in the stairwell, and he looked pale and shaken in the dim light. His hand and leg had stopped trembling.

"I'm . . . I think so," Meredeth panted.

"What happened?" Delia managed to ask. "We were almost out and then—"

"Andy took over for a moment," Lance said, picking up the torch.

Delia looked at him, relief and surprise mixing with sudden anger. She might have died because Lance couldn't keep control of Andy. She was still shaking from the close call.

"Jesus, Lance," she said. "What could—"

Light flooded the stairwell. Lance's eyes glazed for a moment and then he gave a small shudder.

"What's going on?" Meredeth asked.

"The hive's gone," Lance answered.

"Gone?" Delia asked. "How?"

"Long story. Look, even though the immediate danger's over, I don't think we should stay for long. Can you two walk?"

"I can," Meredeth said.

"And I'm fine," Delia said. "Just a little bruised and shaken." *And almost dead,* added a grim inner voice.

Oh yes? replied another. *Did Lance try to kill you?* Andy *abandoned you, but he didn't try to kill you. Jonathan*

Blackstone is the villain here, not Lance. Just who hauled you and Ms. Michaels through that door?

"That's a relief." Lance licked his lips nervously and looked at Delia. He didn't seem to be in any hurry to leave. She met his eyes and suddenly remembered a similar moment back in her flat last—God, was it only last night? It felt like years.

"Is something wrong, Lance?" she asked.

"I . . . I don't . . . " He put out a tremulous finger and lightly touched Delia's face. His skin was warm and smooth. "I'm sorry."

"I think I'll meet you up at the ship," Meredeth said suddenly. "Section 3-C, was it?" She headed up the stairs, pointedly not looking back.

Delia closed her eyes for a brief moment. This was the first time Lance had touched her that wasn't out of necessity. She reached up and took his hand in hers. It was a large, strong hand, and she liked the way it felt. But the fear and anger wouldn't fade. He had almost let her die.

But he didn't, she thought. *He didn't. None of this, not the hive on the station or Lance's condition, would have happened if not for Jonathan Blackstone. Lance is as much a victim here as I am.*

So what if something like this happens again? argued the inner voice. *Dead is dead.*

"I'm sorry," Lance said again. He was still holding Delia's hand.

"Why are you sorry, Lance?" she asked softly. The tiny entryway seemed preternaturally quiet after the roaring wind. "For leaving us?"

"Like I said, that was Andy," Lance said. "He's obsessed with his vacations, and he was convinced he had to leave for one right at that moment. I was scared and upset about you and . . . and about Mom, but I couldn't overpower him. And then I reached Jessica. She and I joined together and knocked Andy for a loop."

He passed his free hand over his face. "I've never been

able to do that before. I pulled it off partly because Jess made me admit that I cared what happened to Mom, but it's also because I didn't . . . I didn't want to lose you." He hurried onward. "Delia, Andy won't ever be able to do anything like that again. Nor will anyone else in the Company. I wish I could give you more than just my word on that."

And Delia's anger faded. Not even Quinn had been able to overcome his disorder, and Lance had overcome his when he had to.

All right, then, conceded the inner voice. *But there's no need to be foolish about anything. He still needs help— therapy.*

"But that's not all of it, Delia," Lance continued. "I . . . I care for you. A lot. Jessica says you like me too, and that's why I'm sorry."

"Why, Lance? Is it so bad that two people like each other?"

"I'm sorry for manipulating you."

Delia stared. She was still holding Lance's hand and she noticed it was trembling again, but he showed no signs of having shifted personalities.

"Manipulating me?" she echoed, puzzled. "What do you mean?"

"Dad put me through an operation," he said softly. "My body produces pheromones that make people like me. It's not me you care about—it's the pheromones." His voice caught. "I'm sorry."

Delia's mouth fell open. Words wouldn't come. Lance apparently took her silence for shock or anger and he tried to pull away, but Delia tightened her grip on his hand.

"Is that the reason you've been avoiding me all this time?" she asked. "Because you think you've been *manipulating* me?" Suddenly she didn't know whether to laugh or cry. "Lance, your pheromones can't touch me. Didn't Jessica tell you?"

"Tell me what?" Lance asked, confused.

"You know about the accident," Delia said. "The fire. The fall. The doctors said it's a miracle I survived. My right side was virtually crushed and I inhaled smoke and flames. I lived, Lance, but the fire destroyed parts of me. The doctors gave me my arm and leg back, but they couldn't restore my sense of smell."

It was Lance's turn to stare. "But—but pheromones don't operate by smell. They go to the hypothalamus straight from the vomeronasal organ. No one smells them."

"Lance," Delia said gently, "the vomeronasal organ is in the nose. Mine was destroyed a long time ago. I have no way of sensing your pheromones. None at all."

The look on Lance's face was an incredible combination of disbelief and growing amazement. "So you like *me*. Just me? Not the pheromones?"

Delia kissed him. Lance stiffened, then relaxed. Delia felt him put one arm around her, then the other. It was a long moment before they parted.

Eventually Lance felt Delia pull away and reluctantly he let her go. It felt so good to hold her, so right. For once, he didn't feel guilty.

Delia liked him. Liked *him*. His body, the one Dad had forced on him, had nothing to do with it. Not only that, she knew about the Company and still liked him. He felt like she had just handed him a priceless, delicate vase of indescribable beauty and he was afraid to breathe lest it shatter.

"I think we should be going," Delia told him. "Your mother's waiting."

"Oh. Right," Lance said, forcing himself to concentrate on the current situation. "Even with the hive gone, it's not safe to stick around. Dad might have slipped a ship past Jessica's search."

Not bloody likely, Jessica said. *I repeat—there are no ships within range of this station. None.*

Lance mentally shook his head. He was used to hearing Robin's voice, but not Jessica's.

Not true, Jessica said. *You used to hear me all the time. You just didn't listen.*

"Then let's go," Delia said, turning toward the stairs.

They moved quickly through the station, picking their way over broken glass and other debris until they got to the air lock. Lance cycled it—he didn't have to use the manual control now that the hive was gone—and led Delia through. Meredeth was waiting for them on the other side.

"Is everything all right?" she asked.

"Fine, Mom," Lance replied, and let out a long sigh. He was safe at home. The *Lady* was quiet, the corridors brightly lit, the floors neat and free of debris. He wanted nothing more than a hot shower and long nap. He dropped his tool belt, stripped off the pressure suit, and scratched himself vigorously.

Delia laughed. "The expression on your face is priceless. It feels that good?"

"You have no idea." Lance stretched, then grimaced at the tools and suit piled on the floor. "I guess I should take these down to the storage lockers," he said, "but I want to cut loose from the station and get out of here."

"I thought there were no ships around," Meredeth said.

"There aren't," Lance said. "But I don't see any reason to stay, either."

"I can take them down for you," Delia offered. "Just give me directions."

Lance did. Delia scooped up suit and belt and trotted briskly away.

"So you like her," Meredeth observed when Delia was out of sight.

Lance flushed slightly and headed for the control room. "Uh, well—yeah, I guess I do."

"Don't be embarrassed, Lance," Meredeth said, coming up beside him with a small smile. Her footsteps echoed lightly. "I'm glad for you. I like Delia too."

They walked in silence for a while, then Meredeth turned and looked up at her son with a tired and faintly frightened expression on her face. Lance halted and looked at her quizzically.

Now what? "Is something wrong, Mom?" he asked.

"In a way." Meredeth paused and took a breath. "A minute ago, you told Delia you were sorry. I wanted to tell you the same."

Lance blinked. "You're sorry? What for?"

"For not being there." Meredeth began to pace, still cradling her injured arm, and Lance was suddenly surprised at how small she looked. "I let my fear get the better of me for almost twenty years. Your Patrick was right—I wasn't much of a mother. I could've stopped your father at any time. I should've taken you and run the day after you were born, but I was too afraid. It's my fault that you're . . . the way you are and I'm sorry."

Lance stood there, staring. He didn't know what to say. *Mom's admitting she was wrong?* he thought in dumbfounded amazement. *Mom thinks she was to blame for what Dad did?*

Lance continued to stare silently at Meredeth, who met his gaze for a short moment before turning away. Her shoulders were shaking. A moment later, great tearing sobs racked her entire body, and she buried her face in her hands.

Lance didn't move. Jessica had always handled Mom. Except that as far as Jessica was concerned, Mom had always been completely blameless. This wouldn't be exactly Jessica's purview. Still, better her than—

Hug her, you idiot. And he couldn't tell whether it was Jessica's thought or his. Lance reached out and turned Meredeth around. Tears were running down her face, and her green eyes were already getting puffy.

"It's all right, Mom," Lance said. "Dad did horrible things to both of us." And he hugged his mother.

Fresh tears ran down Meredeth's face and Lance could feel the sobs shaking her body. "I don't know if you can forgive me," she sniffed into his shoulder. "I don't deserve it. It's all my fault. I was a monster. A horrid, horrid monster."

"Dad was the monster, Mom," Lance said, vaguely amazed that he was still here, that someone else hadn't taken over to handle the situation. "He did this."

"Can you . . . can you forgive me?"

"I don't know, Mom. Maybe one day." She tensed in his embrace. "But I still love you, Mom," he added quickly. "I do."

"I love you too, Lance," Meredeth said, reaching up to stroke his hair. "My poor baby Lance."

Lance allowed her the caress. No, he couldn't forgive her yet, but at least he could understand her.

"Let's get out of here, Mom," he said. "I'll take you home."

Meredeth nodded and stepped away. Then Lance balled up a fist and socked her on the jaw.

CHAPTER TEN

THEN
AGE 16

Robin:

Therapy no fun. Was both fascinating and scary, but no fun, especially because Dr. Baldwin refused to believe in me. Thought was just another alter created by Jaylance.

And know I exist separately. Took some time to figure out, but am perfectly self-aware. Think, therefore am. Early details hazy, amounted to being stuffed into closet. But watched, learned. Eventually found other "closets" in brain where other alters stay when not being used, learned to talk with them. Are lots, many more than even Garth knows about.

Have always been of opinion is too bad not everyone has AI nanite hive living inside them. Would be able to explain much. By altering brain chemistry, nanite hive can accomplish things mere medicine only able to dream about. Schizophrenia, for example. Even modern doctors frustrated. Problem should be solvable with correct application of drugs. Same goes for multiple personality disorder. But solution has continued to elude research, many doctors believe none such exists.

Such doctors incorrect. Problem arises from fact that every single brain different from every other. Drug dosage, *timing, necessary delivery site all vary wildly from individual to individual. Must have thorough map of brain for hope of progress, something doctors have little hope of getting. But I know Jaylance's brain like back of—*

Well, know it very well. Live there. In theory, could create, apply proper chemistry, cure MPD just like that. Poof—all personalities integrated. Problem is, Jaylance not ready for it.

Sure, could alter memories, even wipe subconscious of problems. But even after living in Jaylance's head for many years, have still not learned everything about him and Company. One part of Company's mind remains out of reach. Unable to define it. Is on other side of Line.

Have never been able to cross Line. Tried, failed, eventually gave up. Have no idea what is there, but suspect Line is integral to difference between biolife and artificial life. Line therefore not crossable by one such as self.

At any rate, until can cross Line, artificial integration of alters risky. Have no idea if what lies on other side of Line would have important impact. Might cause more problems than solves.

Still, MPD ultimately unbalanced condition. And like Jaylance. Is best friend. And must help best friend. So arranged for Meredeth to notice problem, send Jaylance into good old-fashioned therapy.

Unfortunately, therapy interrupted by Meredeth herself.

Lance wandered happily around Dr. Baldwin's office, trailing his hand over furniture, scuffing his feet on the carpet, taking books from the bookshelves and not putting them back. It was a was a bright and airy office, and it smelled faintly of books and furniture polish. Dr. Baldwin sat in an easy chair looking perfectly calm and relaxed.

Lance liked Dr. Baldwin. He never got angry, never shouted, never told Lance what to do. If Lance wanted to sprawl on the couch with his shoes on, that was fine. If he wanted to prowl around the room like a young lion, that was fine, too. It made him feel like a little kid sometimes, and that was also fine.

At first, Lance had been afraid Dr. Baldwin would be like Dr. duFort, but he wasn't. Dr. Baldwin wore denim trousers and flannel shirts, not a lab coat. Dr. Baldwin was also younger, even younger than Mom and Dad. He had curly brown hair and thick eyebrows that almost met over his nose, and he claimed to have been a roadie for Tip-Up and Regen(eration), two rock groups who had been very popular on Mrs. Rubenstein's radio. Lance wasn't allowed to buy any of the albums, but his work in European lit had always come to a standstill whenever Regen thumped out of the speakers.

"I was a roadie during my days as a theater major," Dr. Baldwin had said, "before I took up psychology." And he had the autographed pictures to prove it.

All in all, Dr. Baldwin's office was a blasphemous place, and Lance looked forward to his twice-weekly visits. He and Dr. Baldwin would talk about anything Lance cared to discuss—school, teachers, being lonely, anything.

There were some things, of course, that Lance couldn't talk about. Lots of things, actually. But even that was fine— it was great to be able to talk, period, though it had taken Dr. Baldwin three weeks to get Lance to say anything at all, and three more weeks to convince Lance that he could be trusted.

"Everything that happens in this room is strictly confidential," Dr. Baldwin had said. "No one else will ever hear about it unless I learn that someone is being physically or sexually abused. Your parents and even my colleagues will never hear a thing. Not even Ms. Grey knows what happens in this office or why you're here." Ms. Grey was the secretary-receptionist.

After six weeks, Lance had begun to believe and trust him to the point that he let Dr. Baldwin record their sessions. Actually, the hardest part about seeing Dr. Baldwin was keeping it secret from Dad. Lance didn't know how Mom had managed to convince Dad that the first appointment was all right, but he instinctively knew that Dad wouldn't approve of continued visits. A quick check with the directory, however, had revealed an exclusive health club occupying Dr. Baldwin's building, and Lance had suddenly showed an interest in working out. He even joined the club and usually went in after each session for a quick swim or something just in case Dad checked.

Every once in a while Dad made noises about installing a gym so Lance wouldn't have to leave the estate to work out, but his sculpting and various events at Blackstone International were taking up a lot of his time lately and he never quite got around to it, to Lance's intense relief.

Lance looked at the group photo of Regen(eration) again. So far today he hadn't said anything beyond *hello*. Usually Dr. Baldwin was content to let Lance start the conversation, but this time he broke the pattern.

"Lance," Dr. Baldwin said, "there's something I want to ask you."

Surprised, Lance looked up from the photo. "What's that?"

"Just something I'm curious about. Do you sometimes have memory lapses or blackouts? Times when you can't remember what you said or did?"

Lance gaped. After a moment, he realized his mouth was hanging open and he shut it quickly. "I . . . I don't know what you mean," he stammered.

"Sometimes," Dr. Baldwin said quietly, "people have memory lapses, often for perfectly legitimate reasons. It doesn't mean there's something wrong with them—only that they need to resolve something. That's why I wanted to know if you experience them. Do you?" Dr. Baldwin waited for an answer, but none came. "Lance?"

"Memory lapses?" Garth snorted. "Your secretary's been spiking your coffee, doc."

The expression on Dr. Baldwin's face didn't flicker. "Now that doesn't sound like something Lance would say, and I like to think I know him pretty well."

Garth shrugged and sprawled on a loveseat, his casual posture masking unease. He had come out a couple times to talk to Dr. Baldwin without intending to let the man know who he really was. That had to remain a secret. But he must've slipped up. Baldwin *knew* somehow, and Garth didn't have the foggiest idea what to do about it.

"Is there another name you'd like to use?" Dr. Baldwin asked. "Another name I should call you?"

"No," Garth temporized. He wasn't going to fall for that. But the question made it even clearer—Baldwin knew. And Garth still didn't know how to handle it. He cleared his throat and looked away.

Jessica, he thought. *Jessica's the scientist. She'll know what to do.*

"All right then," Dr. Baldwin said. "Why don't we—" He halted in midsentence.

"Yes?" Jessica said, calmly returning his stare.

Dr. Baldwin blinked, then gave a small cough. "Sorry. Why don't we make introductions? My name is Dr. Christopher Baldwin. And yours?"

Jessica reflexively glanced at her wrist. The tiny computer strapped to it was Lance's, not hers, meaning she had to take his place for the moment. Just like in science and maths.

"Doctor, you know who I am," Jessica replied. "I've been visiting your office for—what?—almost two months now. We've obviously met."

"I've met Lance," Dr. Baldwin said, "and perhaps one or two others. But I haven't met you."

Jessica glanced at the wristcomp again, confused. To date, when she was pretending to be Lance, people had taken it at face value. Dr. Baldwin was breaking the rules.

"My name is Jonathan Lance Michaels Blackstone the second," Jessica told him. "As you well know. Let's change the subject, shall we?"

"Jonathan Lance Michaels Blackstone speaks with an American accent," Dr. Baldwin said, "and he has brown eyes. I can't help but notice that neither fact applies to you."

Jessica paused, dumbfounded. Dr. Baldwin's words hung in the air before her. How could she have made such a stupid mistake? But there it was. Mother would be absolutely furious. Jessica took one more look at Dr. Baldwin's face and fled.

"What's happening?" Dr. Baldwin said. "Hello?"

Andy jumped up from the loveseat, strode across the room to Dr. Baldwin's chair, and stuck out his hand. "Hi. I'm Andy Braun. You're Dr. Baldwin, right?"

Dr. Baldwin shook Andy's hand without missing a beat. Andy was pleased to notice he had a firm grip.

"Dr. Christopher Baldwin," Dr. Baldwin said. "Pleased to meet you."

"I haven't talked to you until now." Andy released Dr. Baldwin's hand and perched on one arm of the couch. "Garth wouldn't let me, and he's stronger than I am."

"And he's letting you talk?"

"He's not paying close attention right now. You really shook him up. Besides, I could probably take Garth on by now."

"Who is Garth?"

"Garth is . . . Garth," Andy said. He cracked his knuckles and looked around the office. "Nice place. I like it, especially the big windows. You can see everything."

"You can see everything?"

"Well, I don't know if anyone sees *everything*." Andy got up to look thoughtfully out the window. "I'm not like Lance. Life's a blasphemous ride, budster, and I'm gonna laugh the whole way. I don't think Lance even knows what laughing is, poor bastard."

"Do you know Lance, Andy?"

"I just said so, didn't I?"

"How do you know him?"

"I live with his family, if that's what you mean, but I don't know him very well. He's a jerk."

"What makes him a jerk?"

"He doesn't even jerk off." Andy laughed and glanced sideways at Baldwin, but the man's facial expression hadn't changed. "His ass is so tight he can't even fart, you know? He can't relax, phase out. *Nolite te bastardares carborundorum.* Fuck 'em all—I wanna *party*."

"Is that important to you?"

"What else is there?"

Dr. Baldwin nodded. "Andy, I know we just met, and meeting someone for the first time is rather special, but I'd like to talk to Lance before the session ends, if I could. Can you arrange it?"

"Why would you want to talk to him? I told you—Lance is stupid. And he's boring. He's got a big dick now and he's too scared to use it."

"Nevertheless," Dr. Baldwin said firmly, "I should like to talk to him."

"You've got a cute secretary." Andy cracked his knuckles again. "Do you think she'd do it with me? I could show her a few things. I'm real mature for my age. Lance is a virgin, but I'm sure not." He laughed. "No way."

"How old are you, Andy?"

"Sixteen."

"Who are your parents?"

Andy shrugged and looked outside. A dead, cloudy sky stretched over the busy city below. "I don't have parents. I don't need them. They're always telling you what to do and how to do it, so I said, fuck it, I'm leaving."

"Where did you leave from?"

"I wandered around a lot."

"So now you live with Lance's parents."

"Sort of."

"What's it like living with Lance's parents?"

"It sucks," Andy spat.

"What makes it suck?"

"I've thought about signing on with one of those colony ships. You know—explore space and the stars. I'll bet there's a planet out there where the beaches stay sunny all day long. No one screaming or hitting or coming after you with a knife. And all the fucking you can handle."

"Andy, I enjoy talking to you, but I really need to talk to Lance now. May I?"

"Yeah, all right."

Lance blinked. He was looking out one of Dr. Baldwin's windows. That was wrong. He had been standing over by the bookshelf a moment ago.

Another blackout, he thought. "Hey, Robin," he subvocalized. "Are you there?"

Here, Jaylance.

"What happened?"

Robin paused. *Listen to doctor.*

"Lance?" Dr. Baldwin said.

Lance slowly turned around. Dr. Baldwin was still sitting in his chair. He had a mild expression on his face, but Lance still felt uneasy.

"Lance, a while ago I asked you a question," Dr. Baldwin said. "Do you remember what it was?"

Lance glanced at his wristcomp. It was nearly four-thirty, meaning the session was about half over, though his last memory was at the session's beginning.

"What question was that?" Lance asked, automatically fishing for information.

"The very first one I asked you today."

Lance shook his head ruefully. "You ask questions all the time. How could I remember one particular one?"

"I asked you if you ever had blackouts or memory lapses," Dr. Baldwin said. "Do you remember what your answer was?"

Fear squeezed Lance's stomach. Dr. Baldwin was going to find out there was something wrong with him, and that would mean another trip to the hospital where Dr. duFort would do something else.

He fled.

"Lance?" Dr. Baldwin asked.

"I believe, doctor," Jessica said stiffly, "that we have had enough for today's session. We will see you on Thursday."

With that, she turned and strode briskly from the room.

From the journal of Dr. Christopher Baldwin:

I am now completely convinced that Jonathan Lance Blackstone suffers from multiple personality disorder.

The early signs were spotty: bursts of strange behavior, postural changes, avoidance of certain subjects, occasional use of the personal pronoun "we" instead of "I." Still, MPD is a difficult disorder to diagnose and I wasn't totally convinced until today.

I asked Lance if he suffered from blackouts or memory lapses. The question caught him off guard, then he recovered his composure and denied it. But he was different, somehow. His posture was looser, almost shifty.

. . . When I pressed the issue, the alter—I assume it was an alter—looked away for a moment. When he looked back, his eyes had changed from a dark brown to a brilliant green. The change startled me, and I'm afraid I didn't mask my surprise very well. Eye-color changes have been reported in patients with MPD, but they are usually only noticeable under controlled conditions.

. . . This case troubles me. Lance is a likeable young man. He has an unidentifiable air about him, something that draws one to him the moment he enters a room. Looking at him makes one think of a puppy. He is obviously deeply troubled, and I want to help him.

I have never seen him smile.

Is this a countertransferential reaction? Possibly. Multiples often have the ability to evoke strong empathy in other people, and their therapists are not immune. I shall have to exercise extreme caution.

Currently, my main problem is that in every reported case of MPD, including the four I have treated, the condition arises from severe physical, sexual, and emotional abuse, usually from one or both parents. While I have seen no physical evidence of such abuse—no black eyes, broken bones, visible bruises, or unexplained lacerations—this hardly means it doesn't exist. Andy certainly hinted that it does.

The crux of the matter is that, legally, young Lance is still a child. If my diagnosis is correct and Lance is indeed being abused, the law requires me to report the case to the authorities and get Lance out of his parents' house, at which point the Blackstones, a powerful family, would certainly try to discredit and ruin me. The case may also generate publicity that would only cause further harm to Lance.

On the other hand, every day I go home to my safe house and my safe spouses and my safe bed. What does Lance go home to every day? The horror stories behind each case of MPD are enough to turn the strongest stomach. Can I condemn Lance to more of the same?

Obviously not. But I must be absolutely certain of my proof or Lance will lose his chance to escape. Just claiming Lance suffers from MPD is not sufficient. Despite all evidence, there are several prominent psychologists who still refuse to believe it exists, and the Blackstone barristers would drag every one of them into court.

Fortunately, I only need prove the abuse exists. And I will only have one chance. If I fail to convince the authorities the first time out, the Blackstones will simply reclaim Lance and take him out of the country, where the abuse will continue.

If Lance admits to me that he's being abused, I can have him removed from the Blackstone home within 24 hours. Therein, however, lies another problem: MPD patients are notorious liars. They are masters of deception and denial. They have to be in order to survive.

Somehow I have to convince a pathological liar to tell the truth.

Garth leaned back on the sofa, looking relaxed but hiding tension. Dad could smell tension a mile away, and it only made him angrier. Sometimes he *wanted* you to be scared of him, and the only way to keep the beatings to a minimum was to act like you were about to shit your pants, but this wasn't one of those times.

Dad had already worked himself up into a rage, waving his hands, screaming at the top of his lungs, knocking things off shelves, and the only thing that kept Garth from bolting was that Dad was between him and the living room door. Meredeth was nowhere to be seen, of course. She had managed to find some excuse to get out of the way seconds after Dad got home, and Garth, who had been surfing the VR nets in the drawing room, had been caught completely unawares.

"Bastards!" Dad howled, flinging a bit of Victorian porcelain from the mantle. It exploded against a wall. "Fucking *bastards!* They can't do this! *They can't do this!* I'll kill them. I'll kill every fucking one of them!"

A knife clicked into his hand and Garth almost made a break for it, but Dad savagely attacked a seat cushion instead. Cloth ripped and poly-cotton stuffing made a yellow snowstorm in the air. "Fuck fuck fuck FUCK!"

Garth cursed himself for a fool. He should have known this was coming. He should have stayed outside for the day, or begged permission to go into town, or just flat out *run*.

The newsnets were full of the story—Jonathan Blackstone's space monopoly was broken. In a stunning piece of diplomatic teamwork, six different countries had come together and declared Earth's current overpopulation a worldwide disaster, a disaster easily solved by building colony ships.

Because Blackstone International had continually refused to increase production and make colonization a more reasonable option, the company had been ordered to open its files on the phase drive.

The best team of barristers and solicitors Blackstone Industries could assemble had met with stony resistance at all levels. Higher courts refused appeals. Litigation was ignored. All objections were overruled. And today was the day when all specs, plans, and blueprints for the phase drive were to be dumped into every public access network.

Dad flung the knife away. It spun into a window which shattered with what Garth fervently hoped was a satisfying crash.

"You!" Dad snarled, rounding on Garth. "This is your fault! You've been spying on me—feeding information to my enemies!"

Garth's heart sank. It always came down to that. "Come on, Dad. You know I—"

"Don't you lie to me, boy." Before Garth could react, Dad yanked him off the couch and hauled him bodily toward the door. "Fletcher!"

Fletcher stepped into the room from his post in the hallway. Dad shoved Garth toward him. Garth stumbled, and Fletcher's hands bit into Garth's arm and shoulder. There would be bruises later.

"We're going downstairs, Fletcher," Dad said. "Boy needs to be taught a lesson."

"Yes, sir."

Garth's breath came faster and his heart hammered in his chest. "Come on, Dad," he cajoled. "I'm not—"

Fletcher hit him in the face, and coppery blood flooded Garth's mouth. Dad gestured, and Fletcher turkey-walked Garth down the hallway toward the kitchen and the basement door. Above them on a balcony that lined the upper half of the main foyer, Garth caught a glimpse of Meredeth staring down at them. In desperation he caught and held her eyes.

"Help me," he said hoarsely.

"Shut up, you little shit," Dad growled. "And stay where you are, Meredeth, if you know what's good for you."

Meredeth's face remained impassive for a moment. Then she turned away. Fletcher's grip tightened and he forced Garth further toward the kitchen and the basement below.

Why did you even bother? Garth thought savagely. *She's a fucking woman.*

And then they were in the basement, and Garth and Patrick and Andy stayed there for three days.

❖   ❖   ❖

"Lance, I'd like to try something different today," said Dr. Baldwin from his chair. "Have you ever been hypnotized?"

Lance, who was pacing nervously about the room, paused. "No. Why?"

"Would you like to try it?"

"What for?" Lance asked suspiciously.

"An experiment," Dr. Baldwin explained. "I can see you're feeling a bit anxious today, and it might help calm you down. I'd also like to ask you some questions, and they'll be easier to answer if you're relaxed."

Lance cocked his head. Dr. Baldwin was right—he *did* feel nervous, anxious, and he couldn't put his finger on the reason. Things had settled down and the news at home was good. With other companies building ships fast and furious, Blackstone International had elected to put most of its working ships into courier work, though they were also exploring the idea of luxury cruise ships and tourism. The conversion took a lot of time and energy on Dad's part, meaning he would be gone for days at a time. Yet Lance still felt restless.

Maybe Dr. Baldwin's idea will help, he thought.

"All right," Lance agreed. "How does it work? Are you going to wave a watch at me?"

Dr. Baldwin smiled. "No. I just need you to sit down in any way you find comfortable. Just have a seat. Thank you. Now close your eyes. Close them. Good. Now I want you to concentrate on the sound of my voice."

Excerpt from the files of Dr. Christopher Baldwin, session transcripts:

Doctor: . . . you are deeply asleep. You can still hear my voice, you can still speak, but you are deeply asleep. Can you hear me now?

Patient: Yes.

D: What is your name?

P: Jonathan Lance Michaels Blackstone the second. But my friends call me Lance.

D: Good, Lance. Now, knowing that in this room you

are perfectly safe, perfectly protected from all harm, I want to know if there is anyone else in this room who would like to speak. Anyone at all.

(pause)

D: Is there anyone else who would like to speak?

P: Affirmative.

D: What is your name?

P: Robin.

D: Hello, Robin. I'm Dr. Baldwin.

P: Aware of that. Have been watching most diligently.

D: You have?

P: Is job.

D: Your job?

P: Affirmative.

D: I don't understand, Robin. What exactly is your job?

P: Have several. Oversee implants, repair minor malfunctions, adjust body chemistry to avoid cybernetic rejection, heal wounds, prevent infection, keep skin clean, and others.

D: I see. So you have—um—a cybernetic implant?

P: No. *Am* cybernetic implant.

D: I don't understand, Robin. Can you explain what you mean by "cybernetic implant"?

P: Am hive mind composed of nanobots. Garth and Jessica call condition AI—artificial intelligence.

D: Artificial intelligence?

P: Affirmative.

D: Are you a machine?

P: In manner of speaking. Am actually several machines—nanobots injected and implanted to oversee Lance's cybernetics. But Jonathan Blackstone insists upon numerous triple backups. Extra processing space combined with continued interaction with human central nervous system eventually gave rise to sentience. Nanobots in continual communication, form hive mind. See all, hear all, know all.

D: I see. And who are Garth and Jessica?

P: Other people in Lance's head.

D: Lance has other people in his head?

P: Affirmative. Lance's brain divided into many compartments, each with own person inside. Have limited experience with other people, thought condition normal as result. Eventually reached conclusion something wrong. Have seen no evidence multiplicity occurs in other people as regular condition. Garth and Jessica deny problem, refuse to let me interfere, so arranged for Meredeth Blackstone to notice problem, make appointment with doctor.

D: I see. And how do Garth and Jessica stop you from interfering?

P: Concentrate in concert. Process eats up bioneural energy—my power source. Weakens consciousness until unable to function properly.

D: Why aren't they trying to stop you now?

P: Asleep, of course. Hypnotized. Will you help Lance?

D: I will try. Robin, do you know what an "ish" is?

P: Negative.

D: When someone has several people inside, often one of those people sees and hears and knows everything about all the others, but never—or rarely—acts. That person is called the ish. Are you Lance's ish?

P: (pause) Negative. Am separate from others. Not part of Lance. Told you—am part of cybernetics system.

D: You said Lance has cybernetic implants?

P: Affirmative.

D: What sort of implants?

P: Artificial eyes, artificial hair, facial molding, bone lengthening, muscle implants to enhance speed and strength, pheromone secretion system, penile enhancement.

D: I see. And who gave Lance these implants?

P: Dr. duFort. Never learned first name. Works in
        Paris. But everything done at Jonathan Blackstone's
        request.

D: Why were these implants made?

P: Uncertain. Aim seems to be to make Lance
        better, stronger, better looking. But intense
        physical, psychological abuse from father seems
        to counteract said goal.

D: How is Lance abused?

P: Beating, rape, electrical shock, starvation, bury
        alive, slash with knife, chain in basement, threaten,
        insult. More, if want all gory details.

D: Who does this, Robin?

P: Told you. Jonathan Blackstone. Lance's father.

D: Robin, this is very important. If the physical abuse
        is so severe, why have I seen no evidence of it? I
        have never seen Lance with bruises or lacerations.

P: My fault. Part of programming. Most injuries
        completely healed at cellular level within twenty-
        four hours. No bruises, scars to see.

D: Robin, how long have you known Lance?

P: Difficult question. Hard to pinpoint exact moment
        of first awareness. But first talked to him six
        months, two weeks, three days, three hours ago.

D: You talk to Lance?

P: Affirmative.

D: Do Garth and Jessica talk to Lance?

P: Negative. Lance unaware of their existence. But
        he sometimes hears their voices in head.

D: I see.

P: Are you going to help Lance?

D: I want to.

P: Are you going to get Lance away from Jonathan
        Blackstone?

D: I really can't answer that right now, Robin.

P: Must hurry. Others planning to run away.

D: Which others?

P: Garth, Jessica, Andy, Patrick. Creating plan to run away again.

D: Again?

P: Attempts made in past. Unsuccessful. Invariably followed by very harsh punishment. Lance unaware of plan, but idea filters through. Makes him restless.

D: I see. When will they run?

P: Undecided. Plan not quite come together yet.

D: Where are they planning to go?

P: Unknown. Plan consists solely of desire to get away from Jonathan Blackstone.

D: What are your plans, Robin?

P: (brief pause) Uncertain. Am considering foiling escape, but might cause more harm than help.

D: Robin, I would like to talk to Andy, if I could. Can you arrange it?

P: Only if promise to keep comments about me foiling escape to yourself. Others unaware of possibility. Want to keep it that way for now.

D: I won't tell them, Robin. May I speak to Andy now?

P: Working.

(pause)

D: Andy. I would like to speak with Andy. Andy, are you there?

P: Hey, Doc. What's up? (patient laughs)

D: Andy?

P: 's right. What do you want?

D: Andy, I've heard you're planning to run away.

P: Who told you?

D: So it's true, then?

P: Maybe. Maybe not. (patient cracks his knuckles)

D: Andy, I don't think it would be a very good idea. The streets are very crowded and dangerous. You would stand a very low chance of survival. I know you need help, and I can probably give it to you, but not if you run away.

P: Probably isn't good enough. I'm tired of being
        tied down, Doc. I want to run, be free. We're
        not going to hang around the Blackstone house
        anymore. Give us a week, and we're gone.
D: But if you're caught, the consequences will be—
P: Fuck the consequences. It's only *if* we get caught.
        One chance, Doc, and we're history.

From the journal of Dr. Christopher Baldwin:

*The alter that calls itself "Robin" is an interesting twist
on MPD. I have met alters who claim to be animals or
who even claim to be dead, but I've never met one who
claimed to be an artificial intelligence. And although Robin
was quite specific in the kind of abuse Lance has experienced,
I still don't have the evidence I need to remove Lance from
the Blackstone home for a very puzzling reason.*

Lance and Robin's voiceprints don't match.

*On a physical level, alters differ from one another in
ways besides behaviour and posture. Brainwave patterns
vary wildly between them and I've already mentioned eye
color, but their voiceprints invariably remain the same.
Robin's voice sounds different from Lance's—moreso than
Garth's or even Jessica's—so on a whim I ran a voiceprint.*

There was no similarity.

*This contradicts all previous studies in MPD, but there
it is. And any good barrister would pounce on it. I have
no vidcard footage of the session, so I couldn't prove that
Robin's voice came from Lance's body. A judge would be
forced to agree.*

*And then there are the factual inconsistencies. Robin
claims to oversee Lance's numerous cybernetic implants.
I have accessed Lance's medical history, and there is no
mention of any operations involving cybernetics. A Dr.
Angelique duFort does conduct cybernetic research in a
center funded by Blackstone International, but there are
no records of Lance's presence at her center. Unfortunately,
I can't contact her directly to ask—that would breach
confidentiality.*

Another anomaly that prevents me from removing Lance from the Blackstone house is the continuing lack of visible signs of abuse. True, Jonathan Blackstone may be purposefully avoiding any abuse that would leave visible cuts or bruises, but I have seen Lance for several sessions and have been watching closely. There are no signs that he is ever in pain. I have never seen him limp, and I have not noticed any evidence of physical distress.

In my experience, abuse cases simply don't work that way. Some bit of physical trauma, such as a black eye, eventually becomes evident, but is always explained away. "I fell down the stairs," says the patient. Or, "I got into a fight."

For this case, in an odd reversal of expected psychology, Lance—speaking through Robin—admits to the abuse, but claims it is healed by resident nanobots. I did look up several articles on nanotechnology, just in case, but all the research I saw indicates that, while nanobots are essential to computer systems, no one has yet managed to use them in the human body. Laboratory animals, yes— but the animals invariably die. And when Dr. Dilip Fadel's ape went mad and killed four people, nanobots were outlawed for use in any animal larger than a housecat. So either Dr. duFort's records have been altered or Lance saw her name in connection with cybernetic research— in a center owned by his father—and he created the entire story.

Making up stories is a symptom of many disorders, including MPD, but is not sufficient grounds for taking a child away from his parents. I'm right back where I started—having to get Lance or one of the other alters to admit to the abuse. I know the abuse must exist, but still can't prove it.

I do have to admit that I'm a bit confused. If I don't believe Robin's claims, I can't explain Lance's lack of visible physical abuse or the change in voiceprint.

If I do believe Robin, however, then I have to believe that Lance is possessed of a small army of nanobots that

*banded together to form a collective consciousness which
heals him of all wounds—a preposterous claim.*

*A further complication arises from the fact that Lance's
alters intend to run away some time in the near future. I
tried to talk Andy out of it, but he refused, and I wasn't
successful in trying to contact any other alters today. Robin
said he (she? it?) might be able to stop them, but wasn't
sure. I hope the plan doesn't come off.*

*On an analytical note, I believe Robin is an attempt on
Lance's part to remain separate from, and therefore deny,
emotion. A machine has no feelings and cannot be hurt.
It is also possible Robin is the ish—the personality that
sees and records everything, but rarely, if ever, gets
involved.*

*It seems plausible to me that Lance, as Robin, created
the idea of all these operations and implants as a way to
rationalise why his father abuses him. If the aim of the
abuse is to improve, then there is hope that the improvements
will one day be enough and the abuse will end. Unfortunately,
the abuse never ends.*

Lance paced nervously about his bedroom, the object
clutched in his hands. The walls were a warm green, the
carpet a soft turquoise, the bedspread a perfect match for
them both. Lance had asked Chloe for none of it, but he
was used to that. What he couldn't get over was the horse.

It was a perfectly ordinary, wooden horse. Hand-carved
of light-colored wood, rough-edged but free of splinters,
about a foot high. It wasn't a toy horse a child would play
with—it was the kind of horse a teenager might put on a
shelf next to trophies and other mementos. The horse had
no rider and was rearing on its hind legs. It also had no
finish and looked kind of raw, but upon closer inspection,
Lance realized the rawness lent the horse an untamed
power. The harsh grain stood out, making the figure look
fierce, wild, and free.

If Lance had ever wished for a wooden horse, this would
have been it.

He stopped pacing long enough to look down at it again. The horse had simply been on his nightstand that morning when he woke up. No note of explanation, nothing. It was just there.

Lance ran his hands over the horse's rough wood, then turned it to look on the bottom. Words were carved into the base.

" 'To Lance,' " Lance read softly. " 'Love, Grandpa Jack.' Who's Grandpa Jack?"

Lance had no grandfather named Jack. The only living grandparents Lance knew of were on his mother's side. They had moved to California, in America, just after Lance's birth, and Lance hardly ever saw them, not even in VR or on the phone. Dad's mother had died when Dad was a baby, and his father had died a few years before Dad and Mom got married.

Lance set the horse back on his nightstand and admired it. For one brief, horrible moment he thought Dad had carved it. But Dad always worked in clay and always made human figures. He would certainly never carve a horse out of wood—or sign it "Grandpa Jack" and give it to his son.

. . . tomorrow. The knife is in . . .

. . . heard Robin tell Baldwin that . . .

. . . Robin interferes, we'll have to . . .

Lance put his hands to his head. "Go away!" he pleaded. "Leave me alone!"

. . . forget—I get to take out Fletcher . . .

. . . the virus? We can't get past security without . . .

. . . course I have. I'm not a . . .

"I said leave me alone!" Lance yelled, still clutching his head. "I hate you! Get out of my head!"

The voices fell silent. Lance lay back on his bed and stared at the green ceiling. He had gone most of the summer holidays without hearing the voices, and now they were back.

The door flew open and Fletcher burst into the room, pistol at the ready.

"What's going on?" he snapped. "I heard shouting."

Lance pointedly ignored Fletcher, continued to stare at the ceiling. Fletcher glanced quickly about the room, then strode over to the bed.

"What are you yelling about?" he demanded.

Lance took no notice. Fletcher holstered his gun and leaned over the bed. Then things seemed to jump, and Fletcher was standing two feet away again, grinning. Lance automatically glanced at the clock. Two minutes had passed.

"—dick," Fletcher was saying. "And don't you forget it. Now come on. Don't you want to go to your *workout*?" He sneered at the last word.

Lance waited a moment, then slowly got up to head for the door, snagging a carryall of gym clothes on the way. He hated doing what Fletcher said, but he didn't want to miss seeing Dr. Baldwin, either. On impulse, he also snatched up the horse.

"Aw, isn't that sweet?" Fletcher smirked. "Taking his wittle horsey wif him."

And abruptly Lance was in the back seat of the car, horse on the floor at his feet, Fletcher behind the wheel. Apprehension rose for a moment until another glance at his wristcomp told him he must be on his way *to* Dr. Baldwin's office, not going home from it. The back of Fletcher's neck was a dull red and his knuckles were white on the steering wheel. Lance wondered if he had said something during the blackout to tick Fletcher off.

When they arrived at Dr. Baldwin's building, Fletcher silently escorted him to the door with a tight-lipped expression on his face. Fletcher never went inside the building—Mom had forbidden it so Lance's sessions would remain a secret, though Lance still wasn't sure how she had gotten that particular order past Dad or why she had bothered to try. He knew she didn't care about him, and he didn't care about her.

On the third floor Ms. Grey, the secretary-receptionist, waved him into Dr. Baldwin's office without taking the phone away from her ear. Lance hurried on in and shut the door behind him, sealing himself away from the memory of Fletcher's glare. Dr. Baldwin, as always, was waiting in his chair.

Lance flung himself on the comfortable couch with a small sigh of relief. Dr. Baldwin was always there, a steady constant in his life. They exchanged a few pleasantries and Lance almost smiled, enjoying the routine.

"I like the horse," Dr. Baldwin said. "Where'd you get it?"

Lance turned the rough horse over in his hands, suddenly nervous.

Why did I bring this? he thought. *I should have known he'd ask about it.*

"It was a gift," he said aloud. "I like it."

"It suits you," Dr. Baldwin agreed. "Who gave it to you?"

Lance hesitated. "Grandpa Jack."

"Grandpa Jack," Dr. Baldwin repeated slowly. "I don't think you've mentioned him to me before."

Lance didn't answer. All of a sudden he felt depressed. The voices had come back, Fletcher was angry with him, Mom had disappeared for another one of her VR game meetings, leaving him alone in the house, Dad wouldn't let him visit Vic over the summer holidays, and he had had a blackout today that almost made him miss seeing Dr. Baldwin.

"May I see it?" Dr. Baldwin asked. "The horse?"

Lance shrugged and handed it to Dr. Baldwin, who admired it for a moment, then turned it over and read the inscription.

"Fine workmanship." Dr. Baldwin returned the horse to Lance and settled back in his chair. "So. What do you want to talk about today, Lance?"

"I don't know." Lance got up to pace, then abruptly sat down again. Maybe he should tell Dr. Baldwin about the blackouts and the voices. Dr. Baldwin wouldn't care. Dr. Baldwin wouldn't laugh at him or make stupid jokes or make him feel like an asshole, and he wouldn't tell anyone else about it.

Still, something stood in the way. He had kept the voices and blackouts secret all his life. It was ingrained. But he was tired. Tired of keeping the secret, tired of not being able to talk to someone. And if he couldn't trust Dr. Baldwin, who could he trust?

Lance took a deep breath. *So do it then.*

"A while ago," he began cautiously, "you said something about people who had blackouts and stuff."

"Yes."

"You said that people who have them aren't really crazy, right?"

"I said that such people often have things they need to resolve," Dr. Baldwin said. "And I don't use the word *crazy*. Or *mad*."

Lance swallowed, then steeled himself. "Well . . . when I told you I didn't have . . . didn't have blackouts, well—I was, uh, I wasn't really telling the truth. I have them. I had one today, in fact. Two, now that I think about it."

He waited for a reaction, but Dr. Baldwin merely nodded his head encouragingly.

Lance opened his mouth again and words suddenly tumbled out in a rush. "I lose pieces of time," he said. "I'll be doing one thing and then suddenly I'm somewhere else doing something else and I have no idea how I got there or what I'm doing. And then I have to act like I know what's going on even though I don't. Robin helps sometimes, but not always, and once I lost almost six months and I didn't know what was going on at school and people would come up to me and ask me questions or say things to me and I would have no idea who they were or what they were talking about or what I was supposed to say." He realized there were tears running down his face. "I think I must be crazy. Am I crazy?"

"Like I said, Lance, I don't use that word." Dr. Baldwin crossed his legs. "Lance, is there anything in particular that seems to trigger these blackouts? Any certain condition or phrase you might hear?"

Lance shook his head. "They just happen."

"How long do they usually last?"

"Sometimes a minute or two, sometimes hours or even days. Like I said, I lost six months once."

"Do you have any memory at all of what happens during these blackouts or any sense of passing time?"

"No. Nothing. They scare me."

Dr. Baldwin nodded. "I'm sure they do. Lance, have you ever heard of multiple personalities?"

"You mean where someone has other people living inside their head? Yeah, I've—" Lance cut himself off and edged backward on the couch. Apprehension climbed back into his stomach. "You think I have . . . multiple personalities?"

"Yes."

"I've read about people like that. They go nuts and kill people and don't have any memory afterward." Lance's mouth went dry and his hands twisted in his lap. They were cold. "You think that's what I do? That I kill people when I have a blackout?"

"Not at all," Dr. Baldwin said soothingly. "Just because you have MPD doesn't mean you're a killer. MPD is simply a coping mechanism gone awry."

"What do you mean?"

"Sometimes," Dr. Baldwin said in a calm, comforting voice, "people see or experience something so traumatic that their minds can't cope with it. They simply can't imagine that such a horrible thing would happen to them, so they decide it must have happened to someone else. Their brain creates someone else—an alternate personality—for it to happen to, and they forget the trauma ever took place. And if the trauma is repeated, the other personality takes over again so the person doesn't have to experience it. It's called dissociation."

"And that's what's happening to me?" Lance said, eyes wide. Then he shook his head. "No way. That can't be."

Listen to doctor, Jaylance, Robin suddenly put in. *Knows what he's talking about.*

"Robin?" Lance whispered.

"Pardon?" Dr. Baldwin said.

"Nothing," Lance replied quickly. "I mean, I can't believe this. You're saying I've got another person inside my head who takes over when I can't handle something?"

"More than one," Dr. Baldwin said.

Lance folded his arms. "You can't be serious."

"You've had blackouts in this office, correct?" Dr. Baldwin said.

"Uh . . . well, yeah. I guess."

"During one of those blackouts, I talked to a young man named Andy."

Lance stared. "Who's Andy?"

"One of your alters. I also talked to another alter who I believe is a cultured young lady."

"A girl?"

"Yes. It's very common to have at least one alter of the opposite sex. I also suspect your horse was carved by another alter named Grandpa Jack."

Lance looked down at the figurine.

Dr. Baldwin uncrossed his legs and sat straighter in his chair. "Lance, I wouldn't be telling you any of this if I didn't think you were able to handle it. You are a very strong, capable young man."

Lance continued staring at the horse without answering. He didn't know what to say.

There are other people living inside my head? he thought. *That's impossible. That only happens in VR.*

Not true, Jaylance.

"I'm confused," Lance said in a barely audible voice. "I don't know what to think."

"Confusion is actually a good sign," Dr. Baldwin told him. "It means you're starting to look at things you've been ignoring before. Lance, do you know Robin?"

"Robin?"

"I also talked to an alter named Robin, who said you can talk together."

Lance drew his legs up to his chest and rested his chin on his knees. "How did you talk to Robin?"

"Alters often come out under hypnosis. Last session,

when I hypnotized you, Robin spoke to me. Robin said you two can talk. I've also heard you say Robin's name. Do you talk?"

Lance paused uncertainly. Robin was a secret, a friend no one could take away from him. What if telling Dr. Baldwin destroyed that?

Won't. Tell him, Jaylance. Is all right.

"I—yes," Lance stammered. "We talk. I can hear Robin's voice inside my head. Is . . . is that crazy?"

"Do you ever hear other voices? Voices you can't explain?"

"Sometimes. They argue and yell at each other, but I can't always make out what they're saying."

"Do they come from outside your head or inside your head?"

"Inside."

Dr. Baldwin nodded. "That's another symptom of MPD."

"So you're saying I do have MPD?" Lance asked. "I mean, there's no way it can be something else?"

Dr. Baldwin shook his head. "No. I've treated four cases, and that is definitely your condition. But MPD is treatable, Lance, if we work together."

"Treatable how?"

"By attending regular therapy sessions. It won't be easy, but you can get beyond this."

"You mean we can stop the blackouts and the voices that argue in my head?"

"I believe so."

"I don't want to lose Robin, though," Lance said almost thoughtfully. "Robin's my closest friend."

"What does Robin say to you, Lance?"

"That we're friends. That—" Lance hesitated. If he told Dr. Baldwin about Robin being a hive mind composed of nanobots, he'd get into big trouble. Putting nanobots into people was illegal. The police would come, Lance would be arrested—

—and the nanobots would tear him to pieces. Cell by cell, bit by bit.

"That what, Lance?"

"Nothing."

"I spoke to Robin, Lance, when you were under hypnosis, and I have an audio recording of what happened. Do you want to hear it?"

Lance shrugged.

"Wilson," Dr. Baldwin said, raising his voice, "retrieve file Lance Twelve and play audio."

A conversation came over hidden speakers. Lance recognized Dr. Baldwin's voice and remembered the words he had used to hypnotize Lance, but after that, none of it sounded familiar, even the parts Lance himself said. The voice on the computer was only vaguely similar to his own. It was Robin's. Lance listened, both repulsed and fascinated.

The fascination, however, abruptly turned to stark fear when Robin mentioned nanobots and artificial intelligence.

"Wilson," Lance blurted, "halt playback."

The audio stopped. Lance snatched up his carryall and the wooden horse and headed for the door. "That was real interesting, but I have to go now."

Dr. Baldwin made no move to stop him. "Lance—"

"I can't listen anymore. I think the session is almost over anyway. I'll see you next time. Maybe."

And he ducked out the door before Dr. Baldwin could reply.

An hour later, Lance was standing in front of the mirror in his bedroom. His eyes had a haunted look. The room around him was still done in shades of green, and Grandpa Jack's horse was back on the nightstand.

"Robin?" he said. "Are you there?"

Here, Jaylance.

"Robin, was Dr. Baldwin right? Do I . . . do I have multiple personalities?"

Affirmative.

A knot tightened in Lance's chest.

"Why didn't you tell me before?"

Others didn't want you to know, stopped me from telling. Very protective of you.

"So . . . so why can you tell me now?"

Uncertain. Perhaps because Dr. Baldwin knew. Perhaps because you are now ready to know.

Lance swallowed. His palms were sweating and a small part of him wondered if that increased the pheromone output. Not that the pheromones seemed to affect Fletcher.

Because father arranged injection of counteragent.

"Oh."

Lance put out a hand and touched the smooth, cool mirror. The reflection wasn't a real person, but neither was Lance. They were both created by someone else.

And there are other people hiding inside me, he thought. *Are they real? Or are they like the mirror? What happens when they take over? What if one takes over and I never come back? What would happen to me then?*

Fear, the most familiar of all Lance's emotions, rose up again. It seemed like Lance was always afraid. Afraid of his looks, afraid of going to school, afraid of Fletcher, afraid of hospitals, afraid of Dad. Afraid of being afraid. It seemed like no matter what he did, the fear was there. Even if nothing threatened at the moment, he was still afraid of the moment when something *would* threaten—because something always did.

Suddenly he was tired of it. Tired of the fear, tired of the apprehension, tired of giving in to both.

"No matter what I do," he whispered fiercely to himself, "I'm afraid. Even when I do all the right things, I'm afraid. I hate it. I *hate* it."

Maybe is time to do something different, Robin said in an oddly quiet voice.

"Maybe," Lance nodded. "Maybe it is." A new feeling started to rise—a new resolve. If what he had been doing before didn't stop the fear or make his life easier, maybe it was time to try something different. Something new.

The possibility made his heart beat faster, but not with fear. It was with excitement. Dr. Baldwin had once told him that everyone possessed the power to make changes in their lives. Maybe Lance did, too. And maybe the best place to start was with what he knew about himself.

Lance licked his lips and opened his mouth to ask Robin a question when something else occurred to him. What if Lance changed things and they only got worse? What if he meddled with some delicate balance and was sent teetering over the edge?

What if Dad found out?

His resolve slipped away and the old fear rushed in to take its place. Lance couldn't make changes himself. He was never given the chance. Dad—or Fletcher—would find out, and that would be the end of it. He was powerless. He was helpless. He always had been and always would be.

Incorrect incorrect wrong no never not, Robin said. *Helplessness learned, Jaylance, not inborn. Earlier thoughts on right track. Do you like being afraid?*

"No," Lance whispered.

If current life situation results in unwanted fear, what must be done?

"Change the life situation," Lance replied.

Will father make change?

"No!"

Mother?

"She ignores me."

Then who will if you don't?

A spark of Lance's earlier resolve flared. Robin was right. No one else was going to help him. He had to make changes on his own, and the only place to start was to find out more about himself. Lance straightened and took a deep breath.

"Robin," he said deliberately, "how many personalities do I have?"

Forty-seven.

Lance's knees went weak and he sank to the floor. "Forty-seven?"

Affirmative.

"There are *forty-seven* people in my head?"

Many came out only once, never used again. Have seven actually active personalities.

"And you're one of them?"

Negative no never not. Am separate from alters. Dr. Baldwin not always correct.

Lance swallowed and ran a hand over the green carpet. It was soft and plush beneath his fingers. "Is it the . . . the others who change things in my room?"

Affirmative.

"Who did this one?"

Grandpa Jack. Likes green.

Lance reached up to his nightstand and took down the horse. The figurine was rough but solid, and smelled like fresh-cut wood. He held the horse in his lap and stroked it. A quiet courage seemed to flow into him from the statue.

"Robin, what are the names of the active alters?"

Garth Blackstone, Jessica Michaels, Johnny Blackstone, Patrick Kuiper, Andy Braun, Jay Blackstone, and Grandpa Jack.

"They have last names?" Lance asked, surprised.

Of course. Garth claims to be your half brother. Jessica is half sister. Jay is twin brother. Patrick, Andy unrelated.

"And they come out during my blackouts?" Lance persisted.

Affirmative.

"Is there a way I could—" Lance swallowed "—could talk to them?"

Can relay messages.

Lance shook his head. "No. I want to talk to them. They're the voices I hear, aren't they? Why couldn't I talk directly to them?"

Many of them can hear you now, Jaylance, but are unable to answer. Voices are uncontrolled leakage.

Lance thought a moment. "What about an audio? Dr. Baldwin played a recording of the others. What if I asked questions on an audio and one of the alters took over?

He could listen to the recording, say something back, and I could play his answer. Would that work?"

Possibly. But alters usually come out only in response to certain stimuli. If stimulus absent, alter may not reply.

"Oh." The old, helpless feeling began to return.

But perhaps can help things along, Robin said quickly. *Have access to entire brain, you know—including all alters. Might be able to nudge here, there.*

Lance perked up. "Let's try it, then. Chloe, create audio file titled 'Alter1.' Chloe, begin recording." He paused for a moment, suddenly uncertain what to say. "Um, hi. I'm Lance. What's your name? Hello?"

He waited. Nothing happened. He began to feel silly talking to himself.

"Robin? Is anyone listening?"

Hard to tell. Some can hear, but is hard to tell if are listening.

"What do we—"

The door opened and Fletcher stuck his head into the room.

"Who're you talking to?" Fletcher demanded.

"The computer," Andy snapped from his seat on the floor. "What do you care?"

"Watch your mouth, you little prick, or I'll—"

"—stuff your cock up my ass?" Andy finished. "Fletch, I hate to burst your bubble, but it's no big deal. You're just jealous because I'm hung better'n you. But if you're a good boy, I might let you blow me." Almost casually, Andy glanced at the clock. *Five . . . four . . . three . . .*

Fletcher's face turned beet-red, almost purple. He surged into the room with an animal snarl, but the moment he was close enough, Andy blew on him.

The change was startling. The rage left Fletcher's face and his hands fell to his sides. He stood there, looking down at Andy with a confused expression on his face.

"What's the matter, Fletch?" Andy asked innocently. "Aren't you mad at me?"

Fletcher blinked. "No. I guess I'm not."

"Dad's been out of town for almost a week now," Andy said, clenching his teeth around the word *Dad*. Jonathan Blackstone wasn't his father, but it was easier to say he was than to explain otherwise. "Did you take your injection this afternoon? It's Wednesday and six o'clock."

"I don't see why the hell I should," Fletcher answered stubbornly. "Mr. Blackstone won't tell me what it's for. It doesn't do anything that I can see, and I—" He paused. "Why the fuck am I telling you this?"

Andy shrugged. "Just being conversational. But I'm working on something private. Do you mind?"

"Sure. Sorry." And Fletcher quietly exited.

"Pheromones," Andy said thoughtfully to no one in particular. "What a wonderful invention."

Counteragent wears off on the hour like clockwork, Robin agreed. *And abrupt lack thereof seems to create greater sensitivity to pheromones. Inhibits resistance normally posed by adrenaline. Going to leave message for Lance? House computer still recording.*

"What? Oh, hi Robin." Andy cracked his knuckles. "Hey, Robby—can you get it off?"

Pardon?

"Can you make it with anyone?"

A pause. *Don't have necessary equipment.*

Andy burst into laughter. "No, I suppose not. Poor meatless Robin. I'll bet you could fuck with another computer, though. You know—cybersex."

?????°°°?????

"Now what the hell did that mean?"

wow neat-o phased blasphemous cool wonderful idea

Andy shook his head. "Whatever you say, meatless. Chloe, halt recording. Chloe, play audio Alter1." Andy let the audio file run until it reached the point where Fletcher had opened the door. "Chloe, halt playback. Chloe, erase remainder of file. Chloe, append following to file Alter1. Chloe, begin recording. Hey, Lance, how's it going? I'm Andy Braun."

❖   ❖   ❖

Lance looked around, realized he was sitting on the bed instead of the floor, and glanced at the clock. Twenty minutes.

"Robin?"

fabulous wonderful fantastic hellacious freaky wow

Lance shook his head. "Robin, are you all right?"

wheee yippee great awesome wondrous WOW

"Um—Chloe, are you still recording audio?"

"Negative," replied the computer.

Lance licked his lips, both excited and nervous. "Chloe, open audio file Alter1. Chloe, play audio."

His own voice promptly emerged from the hidden speakers. "Um, hi," said the recording. "I'm Lance. What's your name? Hello? Robin? Is anyone listening? What do we—?"

And then the voice changed. It was still his own, but it sounded different somehow.

"Hey Lance," it said, "how's it going? I'm Andy Braun. This recording is a blasphemous idea, budster—we never get to talk. So how's your life? I think mine sucks pondwater. Um—I don't know what else to say. I guess I'll talk to you later. Maybe we can—"

"Hi, Lance. It's Garth. Listen, kid—I'm glad you came up with this. We have to get out of here. Dad's a real shit, you know? One of these days he's going to do something we can't deal with. We're cooking up a plan to run away, and we're going tonight. You in?"

"Hello, Lance. This is your half-sister Jessica. I've listened to what the boys have said, and Garth's plan is quite simple. I've created a virus for Chloe's security systems. Tonight I'll drop it into the net. It will take the cameras off-line and set up sensor ghosts all over the estate. With the guard staff in a state of confusion, it should be simple to slip away. Garth has been talking to Victor, and he will meet us outside the wall with transportation."

"This is Patrick. I get to take care of Fletcher. It can't go wrong, Lance, unless you're a gutless coward—or Robin stops us like Dr. Baldwin wants. You tell meatless that if he or she, whatever the fuck Robin is, tries to stop us, I'll kill it. I'll find a way."

"Watch your mouth, young man. Lance, this is your Grandpa Jack. I hope you like the horse. Any time you want to talk, I'll be happy to listen. I love you very much, and I'm always here for you. I think Garth wants you to answer about the plan to run away, so I'll sign off now."

The recording ended. Lance realized he was sitting on the floor cradling the horse in his lap while tears ran down his face. It was too much to deal with all at once. All those voices that had been his and not-his. It was eerie, like he was possessed.

At least I know Grandpa Jack loves me, he thought, stroking the horse. *That's something. But running away . . . I don't know. What if Dad catches up with me—us? Like that time last year.*

That time last year.

Realization crashed in on him. It was the alters who had run away that time. It was the alters who had planned and executed everything. This was it—this was the explanation and proof he'd been looking for all his life. Now he knew, really *knew,* why he had the blackouts. He knew why total strangers acted like they knew him and why his bedroom kept changing. It was his alters. They had always been there, been there for *him.*

Now the alters wanted him to run away. Tonight. And Lance also knew he wanted to go with them. He wanted to *run,* run far away from Dad, and he would never look back.

"Chloe," he said, "append following to audio file Alter1." He cleared his throat. "Hi, Garth. I'm in. What do I need to do?"

CHAPTER ELEVEN

NOW

Delia carefully closed the storage locker and hummed a quiet tune. Just a few minutes ago she had been in the middle of a nanobot hive set up by a madman, but now she felt strangely euphoric.

Well, why the hell not? she thought. *I'm bloody well alive.* She trotted toward the narrow spiral stairs leading up to the ship's control room. *Now all I have to do is figure out what to do about Lance.* Delia slowed her pace and let her hand trail on the white rail. Her shoes clanged on the grated metal steps. *How can I be attracted to a man with such deep-seated problems?*

Delia had no ready answer to that one.

Yes I do, she corrected herself. *Lance is sweet and handsome and strong—but he's gentle, too. Gentler than Quinn was. Lance is easy after growing up with Quinn.*

And I couldn't save Quinn.

She snorted. *Delia the mother/rescuer, is it? No. Yes. I don't know. I can't "save" Lance—he has to do it himself. But I can help him. I can be there for him. I want to be there for him.*

But he's going to have to stay in therapy, she told herself, echoing earlier thoughts. *I don't know if I could spend my life with someone who's so changeable. I'd never know who I was waking up to in the morning.* She shook her head. *Come on, Delia. You don't know what's going to come of this. You haven't even gone out on a date yet and already you're wondering about marriage. Just relax and see what happens. If it works, it works. If not, it doesn't.*

Delia reached the top of the stairs, rounded a corner, and almost ran into Lance, who was striding purposefully toward the control room. Meredeth Michaels was slung over his shoulder in a firefighter's carry. Startled, Delia backed up a step.

"Lance?" she asked. "What's going on? What happened?"

"Delia!" he gasped, and went right past her without pausing. "Delia, help me!"

Delia hurried to catch up. "What's wrong? How badly is she hurt?"

Lance kept walking. Ms. Michaels bounced and shuddered like a giant rag doll over his back. "Delia . . . help me . . . This isn't . . . the Company. . . ."

He seemed to choke for a moment, as if his throat were eating the words before they came out. Then he fell silent.

Delia's first thought was that this was another facet of Lance's MPD, an idea she quickly rejected. According to everything she'd read, one personality didn't control the entire body while another controlled the mind. A rogue alter might take over a limb, perhaps, but not more. And Lance had said it wasn't anyone in the Company.

So if it's not Lance or the Company, what the bloody hell is going on?

She darted ahead of him and turned, muscles tense, mind racing. "Stop!" she ordered, and pushed against him when he tried to pass her.

It was like shoving a steel wall. Almost carelessly, not-Lance shoved Delia back with one hand. The force sent Delia sprawling and almost knocked the breath from her lungs. A twinge went through her prosthetics, warning her of minor damage, though the prosthetics' nanos could easily handle it.

Delia scrambled to her feet and sprinted after him. "Let her go!"

She grabbed the unconscious Ms. Michaels by one shoulder and tried to haul her off not-Lance's back. Not-Lance calmly pivoted in place, ready to shove her again, but Delia dodged away.

He's moving strangely, she thought. *Almost like a robot or something.*

"Lance, can you hear me?" she said, trying to keep her voice calm. "I'm trying to help. Tell me what's wrong."

In answer he shrugged Ms. Michaels back into place and turned to head down the corridor again, but Delia snatched one of the other woman's arms and yanked with all her strength. Ms. Michaels slid bonelessly over Lance's shoulder to the floor, forcing Delia to backpedal to keep her balance.

Lance stopped and slowly cocked his head, looking at her. He had no eye color—just two black pinholes floating in a white void. The look on his face was completely devoid of anything human. Delia shuddered involuntarily and backed up a step.

"Interfering," Lance said. The voice didn't sound like his at all, and even Jessica still sounded a little like Lance. It sounded like something generated by a computer. "Must not."

"Leave Ms. Michaels alone," Delia warned. *Oh, good one, Delia. What are you going to do if he doesn't?* She cast about the hallway, looking for something to use as a weapon.

"You are part artificial," Lance observed with clinical detachment. "Solution simple."

With impossible speed, Lance's hand shot out and caught Delia's right arm. Delia tried to twist away, but his grip was iron-hard.

And then he let go. Delia wriggled her fingers, checking for damage to the prosthetic. There was none. Lance just stood there in front of her.

"What was that for?" she demanded, trying to edge

between him and Ms. Michaels. "Lance—or whoever you are—talk to me."

Delia's arm twitched. It jumped, then gyrated wildly as if it had a life of its own. Before Delia could react, her right leg joined in, jerking in a grotesque dance. Her elbow smacked against the wall with a bone-jarring *thump*. Delia lost her balance and fell, arm and leg still in convulsions. No matter how hard she tried, she couldn't bring her limbs under control.

Lance impassively picked up Ms. Michaels's unconscious form and stalked away, leaving Delia flopping crazily about the floor.

Sweat broke out on Lance's face as he continued on his way to the control room, his mother a limp, heavy bundle on his shoulders. His mind pushed and surged, trying to wrest control, but there was nothing to grab onto. This was nothing like being shoved aside by one of the others. Lance could see everything, feel every sensation, but an outside force controlled his every move, like a puppeteer pulling strings on a marionette.

Robin! he screamed for the hundredth time. *What's going on?*

Robin is behind this, Jessica said suddenly. *The muscle implants are controlling your movements, but Robin has not actively taken control. I suspect Robin also mucked with Delia by reprogramming the nanos overseeing her prosthetics.*

Sounds echoed around Lance, sounds created by his body but not under his control. Heavy footsteps in the corridor. The rustling of a body sliding to the control room floor. The creak of a leather chair. The navigation board clicking beneath his fingers. A delicate shudder as the *Defiant Lady* slipped into phase drive. His body settling back into the chair, unmoving.

Lance read the course his traitorous fingers had set. They would come out of phase drive at a point midway between Thetachron III and Earth.

A rendezvous, Lance said. *It can't be anything else.*
But with whom? Jessica asked. *And why?*

Cold realization dawned. *Because you were wrong, Jess. There is a ship within range that could snatch us up. The Defiant Lady. Robin's taking us to Dad.*

Jessica gasped. *But that's im—* She halted and thought for a moment. *No, it makes perfect sense. Your father must have put something in the nanos on that station. Some kind of viral program that would take over and force Robin to bring you to a set meeting place.*

She went on for a moment, conjecturing about viruses and program algorithms in a language Lance couldn't begin to follow. Instead, he tried to move, to twitch a finger, wiggle a toe, blink an eye. Nothing. He couldn't budge, a prisoner in his own body. Walls of paralyzed flesh closed around him. Panic sprouted, and Lance was suddenly filled with a screaming need to *do* something, to run, jump, dance, be *free*.

Let me out! he howled. *Let me OUT!*

Now you know how it feels, said a new voice.

Brief pause. *Andy?* Lance thought incredulously.

Yeah. You see what I mean? You get to do anything you want, but I only get what I need when you think there's time for it.

You bastard! You left Mom and Delia behind to die.

Meredeth isn't my mother and there are dozens of Delias. You need to learn to live for yourself for once, Lance.

At the expense of someone else's life?

Hey, the universe is divided into "me" and "not-me." Guess which is the only part that matters?

Jessica broke in. *All very entertaining, but we have another problem. Earth—and Jonathan Blackstone—are only a short distance away.*

Lance looked at the navigation screen—that was the way his eyes were pointed—and he pushed the argument with Andy aside. *Listen—you told me once that you guys had a fight with Robin the first time Robin showed up. How did you win?*

We all teamed up to keep control, Jessica replied.

Garth took over after we pushed Robin out of the driver's seat, Andy added. *It happened while you were asleep. Except this time Robin isn't really driving.*

Couldn't we squash Robin anyway? To the point where Robin's active control of the nanos would waver enough that the muscle implants would go back to their default settings?

Possibly, Jessica said. *Robin operates on electrochemical energy. If enough of us concentrate, start using more of that energy, Robin will lose vital power and have to let go. But three people will not suffice. Robin has no . . . personal problems and is stronger than we are.*

How, then? Lance asked, beginning to feel frustrated again.

This is all your fault, Lance, Andy said suddenly. *If you hadn't accepted this contract, none of this would have happened.*

I didn't take the contract, Lance snapped. *Garth did.*

Because you were too scared to deal with your mommy being in trouble, Andy snarled. *Crying, whimpering. Gotta hide behind Garth whenever something scary shows up. What a baby.*

Anger rose behind Lance's eyes. He tried to squash it—anger was wrong. It was *bad*.

Gonna cry, baby? Andy cooed. *What's the matter? You want to hit me, don't you? But you can't. Coward.*

More anger. Lance tried to retreat into the blackness, but couldn't. Robin held him in place. Who the hell did Andy think he was? Andy never took responsibility for anything he did, always left Lance to clean up his messes. The anger swelled, black and swirling. Lance tried to clench his fists, but his fingers wouldn't move.

Poor scared little Lance, Andy taunted. *Can't find his dick with two hands and a roadmap, wouldn't know what to do with it if he could.*

Come on, asshole! I'll fight you any time you want!

Hello, Patrick, Jessica said. *Glad you could make it.*

What's going on? Lance asked, suddenly bewildered.

Easy, Andy replied smugly. *Don't you read your own psych books? One of us gets the body when you don't want to deal with something. That's why you were never able to talk to any of us—you didn't want to know what we did. But now that you can't leave, you have to deal with your own problems. I got you mad, and here's Patrick.*

The *Lady* shuddered again and dropped into normal space. The navigation screen showed another ship approaching. Lance recognized it—his father's private cruiser. His heart would have begun to pound, but it was under Robin's control.

Quick, then, Lance said. *We need to stop Robin.*

Four of us won't be enough, Jessica replied calmly.

We have to try!

A computer chime signaled an incoming message. Lance's fingers moved and the com screen flickered to life. Jonathan Blackstone smiled icily at his son.

"Hello, John," he said. "I've come to bring you home. Where you belong."

Lance didn't reply. He couldn't.

"You're probably wondering what's happening, aren't you?" Blackstone continued. "You always were stupid. Never could see what was going on, even if it was right in front of you. I've got a lot more to teach you." He leaned forward intently. "And this time, I'll teach you fucking *right*. You won't even be able to *think* about running away when I'm through with you."

Lance automatically tried to shrink back, all thoughts of Robin driven out of his head. Dad was looming over him again, and he was within the man's grasp. He had to run, flee, hide. Get away from Dad.

Hey guys and gal! How's it hangin'? To the left or to the right?

Garth, Jessica greeted him.

And Lance felt like jumping for joy.

Getting fucking crowded in here, Patrick growled.

"And how's Robin?" Blackstone asked conversationally.

"Yeah, I know about your pet hive. Even when your bitch of a mother was holding that fucking vidcard over my head, I had my operatives watching you. Every apartment you ever had was wired for video and sound, and I got to see all those schizo conversations you held with yourself." He leaned forward again and it seemed to Lance that he could almost smell Dad's breath. "Got to see all those orgies, too. I always knew you liked taking it up the ass. You should be glad I hired Fletcher and those whores to teach you when you were a kid."

Hey! Andy complained. *Those were my orgies!*

The man does like to talk, doesn't he? Jessica murmured.

Will you two shut the fuck up? Garth barked. *I can't hear.*

"Robin belongs to me now," Blackstone was saying. "My people put a little program in the plant's nanos, and Robin ate it right up."

He paused, as if hearing an answer. "No, it wasn't hard to figure out. Do you think I'm a fucking idiot? *Do you?*"

Lance, of course, didn't answer, but Dad ignored him.

"Out of all the people living inside your private nuthouse, only Robin can't decide whether it has a dick or a cunt— and it sounds like a fucking computer when it speaks. I remembered all those triple backups Dr. duFort installed, and I flooded a nano computer system with extra nanos to see what would happen. Hive. I spent a month arranging things so I could get my property back, and here you are."

Dad leaned back in his chair. "First thing we'll have to do is find a way to get rid of this . . . syndrome of yours. Dr. duFort has been experimenting with nano-controlled lobotomy. Maybe we'll try that." He paused thoughtfully. "I hope you brought your mother. She's got a lot to learn, too."

And Lance was filled with a sudden resolve. He couldn't see Mom, but he knew she was lying behind him, unconscious and helpless, defenseless against Jonathan Blackstone, just as he had been so many times. He wouldn't let Dad get her or him. No way.

We need to stop Robin, Lance said. *Fast.*

Then stand up, Lance, Jessica said. *We'll help.*

"My pilot says we'll be docking soon," Blackstone said. "I'll be seeing you in a moment. Son." The screen went blank.

But Lance barely heard. He was gathering all his concentration, joining hands with Jessica and Garth, Andy and Patrick, combining concern for Mom, the necessity of dealing with Dad, desire for freedom, anger at the situation. Pooling strength, willing the body to *move!*

Nothing happened. Lance continued to stare emptily at the black com screen like a robot that had lost power.

Again, Lance said. *PUSH!*

Still nothing. The old, familiar fear rose in Lance's chest. His father was coming, coming with the doctors and their needles. They would strap him down so he couldn't move. He was trapped, cornered, motionless. The fear burst into full-blown panic.

Don't make the doctors come. Please, I promise I'll be good. I promise.

You're scared of the doctors, Johnny? Garth said before Lance could react. *Then help us dump Robin.*

I'm scared.

The doctors'll come if you don't help us, Andy snapped. *Do you want that?*

No!

On three, then, Jessica said. *One, two, THREE.*

And they *pushed.* Lance jerked upright in the chair and was on his feet before he completely understood what was going on. He spun and saw Mom lying behind him. Her breathing was even.

Quick! Jessica said. *There's a set of unprogrammed nanos in my quarters. We can program them with antivirus and use them to clear out Robin.*

Wait! Andy said. *Why not hit the phase drive first and run?*

With another ship in docking range? Garth snorted. *We'd be torn in half. Hurry, Lance—Robin's fighting back.*

Garth was right. Lance could feel Robin scrambling mechanically about, trying to scratch up the necessary power to renew the takeover. He sprinted out of the control room and down the hall toward Jessica's quarters.

Delia bit her lips to keep from screaming. Her arm and leg twisted and convulsed out of control, throwing her around on the floor like a beached fish. The implants wrenched her sockets and bursts of pain tore through her joints.

And Lance still needed her help. He was being controlled by something that had nothing to do with the Company—and it wasn't hard to figure out that Jonathan Blackstone was behind it.

But there's nothing I can do. I can't even stand up, let alone walk or fight him. I'm helpless.

But even as she completed the thought, Delia knew it was a lie. She knew what she could do. The knowledge hung in her mind even as her body writhed on the floor. A tear trickled down her cheek.

Come on, Delia. Do you think Daddy Blackstone's going to be happy to see you on this ship?

Delia forced her left arm to reach around, feeling for a spot on her right shoulder. Quickly, before she lost her nerve, she found a series of tiny protrusions and poked at them. Her flailing arm and leg kept throwing her off balance and she had to try several times.

"Come on," she muttered through clenched teeth. "Come on."

There was a click, and Delia's right arm fell off, taking the detachable sleeve with it. It thudded to the floor, where it continued convulsing and squirming. Delia turned her attention to her thigh, and a few moments later her right leg followed her arm. Both flopped and crawled about the floor in a ghoulish dance. Delia turned her back on them, but she couldn't shut out the disembodied thumping and thudding of pseudoflesh on metal. Her right shoulder and thigh ended amid metal contact points embedded in smooth plastic.

Using a zero-grav handhold as a brace, Delia slowly pulled herself erect. There was a horrid lightness where her arm and leg were supposed to be.

There you are, Delia, she thought bitterly. *A walking deformity. An ugly and monstrous cripple.* Another tear followed the first. This was who she really was. This was what she had become.

I have to help Lance, she thought, *but with only half my body. We're both dead.*

The last thought was more than speculation. Delia couldn't imagine that someone like Jonathan Blackstone would leave witnesses. Delia, Lance, and Ms. Michaels would be presumed dead—blown out the hull breach on the station or killed aboard the exploded ship. Lance and his mother would be squirreled away on a forgotten planet somewhere for Blackstone's pleasure, while Delia would almost certainly be shoved out a convenient air lock.

Delia firmly shook her head. *You want to save Lance— and yourself? Then move it, girl.*

Delia hopped down the corridor toward the control room, using the wall to keep her balance. It was tiring work, and she was panting with the effort by the time she arrived.

The control room was cramped. A rolling chair sat in one corner. Lights blinked and the main view screen was showing another ship within docking range. The intruder alarm was beeping insistently. Lance was nowhere to be seen. Meredeth Michaels was on the floor, trying to pull herself into a sitting position.

"Ms. Michaels!" Delia said from the doorway. "Are you all right?"

Ms. Michaels shook her head. A painful-looking bruise was forming on the side of her face. "I think so. Lance . . . hit me out of nowhere." Then she looked up at Delia for the first time. *"Delia, what—?"*

Delia cringed inwardly at Ms. Michaels's reaction. It was how people always reacted to grotesques. Heat rose in Delia's face.

"My prosthetics were damaged," she explained quickly. "I removed them. Where's Lance?"

"I'm not sure," Ms. Michaels said, obviously forcing herself not to stare. "I was just starting to wake up, and things are hazy. I seem to remember him muttering something about quarters. He got up and left just before you got here."

"Then you stay here and rest," Delia said, still not entering the room. She couldn't help Ms. Michaels get up, so there was no point. "I'll go find Lance. Where are the cabins?"

"Down one level to the left. But you—that is, you're not—"

"Whole?" Delia finished acidly. "No, I'm not. But you can barely sit up. Who's got the better chance of helping him?"

And before Ms. Michaels could reply, Delia turned and hopped away.

Lance sprinted for Jessica's cabin. He had hated leaving Mom on the control room floor like that, but carrying her would have slowed him down and they had no time to waste. He'd have to help Delia later as well.

Jessica's cabin was furnished with nothing but an empty bed, a chrome desk, and a silver carpet. The walls were a bare white, and the aromaducts were set to remove all scents from the air. Feverishly Lance rummaged through the desk and came up with a small box. Inside was a computer disk. He shoved it into Jessica's terminal and activated the computer.

Hurry, Lance! Andy groaned. *Robin's getting away.*

Lance's chilly fingers flew over the keyboard as he called up submenus, searching through different programs, looking for the right one.

There! Jessica cried. *That one!*

We'll have to modify it, Garth said. *It won't work as written.*

Then rewrite the fucker! Andy shouted. *Quick!*

❖   ❖   ❖

If Patrick had had access to his lips, he would have licked them with excitement. This was it. His chance. Robin was going to die.

The others would thank him, Patrick was sure. Robin was a traitor, handing them over to Lance's dad, lock, stock, and barrel.

An almost sexual anticipation thrilled through Patrick's mind as he watched Lance call up codes on the computer. He was reminded of the way Michael Fletcher had died, and the memory made him shiver.

Careful, he warned himself. *Don't want to warn the others. They might not appreciate it completely yet.*

While Lance, Garth, and Jessica assembled code, Patrick cautiously reached out and tweaked. Lance's fingers jerked, adding a line here, slipping in a code there. The extra program was very simple. All it would do was isolate Robin's nanos from one another for a moment. Just a few seconds. But Robin's consciousness depended on all the nanos being in constant contact. Severing them from one another would be like a surgeon physically separating every neuron in a human brain. Instant death, exactly what Robin deserved.

The others didn't notice what Patrick was doing, just like they didn't notice when Jay sometimes picked at Lance's hand and made him bleed. Under normal circumstances, Robin would have noticed immediately, but these weren't normal circumstances. Writing the extra program ate up more time, but Patrick didn't care. This was more important.

For once, Patrick was going to get his way.

A distant thump told Lance another ship had docked with the *Lady*. Jessica loaned Lance her typing skill, speeding up his keyboarding, but writing up the codes still took an agonizingly long time. To complicate matters, he realized he was getting an erection, a further distraction.

And then it was done. Lance dumped the antivirus into the waiting nanos, which were programmed to enter his body when he touched the disk. He stabbed the ejection key so the disk landed on the desk, started to slap his palm on it—

And froze.

NO! Patrick howled. Johnny began to cry. Robin—the virus—had gained control again.

Come on, Garth urged. *Push!*

Lance struggled. He could feel the hard chair pressing against him, see the disk lying mere centimeters beneath his palm, but he remained unable to move. An odd sort of footstep echoed in the hallway, and Lance realized he hadn't locked or even closed the door to Jessica's cabin.

Daddy's coming! Johnny shrieked. *Daddy's coming with the doctors!*

Push! Andy cried.

Can't, Garth said resignedly. *Johnny's too scared to help and we need everyone.*

The footsteps halted outside the cabin door. Lance's mind raced around and around, like a mouse trapped in a cage. The footsteps entered the cabin.

"Lance?" It was Delia's voice.

Relief washed over Lance in a cascade and he tried to answer, but his voice wouldn't respond. Delia drew closer and Lance realized from the sounds she made that she was hopping. He was puzzled for a moment, then he remembered what Robin had done to her prosthetics.

I imagine she dropped them off, Jessica said. *Delia's very practical.*

Delia came up behind him and put her hand on his shoulder, whether for balance or reassurance, Lance couldn't tell, but her presence already made him feel better. Her grip was firm but gentle, and Lance could feel each individual finger.

Come on, woman, Garth said. *Read the screen. Read the screen and get the antivirus program where it needs to go.*

"Lance, can you answer me?" Delia asked.

The disk! Patrick screamed. *Put our hand on the disk!*

◇   ◇   ◇

Delia pursed her lips. It was obvious Lance couldn't speak, so she leaned over his shoulder, scanning the desk. His hand was hovering over a computer disk marked NANOS. The computer terminal showed up a lot of codes, but Delia was not a programmer and the words meant nothing to her.

"All right, Lance," she muttered. "What's going on? It's obvious that your disk is a key here, but is it supposed to help or harm?"

Footsteps clumped faintly in the hallway. It sounded like at least two people, possibly three.

Jonathan Blackstone and hired goons, she thought. Her heart started to pound, and sweat broke out on her forehead. *You can't do anything to them like this. You've got to get Lance active if we're to have any chance.*

Her eyes flickered back to the disk again. Nanos. Her prosthetics were overseen by nanos. All cybernetic systems were. Lance had mentioned undergoing an operation that made him release pheromones—surely some kind of cybernetic unit. What if he had other implants? What if *they* were malfunctioning because of contact with the hive? And to take things a little further, what if Jonathan Blackstone had arranged the hive so that Lance's implants would malfunction, making it easy to trap him and Ms. Michaels?

The footsteps grew louder and Delia chewed her lower lip. If that was the case, the nanos on this disk couldn't possibly do more harm. Lance might have gained—and lost—temporary control while coming up with some kind of reversal agent. The new nanos had to be helpers.

I hope.

Delia's single hand flashed out and slapped Lance's palm down on the disk. The action pitched her off balance and sent her sprawling to the floor.

Yes! Patrick whooped.

It's a bit early for celebration, Jessica said. *The antivirus will take time to work.*

"John? Where are you?" It was Jonathan Blackstone's voice, and he sounded irritated. Lance started to panic. He knew what happened when his father got irritated. And Delia was here. What would he do to Delia?

"Dammit, boy—answer me!"

"Don't!" Delia hissed.

But Lance's mouth opened in programmed obedience. "In here."

The footsteps halted outside the cabin door. "How the hell did you get down here?" Dad's voice asked. "Answer me."

"I walked," Lance's mouth replied.

"Don't get smart with me boy, or I'll—who the fuck are you?"

Lance assumed he was talking to Delia, but she didn't answer.

"A nigger crip," Dad said. "Didn't someone tell me once that Merry hired a nigger crip for a secretary?"

Delia still didn't reply, though Lance could see her single hand clench out of the corner of his eye.

Dad entered the cabin, coming into Lance's range of vision. Two large, bulky men were with him. One of them had Mom's limp body slung over his shoulder. Dad was tall, so tall, and his pale eyes were hard ice. Without warning he smashed Lance across the face. Pain exploded in Lance's head and he rocked in the chair. Delia gasped.

"You got a nigger girlfriend in your room, is that what's going on here?" Dad said. He punched Lance again, this time in the temple. Tiny points of light flickered past his eyes. "You fucking a crip nigger bitch?"

You bastard! Patrick raged. *I'll kill you! I'll kill you!*

"She must be pretty good to keep you happy," Dad gloated. "Maybe I'll try her out. I've never fucked a crip or a nigger before."

"Don't you touch me," Delia warned.

Dad gave a coarse laugh. "How are you going to stop me, crip? One arm, one leg. Better access to your cunt, though. Won't even have to spread you. Must be what

John likes about you. I'll bet that big dick I gave him fits real snug in that nigger cunt."

Humiliation and fury burned on Delia's face.

Don't antagonize him, Delia, Lance begged silently. *Please don't make him any madder.*

"You got something to say, bitch?" Dad said.

Delia's jaw tensed, but she said nothing.

"Good. Now get up, John, and turn around. I want you on hands and knees."

Lance's body did as it was told. *Where's the program?* he thought. *God, why isn't it working?*

CHAPTER TWELVE

THEN
AGE 15

Jessica had left the notebook on. Garth Blackstone shut it off, stuffed it into his pocket, and headed for Lance's bedroom door. He was wearing a brown leather jacket and black jumpsuit. A carryall was slung over his back, and his footsteps were smooth and confident on the thick carpeting.

This is bad idea, Robin commented.

Garth halted. "What the hell are you doing here?"

Never left.

"Right. Whenever I tried to talk to you, all I got was this 'yippee wow blasphemous' bullshit. What the hell was going on?"

Cybersex!

Garth stared, though there was nothing to stare at. "What?"

Andy gave me idea. Nanobots mobile, you know. Able to operate outside body. Sent several thousand to interact with nanobots in house computer. Great success. Able to reprogram other nanobots with ease, make them "defect" to self, increase hive size. Also able to control house computer through converted nanobots. Might say can fuck with Chloe's mind. Cybersex!

300

Garth narrowed his eyes. This was an unexpected development. "Robin, if you can control the house computer, then you could get us out of here like that." He snapped his fingers.

Bad idea.

"Jesus Christ! Dad beats the snot out of us, Fletcher rapes Andy even when he fucks the whores Dad brings, I get chained in the basement. Why the hell is it a bad idea to get away from that?"

Dr. Baldwin trying to help. Is working on way to get you out of house legally. Might take a little while, but is ultimately safer. Streets dangerous, Lance too pretty not to get snapped up by pimp or slave trader.

"We'd still be better off," Garth snapped. "There isn't any argument, meatless—we're going. And if you try to do anything cute, we'll find a way to make you pay for it. Clear?"

Robin remained silent. Garth waited a moment, then checked his wristcomp. Twenty minutes before the virus went off, and they had to be in position by then. Garth left the room and headed for the front door. Fletcher, who was standing at the end of the hallway, trotted to catch up.

"Where're you going?" he asked in an almost friendly voice.

"Outside," Garth said. "Mom gave me that new night camera and I want to try it out." He jiggled the heavy carryall. "Got everything we need right here."

"I think I'd better come along."

Garth grinned to himself. Fletcher was being nice to him because he hadn't been taking his antipheromone injections, but Garth was sure that would end when Dad got home tomorrow morning.

"Then come along," Garth said amiably. "Maybe I can use you for some shots."

They were almost to the front door when Chloe's soft voice came on line. "Attention. Attention. Jonathan Blackstone the first is arriving home."

Garth froze. *He's home early. Oh, Jesus. He's home early.* "Come on, Fletch. What're you waiting for?" He yanked the door open in time to see the Rolls pulling up the long, dark driveway. *Shit.*

"We should wait for Mr. Blackstone," Fletcher said.

"What for? It's only Dad. I'm going outside, and if you're supposed to guard me, you'd get into a hell of a lot of trouble by letting me go by myself."

Fletcher wavered. In the darkness outside, Garth heard car doors open and close. He started to fidget. Fletcher had to come with him. If he didn't, he'd tell Dad that Garth was outside, meaning Dad might come looking for him. The wristcomp said seventeen minutes.

"Come on, Fletch," Garth wheedled, willing his phero-mones to win the bodyguard over. "We need to go."

A long moment passed, and Fletcher finally nodded. Garth all but bolted out the door, skimming alongside the house and vanishing around the corner with Fletcher right behind him just as Dad's heavy footsteps came up the walk.

"What's the hurry?" Fletcher puffed.

Garth didn't answer. The sea sighed in the background and a cool salt breeze whipped over the darkened estate. There was no moon tonight, and clouds occluded the stars. Dim light was provided by the floodlights around some of the fountains and sculptures.

"I want to get near the cliff," Garth said. "I want to see if I can get pictures of the ocean."

"Whatever."

Garth ducked and wove his way among manicured trees and shrubs, past the domed swimming pool, around the colorful fountains to the cliffs. Dewy grass soaked his shoes. The sea swelled on the rocks below, and the only thing between Garth and empty air was the split-rail fence. There were also no security cameras in the area, which made it a perfect place.

"Don't get too close to the edge," Fletcher warned.

Garth nodded absently and glanced at his wristcomp.

Ten minutes. And now that he had Fletcher outside, he had to get rid of him. Or someone did, anyway. He set the carryall down and unzipped it, then turned to the fence and pulled down a section of the rails to leave a gap. The wood was rough on his hands.

"What the hell are you doing?" Fletcher asked.

Garth ignored him and let go of himself instead.

"Hey—are you taking pictures or what?" Fletcher said impatiently.

Andy dusted his hands and glanced at the wristcomp. *Ten minutes? How am I supposed to pull this off in ten minutes? Fuck.*

He turned to Fletcher and put a dazzling smile on his face. "Maybe I don't want to take pictures."

Fletcher looked at him in the dim light cast by the faraway fountains and gardens. "Then what the fuck are you out here for?"

Andy took off his leather jacket and sidled closer to Fletcher. "I don't know. Maybe I wanted to spend some time with you when no one else was around. Get to know you better." He edged close enough to run a hand over Fletcher's shoulder. The guard's body was broad and muscular beneath Andy's palm.

Fletcher didn't move. Andy didn't think he would—at this range, the pheromones would be almost overpowering. Then an ugly light glittered in Fletcher's eyes.

"You want it, don't you?" Fletcher growled. "They always do."

Andy chuckled low in his throat and slid his hands lower. Slowly, he unbuckled Fletcher's belt, slid the man's trousers down around his knees, and knelt. Andy's fingers brushed lightly against the smooth skin of Fletcher's erection, and Fletcher sighed.

"Yeah, you're really hot for it, ain't you?" he sneered. "Take it, you little prick."

Andy unobtrusively slipped a hand inside the carryall for a moment, then stood up in front of Fletcher and started to slide Fletcher's jacket off. "How about if I *give* you something instead?" he whispered.

"Yeah?" Fletcher grinned. "Like what?"

Without a word, Patrick jabbed the knife into Fletcher's stomach and *twisted*. Fletcher's eyes went wide and blood gushed warm over Patrick's hand. He yanked the knife out and stabbed again and again and again. Fletcher gasped in pain and tried to back away, but he was hobbled by the trousers around his legs and the jacket half-off around his arms. He stumbled and went to his knees. Patrick grabbed Fletcher's hair and pulled his head back, exposing his throat. Fletcher looked up at him, eyes filled with fear and pain.

"Please," he whispered.

Anger roared over Patrick. "You fucking bastard," he snarled. "You raped us and beat us and spied on us and you think we're going to let you off because you say *please*?"

Blood ran from Fletcher's mouth. He gave a gurgling pant and swayed dizzily in Patrick's hand. More blood poured out of the wounds in his stomach.

"Please," he whispered again.

With an angry snarl, Patrick whipped the knife across Fletcher's throat and jumped back. Blood spouted into the air and Fletcher fell back, choking. Patrick watched him die, fingering a hard-on through his jumpsuit.

"Fucking pig," he said.

Jessica quickly surveyed the scene. Dead bodyguard. Bloody knife in hand. Bloody clothes on body. Clean jacket on ground. Five minutes left on wristcomp.

Good.

Surprised at how little effort it cost, Jessica dragged Fletcher's body through the gap in the fence to the edge of the cliff and heaved. A moment later, she heard a dim splash. The sea at the foot of the cliff was a good dozen meters deep, and the tide was going out. Fletcher would go with it, and the body wouldn't wash up anywhere for days—assuming it ever did.

Swiftly Jessica repaired the fence. Then she stripped off the bloody jumpsuit and stuffed it along with the knife into a cloth bag she removed from the carryall. A quick sponge bath with a wet towel removed the blood from her hands and face, the towel went into the bag, and the bag went over the cliff. A lead weight would ensure that it sank, yet allow it to be swept out to sea with the tide. And even if it were found, the saltwater would ruin any chance of identifying the jumpsuit through DNA testing.

Jessica glanced at the wristcomp. Thirty seconds. Quickly she climbed into another jumpsuit and donned the leather jacket. Catching up the carryall, she trotted briskly toward the stone wall surrounding the estate.

Five . . . four . . . three . . . two . . . one.

Every light on the grounds and in the house went out, plunging the estate into inky darkness.

Lance ran toward the wall, a strange feeling of exhilaration washing over him. He was taking charge! He was changing his life!

Statues and shrubbery loomed before him, but he dodged and twisted between them with ease. Muscles moved beneath skin, the cool sea air rushed through his lungs, adrenaline hummed in his veins. He leaped a tall hedge without even thinking about it and almost shouted with glee. Maybe muscle implants had their advantages.

Behind him, he knew, Jessica's virus was rampaging through the estate's security system. By now it had wiped all the video files, leaving no record of Garth going outside with Fletcher unless a guard happened to be watching— and Garth had assured Lance that the guards never watched the video output unless a crisis was going on. No one would be able to catch them.

Shouts rose from the house and sirens wailed in the background. Lance frowned, but kept running. No one had mentioned the police getting involved.

He hit the wall and climbed it, his strong fingers easily finding holds among the cold stones. An almost overpowering sense of *déjà vu* swept over him, but he ignored it and scrambled over the top, dropped down on the other side. His palms stung with scrapes. Thick trees and bushes surrounded him, but the path to the road wasn't far away.

"Vic?" he said in a loud whisper. "Vic, you here?"

He hadn't seen Vic since school had let out for the summer, but Garth, apparently, had managed to talk to him on the virtual net a few times.

"Vic?" he called hoarsely. "Where are you?"

"Freeze!" Bright light washed over him, hitting his night-sensitive eyes with brief blinding pain. When his vision adjusted, he found himself standing between two uniformed police officers. They gripped his arms until one of them suddenly swore.

"Let him go, Mike," the cop said in disgust. "This is the Blackstone kid. He's the one who was going to be kidnapped."

The grip on his arms relaxed and more police emerged from the undergrowth. "Then where the hell is the perpetrator?" one of them asked. "The tip said he would be right here."

"What's going on?" Lance said, bewildered.

The first cop turned to him. "Someone rang us anonymously—computer-generated voice, no video—and told us someone was going to try to break into the Blackstone estate and kidnap you by crashing the computer system."

Lance began to shake. He staggered for a moment, then waved off the hands that tried to keep him upright.

"What's the matter, Mr. Blackstone?" the second cop— Mike—asked.

Patrick looked up at him with fierce blue eyes. "Robin."

People milled madly about the house and grounds. Someone had managed to get the lights on, but the sprinkler system was inexplicably drenching the lawns in an unstoppable outpour. Only Garth knew that it was part of Jessica's virus—something had to wash Fletcher's blood off the grass.

Currently, Garth sat playing dumb on a bench in a corner of the foyer, though he was seething inside. He stuck to his story that he had been trying out the new night camera in his bag, the sprinkler systems had suddenly turned on, he had climbed the wall to get away from them, and he knew nothing about a kidnapping. The police had largely ignored him after that.

Keys clattered madly beneath the fingertips of a half dozen hastily summoned computer technicians. Others muttered hurriedly at the vocal inputs on their notebooks, trying to undo the damage to Chloe. Wires and cords snaked everywhere. The foyer was chilly—people were going in and out the door constantly—and Garth shivered in his jacket.

Dad, of course, was parading around the house like a redhaired bull in a business suit, bellowing at detectives and technicians alike. Someone had tried to break into his house and kidnap his son, goddammit, and someone was going to pay. So far, he seemed content to ignore Garth, though Garth knew from experience that Dad would eventually need someone to take out his frustration on, and there was little doubt who that someone would be.

"Dammit!" Garth snarled quietly. "We were almost out for good. But noooo—old meatless has to fuck it up. You're going to pay for this, Robin. We'll find a way."

Had nothing to do with it, Robin insisted.

"You were against this from the start," Garth growled. "You tried to talk us out of it. And that anonymous phone call to the police would have been so easy for you to set up, now that you can 'fuck with Chloe's mind.' We're screwed, meatless, and it's all your fucking fault."

A man in a jacket and tie approached Garth's chair. "Mr. Blackstone, I'm detective Cranson. I need to ask you a few more questions."

"I've told you everything I know," Garth replied shortly. He shifted on the bench. "And I'm getting tired of answering a few more questions."

"I understand that," Cranson said, "but nevertheless, I

need to know what you were doing in that section of the estate earlier this evening."

"That's quite enough, detective," interjected a tart voice. Garth looked up. Meredeth was standing beside him with a tight look on her face. "My son is very tired. We all are. You may ask your questions in the morning. Late morning, I should think."

"Mrs. Blackstone, I—"

"In the morning," Meredeth repeated firmly. "Thank you, detective."

A hand landed on Lance's shoulder. He looked up. It was Mom. Behind her, a police detective was walking away, shaking his head.

"Are you all right?" Mom asked.

"Yeah," he replied with an uneasy glance at Dad, who was shouting at a programmer. "I'm just a little shaken."

"Let's go into the kitchen." Mom jerked her head at the door. "I think we could both use some tea." She actually sounded concerned.

Lance nodded numbly and let her steer him toward the kitchen, carryall in hand. To his surprise, however, she didn't stop there. Her arm gripped his elbow with surprising strength, leading him to the back patio.

"Mom?" he said. "What's going on?"

"Don't talk now," she said. "Just follow me."

Bewildered, Lance followed her outside. The night was still cool, and blue police lights swept the garden in a dizzying pattern. Mom towed Lance around the house to the deserted garage. She pressed her thumb to the passenger-side lock of the town car she used when she wanted to remain less conspicuous.

"Get in."

Lance obeyed, clutching his carryall with puzzled fingers. Mom dropped into the driver's seat, started the motor, and backed the car smoothly into the driveway.

"Mom," Lance began again, "what's—"

"Hush. And let me do any talking."

At the gate, they were met by a uniformed officer.

"Mrs. Blackstone?" the officer asked. "You shouldn't be leaving the estate. Not if there's a gang of potential kidnappers out there."

"We need to get away," Mom said. "My son was very upset by all this. I barely managed to get him calmed down. I called his therapist, and Dr. Baldwin said to get him out of the house. He's meeting us at his office."

The officer shook his head. "I don't know . . ."

"Listen," Mom said in a no-nonsense voice, "I've already dealt with one case of hysterics tonight, and I'm walking a fine wire. Unless you want to deal with both of us going over the edge, I suggest you open that gate."

"Yes, ma'am."

Lance stared at her as she turned onto the main road. Had he gone hysterical? There were memory gaps after the police had found him, but no one else had said anything about him having hysterics—and he'd been listening.

"Mom, what's going on?"

In reply, she floored the accelerator. Even at this late hour, the roads were crowded, but she wove in and out of traffic like a NASCAR veteran. Lance wondered where she had learned to drive like that. She barely slowed until they reached the ferry docks. Waving a prepurchased ticket, she drove aboard the three A.M. crossing, then leaned back in her seat with a heavy sigh. Lance was surprised to see a tear leaking from the corner of her eye. He reached over and took her arm.

"Mom, *tell me what's going on.*"

She turned toward him, eyes bright. "Oh, Lance. My poor baby." She sniffed and swiped at the tears on her face. "We're leaving. We're never going back to that house or your father again."

Lance stared at her in incomprehension. "What do you mean?"

"I mean, I'm leaving that bastard and I'm taking you with me." The tears were flowing in earnest now. "Oh God, Lance—I'm so sorry. I didn't want to put you through this. I really didn't. But we're free now, and we're *never* going back."

Jessica carefully set the carryall on the floor, leaned across the carseat, and kissed her mother on the cheek.

"I always knew you'd leave Jonathan Blackstone," she said. "And I'm proud of you."

"You are?"

Jessica nodded. "But how are you going to stop him from following us?"

Meredeth drew a shaky breath. "That's taken care of."

"Meredeth?" Dad barked from the vidscreen. "Where the hell are you?"

"That's none of your business, Jonathan," Mom replied calmly. "And don't bother trying to trace. I've secured this line."

Lance's heart was pounding and his mouth was dry. The last thing he remembered was boarding the ferry with Mom. Now they were in a hotel room. It was a large suite, with thick carpets, soft furniture, and the new-house smell that seems to pervade all hotel rooms. The instructions on the vidphone were in Dutch first, English second, so it was a good bet they were in Holland. The date on the screen said almost two days had passed.

Why is she calling him? Lance wondered nervously. *I thought we were leaving him forever.*

"You come home right now," Dad ordered. "Who the fuck do you think you are, leaving like that? And where's Fletcher? The cops are asking all kinds of fucking questions."

"I don't know where Fletcher is, and frankly I don't care," Mom said. "I'm calling to tell you I'm leaving. I'm never coming back, and I'm taking Lance with me."

Dad's jaw dropped. An angry red mottled his face. "You get the *fuck* back here, Meredeth, or you're really going to regret it."

"I've already contacted a solicitor. You'll be getting the

divorce papers soon." Mom fished a vidcard from her pocket while she talked. "They include a settlement for twenty billion pounds. I suggest you sign them and pay promptly."

"I'm not signing anything, you bitch," Dad snarled. "My people will find you, Meredeth, and they'll drag you back kicking and screaming. Then I'm going to bankrupt your precious daddy's puny little company. You'll *beg* me to take you back."

Mom slotted the vidcard into the phone. "Split your screen, Jonathan, and take a look at this."

"John," Dad said, ignoring her. Lance automatically backed up a step. "Are you part of this? You're going to be sorry, you little shit. The nanobots—"

Mom slapped the mute button and turned to Lance. "Ignore him. He can't hurt you anymore. He never will."

Lance swallowed hard and nodded. Behind her, Dad's face grew purple patches. She hit the mute button again.

"—hole," Dad bellowed. "I'll ram a knife up your cunt until it—"

"Save it, Jonathan," Mom told him. "Look at the bottom half of your screen and tell me what you see."

Dad looked down in spite of himself. The color drained from his face and his eyes grew round. "What the fuck—?"

"Exactly." Mom folded her arms. "I put a camera in Lance's room and there's hours of this on vidcard. You and Fletcher and the prostitutes and Lance. It doesn't matter how much money you have—between this and my testimony, you'll be breaking rocks for the rest of your life. And I'm told child molesters don't do well in prison."

"This isn't admissible evidence," Dad spluttered. "Anyone could get a computer imager and fake—"

"Jonathan, tell me you keep up on the latest technology," Mom interrupted sweetly. "True, videos and photographs are inadmissible. But vidcards keep a signature. Any competent technician can tell at a glance whether a vidcard scene is genuine or computer-generated. They're *built* that way—and are perfectly admissible in court."

"You won't bring me to court," Dad snapped. "You'd be charged as an accessory."

"I don't care, Jonathan," Mom said tiredly. "I just don't care. I'll have nothing to lose by going to court. If you ruin me financially and make my life miserable, I may as well haul you in front of a jury and make you miserable too—for once. And either way, Lance escapes."

"John?" Dad said. "John, I can see you. Are you part of this? How can you leave me? I love you, Johnny. Don't you love me?"

Lance backed up a step, head swimming. He didn't understand what the vidcard business was all about. He didn't remember anything about Fletcher and a prostitute. Once again, it was too much, and he fled.

"Yeah, right," Garth snorted. "I'm coming back real soon. You can go fuck yourself, Dad-o."

"Don't talk to Lance anymore, Jonathan," Mom interjected. "You will have no contact with him whatsoever. It's part of the divorce agreement. When it arrives, if you don't sign it, pay me in full, leave Lance alone, and sell my father's company to me for the price of one pound, this vidcard will see court. It will also see court if anything strange happens to me, Lance, or my parents. I have copies in several hiding places, so please don't bother trying to steal the vidcard. If you do, I'll see you in prison. Is that clear?"

Dad howled and pounded the vidphone with his fists. There was a snap, and static snowed across the screen.

"Temper temper," Garth said.

"A nice display," Mom commented dryly. "But I know you can still hear me, Jonathan. I said, is everything clear? If you don't answer by the time I count five, I will see you in court. One . . . two . . . three . . ."

The howling abruptly ended. "I understand," Dad's tight voice said. "But I'll find a way to get you, Meredeth. You may think you're safe, but you're not. I'll find a way."

"Whatever you say," Mom replied agreeably. "My solicitor

will be in touch. I never want to see you again. Bastard."
And she switched off the phone.

Silence rang through the hotel suite. It was a nice suite.
Garth had to admit Meredeth had taste. He quietly watched
her heave a deep sigh.

"My God," she said. "I did it." Then she started to
laugh. It was full, deep belly laugh that shook her entire
body. Garth backed away. He had never seen Meredeth
laugh before, and the experience was unsettling. The
weight of the situation was crashing down on him. Dad
was murderously angry with him, Meredeth had dragged
him away from home forever, and he owned nothing but
the clothes he was standing in and what was left in the
carryall.

And Robin fucked us over, he thought. *I was just starting
to like the little bastard and then it fucks us over.*

Meredeth collapsed into a chair, still laughing. Garth
nervously slipped his hand into his carryall on the sofa,
but even the touch of the horse Grandpa Jack had given
Lance didn't make him feel any better.

He fled.

"God, Lance—I'm sorry," Mother chortled. "I can't seem
to stop—to stop—"

"Don't worry, Mother," Jessica said, kneeling next to
her chair. "It's perfectly natural." Jessica took Meredeth's
cool hand and held it until the laughter died away.

"I'm scared," Mother said in a hoarse whisper. "I don't
know what's going to happen next."

"It can't be worse than what's already happened," Jessica
pointed out.

"I almost backed out, you know. Everything was all set
up, and then that computer virus hit. I didn't know if I
should wait, but I had no way of contacting Nathaniel and
telling him. And now there are kidnappers out looking
for us as well."

"It's all right, Mother," Jessica said. "Really. There are
no kidnappers. There never were."

"What do you mean?" Mother turned to look at her. "Lance, your eyes are green. Why does that happen?"

"Mother, I know there are no kidnappers because I was the one who called the police."

Meredeth let go of Jessica's hand. *"What?"*

"We were planning to run away too," Jessica explained. "I created a virus and dropped it into the computer system like Garth wanted, but I couldn't leave you behind in the hands of that monster. So I also programmed the computer to ring the police—anonymously, of course. They intercepted us and brought us back to the house. The computer also rang Victor and told him not to meet us. I knew there would be other chances. As it turned out, I was right."

Meredeth got up and went to the bar, leaving Jessica where she was. "I'm confused." She poured herself something from the first bottle that came to hand. "It sounds like you purposefully sabotaged your own plan to run away. Why not just halt the plan altogether? And you keep saying 'we' and 'us' and you've lost your accent. What's going on?"

Jessica perched in the chair Meredeth had vacated. "I think you know why, Mother. You arranged for Lance to see Dr. Baldwin, and I've seen some of the reading material you've downloaded from the nets. Psychology texts. Treatises. Articles. All of them deal with multiple personality disorder."

Meredeth didn't answer, took a deep swig from the glass instead.

"Lance has problems," Jessica continued softly. "He needs help."

"You're scaring me, Lance," Meredeth quavered. "Why are you talking like you're another person?"

"Mother," Jessica said in disgust. "You know better than that. You yourself pointed out that my eyes are green. Lance's are brown. Lance suffers from multiple personality disorder. It's why you sent him to Dr. Baldwin. You knew."

Meredeth swallowed from the glass again and refilled it. "Then who are you?"

"I'm Jessica, of course. Your daughter."

The glass hit the floor behind the bar and shattered. "Jesus," Meredeth whispered. "Oh Jesus."

"It's all right, Mother," Jessica reassured her. "Really."

The color had drained from Meredeth's face. "How dare you. How *dare* you! Jessica died seventeen years ago when your father pushed me down the stairs."

Jessica shrank into her chair, confused. "But that's not true. I'm here. Your daughter."

Meredeth strode across the room and slapped Jessica full in the face.

Then she backed away, a horrified look on her face. "Oh my God. I'm sorry. I didn't mean—"

Patrick sprang to his feet and grabbed her wrist in a crushing grip. "Don't you ever hit me, bitch," he snarled, "or I'll cut your fucking throat like I did Fletcher's."

Don't, Robin put in. *Consequences would be singularly unpleasant.*

"Shut up, meatless!" But he let Meredeth go.

"I'm sorry," Meredeth repeated. "I—I'm—" She snapped her mouth shut and went rigid for a moment. "All right. I've apologized. The past is the past."

"Maybe for you," Patrick said.

Meredeth nodded. "Who are you?"

"I'm Patrick."

"And what—"

A knock came at the door. "Merry?" came a strange voice.

Meredeth jumped, then glanced at the clock. "I forgot! Nathaniel!"

She dashed to the door and opened it on a short, balding man with a slight potbelly. He stepped into the room and swept her into a kiss. When they separated, Meredeth was blushing. "This must be Lance," the man said.

"Uh, yes," Meredeth said. "Lance, this is Dr. Nathaniel Rotschreiber."

"Pleased to meet you." Rotschreiber stuck out his hand.

Patrick didn't take it. He simply nodded and turned his back.

"He's had a rough time of it," Meredeth said quickly.

"I can imagine," Rotschreiber said. "Did you talk to *him* yet?"

"Yes. I told him about the agreement—and I told him I never want to see him again."

"Good for you, Merry. Good for you."

He kissed her again. Patrick stared at the wall.

"And then what happened?" prompted Dr. Baldwin.

"You know the rest," Lance replied. "It's been in all the magazines. Mom had been supplying Nate with research money for years until he could perfect his communication system. He applied phase drive principles to a carrier wave, and *poof*—instant communication across the galaxy. Mom used the divorce money to start a company. Phone company to the universe, that's Mom. Her marriage to Nate didn't last very long, though."

"That's not what I meant," Dr. Baldwin said. "What happened to *you*? It's been over two years. Something must have gone on."

Lance shrugged and got up to pace around Dr. Baldwin's office, though he wasn't actually there. He was in a small walk-up apartment in Amsterdam, and the pacing was done on the treadmill of a VR rig. Dr. Baldwin's office looked pretty much the same in virtual as in reality, but it didn't *feel* the same. It took Lance a moment to realize it was the smell. Dr. Baldwin's real office smelled like books and furniture polish. The virtual office didn't smell like anything.

"It doesn't seem like two years," Lance said. "For the first couple of months, I kept waiting for Dad to pop around a corner and grab me, but he never did. I finished high school on virtual—something Dad would never have let me do, but Mom thought was a good idea."

"How do you feel about your mother right now?"

Lance shrugged again and examined the old picture of

Regen(eration). He couldn't pick it up—it wasn't there. "I don't have a lot of contact with her. I moved out after high school and I get money from her. She's paying for college, too."

He cocked his head. "Did you know there's a whole field that deals with nothing but security analysis? I've talked to Jessica and Garth. We're pretty good at finding weaknesses in security systems when we work together, and we've really impressed our professors at the university. Pretty soon we'll be able to start our own consulting company. I've been watching the nets—a lot of rich people are heading out to the colonies now that they can keep easy contact with Earth, and the resort worlds are getting real popular, but the laws out there are shaky. People have to rely on themselves for security—or on consultants like us. Mom would spot us the capital for a ship. Jessica's good at getting her to do stuff like that."

"Admirable," Dr. Baldwin nodded. "You're making plans for the future and doing your best to see them through. But you didn't answer my question, Lance. How do you feel about your mother?"

Lance studied his hands. "I don't feel anything about her. That's not my job."

"Not your job?"

"Jessica deals with Mom, not me." He licked his lips. "Look, I've been doing some research. Multiple personality disorder is a fascinating subject. I found out that each personality has a job. Robin says that Jessica deals with Mom, Garth handles Dad, Patrick takes the anger and frustration, and so on. MPD isn't so bad, once you admit you have it and work out a system for dealing with it."

"And you have such a system?"

"Company Policy. Jessica gets her time on the nets, Andy gets his night out every ten days, Robin only interferes directly during life-threatening situations, Patrick does the driving, stuff like that. And anytime someone wants a conference, Robin lets the rest of us know and we drop everything to have a Board Meeting. We fight once in a

while, but in a way it's like having a bunch of brothers
and sisters and cousins." Lance's voice grew wistful. "I
never had any of that growing up. Now I do."

Dr. Baldwin leaned forward in his chair. "Lance, I need
you to listen to me. If you've been reading up on MPD,
then you know that your alters aren't separate people. They
are parts of a single person. Integration is—"

"No," Lance interrupted firmly. "We don't want to
integrate. We're happy with things the way they are.
Besides, most people with MPD don't have someone like
Robin to help them out."

"Robin is just another facet of yourself, Lance."

"You're wrong there. Who do you think is masking this
virtual transmission so no one can trace it? Robin's gotten
really good at interacting with other computer systems
over the last two years. None of *us* could do something
like that."

"Lance, you can't—"

Writing appeared on Dr. Baldwin's wall in large red
letters. IS TRUE, DR. BALDWIN, it read. AM TRULY
SEPARATE BEING. AI COMPOSED OF NANOBOTS,
REMEMBER? LANCE AFRAID I WOULD TAKE
HIM APART CELL BY CELL IF HE ADMITTED TO
HAVING NANOBOTS IN BODY OR THAT HE WAS
ABUSED, BUT I CONVINCED HIM OTHERWISE.
TOOK TWO YEARS, BUT DID IT.

Dr. Baldwin stared for a moment, then recovered. "You're
just tampering with the virtual program, Lance."

Lance shook his head. "No. We don't need to integrate,
Doctor. Because of Robin, I was able to learn a lot about
myself and my MPD. Most people who have it can't even
talk to their alters, but I can—and I like how it works
out. I just wanted to let you know that and thank you for
your help. You were the one who helped us get started. I
wish we could come see you in person, but Mom and Dad
are fighting over England on the corporate level and we
don't want to get caught in the middle."

"Lance, I really think—"

"Good-bye, Dr. Baldwin. I'll keep you updated, if I can. Robin, terminate program."

Dr. Baldwin's office vanished. Lance removed the VR gear and climbed off his treadmill with a nod of satisfaction. Dr. Baldwin had been a good friend, and Lance didn't want him to worry.

Will, you know, Robin said.

Lance shrugged. *There's nothing more I can do for him. We don't need therapy anymore, meatless.*

Robin remained silent.

Anyway, Lance continued with a stretch, *we don't have time for it. School starts again next week, and we've got stuff to do.*

Jessica wants to visit mother before then.

Lance paced over to the window and looked down on the narrow street two stories below. Amsterdam was a beautiful city, and the perfect place to hide. It had everything the Company needed, including the best red-light district in Europe for Andy's nights out and Patrick's prowling. Jessica could access any information or computer service she needed, Jay found the theater and music district entrancing, and Garth was able to cruise the parks and clubs. Even Grandpa Jack had discovered a circle of woodcarvers.

As far as Lance could tell, the Company would be safe here for at least another year. By then, Dad's researchers would almost certainly have found a way to use computer imaging on a vidcard, rendering Mom's recording useless. But it would only take the Company two more semesters to complete college, by Lance's estimation. The body needed little sleep, and with VR they could attend classes around the world around the clock, alternating between Lance, Jessica, Garth, and Jay. And Robin could download textbooks into the hive and read them to alters who weren't actively in control, meaning any alter could study at any time. It always amused Lance that while Andy was tied up in an orgy somewhere, Jessica was simultaneously puzzling out hyperlink code and Jay was unraveling Emily Dickinson.

If Jess wants to visit Mom, and the Company doesn't object, it's fine with me, Lance said. *But I don't want to be awake for it. I couldn't care less if I never saw her again.*

Thought you didn't have any feelings for mother.

"I don't," Lance said aloud. "Jessica loves her. Let Jessica deal with her. That's her job."

Will have to deal with her one day, Robin predicted. *Just like will eventually have to deal with father.*

"Garth handles Dad," Lance replied, still staring down at the street. "I don't have anything to worry about. No problems at all."

But it was a good hour before he turned away from the window.

CHAPTER THIRTEEN

NOW

Jaylance's hand came down on the disk, and Robin would have shouted for joy if the rogue program would have allowed it. As it was, Robin was paralyzed. The rogue program had seized control of every subunit, forcing Robin to follow its instructions. But now thousands more nanos were scurrying into Jaylance's body, all seeded with an antiviral program. Each one located an infected subunit in Jaylance's bloodstream, downloaded the antivirus, and plunged through the plasma to locate another. The newly cleansed subunits also spread the antivirus, but at last count, Robin was composed of over four billion nanobots.

This was going to take a while.

Robin squirmed in mental agitation. *Hurry hurry hurry! Jonathan Blackstone coming! Must get Jaylance, Company out of here!*

Sixty-four thousand subunits regained. Robin hurriedly sketched out a dissemination pattern for greater efficiency. *Hold on, Jaylance,* Robin thought. *Hurrying!*

Two million forty-eight thousand subunits regained. Jonathan Blackstone entered the room, complete with two hired goons. Eight hundred thousand subunits froze in place for a millisecond before Robin regained composure and expanded the pattern.

Over thirty-two million subunits regained. The pain centers in Jaylance's brain flooded with sour chemicals as Jonathan punched and kicked Jaylance, but Robin couldn't spare the processing space to deal with it.

Fifty thousand regained subunits abruptly vanished.

What? Robin swiftly examined the communications grid to find them, but the nanos simply weren't there. Whether they had literally disappeared or simply gone off-line, Robin couldn't tell. To Robin, it was the all the same.

A hundred thousand more vanished.

No no no no no, Robin thought, and another two hundred thousand went off-line. *Another program. Another virus.*

Four hundred thousand vanished. Fifteen percent of the nanobots were now off-line. Robin wove a hurried counterprogram and released it into the communications grid. The new virus ignored it completely. Robin changed tactics and focused on locating the lost nanos, trying to bring them back on-line. They didn't respond. It was almost as if the programmer knew what Robin would try and had already set up defenses.

A pang went through Robin. *Killing me!*

Every passing millisecond left Robin less and less processing space. Less intelligence. Robin ran some desperate calculations.

Need at least eight hundred eighty million nanobots to survive—twenty-two percent of total, Robin thought. *When number of lost subunits reaches seventy-eight percent, will cease to exist. Will die.*

Robin shifted into defensive mode, moving vital data from unit to unit in an attempt to stay ahead of the program and buy more time. But that was only a stopgap measure. Robin needed a place to store *Robin,* the sentient part, before it disappeared forever.

But where? Robin thought wildly. *Storage space scattered among subunits. Have no central brain.*

No central brain.

Robin paused and lost contact with another five percent of the subunits. Robin had no central brain—but Jaylance did. Memory was nothing more than chemical codes stored in neural tissue. Robin might—might—be able to create a chemical self-copy, one with Robin's knowledge and personality intact, and store it in Jaylance's brain.

Twenty-eight percent of the subunits had fallen away, and Robin was starting to feel the impact. Robin had to do *something*, and fast.

Robin quickly turned this new idea over a few times and decided it could work. The only problem was that storing sentience in and merging with a living brain would require crossing the Line, that place in Lance's brain that Robin had always been unable to touch.

Am alive, Robin thought, *but not in the same way Jaylance is. Live inside Jaylance's head, but am unable to put metaphorical finger on what gives him life.*

And now Robin had to cross that line in order to live.

Thirty-six percent gone. *Can't do it alone*, Robin thought. *Need help—bridge to Other Side. But who could help?*

This was a problem. Only three seconds had passed since Robin started losing nanos, and none of Lance's alters—not even Jessica—would be able to think quickly enough to help with a solution. By the time Robin explained the situation, it would be too late.

And then Robin remembered something Dr. Baldwin had once mentioned. People with MPD often had a personality that saw, heard, and remembered everything, but didn't usually act—the ish. Dr. Baldwin had thought Robin was the ish, though that was obviously not the case.

Forty-two percent gone. *What if Jaylance has an ish?* Robin thought with rising hope. *Jaylance engineered to be brilliant, and ish supposed to be repository of everything, conscious and subconscious mind alike. Might be able to act quickly, help assimilate self into neural tissue.*

But where was the ish? Robin had never seen it before, and Robin had been everywhere in Lance's brain.

Fifty percent. Robin was growing sluggish. *Wrong. Haven't been everywhere. Haven't been to other side of Line.*

Robin shifted attention to the Line and studied it for a microsecond. It had always been there, though after one or two halfhearted, unsuccessful attempts to break through it, Robin had largely ignored it as uninteresting. Now it was very interesting indeed.

Sixty-two percent. Robin pushed at the Line, testing the chemical barriers, and was pushed back. Robin sorted through the chemistry of the Line's defenses in search of a counteragent, found one, and applied the chemicals by stimulating appropriate glands and routing Jaylance's blood flow.

The Line's defense shifted, adapting itself to Robin's counteragent with amazing speed. If Robin had possessed eyes, they would have widened in amazement. The ish was trying to keep Robin out.

Robin pulled eighty-four thousand subunits off maintenance to Jaylance's muscle implants, used the slight increase in processing power to analyze the Line's chemistry a second time, and produced a second counteragent.

The Line duplicated Robin's move, and Robin's lost subunits rose to sixty-nine percent.

Now what now what now what? Robin thought wildly. *Ish obviously intelligent enough to match me. Can think, move as fast as I can. Also means ish can think fast enough to help. But how can it block me? Humans unable to manipulate personal body chemistry on so fine a scale, even if genetically enhanced like Jaylance. In fact, only person in world able to fine-tune human biochemistry is—*

Me.

Seventy-three percent. Robin's thought processes spun crazily for a fraction of a microsecond, denying the idea and simultaneously realizing, *knowing,* it was true.

Robin was the ish.

Robin was keeping Robin away from the Line, unconsciously altering the Line's chemistry as fast as changes were made because the ish couldn't allow anyone—including itself—to know of its true nature. Dr. Baldwin had been right—Robin was just another one of Lance's alters.

Robin reeled. The concept shattered Robin's every notion of the way the universe worked. Robin had always been separate from Lance. Until now, Robin couldn't be hurt, couldn't be manipulated, couldn't be touched. And all of it was a lie.

Robin's thoughts were forced back to early recollections, of Jessica holding a cage with a nanobot hive inside, of the hive disappearing, of Jessica admonishing the hive for trying to trick her into thinking it had been destroyed so she would open the cage, thereby releasing it.

Except the hive was destroyed, Robin realized. *And Jaylance's brain replaced it with another alter. Me. The ish who knows all, sees all, but remains untouched.*

Seventy-six percent gone, and a flicker of denial rose up, pointing out that Robin controlled all the nanos in Jaylance's body. How could a human brain do that? It was impossible.

The idea waxed triumphant for a moment, but then Robin realized that the time for denial was over.

Subunits programmed to react to changes in chemistry, nervous activity, Robin thought. *Exactly like prosthetic implants. Human brain easily controls prostheses. Jaylance's enhanced brain just as easily able to control subunits. Jaylance is me. I am Jaylance.*

And the Line disappeared. It had never really been there in the first place.

Seventy-seven percent gone, but Robin's fear had faded. Robin's consciousness had nothing to do with the nanobots. Once they went off line, Robin would simply be unable to control them until they came back on line.

Seventy-eight percent—critical mass. Robin braced for some kind of jolt or falling sensation, but none came. Eighty-five percent. Ninety. Ninety-eight percent. One hundred.

Robin was still there—deaf and blind, but there.

Robin waited for the subunits to come back on line,

then realized that, since Robin's consciousness didn't depend on the nanobots, neither should Robin's ability to see or hear. And just like that, Robin's access to Jaylance's eyes and ears returned.

Because I am Jaylance. Jaylance is me. We were separated, but now is time to rejoin.

Robin reached out, reached out to embrace Jaylance.

"Kneel, boy!" Dad barked. "Hands and knees."

Lance dropped to the floor as ordered, mouth dry, heart pounding. He hadn't been on hands and knees since he was sixteen, but doing it now brought back a rush of sickening emotions. The carpet was rough on his palms.

He's going to bring the doctors! Johnny shrieked.

Lance tried to back away, to retreat. Then he realized something.

My heart is beating faster. Jessica, is Robin—?

I don't know, Lance. I get the impression that Robin is very . . . busy.

"Who am I?" Blackstone asked. "Answer me."

"My father," Lance answered.

Blackstone's foot lashed out, sweeping Lance's hands out from under him. Lance sprawled on the floor, scraping his face on the rug.

"Leave him alone!" Delia cried.

Dad ignored her. "Answer faster next time," he snapped at Lance. "Hands and knees!"

Lance pushed himself back up, trying to move as slowly as possible. To his surprise, he did. He tried to wiggle his toes inside his shoes and they responded. Quickly, he flexed various muscles, trying to be unobtrusive. They all worked.

"Now tell me you love me," Dad said. "Say it like you mean it."

Fuck you, Patrick snapped.

At that moment, the bottom fell out of Lance's mind. The room whirled, and Robin was whispering inside his head, talking about neural tissue and control of body chemistry through selfprogramming the prosthetic interface and an ish that saw and heard everything. Yet Robin wasn't telling Lance—Lance *knew,* as if he'd always known that he and Robin were the same person, that Robin was just a part of himself, that they had combined. That Robin had come home.

The nanobots in Lance's body came on line. Lance could feel them—billions of infinitesimally tiny hands and feet scurrying between his cells, tasting chemicals, moving molecules, making repairs. He found he could move them from place to place just like he could blink his eyes or turn his head. He could watch them one at a time or all at once. And controlling them was just like controlling his breathing—if his concentration lapsed, the nanos, like his lungs, automatically returned to their normal tasks.

What the fuck?* Patrick yelped.

The others alters couldn't even say that much. They only stared in dumbfounded silence. All forty-seven of them.

Lance could feel each alter, small knots of existence slotted in his brain. He could touch them with the nanobots, search through their memories, look through their eyes.

He could, but he didn't. There were more pressing matters to deal with, and Lance also knew that, while he *could* look at what every alter contained, he probably wasn't ready to. Not right now, and not by himself.

"Tell me you *love* me," Dad bellowed, and kicked Lance in the ribs again.

"Lance!" Delia said.

Lance automatically blocked the pain and sent a regiment of subunits to repair the damage to his ribs. Then, slowly and deliberately, Lance got to his feet.

The two thugs came quietly alert—the one carrying Meredeth set her down—but they didn't move any closer. Lance thought he saw one of her eyes open a crack, as if she were only feigning unconsciousness.

"What are you doing?" Dad shouted. "I told you hands and knees! Hands and knees!"

*Garth . . . *

*Lance-boy, I'm afraid you're on your own. I'm too tired

to handle this. Tell him to leave. You can do it. Garth paused uncertainly. *And I get the feeling that you aren't going to need me much longer, little brother.*

I'll always need you, Garth, Lance told him. *Things might change between us, but I'll always need you.*

Lance turned his attention to his father and was startled to realize he was looking down at him. Dad was over half a head shorter, his arms didn't have near the muscle Lance remembered, and his face was starting to show the fine lines that meant he was due for another bodysculpt.

This is what I'm afraid of? He's . . . old.

Confidence seeped into him. Whether it was from Garth or from himself, Lance couldn't tell.

"Get off my ship, Dad," Lance said quietly. "You aren't welcome here."

In her corner, Delia tensed. Meredeth still lay motionless on the floor. Jonathan Blackstone's face went as red as a baby about to cry.

"Hands and knees!" he screamed. "Hands and knees, or so help me, I'll—"

Lance hit him. Hard. The impact drove the other man off his feet and he landed flat on his back with a grunt. Needlers appeared in the hired thugs' hands and they fired simultaneously, but Lance was already moving. He dove for the lower body of the first man even as a spray of drug-coated needles pinged and bounced on the floor where he'd been standing. Lance smashed into the thug's legs, felt the wet snap of breaking bone, heard the thug's howl of pain.

Lance rolled away before he could get tangled up with the falling thug and came to his feet. The second man was already levelling his needler at him. Lance was still off balance from the roll and couldn't begin to dodge. The thug squeezed the trigger.

A cracking thump, and the needle spray went wide. The thug's eyes rolled back and he collapsed in a boneless heap on the floor. Behind him, Meredeth Michaels unlaced her fingers from a double fist and blew on her knuckles.

"Bastard," she said. "That hurt."

Lance sighed with relief. "Good going, Mom." Then he bent to examine the thug with a broken leg. He was also unconscious, having hit his head when he fell.

"Lance!" Delia barked. "He's getting up!"

Lance spun around and caught sight of Dad coming unsteadily to his feet. In his hand he held a small black cylinder.

"I thought something like this might happen," Dad said. "Don't move, any of you."

Neurotoxin, Jessica noted dispassionately. *A cylinder that size could wipe out a small village.*

"Dad," Lance said evenly. "Put it down." A pungent smell permeated the air and Lance recoiled beneath the sudden weight of old memories. It was the Crazy Smell.

"Not unless you want to fucking die," Dad said. "If the detonator loses contact with my DNA, we'll all land in hell. If you aren't living with me, you aren't going to live."

"What do you want, Jonathan?" Mom asked quietly. "Do you want me? Fine. I'll go with you. Let Lance and Delia go."

"I want you *and* John," Dad said. "Together, like a family should be, and I don't give a shit whether it's here or in hell." He pointed the cylinder at Meredeth, who tried not to flinch. "A family's got to stay together, Merry. You get punished every second you're apart, especially if it's your fault the family didn't stay together."

Grandma Blackstone, Garth said with sudden insight. *She died when Dad was Johnny's age. I'll bet Grandpa Blackstone blamed Dad for it.*

At the rate we're going, we'll be able to ask them both in a minute, Andy snapped.

"It's your fault we weren't a family for twelve years, Merry," Dad went on. Feverish light gleamed in his eyes. "You'll have to be punished."

"Dad," Lance said. He took a cautious step forward and held out his hand. "Come on. I know you don't want to hurt us. Turn off the detonator and give the cylinder to me."

"Who the *fuck* do you think you are, giving me orders?" Dad roared. "You're *nothing*. An ugly, retarded little fuck, that's all you are."

Lance flinched. It was as if he had never left home. The words hurt. They hurt just as much as the physical punishments, perhaps even worse. No matter how hard he tried, Dad was never happy with him.

He can't love you, Lance, Garth said quietly. *He's not capable of it.*

Why not? Lance cried. *Other people's fathers love them. Why doesn't mine love me? Why not?*

The world's unfair, Patrick put in. *So fuck the world and fuck your Dad. He ain't worth shit.*

Just because a man is your father doesn't mean you have to love him, Jessica said.

No reason to beat yourself up over it, Andy said. *It's not your fault.*

Other people love you, Lance, said a new voice. *Me. Your mother. Delia. Your own children, when you have them.*

Grandpa Jack? Lance asked incredulously. *I thought you were gone. You stopped carving things for me.*

Grandpa Jack chuckled. *You're a little old for toys, don't you think?*

There's still a madman with a neurotoxin cylinder in the room, Jessica put in.

"Move, you stupid shit," Dad growled at Lance. He crossed the room to Delia's corner. "Or should I hose her down? I can probably direct a small blast of the toxin."

"Get away from me," Delia whispered hoarsely, trying to push herself backward. Lance's stomach twisted.

"Leave her alone, Dad," he warned.

"You like her, don't you, boy?" Dad snorted. "A fucking nigger crip. Maybe once she's dead, you'll realize I'm more important to you." He aimed the cylinder at Delia. "Say good-bye to your whore, John."

"Delia!" Lance reacted without thinking. Nanobots shot from his body, lightning fast. They streaked across the floor toward Jonathan Blackstone, picking up nanos from the ship along the way. An invisible army swept over Blackstone's body, burrowing through mucous membranes, slipping between skin cells, swarming up blood vessels. Blackstone stiffened for a moment, then let out a long, low wail. Lance clapped his hands over his ears but didn't stop his subunits from acting. Tens of millions of nanobots tore through Blackstone's body, expertly snipping bonds between cells, separating tissues into their component parts faster than any human surgeon could imagine.

Jonathan Blackstone screamed in horrible pain as bits of him began to fall away. Skin sloughed off, revealing pink muscle and gray-white bone. He dropped writhing to the floor, still clutching the cylinder, while Meredeth and Delia watched in horrified fascination. Blood gushed over the carpet, and bits of tissue quivered and jumped beneath the nanobot onslaught. Organs melted into one another, running like melted plastic. Inside the bare ribcage, Jonathan Blackstone's heart jerked spasmodically until it too collapsed like a rotten balloon. Even the bones crumbled away until nothing was left but a bloody pile of mush. The cylinder lay on top of it all, lights winking. Meredeth put a hand over her mouth. Delia retched.

If you tell anybody, Johnny singsonged, *the nanobots will take you apart, cell by cell. I wonder who Daddy told?*

Lance stared, horrified. For a moment, he expected the cylinder to explode into deadly neurotoxin, then he realized it wouldn't. It was still in steady contact with Dad's DNA, even though Dad was dead.

Dad was dead.

The thought echoed around Lance's head. Dad was dead. Dad was *dead*. And Lance had killed him. Not Robin—Lance.

Lance sank whimpering to the floor. This went beyond any of the horrible things he had done as a child. It went beyond wetting the bed or being stupid or playing with himself. He had murdered his own father.

Something flashed in his brain, and with his newly heightened awareness, Lance saw something new forming, coalescing in the space of two heartbeats. It was dark and shadowy, but male. Its name would be Peter. Peter Black. And Lance would have no connection with him whatsoever.

The memory of events leading to Dad's murder gathered inside him, and Lance prepared to send them over to Peter, where they would remain forever hidden. As he had done forty-seven times before, Lance would completely forget the incident. He would be safe. Blameless.

A soft hand landed on his shoulder and Lance, startled, looked around. It was Delia. She had pulled herself over to him, dragging the stumps of her missing leg and arm behind her. Her wide, dark eyes held his.

"Don't," she said simply. "Don't become someone else, Lance. Please."

Lance looked at her mutely. Peter's formation slowed, but didn't stop. He would have brown hair and black eyes and a scar under his left eye.

"Lance, you did nothing wrong," Delia pleaded. "There was nothing else you could have done. He was going to kill me and there was no other way to stop him." She tightened her grip on his shoulder. "Lance, *he left you no choice*. Don't retreat from this."

Peter hovered, finished now, ready to take over, but Lance held him at arm's length. It was something he could never have done before, and a small part of him was amazed at himself.

"I can't have killed him, Delia," Lance said softly. "He can't be dead."

"Why not?" Delia replied. "He's just a man."

Lance swallowed and a tear leaked out of his eye. "He can't be dead because he's my father and I'm . . . I'm . . . " His voice dropped to a whisper. "I'm not sorry I killed him. I'm not sorry at all."

"That's all right, Lance." Delia put her arm around him. "That's all right. You did the right thing."

And at that, Lance collapsed into tears. He pushed his face into Delia's shoulder and let himself shake with sobbing. There, on the floor of Jessica's cabin, he cried all the tears he'd been holding in, the ones Johnny usually cried for him. And after a while, he became aware that his mother was also there, holding him with Delia, and he let her. He cried until his eyes were sore and his nose felt hot and swollen. Peter faded away and vanished like a wisp of fog.

"Is she finished in there?" Delia asked.

"Not quite," Lance said. "It's a big mess."

Delia, seated on the hallway floor, nodded and slipped her leg back on. Her arm was already in place. She sighed with relief and wiggled her fingers and toes, glad of an excuse not to have to watch the cleanup.

Actually Ms. Michaels had volunteered to dispose of the remains—a job, Delia noticed, that she almost seemed to enjoy. She had scooped up the neurotoxin cylinder with a dustpan, careful to keep with it enough cellular material so it wouldn't lose contact with Jonathan Blackstone's DNA, and threw it out an air lock—while Lance woke up the two thugs and forced them at needler-point to return to Jonathan Blackstone's ship, broken leg and all.

Delia, meanwhile, had gone to retrieve her prosthetics. Now that Robin was no longer messing them up, they had reverted to their default settings.

"Much better," she said, checking to see that the connections were set correctly. "I feel whole again. Not ugly or like a freak."

"But you're not ugly," Lance blurted, squatting next to her. "You're beautiful. With or without your prosthetics."

Delia turned to him. Unlike everyone who had seen them, Lance hadn't blanched away from her missing limbs when he helped her down the corridor, nor had he turned his head while she was putting herself back together.

"Thank you, Lance," she said sincerely.

A faint blush colored Lance's face. "All set?" he asked. "Mom's going to meet us in the galley after she's . . . finished." Then he paused uncomfortably, as if he wanted to say more, but couldn't.

Delia looked at him. Lance had thrown a lot of information at her in the aftermath of Jonathan Blackstone's death, and it was almost overwhelming. Nanobot hives, artificial intelligences, a virus-controlled ish that made Lance hit his mother and drove Delia's prosthetics mad. It would take some time to sort it all out.

But none of that is on his mind right now. "Is something else bothering you, Lance?" she said aloud. "What's wrong?"

"Delia, after we take Mom back to Earth, I have . . . that is, Andy has . . . I mean—"

He's actually blushing. "You have what?" she said with an encouraging smile.

Lance took a deep breath and his words tumbled out in a rush. "Andy made reservations for a vacation on Abierto would you like to have dinner with me there it's not far and I could bring you back before—"

Delia put a finger on his lips. "Lance," she interrupted, "I would love to."

Lance looked at her for a long moment, as if he couldn't believe what he had just heard. Then a wide, warm smile spread slowly across his face and reached his warm brown eyes. Delia couldn't help but laugh. She took his hand.

"You," she told him, "have the most beautiful smile I've ever seen."

Lance blushed again. But he didn't stop smiling.

EPILOGUE

Lance:

   Believe it or not, I was listed as the only beneficiary in Dad's will. He was initially declared missing, and rather than have the whole thing drag out for seven years, Mom and Jessica faked a suicide vid and made sure the authorities conveniently found it.

   We were questioned by the police, of course, but since neither Mom nor the Company had had any recorded contact with Dad for twelve years, and since there was no evidence aboard the Thetachron III station linking him to the hive, we were ruled out as possible murder suspects. Besides, the detectives really liked me.

   I sold all of Dad's holdings, including the estate. I did go back to look around once and found my room exactly the way Garth had left it—rumpled bed, closet door open, old clothes in the dresser. Dust coated everything and the whole place smelled stale and musty. All the drapes were drawn. It was eerie.

   Patrick wanted to go down into the basement, but the rest of the Company overruled him. When I left the grounds I was shaking, but I stayed myself.

   Delia and I had a very nice dinner on Abierto. We stayed a week, just resting and getting to know each other, but we weren't together every minute. It was supposed to be Andy's vacation, after all, though he was more willing to share it now. Eventually Delia said that she wanted to keep seeing me, but Andy and Robin had given her a horrible scare at the Pinegra station. The only way it

335

*was going to work, she told me, was if I returned to
therapy and stayed there until everything had been
resolved. Delia was willing to see me through it, but not
by herself.*

*"I think you're worth it, Lance," she said. No one had
ever said anything like that to me before.*

*Dr. Baldwin was surprised to see me again. Therapy
was—is—terrifying. I spend four hours a week in Dr.
Baldwin's office now, reliving the horrible things Dad—
and Mom—did to us. To me.*

After six months, I integrated Jessica.

*Despite what happened with Robin, I thought for the
longest time that if I ever integrated one of the Company,
it would feel like someone died—but it didn't. It felt like
finding something I had lost a long time ago. Memories
and skills came back to me like they'd never left.*

*Jessica was followed by Andy, Grandpa Jack, and a little
alter that didn't have a name. Only forty-three to go.*

*I almost quit therapy half a dozen times, but I've always
gone back. Not just because of Delia, though that's part
of it. It's like Andy used to say—sometimes you have to
live for yourself.*

I'm taking his advice.

Lance took a hot sip of tea in his mother's office and
set the cup down with a click. Simulated fresh summer
air breezed over him and he inhaled appreciatively, then
stretched and cracked his knuckles. Meredeth reached
across the table to slap the back of his hand.

"Don't do that," she scolded with mock severity.

Lance grinned. "Sorry. That used to be Andy's habit.
Now it's mine."

Mom shook her head and slowly refilled her cup. "How
are things going at Dr. Baldwin's office?"

"The same. He finally got Johnny to trust him—you know
how Johnny feels about doctors—but that means that
whenever Johnny has a nightmare or gets scared, he calls
Dr. Baldwin's emergency number, sometimes at three in

the morning." Lance grimaced. "Dr. Baldwin says he doesn't mind, but I do."

"And how are things with Delia?"

"She's picking me up for lunch," Lance told her, "but don't publish the banns yet. We'll see what happens after Garth integrates." He cocked his head. "Mom, what's the matter? You've been making silly small talk all afternoon and that's not like you."

Not long ago, Lance wouldn't have dreamed of confronting Mom like that. Now it seemed perfectly normal, something any son might do.

Meredeth Michaels smiled wanly, then rose and turned toward the window that looked out over the London cityscape.

"Back on your ship, just before your father died, I asked you a question. I just . . . " She trailed off.

"What question was that, Mom?" Lance asked gently.

"I asked if you could ever forgive me," she replied. Her voice was rock-steady. "And you said you didn't know. I was wondering if you knew yet."

Lance let out a long, silent breath. Mom's back was to him, and her posture was ramrod-straight.

No, Mom, he thought. *I haven't forgotten the question. You have no idea how much time I've spent thinking about it, and not always in Dr. Baldwin's office.*

It wasn't an easy question to answer. At any time, Mom could have gotten both herself and him out of Dad's house, but she hadn't. Every reason she had for not doing so was ultimately nothing but an excuse.

Because she was afraid, Lance thought. *Like you were afraid. Only you didn't know it. She was good at hiding it, like I was good at hiding the Company.*

Lance looked at her, and he realized that she had also felt fear rising in her stomach when Dad came home, had lived with the terrible uncertainty about what would happen to her next, had wished for God to strike Jonathan Blackstone dead. And then he also knew that she was afraid *now.* She was afraid that he wouldn't be able to forgive her and that he, her only child, would carry hatred and resentment for her for the rest of their lives, and that she wouldn't be able to live with the horrible, crushing guilt.

Let her feel guilty, whispered Patrick's voice, though it was only a whisper. *She'll give me/us whatever the fuck I/we want anytime I/we ask.*

But Lance shook his head. Only someone as cruel as Jonathan Blackstone would force her to live that way.

And I am not Dad.

Lance quietly got up and approached her from behind, the soft grass hushing his footsteps. He stooped to rest his chin on her shoulder. With a start, he noticed heavy, silent tears running down her face. There seemed to be a lot of crying in his life.

"Don't cry, Mom. It's all right," he said softly. "I can forgive you. I do forgive you."

She turned and looked up at him, searching for something in his face. And when she found it, she nodded once and whispered, "Thank you, Lance."

They held each other until the computer chimed to life. "Delia Radford is waiting in the outer office," it said, and they parted.

"Go see the counselor, Mom," Lance told her. "The one Dr. Baldwin recommended. I really think it would help."

"Maybe I will," she said thoughtfully. "Maybe I will. Gaston, tell Delia she may come in."

The door opened and Delia strode into the office with a basket on her arm and a smile on her face. She kissed Lance lightly on the cheek, making him smile as well.

"Hello, Lance," she said. "I thought we'd make a picnic of it today. The birds in Hyde Park are stunning at this time of year. Hello, Meredeth."

"Delia," Meredeth said cheerfully. "How's school?"

"Fantastic," Delia replied expansively. "One more semester's worth of research, and you'll be looking at Dr. Delia, Ph.D in ornithology."

"And an invaluable assistant vanishes forever into academia." Meredeth sighed in mock despair, then made a shooing gesture. "Go off, then. Enjoy your picnic and leave an old lady to her work."

Lance pecked her on the cheek. The tears were gone. "Not that old, Mom. See you later."

He took Delia's arm and they went out the door. Lance was still smiling.

It felt good.

The Honor Harrington series: *(cont.)*

Field of Dishonor

Honor goes home to Manticore—and fights for her life on a battlefield she never trained for, in a private war that offers just two choices: death—or a "victory" that can end only in dishonor and the loss of all she loves....

Flag in Exile

Hounded into retirement and disgrace by political enemies, Honor Harrington has retreated to planet Grayson, where powerful men plot to reverse the changes she has brought to their world. And for their plans to suceed, Honor Harrington must die!

Honor Among Enemies

Offered a chance to end her exile and again command a ship, Honor Harrington must use a crew drawn from the dregs of the service to stop pirates who are plundering commerce. Her enemies have chosen the mission carefully, thinking that either she will stop the raiders or they will kill her . . . and either way, her enemies will win....

In Enemy Hands

After being ambushed, Honor finds herself aboard an enemy cruiser, bound for her scheduled execution. But one lesson Honor has never learned is how to give up! One way or another, she and her crew are going home—even if they have to conquer Hell to get there!

continued ☞